NO
TURNING
BACK

Also by Sam Blake

Little Bones
In Deep Water

Sam Blake is a pseudonym for Vanessa Fox O'Loughlin, the founder of The Inkwell Group publishing consultancy and the hugely popular national writing resources website Writing.ie. She is Ireland's leading literary scout who has assisted many award-winning and bestselling authors to publication. Vanessa has been writing fiction since her husband set sail across the Atlantic for eight weeks and she had an idea for a book.

Follow Vanessa on Twitter @inkwellhq, @samblakebooks or @writing_ie.

SAM BLAKE

NO TURNING BACK

ZAFFRE

First published in Great Britain in 2018 by

ZAFFRE PUBLISHING
80–81 Wimpole St, London W1G 9RE
www.zaffrebooks.co.uk

A CIP catalogue record for this book is
available from the British Library.

ISBN: 978-1-78576-081-5

Also available as an ebook

1 3 5 7 9 10 8 6 4 2

Typeset by IDSUK (Data Connection) Ltd
Printed and bound in Great Britain by Clays Ltd, Elcograf S.p.A.

Zaffre Publishing is an imprint of Bonnier Zaffre,
part of Bonnier Books UK
www.bonnierzaffre.co.uk
www.bonnierbooks.co.uk

This book is dedicated to the seventy-one victims of the Grenfell Tower fire, and to Nicole Dressen, who helped to make a difference.

O, what a tangled web we weave,
when first we practise to deceive!

Sir Walter Scott, *Marmion*

Prologue

Thursday, 10.30 p.m.

The sea wind cut through her coat as she hurried along in the icy darkness. She pulled the shiny black fabric around her, trying to shut out the cold. The pavement was narrow, uneven, and as she drew level with the little harbour, the wind whipped her pale hair into her face. She was exposed here; there was no protection.

Her stomach felt hollow, churning with fear. He'd texted her directions, telling her where to get off the DART; to walk down into the village and take the second right, to keep going to the park. It would be too late for walkers by the time she got there. When she was inside the entrance she needed to turn right and follow the path to the end, to the narrow overgrown track that curled around the headland.

They could meet there, where they wouldn't be seen from the road.

Shivering, she ran the instructions through her head as she hurried on, wishing she'd worn jeans instead of a skirt. Wishing that she'd never opened the first email on Monday; wishing none of this had ever happened. She'd thought she could fix it, that she wouldn't have to tell him, but as she'd lain tossing and turning in bed unable to sleep, she'd realised she had to. She had no choice.

Lauren pulled at her fringe, at the place where it parted, smoothing it, tucking the stray strands of heavily highlighted hair behind her frozen ear; her hand went to her button earring, twisting it. The image of her trying on the new underwear was imprinted on her memory like one of those horror films that stayed with you, no matter how much you tried to forget. How had they got a camera into her room? How much more film of her was there? Her stomach contracted like she was going to vomit. She'd ordered the black lace bra and thong online, remembered her delight as she'd opened the plain brown cardboard box in her room, thrilled it had arrived in time for their next meeting. She'd pulled the curtains and slipped off her sweater and jeans to try everything on. Lace and mesh and leather. She'd known immediately how much he'd like it, how the bra and pants showed off her narrow waist and full breasts. And she'd crashed out on the narrow single bed laughing, imagining his face when she pulled off her sweater. She'd leaned over to hit the playlist on her phone, filling her tiny room with seductive music.

And it had all been captured on camera like the worst amateur porn.

He'd told her never to call, just to text their special number, but she'd been desperate. When he'd finally called back he'd been quite short with her, told he loved her but to calm down, like she was overreacting. But then he'd texted her back arranging to meet – and she'd known that he really did care; he must have been just as shocked as she was. She'd been sick with anxiety for days. Someone had been watching her and now they wanted money, wanted her to pay to stop them from putting the images online.

Lauren felt her stomach drop. How long had they been filming her? Whoever it was had sent her stills of her after a shower, getting dressed. Was he on video somewhere too? He'd only been to her room once but she knew that must be what he was thinking. That was what made this problem even more catastrophic. Tugging at her fringe, smoothing it flat, tucking it anxiously behind her ear, she increased her pace, tried to focus on the huge ships anchored out at sea in the blackness that was Dublin Bay. One looked like it was about eight storeys high, lights gleaming from the back like a tower block. What dramas did they have on board? She bet it was nothing close to what went on here, on shore. Out at sea the mist was even thicker than inland; it sat heavy and cold, far colder than she'd expected, much colder than in the centre of town.

Her head down, she kept walking. He'd said it was only about fifteen minutes but it felt longer. Thank goodness it was a Thursday night. The village had been quiet, and now that she was leaving it behind her there was nobody about, only the odd passing car, headlights picking her out like a target in the darkness. The houses were huge here, lights glowing warm behind solid walls and gates. She was relieved he'd told her to come to meet him; it showed he understood how important this was. Part of her had been dreading him saying that he'd come out to see her. How many times had he let her down, saying he'd call over but never arriving? How many nights had she sat and waited for him, make-up and hair perfect, and he hadn't even texted to explain?

She couldn't risk that now.

She needed help with this, needed him to sort it out for her. There was no time.

Whoever had the video had said they would post it to Facebook in seven days unless she found €1000. She was a college student, she didn't even have a job, where was she going to get that sort of money? Maybe that proved that they did know about him, knew that he had easy access to that amount of cash. Lauren couldn't take the risk of the tapes being broadcast to the Internet. She shrivelled inside at the thought. She knew he loved her, that if things were different they could be together, but his family ... She couldn't let his reputation be damaged, couldn't let the press tear him apart, she loved him too much. But she couldn't become the laughing stock of college either – if it got into the papers her parents would find out. She felt bile burn the back of her throat. Life was different in Longford on the farm, they'd never understand. It was all so complicated. She didn't understand why someone would want to ruin her life like this – ruin everything.

The vodka she'd had before she'd left had been to calm her nerves, but now it was churning in her stomach as she walked quickly on through the darkness. The street lamps became fewer and fewer as she got further out of the village. She couldn't run in case someone saw her, she needed to be invisible.

He'd sort it out, she knew he'd help her, she just knew he would.

The car passed again, slowing as it neared her, but Lauren was too preoccupied to notice.

Chapter 1

Friday, 8.15 a.m.

'Have you seen this?'

Detective Garda Cathy Connolly slammed the letter onto Detective Inspector Dawson O'Rourke's desk. Behind her his office door ricocheted off the wall and slammed closed with the force of her arrival. She didn't notice; she was too busy glaring at him, her blue eyes blazing. Still wearing his heavy navy wool coat, he turned and looked speculatively at the dent that the handle had made in the cream wall.

'Has anyone ever pointed out that you're supposed to knock when you enter a superior officer's office?' His soft border accent was calming in most circumstances. But not this morning.

Her dark curls a riot of temper, Cathy pulled an unruly strand away from her face, hardly pausing for breath. Her hair was still damp from her shower after the gym where she'd beaten her roundhouse kick personal best. She'd been feeling good. Then she'd come in to the station to be met by Thirsty, who had presented her, wordlessly, with the printout that she'd just thumped onto O'Rourke's desk.

'Did you know? And not tell me?'

He shouldered off his coat and hung it on the back of the door before sitting down. Picking up the printout, he scanned it quickly. She put her hands on the edge of the desk and leaned over it, lips pursed. He opened his mouth to answer but she didn't let him.

'How could you? How could you not tell me? Really?'

Standing up straight and crossing her arms, Cathy turned her back on him and looked out of the window that filled almost the entire end wall of his office, trying to control her fury. She knew she wasn't doing a great job of that, but at least she hadn't hit anybody. Yet. It had been just as well that it had been Thirsty who had handed the news to her. Dun Laoghaire's Scenes of Crimes Officer had more years in the job than she did on the planet; his nickname was an ironic twist on his renouncement of alcohol. His vice was cigarettes, and as Cathy kept telling him, they'd be the death of him; she could hear it in his chest every time he spoke. They'd come a long way together and she knew he looked out for her. And she'd known something was wrong from the moment he'd met her at the top of the stairs and she'd seen the tension in his face.

Uncrossing her arms, she shoved her hands into the pockets of her camouflage combats and focused on her breathing, on trying to keep calm.

She didn't know if she was more angry or upset. *After everything she and O'Rourke had been through, how could he? He must have known; how could he not tell her?*

She'd thought they had a thing – she didn't know what it was, but they had a special relationship. She'd taken a bullet for him back in the day, and he'd been there for her the previous year, after the bomb blast that had almost claimed her life. He'd pulled out all the stops when her best friend Sarah Jane had gone missing a few months before. They had history and he hadn't told her. Hadn't given one iota of a hint.

Did he not care at all? Cathy didn't know which was worse. The news, or him not telling her. His voice cut through her thoughts.

'I didn't know.' Dawson O'Rourke cleared his throat. 'I only found out about ten minutes ago when I walked in the front door.'

She turned to look at him, disbelief written all over her face. 'Really? And Niamh? She didn't know either?'

'Come on, Cat, she might be your sister-in-law but she's the Assistant Commissioner too. She's been working night and day trying to negotiate a pay deal and prevent an all-out strike – the Garda Representative Association might call it blue flu, but we all know the score. The entire country having no police force even for ten minutes is a bit more catastrophic than you not getting your promotion.'

Cathy narrowed her eyes. 'That depends on your point of view really, doesn't it?'

'Sit down will you, you're making me nervous standing up.'

Arching her eyebrows, she pulled the guest chair out from in front of his desk like a belligerent teenager. And like a belligerent teenager, she sat and immediately leaned back until it tipped precariously on its back legs. O'Rourke looked at her witheringly.

'If that chair falls over, Cat Connolly, and you injure your wrist trying to break your fall, you're going to have a lot of explaining to do to McIntyre. When's that fight?'

'Middle of April.' Cathy abruptly set the chair straight.

He was right. The Boss, Niall McIntyre, her friend and coach, would kill her if she injured herself. As a result of the explosion she'd been off the kick-boxing competition circuit for a year. Now she was fit again and they were putting everything they had into getting her ready for the next National Championships. She was going to win back her title and she was going to wipe the floor with her rival, Jordan Paige.

'That's better. Now let's look at the promotion list properly, shall we?'

O'Rourke flipped open his laptop and pulled up the members' portal on the Garda website, running his eye down the list to 'Forensic Profiler'. It was a new position, listed last after other roles and ranks: Sergeant Sub-Aqua, Warrant Officer, Dog Handler, Community Liaison. It was the first time An Garda Síochána had created the position, mainly through lobbying from Cathy and her report on their last case. Uncovering a trans-European criminal empire had been an added bonus to finding her best friend alive, despite getting shot at twice during the process.

And everyone reckoned that the job was made for Cat Connolly. Very few applicants had her specific training in forensic psychology, her experience. She'd got a first in every single assessment she'd handed in for her Master's. The final piece, due in May, would give her the formal certificate in Forensic Psychology, but her tutors were confident it was a foregone conclusion, had written her a glowing recommendation. She'd ploughed through ahead of most of her classmates, knowing her time wouldn't be her own when she was back in the unit and fully operational.

'So who got it? Who's the wonder boy?' Cathy didn't even try to keep the sarcasm out of her voice, pulled her necklace from the neck of her black sweater, running the Tiffany dog tag along its silver bead chain as she waited for him to answer. She couldn't look at him.

O'Rourke stared at the name on the list for a long moment. Running his hand over his chin, smoothly shaven today, he took his time replying.

'Well?' Cathy stared at him suspiciously. At times like this his broken nose and military buzz cut made him look seriously shifty, but he couldn't hide anything from her; after all these years she could read him too well. 'What are you not telling me? One of the lads said he was from Donegal. Why have I never heard of him if he's gone and got my fecking job? Has he trained with the Met or something?'

'You've done that.'

'I know, but . . . What?' She could tell from O'Rourke's face that something was wrong.

'He's a sergeant. He was stationed on the border.'

'So he's got a rank on me.' She looked at him; she could almost feel her mouth turning down at the corners. Glum, that was the word.

O'Rourke glanced at her. 'He's in his thirties.'

'So he's got a Master's or a PhD, has he?'

O'Rourke shrugged. 'Maybe.' He hesitated. 'He's the Taoiseach's nephew.'

'*What?*' Cathy's reaction was explosive. 'Holy fecking God, what sort of state do we live in? Are you *serious*?' She pursed her lips. Niamh, her sister-in-law, was one of the most vehement and public voices against 'jobs for the boys', so this decision must have been made at a higher level, deliberately keeping her out. At least that meant that she hadn't been keeping it from Cathy. And

Cathy knew Niamh would be as furious as she was. 'I hope he's going to be fecking good at his job . . .' She trailed off, scowling.

'Or he'll have you to deal with?' As if he'd read her thoughts, O'Rourke continued, 'He'll have me and Niamh breathing down his neck too, so let's hope he does know what he's doing, shall we?'

'Jesus, what do you have to do to get on in this country? How many times do you have to put your life on the line before someone notices you?'

'I don't think almost getting killed is exactly something I'd shout about. What's that Oscar Wilde line about losing handbags?'

'It's parents, and it's careless to lose two.'

A knock on O'Rourke's office door interrupted her before she could say more, and Jamie Fanning stuck his blond head around the door, his fringe flopping into his eyes.

'Alpha Foxtrot One's here for you.'

Cathy turned to O'Rourke in question. His face was grim. 'Hit-and-run in Ulverton Road this morning, opposite Our Lady's Manor. Starsky and Hutch attended. Traffic reckon there are skid marks that indicate that it wasn't an accident. I need you to accompany Starsky to talk to the family. I have to go into the Park for a meeting but Frank will get the incident room set up.'

'At least I'm useful for something.' Cathy slid her chair back abruptly. 'While you're up at the Phoenix Park, *at headquarters*, you might enquire about the promotion procedure for decorated members?' She glared at him, then turned to Fanning. 'Starsky downstairs?'

'I'll let him know you're on the way,' Fanning said, looking at Cathy for another second as if he was about to say something, and then vanishing as quickly as he'd appeared. He had the best intentions, Cathy was sure, but he'd been at the sharp end of her tongue more than once and she could tell from the look on his face that she wasn't hiding her feelings well. No doubt news of the promotions list had circulated around the entire station by now.

O'Rourke pursed his lips before continuing, 'The hit-and-run victim is Tom Quinn, father owns that radio station, Life Talk . . .'

Cathy interrupted, frowning, 'And his mother owns a portfolio of companies, one of which is one of the biggest recruitment companies in Europe. She's well known for being a ruthless businesswoman, has won loads of awards.'

He didn't rise to her bait. 'Quite right. And the press will be all over this one when they find out who it is, so make sure you cross all the t's. Traffic have closed the road, they're waiting for the collision investigators to start the forensic analysis and to survey the location.'

'Of course.' Cathy didn't know why he thought she'd treat this one any differently from any other case, be any less than thorough, but he was obviously tense about something more than the promotions list. 'The CCTV at the petrol station should have picked him up on his way home if he was in one of the pubs in Dalkey – if we're lucky that'll give us a time frame. It might have picked up the vehicle involved too.'

'I'll get Frank on to it while you're out. We'll get the tapes from any buses that went down Ulverton Road too, their on-board cameras pick up everything outside as well. They're like mobile CCTV units.'

'I think there's another camera at the other end of the road, in Sandycove, at the Spar?'

O'Rourke nodded curtly, his mind obviously on the next problem. Cathy stood up and headed for the door. As she reached it, she turned to him.

'Make the most of me while you can. The minute I get back I'm putting in an application for the Emergency Response Unit. Reckon the Taoiseach's got any nephews who can cut it out in the wild?'

She only caught a flash of O'Rourke's face as she let the door fall closed behind her. He thought she was joking.

Chapter 2

Friday, 9 a.m.

Sean O'Shea was already in the yard behind the station when Cathy got to the bottom of the stairs. Nathan Walker, his observer in the patrol car this morning, was still at the scene. Nicknamed Starsky and Hutch, Sean O'Shea and Nathan Walker could have been poster boys for the force in the unlikely event the commissioner decided to do a glamour calendar. Although the truth was something different. O'Shea was yawning as Cathy swung out of the glazed back door of the station and pulled open the car door. She grinned. 'How are the kids?'

O'Shea rubbed his hands over his face. Between them, Starsky and Hutch had seven children under six – sleep was at a premium in both their households.

'Sick, all of them, Eimear too. It's like a scene from the zombie apocalypse in our house. Her mum's come down to take over.'

'I hope you're not contagious.'

'You're grand, I had it last week.' He flashed her a grin and started the engine. 'Do you know the Quinns?'

'Only by reputation. What's the scoop?'

'We got a call at seven saying that there was a lad lying seriously injured on the pavement, opposite Our Lady's Manor nursing home. Man out with his dog was heading down to Bulloch Harbour for a walk.' Cathy grimaced; dog walkers had a special place in the hearts of police officers. 'Paramedics did their best but he died shortly after arrival. They reckoned it was a hit-and-run – looked like he went right under the wheels.'

O'Shea reached the security barrier and punched in his number as Cathy said, 'Weird he wasn't found earlier?'

He shrugged. 'He looked drunk. Was lying on the pavement. Not many people would cross the road these days to help a homeless drunk. If anyone saw him, I'd guess they steered clear.'

'Helpful.' Her tone reeked sarcasm. 'So he's in Vincent's?'

'Yes, they took him straight in. Poor bastard. Parents have been notified, post-mortem will be later today. He had his student card on him so at least we were able to identify him pretty quickly.' *That was something.* Cathy exhaled as O'Shea continued, 'Traffic think the skid marks on the pavement indicate that the vehicle was driven straight at him, knocked him down, and then reversed and ran right over him as he was lying there. Could have been a drunk driver but . . .'

'It sounds a bit too calculated for someone not completely in control.'

Cathy finished the sentence for him.

As O'Shea pulled the Dun Laoghaire patrol car up to the Quinns' ornate cast iron gates, they immediately began to slide open. They looked like they'd been imported from a French palace: complex scrolls and leaves painted navy blue; a gleaming brass plaque announcing the name of the house, St Gabriel's. Whenever Cathy had passed before she'd always wondered if it had been a convent at some stage; it was certainly big enough.

'They like their privacy.' O'Shea indicated the eight foot cut stone wall on either side of the gates.

'Have to say I'd prefer to meet Orla Quinn under different circumstances. I've always thought she was pretty amazing. She was on the Irish Olympic pentathlon team until she got injured in a riding accident, then she started ProForce Recruitment in her back bedroom.'

Cathy had read an interview with her years ago – when her sporting career had ended, Orla Quinn worked her way up from leading corporate team-building events to management recruitment, had expanded into media and tech, placing Irish graduates into some of the biggest companies in the world. She was focused and driven, and had a reputation for getting exactly what she wanted. Cathy had huge respect for her and all the good she did, using her company's might to lobby the government over the homeless crisis, getting the ladies who lunched to seriously think about the city they lived in.

'She's a smart lady.'

'Success doesn't make losing your child any easier.' Cathy paused, thoughtful for a moment. 'What's the story with the rest of the family?'

'Only son.'

Cathy blew out a sigh. 'This is one of those days that just keeps on giving.'

O'Shea pulled up onto a gravel drive that swept around the front of the house. It had an uninterrupted view of the sea, a broad lawn sweeping down to meet the water. A brand new silver Mercedes sport was parked at the bottom of an imposing set of stone steps leading up to the Georgian front door. O'Shea glanced at the car.

'That's hers. Bet it's a fabulous drive.'

The housekeeper opened the door almost the moment they rang, her eyes bloodshot and red. Cathy guessed she was Eastern European from her accent. Attractive, late thirties, her dark blonde hair was shoulder length, pulled back in a low ponytail. The Ralph Lauren logo brightened up her simple dark grey sweater. She obviously wasn't on minimum wage.

Inside the house the scent of lilies filled the high-ceilinged hall from a massive display on a circular antique walnut table. Cathy glanced into an enormous farmhouse style kitchen to the left. A huge golden retriever lumbered to the kitchen door to stare at them mournfully as they followed the housekeeper across the pale coir carpeting.

'She's very upset. This is just so terrible.' The housekeeper crossed herself quickly in an unconscious movement, her eyes filling with tears.

The living room was homely but elegant, massive picture windows taking advantage of the view of Dublin Bay, letting in the morning light. Polished occasional tables were crowded with family photos: Tom at various ages, in rugby gear, sailing gear, school uniform, with his mum. One posed shot of both parents at some sort of a charity event. Another of Orla in a showjumping ring.

Sitting beside a white marble fireplace, the flames licking at huge logs, Orla Quinn was staring blankly at her phone as if she was expecting it to ring. Her face was flawlessly made up but she'd obviously been crying, her face bleached white under her make-up. Cathy reckoned she was in her early forties, but she looked ten years younger, her hair expensively highlighted, pulled back with a tortoiseshell clip. Wearing skin-tight navy jeans and a plain navy silk blouse; diamonds the size of marbles flashed from her fingers. On the sofa opposite her, sat a man Cathy recognised from the press, her husband Conor. He was slumped forward, his elbows on his knees, staring into the flames. He turned as they entered the room. He looked like he hadn't slept, eyes wet with unshed tears.

'It's the Guards, Mrs Quinn.' The housekeeper stood to one side, ushering them in.

Something Jamie Fanning had said on the way out of the station clicked in the back of Cathy's mind – Conor Quinn had been in a rock band in the 1970s. Then he'd bought a string of nightclubs in Dublin, and one in London. She could see that he was older than his wife, slightly overweight, his hair unnaturally dark, slicked back. He'd had a big career before they met – did he still own the clubs? She wasn't sure. She'd have to ask Fanning. Cathy thought back to another society face she and Fanning had met not too long before – Richard Farrell with his A-list restaurant and indoor swimming pool – but he'd had plenty to hide. She wondered what was simmering below the surface in this house.

'We're very sorry for your loss. I'm Detective Garda Cathy Connolly, this is Garda Sean O'Shea.' Cathy held out her hand.

Orla Quinn stood up, her face a mask of politeness, and returned Cathy's handshake.

'It's Orla, and thank you for coming. Please sit down. Mira, could you organise some tea?' Her grip was firm despite the huskiness of her voice. Conor Quinn glanced at Cathy stonily.

Cathy turned back to smile at the housekeeper. 'We'll be fine, there's no need to worry.' Then turning to both of them, she said, 'I'm sorry we have to meet like this, but as you know there was an incident earlier today involving your son, Tom. We just want to be clear that we have the full picture.'

Orla frowned. 'But it was an accident?'

Cathy kept her face impassive. 'We're not completely sure what happened. We want to understand the reason why Tom was struck, and why the driver left the scene. As it stands it's a hit-and-run, a crime that carries a custodial sentence.'

'But who? How could they have hit him? And why would they drive off?' Conor Quinn stood up abruptly and walked over to the window, his hands thrust in the pockets of his jeans, his voice hard-edged. Tears began to slip down Orla's cheeks. She caught them with a French polished nail.

'That's what we need to find out, Mr Quinn. Which means we have to ask you both some questions.'

'Of course. Conor only got back from New York late last night. I was at a fundraiser.' Orla sat down on the sofa, her hands open as she spoke. 'I don't know what I can tell you. Oh God. Tom's been so happy recently. He was just away for New Year; he was loving college . . . I just . . . I'm sorry.' She took a deep breath, closing her eyes for a second, as if she was centring herself. When she spoke again her voice was more controlled, determined. 'I want you to look at everything, to find out precisely what happened. I need you to find out why and to punish whoever did this. If they had stopped, he might have survived.'

Cathy sat on the edge of the sofa. These interviews were never easy, no matter who the parents were; they had lost a child and the grief, the recriminations, the need to blame, were universal. This case was further complicated by the fact that, as O'Rourke had said, as soon as the press heard about it, they'd be camped at the gate. Grief was never something that should be public, whatever had happened, no matter how high profile the participants. The public had an apparently insatiable curiosity for the macabre but Cathy had always made it her priority to ensure that the victim was awarded the same dignity in death as they would have expected in life.

'That's what we're here for. There will be a special family liaison officer appointed to look after you – Marie would have been here herself now, but she's on a course today. As soon as she can she'll call in to you. It's her job to keep you fully informed as to what is happening with the investigation, and if you think of anything relevant, you just need to let her know.' Orla acknowledged this silently as Cathy continued, 'You mentioned you were out last night?'

Beside her, O'Shea pulled a black notebook from his jacket pocket and flipped it open.

Orla's lip trembled as she replied, 'Yes, I set up a charity that provides schooling for girls in underdeveloped countries. We work in South America and Africa.' She tried to gather herself. 'We have an annual fundraising dinner and hook up a lot of the sponsors with the girls they are sponsoring by satellite, we live stream the whole event to the Web so our contributors worldwide can see exactly what they are supporting. Ronan Delaney, one of the DJs from Life Talk, hosted. He and his wife Karen are close family friends – it was a great night . . .' She shook her head. 'Sorry, you don't need the details, I'm sure.'

Cathy smiled. 'Tell me everything you can think of. What time did you get home?'

'Around eleven, I think.'

'And Mr Quinn – Conor – when did you get back?'

His back to them, Quinn shrugged. 'Just after nine, I think. I had to go straight out to a meeting that was rescheduled – my plane was delayed. I got back in later, just after Orla.'

'And was Tom home then?' Cathy looked at each of the Quinns as she spoke.

Orla shrugged. 'I thought he was – his room's right at the top of the house, though. We have an internal phone system as there are so many flights of stairs.' She hesitated, speaking more slowly. 'When I got out of the car I could see Tom's light was on from the driveway. I texted him to say goodnight and he texted me back asking if he could get a lift in to college this morning if I was going into town.' She shook her head.

'And did you see him this morning?'

Orla shook her head. 'I had a meeting, I was running late after last night and when Tom didn't come down I thought he'd just slept in. I wasn't worried because he had loads of time to get the DART. He doesn't have any lectures on a Friday, just a study group in the morning with Anna – sorry, Professor Lockharte, his tutor.' She drew in a shaky breath. 'I left at eight, and was heading into town when the hospital called.' A sob tore through Orla. 'I should have gone up to him, I should have checked . . .'

Cathy smiled, trying to look as consoling and sympathetic as she could. She knew it didn't matter what she did or said, she couldn't bring him back.

'If Tom was home at eleven, would it have been normal for him to go out late at night or very early in the morning? We need to find out where he was between eleven and when he was found at seven this morning. Could he have gone out for a last drink in the village before closing? Several of the pubs in the village have an extended licence.'

Orla shrugged. 'He might have done, but most of his friends are in town. He wouldn't have gone to a pub on his own. He did go for late night walks, though, I think it helped clear his head when he was studying.'

'Did he go anywhere in particular?'

'I'm not sure, he'd usually stick his head in here on his way out, it could have been any time – I suppose he'd go down to Bulloch Harbour, or around the village.'

'Would he be gone long?'

Conor Quinn interrupted. 'Why all these questions about Tom's movements? Shouldn't you be out looking for the car that hit him?'

'My colleagues are doing exactly that, Mr. Quinn. It's my job to establish who the last person to see Tom alive was. To do that, I need to identify where he went last night.'

Orla glanced at her husband and continued as if he hadn't spoken. 'I suppose he sometimes went for quite long walks. He has his own key, but he'd be out for at least an hour, sometimes two.'

Cathy kept her face impassive as she took this in. Did Tom feel the need to get away from home, his family or maybe his studies? Perhaps walking really had helped clear his head. Or perhaps he was meeting someone? Cathy was sure his friends would know.

'Did he have a girlfriend? Any close friends we could chat to?'

'No, no steady girlfriend, but he was very popular.'

Cathy smiled encouragingly. 'Tell me more about him.'

Orla's sigh was ragged. 'He's nineteen, would be twenty next month, in his second year at Trinity studying politics and economics. We wanted him to join Life Talk, but he insisted he needed an academic degree first.' She half-smiled. 'He got a part-time job with Ronan Delaney. Ronan does lots of mixing for commercials and things, he has a sound studio in his garden, Tom's been helping him out. He was really enjoying it, seemed to be there every spare minute.'

She bit her lip. 'But he loves his course, adores his tutor – Anna Lockharte – she's quite brilliant, a real high-flyer in her field. She was at the event last night, her family are very influential in international politics, they helped get the project off the ground. I met her a few years ago in London at a conference. She's been fantastic. And she's really looked after Tom since he started at Trinity.' Orla faltered. Cathy could feel that she didn't really know how to continue. Orla cleared her throat. 'He's got loads of friends, I can give you a list but I'm sure Anna will be able to tell you more about who he hangs out with at Trinity. He doesn't have a girlfriend at the moment but he's not short of offers. He was talking about taking some of his friends to our house in France – it's near Nice. He loves France, we used to spend all our family holidays there.' She took a deep breath. 'He really had no worries that I knew of, money isn't a problem. I'm not a brilliant mother, I work long hours, and I know Tom's had to look after himself a lot, but I try to be here for him as much as I can . . .'

'I'm absolutely sure this is nothing to do with your working hours, Orla. I know how hard this is.'

Orla's eyes filled with tears. 'I've never seen him so alive as this term.' She pulled her hands out from between her knees and wiped away her tears, shaking her head. A moment later she said, 'It's just so horrific that someone would do this.' She looked directly at Cathy, balling her hands into fists on her knees. 'He was my son, my beautiful boy.' Her voice changed, becoming flint edged, 'I need you to find out who did this and make sure they understand what they've done. They need to pay the full price.'

Cathy glanced at O'Shea. They had no argument with that. Nodding, he closed his notebook.

'Thank you. We're going to find out exactly what happened. We'll be in touch when we have more information for you. If you could make a list of his friends, that would be very helpful.'

Cathy stood up, turning to speak to Conor Quinn, but he spoke before she could.

'Mira will show you out.' *Friendly.*

Outside in the hall, pausing beside the front door, Cathy smiled warmly at the Quinns' housekeeper.

'Have you worked for the Quinns for long, Mira?'

Mira nodded. 'Yes, since Tom was little. Orla had very serious postnatal depression. I came first as a nanny to help out. And then as her business grew I got more involved – became her and Conor's PA.' She drew a breath, steadying her voice. 'I run the house now and co-ordinate the office staff who are based here. Orla works from home; she goes into Dublin for meetings but most of her time is spent here so she can be near the family.'

Cathy smiled sympathetically. 'Where are you from?'

'Sarajevo, I came here during the war. He is – was – such a lovely boy . . . This accident is terrible. Do you know if it was instantaneous?' Her face was troubled, her imagination no doubt coloured by sights Cathy was sure she didn't want to remember. She knew Guards, men and women who had served with the UN in Bosnia during the war. Many had returned with PTSD. Man's inhumanity to man defied imagination.

Chapter 3

Friday, 11 a.m.

Anna Lockharte leaned back on her office windowsill, her mobile phone loose in her hand, unable to focus, the conversation she'd just had still sinking in.

She'd smiled as Orla Quinn's name had flashed on to the screen, thinking she was calling about the charity benefit last night, but the moment Anna had answered she'd heard Orla swallowing tears, her voice cracking. The smile had gone out of her own voice as she'd found herself paralysed on the edge of her chair, one hand gripping the edge of the desk, as Orla had taken a breath and launched into what had happened that morning. Anna had watched her knuckles whiten as her grip had tightened, half-hearing what Orla was saying, half of her back in the time when she'd been told her own bad news. Then it had been her brother-in-law Charles, confirming what they had all feared most, that her sister Jennifer had died from the injuries she sustained in the terrorist attack that had changed all their lives.

Anna turned around, leaning her forehead on the cold window glass, her emotions jumbled, trying to focus on what Orla had said. She'd been surprised when Tom hadn't turned up for their study group, but she'd assumed he was unwell – or nursing a hangover, which was the usual problem with morning tutorials.

How could a tragedy like this happen? How could someone hit him and just drive away? She fought away an image of his blood-soaked body lying on the pavement. She knew that picture would lead to more images fighting for her attention – images of a bank in Paris, memories she tried hard to bury – but the awfulness of the news had sent her spinning. The counsellors Charles and the embassy had brought in after that day were the best in the world. They'd explained that post-traumatic shock disorder could creep up on her at any moment. There would always be a trigger, something that took her back to the scenes inside the bank, replaying them like a movie inside her head. A horror movie.

Anna took a deep breath and wiped away a tear, unsure who it was for – for Tom, for the loss of her sister Jennifer, for Hope, her incredible niece who was rebuilding her life piece by piece, for Charles, for herself? Death touched so many, and violent death left a stain so deep it could never be removed.

But how could Tom Quinn be dead? Lovely, vivacious Tom who had everything. He looked like a Calvin Klein cover boy, had brains to burn, came from one of the most influential and wealthy Dublin families. His death was just so tragic. He was a perfect pupil, diligent, intelligent, questioning. He'd only been sitting in her office last week discussing his hopes for the coming year, telling her about the fun he'd had at New Year.

Anna shook her head and pushed an unruly mass of red curls out of her face, sliding her fingers into the roots and grasping a handful. It helped her concentrate, to stay in the moment.

She looked out of the rain-smeared window over the central green in the middle of the ancient university. A few bedraggled students were heading to their next lecture, heads down against the January weather.

Orla had said a detective, a Cathy Connolly, wanted to speak to her. But what could Anna possibly tell her?

Staring out at the wet quadrangle, Anna thought back to the last time she'd seen Tom – after college a couple of nights earlier. She'd hadn't been watching the time, had been working in the office late and suddenly realised that she needed to get moving or she'd be there all night. He'd been walking ahead of her with another student. They'd been some distance in front of her, their heads close together, laughing as they looked at a smartphone screen. Unaware of her presence, her Converses silent on the gravel, they were far enough away that she couldn't catch their conversation.

The streamlined radiator below her office window gurgled and Anna felt her skin go clammy, the sound echoing to an all too familiar soundtrack inside her head. And the memories that had tried to jump into her mind the moment Orla had told her about Tom came back in technicolour. Broken bodies lying on the ground.

The first bullet had passed her hot and fleeting. She could feel the path as it seared across her cheek, hear the dull thud as it embedded itself in the chest of the man standing in the queue behind her.

But she hadn't been about to turn around to look. Instead she had been in mid-dive, her arm wrapped around Hope, their red curls mingling as they hit the black and white tiled floor of the Banque Nationale de Paris. Through the teenager's thin sweatshirt, Anna could feel that Hope had gone rigid, fear paralysing her. She'd pulled the girl to her, covering her with her body, focusing, her senses heightened, every sound, every scent magnified. Floor polish and aftershave, the bitter odour of urine. Focusing and hoping with every cell in her body that her sister Jennifer, who was over beside the bank's lobby, was OK.

Anna had changed so much since that day in the bank. Life had changed so much. She'd learned later that Jennifer and her personal protection officer had been killed in the first wave of gunfire – had been, when the authorities had investigated, the suspected target. The very thought of Jen being gunned down in order to influence the US government made Anna want to retch. There had been so much confusion, so many dead. She'd tried to help and then she'd had to speak to the police, relaying in detail what she'd seen and heard. Then someone had found her to tell her Charles was trying to call, and when she had finally spoken to him, he had told her the news. Now Anna's sole focus was Hope, on ensuring that she achieved all that Jennifer had wanted for her. Moving Hope to Ireland had been her own mother's idea. Even after sixty years in New York – sixty years in which she had never lost her accent or picked up an American one – Anna's mother still thought of Ireland as her home, an island with a small population, with political neutrality at its core. Her old school, Hope's new boarding school, was exclusive, intimate and safe. There were other embassy kids there and Hope had jumped at the opportunity to move from her international school in Paris to a place where no one knew her or what had happened.

Hope had adored Paris but, after everything, it no longer felt safe.

Anna hadn't hesitated to step in as her guardian while she was in Ireland, and when an assistant professorship had opened up in Trinity College Dublin, it had been a perfect fit. After school in Boston, a year in the Sorbonne, Cambridge University and then the LSE in London, Anna hadn't expected to come to Ireland, but it had been a natural move. She had always felt and sounded more European than American, despite being born in New York. It was just what they needed. Anna didn't want Hope constantly looking over her shoulder, worrying about what might happen next. It was vital she felt safe. After that day, Anna's own anxiety level was permanently high. She knew how debilitating it could be.

Charles had organised for Anna to get some high-level personal training, so she could handle herself now, armed or unarmed, and that had helped build her confidence. She'd been trained to see what was going on around her, to question, to look for anomalies and to assume nothing. She'd rejected it all to start with. No one could live with a siege mentality; it had all felt so bizarre. But as it had been patiently explained to her, as long as Charles was a serving ambassador, she and Hope were potential targets for any enemy of America, as incredible as that seemed. Targets who had already been between the crosshairs once.

Death could come at any time. Look at poor Tom.

Chapter 4

Friday, 2 p.m.

'You nearly here?'

Wherever O'Rourke was standing, Cathy could hear his phone being buffeted by the wind, a sound magnified by her car speaker. That, and the level of irritation in his voice. She didn't rise to it; it wasn't like she hadn't been bloody busy all morning.

'Be there in five.' She hung up.

What is it about today?

She'd been in Blackrock Station checking in with the sergeant who ran the Traffic unit about the Quinn hit-and-run when O'Rourke had called. His words – 'a body's been found' – were still ringing in her ears. She hadn't asked him for details, had instead headed straight out of the station for her car. *Another body?* One thing you could safely say about this job was that you never knew what was coming next.

When Cathy arrived several patrol cars and O'Rourke's BMW were already lined up along the narrow winding road that passed Dillon's Park. The park itself was little more than a sloping green that ran down to the cliff edge, patches of trees already beginning to cast shadows in the winter sun. An ambulance had pulled up across the entrance, blocking the path, its back doors open, the paramedics sitting in the back on stand-by.

Cathy pulled over higher up the hill, and grabbed a grey marl scarf off the back seat as she jumped out of the car. Despite her thick leather jacket, it was wild this close to the sea. Wrapping the scarf around her neck, she realised that the last person who had worn it had been O'Rourke; the scarf still smelled of his after-shave. She'd lent it to him one freezing night to wrap around his face in the hope that it would block the foul stench of the fifty cats who had found themselves locked in a pensioner's apart-ment with only his body for food.

Pulling the scarf up over her nose, Cathy followed the low stone wall dividing the park from the pavement, and nodded to the two paramedics as she skirted the ambulance. A narrow concrete path bisected the grass, a lonely bench in the middle facing out to sea. It never failed to surprise Cathy how close Dalkey Island seemed right here, almost like you could reach out and touch it. Ahead of her, through the naked trees, she could see the heads of seals bobbing out at sea, watching the activity ashore, seagulls swooping above them.

Cathy stuck her hands deep in her pockets and braced her shoulders against the wind, swinging around to her right and crossing the grass to where she could see flashes of blue and white crime scene tape and white forensic overalls through the thick bushes. She'd played here with her brothers when they were little, scaling the sheer rocky crags like goats, hopping in and out of the huge rock pools. They'd tried to fish, their lines inevitably getting tangled with the thick weed, breaking over and over again. It was a popular spot for sea fishermen, regulars who had staked their pitch and were often here at dawn to cast their lines with more success than she'd ever had.

Reaching a broad plateau of rock beside the path that was a natural lookout post, Cathy hopped up onto it, looking for O'Rourke.

To her right the crime scene tape marked the top of a narrow path that looked like it had been recently cleared. It descended into thick bushes. She was about to pull out her phone when O'Rourke suddenly appeared from the undergrowth, ducking under the tape, striding up the steep hill, his coat flapping, phone clamped to his ear. Glancing up and spotting her, he stopped, and gestured to the path that he'd just walked up. She jumped off the rock and headed down to join him.

'Girl's body's been spotted on the rocks. Fisherman saw her from the sea and called 999. He reckons we're lucky she wasn't washed away by the tide.'

'Jumped or pushed?'

'Only time will tell. We were co-ordinating with the lifeboat to see if they could get her off, but the rocks down there are brutal. We're waiting for the rescue chopper instead. Apparently there's a storm coming in. We need to move fast. Go take a look, but be careful.' He indicated she should follow the path cut between high gorse bushes, and put the phone back to his ear. 'I'll be with you in a minute, the bloody mobile reception's terrible around here.'

The path was steep, more like a goat track than a path, shreds of ivy, russet fern fronds and exposed roots carpeting the passage. An overhanging bush leaned forward creating what looked like a dead end, but as she got closer Cathy could see the path narrowed even more and changed direction beyond it. She glanced back at the way she had come, at the sight lines from the road. This part of the park was completely hidden from the houses overlooking it, was invisible from everywhere except the near end of the path. Watching her footing, Cathy ducked under the bush to be greeted by Thirsty coming from the other direction, his forensic suit bright white against the foliage.

'Afternoon, lass. Here you go.' He handed her a pair of blue plastic shoe covers. 'See what you think. I'll be back in a sec.'

Taking the booties and slipping them over her Nike high-tops, Cathy stepped carefully on to the plastic markers that Thirsty had laid down to preserve the scene. She immediately found herself at the top of a sheer drop, the sea boiling below. The wind stung her face as she recoiled. She moved slowly back to take a look over the edge. Patchy grass grew between the rocks, the hebe and ivy losing its grip for a metre or so before it grew wild and thick again further on, purple flowers bright against the dark vegetation and grey of the stone.

The drop was so steep the body was difficult to pick out at first. About thirty feet below the girl lay face down on the jagged rocks, her padded coat wrapped around her like a black shroud, camouflaging her, making her look like a dark fissure in the rock. Blonde hair straggled across it like tendrils of seaweed. She'd obviously fallen head first and was facing the sea, one arm folded unnaturally underneath her, the angle painful. She was wearing dark tights, must have lost her shoes along the way. It looked to Cathy like she was above the waterline, but she knew the tide was fast in the sound and in bad weather the waves crashed right over this whole outcrop. In summer she would have been found quickly, this area crowded with anglers, joggers, walkers, and every shape and size of dog from early in the morning, but in January it was lonely, only the occasional dog walker venturing this close to the exposed cliff edge. If the fisherman hadn't seen her, she could have been lost completely.

Cathy could see clouds gathering in the distance. She didn't need to be told that heavy rain could obliterate vital evidence and would hamper their chances of getting the girl off the rocks today. Leaning further out, trying to take in the details of the scene, Cathy caught a flash of orange to her right – the Dun Laoghaire lifeboat was anchored off Killiney Bay. The girl was in a precarious position, totally inaccessible from the land without some serious climbing gear. Even with it, getting her up would be a challenge. Waves slapped angrily at the rocks below, the sound magnified by the cliffs.

Cathy heard a movement in the bushes behind her: O'Rourke and Thirsty returning. She stepped away from the edge, checking where she was walking as she moved further up the path to give them room.

'Any idea who she is?' A gust of wind whipped the words out of her mouth and O'Rourke had to lean in close to hear her as she repeated the question. He shook his head.

'Not at this stage. No relevant missing persons reports. We can't even be sure she's dead until we can get a doctor down there.'

Cathy shuddered. If the girl was alive but unconscious, hypothermia could set in within hours. And they had no idea how long she'd been here. O'Rourke said something else she didn't catch but before he could repeat it, he was interrupted by the *thup* of helicopter blades. The three of them looked up as a red and white rescue helicopter appeared, skirting the coast, nose down, tail rotors whirring. The side door was open, a crew member leaning out, his orange suit luminous. Using the life-boat as a marker she could see him searching the rocks, then as the chopper drew parallel with them, he spotted the girl's body and them standing above her at almost the same moment. He waved to them and signalled to the pilot to hover.

The noise from the chopper grew as it closed in above the rocks. Cathy pressed back into the undergrowth away from the edge. The Coast Guard search and rescue team were based at Dublin Airport and regularly practised over the Wicklow Mountains and this part of the coast. She'd met the crews many times. Too many times. Often their missions didn't have happy endings. Feeling branches pushing at her back, the down draught from the chopper lashed the bushes around her, sending loose tendrils of her hair across her face.

The winchman appeared at the open door, a body board in his hand.

Cathy moved a fraction closer to O'Rourke, hoping his bulk would block her from the wind. There was no way anyone would survive for long out here at this time of year if they were seriously injured. Cathy prayed that the fall had killed the girl outright, that she hadn't lain there conscious, dying of her injuries but unable to call for help.

They'd know soon enough.

The question was, what was she doing here in the first place?

Chapter 5

Friday, 2 p.m.

He watched the reflection of the room in the glass screen of the monitor as he got to work. The library was always quiet early on a Friday afternoon, the librarians chatting at the main desk behind him as they wound down to the end of the week. The building was old, broad stone steps flanked by pillars at the front door, but inside it was modern and warm, thousands of books housed in shelves on wheels, low comfortable seating inviting quiet contemplation. And a bank of computers with excellent Internet access.

Behind him he could hear the staff discussing their plans for the weekend, their accents a sing-song mixture of regions, town and country. He didn't come here that often; he had a series of libraries that he visited on a random rotation – the busier the library, the less likely anyone was to remember him. People were nosy in Dublin, asked too many questions, but while the Internet wasn't fast in a lot of places, the libraries were great. He used a VPN, a virtual private network, so he was totally invisible online, but just in case, using a library terminal with a group IP address made him even harder to find. He was polite to the staff but never engaged, just got in and out as cleanly as possible. He glanced at the reflection in the monitor again. He could see an elderly woman had gone up to the desk, was asking a question, keeping everyone busy.

That was good. This was always the bit that made him nervous. The monitors were lined up along the wall facing into the library so anyone could look over his shoulder and see what he was doing. Not that they'd understand the strings of code, or have any idea that to get to the back end of the sites, he was slipping through all their security on to the Dark Web. He half-smiled to himself. Their idea of security was like a stable door, the top swinging wide open, the bottom left on the latch.

A moment later he'd opened up the Discovery Quay site, the admin area flashing with messages. He could relax now. He didn't have too much to do this afternoon, just check through the main issues, hook up some new video feeds and set up a new vendor on Discovery's parent site, Merchant's Quay. He'd be in and out in an hour assuming there weren't any problems. There rarely were. He'd built both sites from scratch and they were solid, the payment gateways totally secure.

Right from the start he'd encouraged users to rate their purchasing experience, the products they bought. He knew how this worked. Building a reputation was vital to success online. They were the best on the Dark Web and he intended that they stay that way.

Security was his greatest concern. It was the key to everything. His fingers hovered over the keyboard as he thought. He couldn't take any more risks. It was as simple as that. Secrecy was vital. Nobody was going to stop him; it didn't matter who they were. In this world he was king. But there only needed to be one slip and it could all come tumbling down – he'd been stupid before and look what had happened. There really was no room for mistakes.

He'd been hacking since he was ten, was one of the go-to guys for the world's biggest cybersecurity companies to test their clients' vulnerabilities. He and Karim were the A-Team. If companies knew that he and Karim got their kicks finding the vulnerabilities and infiltrating their clients' sites in the first place, only to be paid to lock each other out, they might not be impressed, but cyberspace was their playground, a playground where they made the rules.

The money was here in the sites but commercial work kept him sharp, and it was vital that he was always at least one step ahead of anyone who could be a threat. The traffic was increasing every day. Customers who were looking for the latest incarnation of Silk Road came to Merchant's Quay and found the Discovery Quay portal in the sidebar. But he and Karim had been careful. Every mistake Ross Ulbricht had made setting up Silk Road he had locked down. It was small money to have Karim's group, Unanimous, constantly looking for weaknesses. One of the leading hacker squads in the world, they constantly vied with their competitors to be the best. If they couldn't find a way in, the authorities wouldn't be able to either.

He grinned to himself as his fingers flew over the keyboard again. It had taken a few years, but he now had everything sorted and could enjoy all the added benefits of being the one with complete tech control. Not that he'd be doing anything silly in a public library. Adjusting his eyes to look at the screen, he glanced at the reflection again, checking to see where everyone was. He could imagine the shock on their faces if they could see what was on Discovery Quay. His mouth twitched into a smile as he fought the laughter.

Boy, that would blow away the cobwebs.

Soon Merchant's Quay would be the biggest trading site on the Dark Web and Discovery Quay would be the biggest live camera portal – the traffic was increasing daily, the amount of time each visitor spent browsing on the site increasing with it, as was the number of returning visitors. That was currency.

As he inputted another line of code his mind wandered back to the blonde bitch. She'd been nothing but hassle, had been the reason for a row he hadn't expected and would definitely rather have avoided. Fortunately the bit of the live feed he'd shared had been recorded, so it had looked like he'd found it randomly on Discovery Quay. He'd thought it would be a laugh, but he'd got that wrong. Instead he'd hit a nerve.

He couldn't bear people telling him what to do. Or underestimating him. No matter who they were. His father was the worst, calling him stupid because he couldn't remember capital cities or the length of a river, the boring useless stuff you were never going to need to know in the real world. But he knew he was clever; the magic flowed from his fingertips. Without him there would be no sites – when he was online he had power. And as a result, he was making more money than his father could dream about. One day he'd show him.

It was all about control. Like the blonde. He'd been watching her face as she'd clicked to open the email. He'd seen her fear and it had made him hard. She'd thought he wanted money, but he wanted more than that. He knew she couldn't pay – not in cash, that was the whole point. She was one of the special ones, he'd already decided by then. And nothing stopped him once he'd made a decision. Nothing.

When he got back tonight he needed to find some new feeds, and check what his links had already yielded. 'Sexy, Stunning & So Simple: The Perfect Makeover' was the best yet, and was now installed on at least twenty beauty sites and blogs. It never ceased to amaze him that webmasters didn't spot the appearance of new links. The minute the user clicked through, his malware was already working its way into their system. He could have set up a plausible beauty site but that was too much work, the 404 worked just fine. Women only excited him when he could watch them – that link was so good it was like picking flowers in a field. And he wasn't alone in wanting to watch, if the views on Discovery Quay were anything to go by.

It would always be better for him, though, because he knew who they were, where they were. He could literally walk into the picture with them.

It was all about being in control.

Chapter 6

'So what do you think?'

They were sitting in O'Rourke's car, the engine running, the heating on full. The helicopter crew had, with some difficulty, got the girl onto a body board and winched her up. She'd been taken directly to Beaumont Hospital but the crew had known from the moment that they'd pulled her on to the board that life was extinct. She'd be on the way to the morgue by now.

As she warmed up, Cathy unwound her scarf, appreciating the heat, appreciating that he knew she needed it. She thought for a minute before she answered.

'It's a strange place to choose to jump, isn't it?'

O'Rourke shifted in the seat, screwing up his face, his fingers gripping the steering wheel. 'Pretty awful way to go.'

Cathy looked out of the window, frowning, thinking of the girl's body on the rocks, of her own essay on suicide as part of her Master's in forensic psychology. Years ago her biology teacher had explained that the human body had a self-preservation system that kicked in when the body was threatened. To commit suicide someone had to override every single element of that inbuilt trigger system. It was a massive simplification, but that alone – apart from all the other, devastating ramifications – had always struck her as a massive thing in itself.

She turned back to him. 'Most suicides aren't really thinking rationally, it has to be said. But if she really wanted to do the job there are definitely better places that are higher and less messy to jump from. Across in the quarry or from the cliffs at Howth or Bray Head would be better. It's not really high enough here to guarantee a quick exit, is it?'

'Maybe that's it, maybe she didn't really want to die this way.' O'Rourke grimaced. They had both attended suicides where it had been pretty clear that a cry for help had gone badly wrong.

'But that doesn't make much sense. Jumping onto really jagged rocks, you're going to at least do yourself a serious injury, aren't you? And the chances of being found at this time of year . . . Never mind about jumping closer to the main body of the park – I know it's not as high, but between the dog walkers and the overlooking houses there would be a chance of someone seeing you. Down there she could only be seen from the sea, and if there was a really high tide, she could easily have been washed away.'

O'Rourke pursed his lips. 'I've asked Saunders to put a rush on the Quinn PM. He's doing it now so we should have his official report by this evening.'

'He'll be pleased we're keeping him busy.'

'Won't he?' O'Rourke rolled his eyes. The Irish State Pathologist, Professor Saunders, had a special place in both their hearts – they'd both felt his personal brand of scathing sarcasm. 'We'll keep the scene here secured until we know more.'

'Did anyone find anything left on the path? A note, or her phone or clothing? Something to mark that she was there.'

'Nothing. But in this weather, it could have been blown away.'

'Maybe.' Cathy swung the car door open. 'See you back at the station?'

O'Rourke nodded. 'Don't be long, we'll go in to see Saunders together. I'm hoping he'll be able to slot her in as soon as he's finished Tom Quinn. Two teenagers dying within a few hours of each other is reason enough for him to reorganise his list. And you know what he's like for punctuality.'

'I sure do. I just want to drop into Dalkey on the way, have a quick chat to Karen Delaney about Tom. He worked part-time for her husband at a studio in their house – her salon is on my route back.' She climbed out of the car, ducking back inside for a moment to say, 'I was half-wondering if he might have been intimidated by someone, maybe was involved in the student drug scene? He certainly had the money. I'm wondering if there's a bigger picture here that we aren't seeing yet. If his mood had changed, he might have hidden it from his mum. I'll be super quick, promise.'

Dalkey village was buzzing as Cathy pulled in on her way back from Dillon's Park. Professor Anna Lockharte was actually next on her list for interview in relation to Tom Quinn's death, but now, with a whole new investigation unfolding, Cathy knew the team was going to be stretched and she wanted to make the best use of every minute.

Cathy was hoping that Ronan Delaney's wife, Karen, might be able to give her a bit more background on Tom and his working life. It was a fact that women were usually much more intuitive than men, and if there had been something bothering Tom, Karen may have picked up on it.

The minute Orla Quinn had mentioned the Delaneys, Cathy had known exactly who she was talking about. Karen Delaney had been big in Irish TV until a few years before. The anchor for *Style*, Irish broadcaster RTE's lead fashion programme, she'd been a key face at every celebrity gathering and on every game show, but then she seemed to have decided to take a back seat from TV. She'd opened her own beauty salon, Allure, and Cathy's best friend, Sarah Jane, was a regular visitor there. Despite being a student, Sarah Jane was never far from her all-American roots and getting her nails done was almost as important to her as her detox diet. When they'd first met, Cathy had been constantly impressed with Sarah Jane's apparently effortless style, but as they'd got to know each other Cathy had realised looking good without trying actually took a whole lot of time and effort. Time that Sarah Jane spent a good bit of, being waxed and buffed in Karen Delaney's exclusive salon.

Allure's opaque glass door tinkled as Cathy pushed it open, greeted by a wave of lavender-scented warm air and gentle music. She breathed in as she let the door fall closed behind her. She could immediately see why Sarah Jane loved coming here. The decor was silver-grey, inspired by the logo, a pile of soft grey pebbles, an image that had been blown up and filled the wall behind the glass reception desk. It was soothing somehow, the colours relaxing, and the attention to detail gave everything an air of luxury. A young girl with ramrod-straight glossy red hair appeared from a back room, smiling warmly.

'Good morning, how can we help you?' She didn't say 'Happy Friday' but Cathy almost expected her to.

'I was wondering if Karen Delaney was available for a quick chat.' She flashed her badge. 'Gardaí'.

If the girl was curious she hid it well. Her smile didn't leave her face. 'I think she's in the office. Would you like to sit down? I won't be a minute, I'll call and check.'

As good as her word, less than sixty seconds later the girl reappeared from the room behind the reception desk. 'Karen's upstairs, would you like to go up?'

The office was several flights up, in what must have once been the servants' quarters of the Victorian building. Cathy passed numerous floors, each of them opening to grey carpeted corridors leading to the treatment rooms. Cathy wondered if the workout on the stairs was all part of the treatment process too, but perhaps this was Karen's way of keeping her office private. Being a regular face on daytime TV made you public property.

At the top of the final flight, Cathy pushed a panelled door open to find an airy open-plan office. The light from huge Velux windows, limited on this grey day, was supplemented by designer pendant lights that ran in two rows across the room. Unlike downstairs, this level was all business, steel grey filing cabinets surrounding a huge white desk that rested on spindly legs. As Cathy entered, her Nikes silent on the polished wood floor, Karen Delaney stood up, her hand outstretched. Her dark brown eyes were almost the same colour as her hair, tied up in a glossy ponytail.

Cathy had googled her quickly from the car and one thing was for sure: Karen Delaney was looking very good for forty-three.

'Hello, I'm Karen, how can I help?'

Smiling, Cathy accepted her handshake. 'Thanks for seeing me unannounced. Cathy Connolly – I'm with the Detective unit in Dun Laoghaire. We're investigating a serious traffic accident that took place last night on Ulverton Road in Dalkey.'

As she said it, Karen Delaney's face fell, her eyes filling. 'Orla called. I can't believe it. It's too awful.' Taking a ragged breath, she added, 'Please sit down.' She indicated a grey marl sofa to Cathy's left, an expensive red leather handbag abandoned at one end.

'Thank you.' Cathy sat as Karen pushed a designer armchair over and sat down herself, her hands clutched together.

'How can I help you? Orla said it was a hit-and-run.' Karen's voice cracked. 'Please tell me it was fast, that he didn't suffer.' Her face contorted with grief and she turned to reach for a box of tissues on the corner of her desk.

Cathy had been in this situation many times during her career. When you met someone new and mentioned you were in the job, all they could talk about was parking tickets, speeding fines, the latest episode of *CSI*. But her job wasn't often about any of those things; it was about people and moments like this. Cathy could deal with the action, could deal with running across fields in the mountains in the dark, being shot at, but dealing with a relative's grief, that was the most challenging part of her job, the side nobody ever saw. Catching criminals, tracking down suspects, was the easy bit compared to this. No matter what the outcome of an investigation, Cathy couldn't take away the pain, and that could be overwhelming. But not knowing what had happened to a loved one made it a whole lot worse and she knew the only way to get through this situation was to focus on what could be done, on finding answers. She smiled, sympathetically she hoped.

'I'm afraid we don't have very much information yet, but I was speaking to Tom's mother earlier and she mentioned that Tom worked for your husband?'

Karen's eyes filled again. 'He was brilliant, he picked up everything so fast. But then he was very bright.' She drew in a breath. 'His dad, Conor, wanted him to have a part-time job while he was in college. He'd interned at Life Talk but the studio is in town and their hours are irregular. So between them, Conor and Ronan came up with the idea of Tom helping out with Sound Stream, Ronan's audio company. Ronan does voice-overs and audio books, that sort of thing, we've a studio at the bottom of the garden. It was ideal – Conor really wants to grow Life Talk and Ronan's his key DJ, so he was being pulled in more and more. Tom was able to pick up the slack so Ronan didn't lose any business, and he could learn how things worked at the same time.'

'They are friends? Conor and Ronan?'

'Yes, well, we all are, we go on holiday together. But Conor and Ronan were at school at Blackrock College, they've known each other for years. They're like brothers, two peas in a pod. Ronan was the first person Conor called when he was made CEO at Life Talk. He's got huge plans for the station. That's why he was in the US.'

'And Tom enjoyed working for your husband?'

Karen smiled sadly. 'He was always popping over – he had his own key to the studio. Ronan showed him what to do, how to mix the audio tracks, and it was like he was born for it.'

'Did he ever call in the evenings or at night?'

Karen shrugged, dabbing her eyes with the tissue. 'Sometimes. He didn't need to tell us when he was coming, the garden gate isn't locked. The studio is totally self-contained.'

Perhaps this was where Tom had been going on his late night walks? It was part of an explanation, but Cathy wasn't sure it was the full answer. *Where else had Tom called into during his nocturnal ramblings?*

Cathy smiled warmly. 'He was obviously very dedicated.' She paused. 'How did Ronan keep track of his wages if he didn't know when he was there?'

'Most jobs are fixed fee, you just get the time in and it's all done. We work with an audio book company who are based in Australia, so it helps sometimes to be working their hours. Tom really enjoyed it, but to be perfectly honest I think he saw the audio stuff as a hobby, just some pocket money. He wanted to go into politics. He really could do anything he wanted, but being good at running a sound desk didn't mean he saw it as a career choice.'

Cathy had a feeling that might be news to his parents. Politics and the media were uneasy bedfellows at the best of times.

'So he chatted to you a bit when he was there, it wasn't all work?'

'I suppose so, I never really thought about it. I think you sometimes talk more to people who aren't your parents. I used to make him tea and take it down if I was at home when he was there, catch up on his news from college.'

'Had you noticed if anything was bothering him recently? If he was worried about anything?'

Karen looked surprised. 'Not at all, he was very happy . . .'

His mum had said the same thing. *So perhaps that was her drug link theory put to bed.* The last time she'd been involved in a case concerning Trinity College, Cathy had been undercover at a student party in the Pav, the student bar, trying to identify a dealer who was trading a drug called Modafinil, an upper a lot of the students were taking to get through their exams. Only wherever he'd bought his supply, the tablets he was dealing were weapons grade and had caused some near tragic side-effects.

She'd half-wondered if the hit-and-run could have been drugs related – someone making an example of Tom. The criminal gangs in the north inner city had a constant feud going on that involved picking off rival members. But if Tom had upset someone badly enough to get himself killed, Cathy was sure that he would have shown some outward sign of anxiety in the run-up to last night.

Karen opened her mouth to say more but a phone began to ring from the depths of the red handbag at the end of the sofa. A shadow flitted across Karen's face – concern, worry? Cathy wasn't sure what. As the sound grew, Cathy smiled.

'Go ahead, take that.'

Karen reached for the bag as the phone stopped ringing. She pulled it out. 'Oh, it was Ronan.' She hesitated for a moment. 'It's fine, I can call him back.'

There was an awkward pause, which Cathy filled quickly. 'He's doing very well at Life Talk, he's always in the papers.' Sometimes during her break Cathy would leaf through the tabloids kicking around the station canteen. Ronan Delaney's was a regular face, one that appeared to be constantly surrounded by glamorous models at various society events.

'He is, his career's really taking off. He loves the limelight.'

There was something about the way she said it . . . 'Do you miss being on TV, being in the limelight yourself?'

Karen's face clouded for a moment. 'Sometimes. But it's a tough world. And there's huge pressure to be perfect. Not that there isn't the same pressure in this business, and as Ronan's wife I need to stay looking good, but being constantly in people's living rooms makes them feel like they know you personally. Not that that isn't lovely – but they've no qualms about asking probing personal questions or sharing their thoughts on what you're wearing or how you're looking. You do sacrifice a level of privacy. It can be exhausting.'

As Ronan's wife I need to stay looking good. The sentence jarred with Cathy. On many levels. Here was a beautiful, successful woman who would always be a household name in Ireland, but who saw herself as just 'Ronan's wife'. And who needed to look the part. Cathy wondered how the parade of twenty-something glamour pusses who hung around her husband made Karen feel.

'You're doing very well here, though. Your salon has a national reputation.'

Karen blushed. 'It does, it's been a lot of work and long hours, but it keeps me sane. I've amazing girls working for me, they're a brilliant team.' Before she could continue the phone rang again. The bag was still on her knee. She pulled the phone out. 'I'm sorry, that's Ronan again, do you mind?'

'Of course not.' Cathy shook her head.

Karen swiped the screen to answer, and despite the fact she had her ear to it, Cathy could hear Ronan Delaney's distinctive voice booming out. He obviously had his wife on speakerphone.

'Why didn't you pick up?'

Cathy pulled out her notebook and pretended to flick through the pages, as if she couldn't hear. In her peripheral vision she was sure she could see Karen's hand shaking as she held the phone.

'I'm with someone, I'm sorry. The phone was in my bag.'

Ronan Delaney didn't give her a chance to explain further. 'I'm always telling you to keep it somewhere sensible.' His tone was pure acid. 'There's a reception tonight, Emirates Airlines, make sure you get your hair done. Conor and Orla can't go, they want us to go instead. It's important, the airline are interested in sponsorship. We need to wow them.'

Across the room, Cathy strained her ears, keeping her eyes firmly fixed on her notebook. Delaney didn't let his wife get a word in edgeways.

'Wear that black dress, the one with the high neck. This isn't the type of thing we need you flashing your tits at.'

Cathy cringed inwardly, embarrassed for Karen and wondering who else could hear the call at the other end. *Delaney was some charmer.*

He continued, 'Did you hear, Tom got hit by a car last night on his way home?' Hardly pausing, he continued, 'Make sure you aren't late. If this comes off, we'll get some flights thrown in too. Damn sight warmer in Dubai than it is here.'

He hung up.

For once Cathy found herself speechless. It was just as well Orla Quinn had already called Karen about the accident – was that any way to break news like that to your wife? Then the end of his sentence hit her: '. . . we'll get some flights thrown in too'. Cathy shook her head mentally. At a time like this, you'd think he'd be more focused on the tragic death of his best friend's son than on getting freebies from a sponsor. Cathy wondered if the 'we' would be more likely to be some of the wannabe models and hangers-on that flocked around him than his wife.

Before she could comment, Cathy's own phone began to ring, O'Rourke's name flashing up on the screen.

'Sorry, my turn.'

Cathy kept one eye on Karen as she answered her own phone. At least it gave Karen a moment to recover her dignity. O'Rourke had Cathy on speakerphone himself, but at least he didn't share Ronan Delaney's need for an entire world to hear his telephone calls. Cathy could hear his car radio in the background.

'Saunders is starting the post-mortem in half an hour. I'll pick you up, I'm on the main street. You can come back for your own car later.'

Chapter 7

Friday, 4 p.m.

Cathy felt about as comfortable in the morgue as she did in a hospital. The bright lights, the smell, the squeaky floors, all brought her back to waking up in the intensive care unit after the explosion that had nearly killed her and had murdered her unborn baby. It had left her – for what felt like a lifetime – trapped in a room smelling of disinfectant with no soft surfaces: cream painted walls, shiny lino, a steel bed. A world with no colour.

The nurses had been amazing, keeping her going with hospital gossip, trying to keep her cheerful, but the black dog of depression had been snapping at her heels. Between them, McIntyre and O'Rourke had pulled her through. Her family had been fantastic too, but not like them. And O'Rourke was the only one who knew the full story.

Now, well over a year on, she had one more assignment to go to complete her Master's in forensic psychology and *had* thought she would be moving into a new position with the publication of the promotion list. But obviously the universe had other ideas for her.

Cathy could feel her temper rising again at the thought of the promotions list as she followed O'Rourke into the state pathologist's office. She focused on counting slowly to ten. See-sawing emotions were another result of the explosion, and losing her temper was the main one. She regularly felt a lot like punching people. But it was getting better, and she hadn't punched anyone badly recently, except her opponents in a couple of exhibition fights that McIntyre had organised in advance of the National Championships; she'd wiped the floor with all of them.

Now the business of not getting the profiler job, coupled with that horrible feeling she got in hospitals, was making her feel very narky indeed. O'Rourke glanced at her as he held the door to the office open for her.

'You all right? You're uncharacteristically quiet.'

She raised her eyebrows. That sounded like a challenge. 'Are you suggesting I talk a lot?'

His lined face cracked into a grin. 'I wouldn't dare.'

Cathy took a deep breath as she followed O'Rourke into the pathology theatre, both of them gowned and masked. He'd offered her an extra strong mint earlier and she rolled it around her mouth. It didn't do much good – cotton wool plugs in her nose would have been a whole lot better – but she didn't want to give Saunders any room for his usual sarcasm. The professor looked up as they appeared, nodding sharply to O'Rourke.

'Well, well, Garda Connolly, is it? And how are you? You seem to be generating a lot of work for me today.'

Cathy acknowledged him with a polite nod. Professor Saunders was a short, slightly rotund man whom Cathy disliked with a passion. Almost as much, she was sure, as he disliked her. Sassy women who could carry their weight in the ring were creatures he neither could, nor wished to, understand, and he made his thoughts plain whenever he met her. But a bedside manner wasn't important for Saunders; all his patients were past caring.

Like an operating theatre designed for the living, Saunders' eyrie was brightly lit with huge circular lights hanging from the ceiling like hovering spaceships, illuminating stainless steel counters running along the walls and a stainless steel trolley crowded with instruments that would have looked at home in the average DIY enthusiast's garage: saws, clamps, pliers.

'Nasty one this morning. Massive crush injuries. He probably would have survived the initial impact if the driver hadn't run right over him again. You'll see from my photographs there are tyre marks right across his back.' Saunders tutted, half to himself. 'Regrettably his clothing was too thick for a clear imprint so I don't think you'll be able to get much on the make and model, but there's no question in my mind that it was deliberate. I'll finish up my report when I get this one finished.'

At the end of the table Saunders leaned over and pressed a button to test the Stryker saw, its lethal teeth rotating in a blur of silver. Cathy gritted her own teeth, the mint on her tongue pressing painfully into the roof of her mouth.

The one part of all of this that always made her feel physically sick was the sound of that saw on the bones of the skull, slicing off the top of the victim's head to give the pathologist access to the brain.

She averted her eyes, fixed them on the grey hairs protruding from Saunders' right ear, and sucked hard again on the mint. If she'd had time for lunch today, she was quite sure she'd be struggling with it by now. She'd seen hundreds of post-mortems and it never got any easier, but there was no way she was going to let Saunders see her vomit.

On the steel table in the middle of the room, the girl lay naked, her clothes neatly folded on the counter to their right. Her face was a mess of flesh and bone where she had hit the rocks, the skin on her face, neck and shoulders stained purple with post-mortem lividity, where her blood had pooled at the lowest point. It wasn't pretty. But then death rarely was. For a moment Cathy's mind shot back to a wooded hillside, to finding another girl's body, a girl around the same age as this one. She shook the image away.

She still felt guilty thinking it, that it could have been so much worse, *it could have been Sarah Jane's body*. When Sarah Jane had disappeared everyone had known the chances of her winding up dead had been statistically higher than those of them finding her alive, but Cathy had blocked that thought out. The day that she had had to go up into the Dublin mountains to identify a body that could have been her best friend's was one that still gave her nightmares.

Thank God O'Rourke had been beside her through the whole investigation, pushing it forward earlier than he should have, saving valuable time. Neither of them had expected it to go the way it had, that Sarah Jane would get shot and injured. But everything that had happened had brought her and O'Rourke closer together.

Not close enough in her opinion, but she was still working on that.

It had all happened so fast – their lives had been turned upside down literally in a few days, and the four months since had been insanely busy. The trafficking network they'd uncovered had stretched right across Europe; with the evidence they had gathered in Dublin, O'Rourke had been liaising with law enforcement across five countries and two continents to close down the supply chain. It was a mammoth task, one that had him travelling all over the place, but it was one that he had relished. Cathy had a strong feeling that he was getting bored in Dun Laoghaire and needed more of a challenge – he'd been there two years, he had to be thinking about the next move. Which wasn't one she wanted to think about.

Saunders cleared his throat noisily and Cathy was brought back to the job at hand as he nodded to his assistant to wheel over the steel trolley full of instruments. Parking it with practised skill, the assistant returned to photographing the girl's clothing, his thick rubber soled shoes squeaking on the grey tiled floor. Cathy really didn't need to see the first incision, and as Saunders picked up his scalpel with a flourish, she transferred her attention to his assistant. He was a tall man – young, she'd always thought – but now she realised she wasn't sure if she'd ever heard him speak, or ever seen his face for that matter. He'd always been wearing a surgical face mask whenever she'd met him.

As a wave of classical music began to fill the theatre, Saunders humming tunelessly to it, she watched as the mortuary assistant began to unfold the girl's coat, checking her pockets. Oblivious to everything else around him, Saunders began speaking into an overhead microphone.

'The body is that of an adult female, one hundred and sixty five centimetres in height and of slim build. She was wearing a black nylon coat, purple long-sleeved T-shirt and a short denim skirt with navy blue tights when found. She was wearing a black bra and pants which were soiled. She has medium length blonde hair and her ears are pierced, nails: two to three millimetres . . .'

In her peripheral vision Cathy could see Saunders making a Y-shaped incision across the girl's chest, skirting her navel with his scalpel.

'Do we know how she got onto the rocks?'

Saunders' question made Cathy jump and she turned back to see him opening the girl's stomach cavity. Cathy sucked hard on the mint to combat the smell that was rising from the body and glanced hastily at O'Rourke, who seemed to be studiously looking at the girl's hand as he answered. Her nails were a delicate pink.

'That's what we have to find out. We're not convinced it's a straightforward suicide.'

'When are suicides ever straightforward, Inspector?' Saunders looked at him disapprovingly over his half-glasses, his eyebrows raised, and pursed his lips. 'She seems physically very healthy, toxicology will tell us if she was taking antidepressants, or anything else that might have interfered with her reasoning.'

As Saunders opened her chest cavity, Cathy transferred her attention to Saunders' assistant, who was patting down the side of the girl's coat. He reached into the pocket again and began wriggling something up from the inside of the lining. Pleased for the distraction, Cathy took a step over to him.

'Got something?'

He turned to her, his voice muffled by the face mask, his eyebrows furrowed.

'There's a hole in the lining of her pocket, something has slipped down inside . . . Here we are.' He pulled his gloved hand from the coat pocket, holding a plastic identity card between his fingertips. Cathy leaned over to take a look.

'Assuming this is *her* student ID card.' Cathy glanced across at O'Rourke, who had turned to see what she was doing. 'Her name's Lauren O'Reilly, nineteen. She was a second year at Trinity.'

'You serious? The same year as Tom Quinn?'

'So it seems.'

Chapter 8

It was late afternoon and raining hard by the time Cathy and O'Rourke arrived at Trinity College. When she'd called earlier, the university had confirmed they had all Lauren O'Reilly's medical contacts on file and Saunders' secretary had caught Lauren's dentist between patients. Her X-rays had been emailed before the pathologist had even finished up the post-mortem. Even he had been impressed at the speed at which they'd been able to confirm her identity.

Now local Gardaí in Longford had the unenviable task of notifying her parents, and before they headed back to Dun Laoghaire, O'Rourke wanted to have a chat with Professor Anna Lockharte. As Cathy had been talking to the bursar in Trinity, it had quickly become apparent that Lauren O'Reilly was not only in the same year as Tom Quinn, but she was also studying the same course.

They must have known each other.

Friday afternoons were always busy in Dublin city and today was no exception. Headlights and tail lights blazed through the rain and winter darkness, creating a feeling of chaos. On Nassau Street the side entrance to Trinity College was thronged with students, hoods up, umbrellas jostling with backpacks, their numbers swelled by a group of Japanese tourists in plastic macs, their guide trying to herd them quickly along the street.

They'd parked off Dawson Street and as they walked down, Cathy pulled her collar up, shivering, cold despite her padded leather jacket. She hated January; actually she hated the whole of winter, but at least in November and December you had Christmas to look forward to. At this time of year Cathy felt like she went to training in the dark and came back from training in the dark. It wasn't surprising people got depressed.

Ahead of her O'Rourke crossed the road, stopping at the mouth of the broad tunnel connecting the outside world with the ancient interior of the sprawling university.

'Arts block is this way. That's where she said her office was?'

Cathy nodded. 'She's usually over in Foster Place but they're redecorating or something. She said she'd wait for us.'

O'Rourke's phone began to ring in the depths of his overcoat pocket as, dodging students, they headed down the tunnel. He rolled his eyes and took a step backwards as they reached the other end, to take the call.

Tom's mother had sent Cathy a list of his friends, but she was quite sure there were people Tom had come into contact with that his mother knew nothing about. Kids his age had a way of not quite telling their parents everything. Especially – assuming Karen Delaney was right – when their career plans were diametrically opposed to their parents' ideas. As she scanned the quadrangle, Cathy wondered what scandals this place had seen since it was built in the sixteenth century; how many students had passed through its gates and what problems they'd faced. People's lives were messy in any era. Even perfect families had secrets.

She technically only had thirty minutes left of her shift but it seemed crazy to come back into town when they were both here already. Right now, their main concern was to find out how well Tom and Lauren knew each other, and who the last people to see them both alive might be. Which, at the very least, was something Cathy needed to know in order to fill in the gaping spaces in the Sudden Death reports.

Finding out who had seen Tom last was crucial to moving this investigation forwards. Whoever it was might be able to give them information on the vehicle involved in his accident – although in real terms they were equally likely to have been driving the car that had hit him. It would take at least a week for forensics to come back with a match on any paint samples or glass particles that had been found at the scene – a week in which the vehicle could be repaired.

Standing at the top of the steps outside the concrete and glass Arts block, Cathy's thoughts turned to Lauren. Someone knew why she had been in a freezing cold park in the middle of the night. Had she and Tom seen each other on Thursday evening? Was that why she had gone to Dalkey in the first place? Saunders hadn't been able to give them an exact time of death yet, only an approximation that she had died within the twenty-four hours previous to her being found. He wanted to check temperatures and assess the environmental impact before he committed himself. Appearing beside her, O'Rourke's voice cut into her thoughts.

'This way, I think.'

Finding Anna Lockharte's office turned out to be easier than Cathy had expected. All the corridors in the Arts building looked exactly the same – grey concrete block walls and grass green carpet with hundreds of turquoise doors – but everywhere was clearly marked. Whoever had chosen the colour palette had interesting taste. The walls in the stairwell were painted bright red to the halfway mark and bare concrete above, the stair treads covered in equally bright blue rubber matting. But the green carpet was a triumph of strangeness.

When they found the right door, O'Rourke's knock was met with a muffled 'Come in.'

Despite the darkness outside, the room was brightly lit. Modern, like the rest of the building; two desks were set at right angles, the walls crammed with bookshelves and filing cabinets. O'Rourke filled the space as he stepped inside.

Coming out from behind her desk, Anna Lockharte held out her hand, her face creased with concern. In her early thirties – Cathy wasn't sure if she was even that, but she couldn't be younger with her qualifications – she was wearing wide, pale grey herringbone trousers, cinched at her narrow waist with a slim belt, and finished off, rather surprisingly, with a pair of red Converse runners. She was about twenty years younger than Cathy had expected and, while clothes weren't something that Cathy took a lot of interest in, she could recognise quality when she saw it, as well as good taste.

'Good afternoon, Professor, thank you for hanging on for us. I'm Detective Inspector Dawson O'Rourke, this is Detective Garda Cat Connolly . . .'

'You're soaked. Let me hang your jackets up so they dry a bit. Did you find me OK? I feel like I'm in the land that time forgot at the end of this corridor. Do sit down, please.' Anna had a strange accent to Cathy's ear, sort of cultured mid-Atlantic, not quite American but not British either.

Shaking the rain from her hair as she slipped her jacket off, Cathy passed it to Anna, who jiggled a coat stand closer to the radiator beside the window and hung up their coats. Cathy watched her, fascinated. Anna Lockharte had a sort of luminosity that drew you in. And to be a professor at her age, she was obviously very bright.

'That should help.' Anna hesitated. 'All of this really is so awful.' Cathy could see the pain in her face as she headed back around to her desk chair. 'Orla called me this morning. Tom was such a lovely boy, it's just such a terrible waste. How can I help?'

O'Rourke cleared his throat. 'I'm afraid we've got some more bad news for you, but it's news that needs to be kept confidential for the moment.' Anna froze as he continued, 'I believe you have another student named Lauren O'Reilly on your course?'

Anna nodded wordlessly. Cathy could see the colour draining from her face.

'What's happened?'

'I'm very sorry to have to inform you that Lauren's body was found on cliffs below Dillon's Park in Dalkey earlier today. Her identity has been confirmed and her parents are being informed this afternoon.'

'Oh, my God.' Anna's hand shot to her mouth. Her eyes filling with tears, she couldn't speak for a moment as she struggled with her emotions. 'How . . .?'

'We aren't sure at this stage, investigations are being launched into both Tom's and Lauren's deaths. We'd like you to tell us as much as you can about them, who their friends were, and if they knew each other.' Shaking her head, Anna ran her fingers into her hair as he continued. 'I know this is very distressing for you, but the early hours in any investigation are crucial and we want to build a picture of both victims as quickly as possible.'

Cathy sat forward in the chair, her notebook open on the desk. 'Anything you can tell us will help us understand what happened.'

'My God.' It took Anna a moment, but then she seemed to centre herself. 'I'm sorry. It's such a shock. But – Tom first?' O'Rourke gave a gentle nod as she continued. 'He was doing so well in college, having a great time. It's a cliché but he was the life and soul of the party. I don't understand how anyone could run him over and just leave him.' She paused. 'If they'd stopped, could they have saved him?'

'He certainly would have had a much better chance if he'd got medical attention immediately.' O'Rourke kept his face impassive. Cathy knew exactly what he was thinking: whoever had hit Tom had a lot of explaining to do, and not just about leaving the scene.

'Can you tell us who Tom's friends were, who was in his tutor group?' Cathy asked. 'His mother said he often went walking in the evening – it might have been a way he found to relax when he was studying, but we wondered if he could have been meeting someone in Dalkey village for a drink before walking home.'

'It's possible, I really don't know. I'm year tutor so I look after the welfare of students as well as teach. I can give you a list of everyone in their tutor groups.'

'They were both studying international politics?'

'The course is actually philosophy, political science, economics and sociology.' Anna nodded at Cathy's raised eyebrows. 'I know, it's a mouthful. Trinity College is the only university in Ireland that offers that combination. It's a four-year course, students specialise in two areas in the second two years – Tom was planning to focus on international politics. I'm not sure what Lauren wanted to do, she was still finding her way, I think.

'The course examines the way societies are organised and create wealth. My PhD was in international terrorism so I cover some of the sociology modules too – race, ethnicity and identity – but my main area is international politics.' She continued, 'Tom was enjoying the whole course. He was very bright. His French was excellent too – in the third year students can go and study abroad as part of the Erasmus scheme. He wanted to go to France, so quite often we'd have our one-to-one seminars in French.' Anna stopped herself. 'Sorry, that's probably all irrelevant. Information overload.'

Cathy shook her head. 'Everything is useful to us. Do you teach French as well?'

She shook her head. 'No, I was at the Sorbonne before I went to Cambridge. My sister . . .' She hesitated for a split second and Cathy sensed O'Rourke shift marginally in his seat. Then Anna continued, 'My sister lived in Paris. It was like my second home.'

She stopped speaking and there was a moment's silence. Cathy's antennae twitched. She got the distinct impression there was more to tell, but Anna continued anxiously before Cathy could ask.

'So they were both in my second year political science class. There are a couple of lectures a week and then tutorials once a fortnight. It's a big tutor group, around twenty-five students. Tom seemed to have lots of friends. Lauren was much quieter but I've seen him chatting to her – I think he knew her pretty well. Actually, I think she interned at his father's radio station over the summer, so they would have worked together at some stage, I know he helped out there. There are others in the group – Michaela O'Brien, Paula Garcia who I've seen with Lauren – I can give you a list.'

'Were either of them on any sports teams, or in any of the societies?'

Cathy was suddenly realising that getting a full background and finding out who may have last seen both Tom and Lauren would mean talking to an awful lot of students. It wasn't the number of interviews that worried her – one investigation she'd worked on had ended up with over three thousand statements. It was the time. Witnesses forgot things, and the longer it took for the police to reach them, the fuzzier events became.

Anna shook her head. 'Lauren seemed to keep very much to herself. She was quiet, quite shy, worked hard, was getting good grades. Tom was more involved – he was very techy, had friends studying computer science and engineering. I know he was a member of Amnesty and the French society, the Internet society too. Perhaps others, I'm not sure – we've over a hundred societies here, from juggling to knitting, there could have been more he was signed up to.'

'Any close friends we need to know about?'

Anna shrugged. 'Tom didn't have a girlfriend that I know of – he was very good looking so he was obviously popular, but students these days seem to be very gender fluid; dating isn't as simple as it was when I was in college.'

She grimaced, her look making Cathy smile. Dating was never simple. When Orla had told her that Tom went out for late night walks she had immediately wondered if he was meeting someone he didn't want his parents to know about.

'So, boyfriends?'

'I haven't seen him with anyone – you could ask Olivier Ayari, he might know. They hung out together – he's one of the international students. Olivier's family is originally Tunisian but his family live near Paris, I think. His brother Xavier is here too, doing a PhD. Their family paid for the new science block, the Ayari Building.'

'That must have cost millions.' Cathy couldn't keep the surprise out of her voice.

'I think they are very well off. Xavier drives a BMW.' Anna raised her eyebrows. 'Most students don't even have the money for the DART. They've got a family home in Killiney too, I think. I heard someone say Xavier has a yacht in Dun Laoghaire as well.'

Cathy made a note to check that out. 'And Lauren?'

'I haven't seen her with anyone, but her friends would know. I don't think she and Tom were dating each other, anyway.'

'So what's the best way to get in touch with their friends? Do they live on campus?'

'Most of them are second years so they are either in private rented accommodation or they live at home. Olivier and Xavier Ayari have an apartment in the International Financial Services Centre, I believe.'

Cathy raised an eyebrow. The IFSC was the heart of the Dublin business district, surrounded by five-star apartment complexes that only the super-rich could afford.

Seeing her reaction, Anna continued, 'I think their father is a trader of some sort, or works for one of the international banks, I'm really not sure – perhaps their family is in oil?' She shrugged, 'I know the money for the science block came from a company in the Cayman Islands, Ayari Enterprises. Xavier and Olivier were both at the opening representing their family. Their father works in the Far East apparently and couldn't get away from whatever project he was busy with.'

Cathy nodded. There were some very wealthy people in this world, people who had their businesses registered in tax havens and thought thirty million was small change. She knew there were individuals living in the Dun Laoghaire station district who could buy and sell small countries. She'd been inside their houses. Anna continued, 'I know Lauren's family are farmers, from the midlands. She was staying in halls for a second year rather than moving out with friends – she's a first year "mother", helping with the new students.'

'And when did you see them both last?'

Anna grimaced, trying to remember. 'I saw Tom on Wednesday evening, with Olivier. I was working late and I was heading home about eight. They were walking ahead of me ... And Lauren? It must have been in our tutorial meeting on Tuesday. She was very distracted; said she wasn't feeling well. She looked like she'd slept very badly.'

'So something could have been worrying her?'

Anna nodded as she remembered. 'Yes, definitely. She was doing really well in all her subjects, was on top of her work, so I don't think it was a study issue. It must have been something else.'

Chapter 9

Saturday, 7 a.m.

Cathy looked at the second hand on the clock on the wall of the Phoenix Gym, unconsciously swinging the skipping rope, her trainers rhythmic as they pounded the wooden floor. Squats were next but she had another three minutes here first. The gym was surprisingly busy for this early on a Saturday morning but after Christmas excesses and New Year's resolutions, a legion of determined faces always appeared in January.

Cathy checked the clock again – she knew she'd fly down the M50 to the station on a Saturday but part of her knew her workout time was limited. With two investigations running in parallel, getting over to the gym regularly and for long enough would be a challenge. Last night it had been nine by the time she'd finally written up all her notes on their various interviews and left the station; she'd only been fit for bed. Her Nikes squeaking as they hit the boards, she kept skipping, the sweat starting to run down her spine under her sports bra and black lycra vest top. With the championships on the horizon she knew she needed to keep her hours up.

From the other side of the gym, her coach Niall McIntyre looked up to check she was still hard at it. Five foot six of sinewy muscle, McIntyre was an ex-para from Belfast who had joined the British Army and then been posted right back home. By the time he retired he'd seen active service all over the globe and had ended up training some of the world's most elite troops. A twist of fate had landed him in Ballymun, and knowing how good boxing was for keeping lads off the street, he'd opened the Phoenix Gym and never looked back. Nicknamed 'The Boss', he'd trained all her brothers and had taken her from a shy ten-year-old to national champion. He was her friend, mentor and her rock.

She grinned across at him. It wasn't a proper grin, more of a grimace. As if he sensed something was wrong, McIntyre turned to speak to the overweight middle-aged man he was demonstrating punches to. Indicating that the man should work on his own, he headed over towards Cathy. She finished her skips as he reached her and they fist-bumped before she hung over at the waist, catching her breath.

'Looking good, girl.'

'Easy for you to say.' She straightened up, scowling.

'What's got your goat, young lady?'

She took a deep breath. 'Promotions list.' She opened her mouth again, but she couldn't say it.

McIntyre knew exactly what she wanted, what she'd been working for. Telling him was almost harder than telling her parents. She still couldn't believe that, after everything she'd given to the job, she'd been passed over. Was it because she was a girl? She sure as feck hoped not. There were winners and losers in every walk of life. And with every skip this morning she'd been surer than ever that there was no way she was going to become one of the losers.

But she didn't need to spell it out for McIntyre. He'd been with her every step of the way: helping her in the aftermath of the explosion; pushing her for a first in her Master's; holding her when she broke down when Sarah Jane had disappeared. He threw his arm around her shoulder. She stared ahead, avoiding his eye, conscious that her voice was full of emotion.

'Taoiseach's fecking nephew got my job.'

There was a pause while he digested the news. 'You'll have your moment.' His voice was low, his Belfast accent harsh. But he sounded sure. Absolutely sure.

Cathy didn't answer. She knew he was her champion, and that he was absolutely right. There would come a day when the gormless eejit who had got her job would make a Horlicks of something and she'd be the one to step in. She knew it with unwavering certainty. She took a deep breath, controlling her emotions. She'd got past the raw anger that had had her stamping up the stairs and slamming doors in the station. She still wasn't happy, but now she felt like she was in target mode, calm and precise like an Exocet missile locked on the enemy. She'd have her moment. He was damn right about that.

She'd work out what it was she was going to do and she'd use all the negative emotion to get her there. It was like that moment in the ring when your opponent scored a lucky punch that pissed the hell out of you and gave you that extra bit of fight to hit back and win. Sarah Jane had told her venture capitalists called it pivoting – that moment when everything was going to shit so you sat down and regrouped and came up with a whole new plan. That's what she needed now. A plan.

'What does O'Rourke say?'

'Haven't had a chance to talk to him about it properly yet, we've got two suspicious deaths in Dalkey. We've been flat out.'

McIntyre took this in. He knew Dawson O'Rourke, knew his job was complex even on a good day.

'You need to work out what you're going to do about it.'

'I sure do.'

'But first you're going to be National Champion. Let's see some more skipping, then some squats and *then* you can let rip on a bag.'

Cathy's face cracked into a proper smile, he hadn't said *imagine the bastard's head on the bag*, but that's what he meant. *She could do that.* And while she was doing it she'd have another think about her options.

Glancing at the clock high up on the red brick wall, Cathy flicked the rope behind her, feeling it smack off her ankles. McIntyre patted her on the shoulder and headed back across the gym to his new pupil, who was by now sweating profusely and hitting the bag in what looked like slow motion.

She started skipping again, getting into a rhythm, burning fat, increasing her cardiovascular activity, giving her mind space to wander.

But it didn't wander to the promotions list, it wandered right back to the case. What the feck was going on in Trinity College that two of its students had wound up dead? Tom Quinn had had it all. Looks, and from what she'd heard, the personal determination vital for success. He would never have any money worries; he was in his second year, so had no real exam worries. What could he have done to piss someone off enough that they drove up onto a pavement and hit him from behind, and then reversed over him to finish the job? They'd get a lot more information when they found the car – the point of impact would determine the speed, and whether the car had clipped him or driven straight at him. The Traffic Corps had a lot of years' experience forensically examining accidents like this; there wasn't much they hadn't seen and even less that they missed.

Cathy pursed her lips, her eye still on the clock, watching the second hand shudder from minute to minute, the rope spinning so fast she couldn't see it. She had asked the technical bureau to check both Lauren's and Tom's Facebook, Twitter, Instagram, Snapchat, looking for anything that might give them a lead.

McIntyre's voice came like a pistol shot across the gym. Cathy threw the rope down and hit the boards, her arms spread wide, her legs pumping. It wasn't the most elegant pose but as she hit the wall, her body screaming, she didn't care. She powered through it. On the other side of pain was gain, she smiled to herself. When she'd been over to the Met to join their anti-terrorist course she'd been recommended a gym in Farringdon. Gym Box with its yellow neon lighting and industrial architecture was the 'office' of ex-heavyweight champion boxer Sweet D. Williams. Their sparring session had been one of the toughest she'd ever had – he was six five, with the longest reach she had ever seen, but it had tested her speed and agility and his power talk still echoed in her head. A second generation Jamaican, his upbringing in Peckham – then one of the roughest parts of London – had forced him to create his own opportunities. Opportunities that had led him to New York, to train with legendary promoter Don King, to make a real name for himself. His boxing was different from hers but his philosophy was the same. Training was about winning. Everything was about winning.

'Well done, girl, take a break and then on to the bag. I've got a couple of lads lined up for you to spar with. Is Sarah Jane coming in tomorrow or Monday?'

Cathy picked up her water bottle, slices of lemon and chunks of ice swirling in the bottom. She waited until she got her breath back to answer.

'Tomorrow morning, because of this case. We'll be even more swamped by Monday.'

The Boss patted her on the shoulder. 'Great, I'll tell them. Keep this up and you'll wipe the floor with that Jordan Paige.'

Cathy grinned. That's what Sarah Jane kept telling her. Her best friend had been a tougher coach from the ropes than McIntyre had ever been. It was like they were in collusion. Sarah Jane was getting her fitness back after the surgery to remove the bullet in her shoulder. It would be a bit longer before she could compete with Cathy in the ring at the same level she had been at four months earlier, before she'd been shot.

Her gloves on, Cathy headed for the row of punchbags hanging by chains from the rafters, her mind still on Tom's death, on Lauren's fall, rolling the events of Friday back through her mind.

O'Rourke looked harassed when Cathy appeared in his office shortly after 8.30. He'd obviously been in a while; he'd slung his navy pinstripe jacket around the back of his chair and had rolled up the sleeves of his pale pink shirt, a half-eaten breakfast roll beside his laptop. She'd knocked this time but, getting no response, had stuck her head around the door. Glancing up, he gestured her in, his phone clamped to his ear. He finished his call as she slipped a fresh cup of coffee onto his desk.

'Thank you, I need that.'

'You look like you're trying to do too many things at once.'

He took a sip of his coffee. 'That's what it feels like. Most people are still in bed at this time on a Saturday morning. And I've got an inbox that I'm very unlikely to get through before Monday.' He took a sip of the coffee. 'As if there hasn't been enough happening already this week, last night there was another shooting in town, an attempted armed robbery in Dunne's Stores in Cornelscourt, plus a fatal traffic accident on the N11. And some scrote's breaking into boats on the marina again. If I had twice the number of operational bodies we'd have half a chance of getting through the paperwork alone. Some days I really don't know where to start.'

She grimaced and took a sip of her own coffee, pulling out the guest chair in front of his desk.

'How about with your breakfast, you'll function better with fuel.'

'Thank you, Mother.' He scowled at her, his tone rich with sarcasm. It didn't bother Cathy; she put her cup down on his desk and sat down, pushing his roll towards him.

'Come on, eat quick, or I'll eat it and then I'll be in the shit with McIntyre.'

O'Rourke narrowed his eyes, fighting a grin, grabbed the roll out of her reach and, taking a bite, spoke with his mouth full.

'After we left, Saunders' man went through Lauren O'Reilly's pockets again. He found a note in an envelope with "I'm sorry" printed on it. Standard type, Times New Roman, but big, I'm not sure of the font size. It's up with the technical bureau now.'

'You serious? Did it look like some sort of suicide note?'

O'Rourke shrugged, still chewing. 'I haven't seen it, but apparently it was printed in block caps. Weird sort of suicide note if you ask me. We should know more later this morning.'

He reached for his coffee again, taking a sip. 'We're still waiting for Traffic's final report on the Quinn incident.'

'His mum thought he might have gone out for a walk to clear his head. I told you, when I spoke to Karen Delaney, she said he used to call over there, sometimes at night.'

'He do that a lot?'

'Apparently so.'

As she spoke he picked up the pen on his desk and started clicking the nib in and out. He was thinking. The pen in his hand was a slim black US Army issue that wrote one mile of ink; the press button on the end was the exact length of a two-minute fuse; the length of the pen itself measured one nautical mile on a sea chart, and the plastic casing could be utilised in an emergency tracheotomy. O'Rourke had laughed when she'd given him the box of ten. He could never find a biro when he needed it, and rarely took the gold pen she'd bought him for Christmas years ago out of the office. She'd stumbled over a Reddit post about them and had ordered them from Amazon – someone in the comments had said that whatever shit was hitting the US Army, wherever they were in the world, and no matter what else they were missing, these pens were the one thing you could rely on. In Cathy's mind O'Rourke was a bit like that. You knew what you were getting with him – there was no messing, no bullshit.

She tucked a strand of hair back into her ponytail, trying to focus back on the office, on their conversation. O'Rourke had a unique ability to distract her that sometimes really wasn't helpful. She cleared her throat.

'We need to talk to Tom's friends. If he was worried about something he might have let on to one of them. I'm going to go through Anna Lockharte's list.'

Cathy could have been wrong but she thought she saw a glimmer of something pass across O'Rourke's face. He hid it well but she wasn't the type to let things drop.

'So what's the story with Professor Lockharte? Have you come across her before?'

He tried to look nonchalant, but his offhand tone wasn't fooling either of them.

'Not really. I've just heard her name mentioned. Confidentially.' He looked at her pointedly. She scowled at him, then held up her hands in mock surrender.

'Need to know only, I've got it.'

'Sorry, it's nothing big that affects this case as far as I can see at this stage. If it's relevant I'll fill you in.'

'Got it.'

Cathy smiled inwardly. He was such a bad actor. He might fool other people but she knew him too well – there was obviously something very interesting about Professor Anna Lockharte for her name to be mentioned in senior Garda circles.

O'Rourke cleared his throat; he might as well have said 'moving swiftly on' out loud.

'You still mad about the promotion list?'

Cathy scowled. Mad was a great place to be when you needed to get your shit in gear. She had a lot to think about but she already had an idea about what she was going to do next. She just needed to channel her anger and use it to get where she wanted to be. Then everyone had better watch out.

'Don't go there. I'm madder than hell. I'm just praying I don't ever have to work with that twat.'

He held up his hand. 'Got it. Give him six months and see what the story is.'

'If he's crap, which,' she paused deliberately, 'he will be . . . In six months they'll decide the job is a waste of money and revert to bringing in profilers from the UK. And then there will be no job here. For anyone.'

He shook his head emphatically. 'But the whole point is that the guys from the UK don't have the same ability to get inside the Irish psyche that a native has. To be effective, this has to be filled from inside the job.'

'They might be English but they've been bang on in the past helping us to narrow down suspects.'

'I'm not saying they aren't any good, that we don't need profilers per se. Just that we need good *Irish* ones. Isn't that your whole argument?'

'Yes. It is. "Good" being the operative word here.'

'Right. The incident room awaits us.' O'Rourke checked his watch. 'Everyone should be ready by now. Let's get this show on the road.'

Chapter 10

Saturday, 9 a.m.

In her office in Trinity College, Anna Lockharte looked at her laptop computer and frowned. She'd come in early, supposedly to catch up on her marking, knowing she couldn't sit at home or thoughts of Tom and Lauren would close in on her.

With one hand on her mouse, the other pressed thoughtfully against her lips, she clicked to open the email and a moment later a dialogue box appeared in the corner of her screen: 'Trojan attack detected.'

Anna frowned, not sure whether the virus had come from the email or from one of the web pages she had opened in her browser. Had her antivirus software dealt with it? She read the email again slowly.

Outside her office, the rain was streaming down the window, the sky dark with storm clouds. She had all the lights on, even the one on her desk, and sitting here alone, the lighting made her feel a little like she was in a fishbowl, with people outside peering in. Unlikely, given that she was on the fourth floor, but as Tchaikovsky's overture to *Romeo and Juliet* gathered momentum from her laptop speakers, her nervousness grew with the sound.

The email was completely innocuous – just a request to speak at a conference – but something about it was definitely odd, quite apart from the virus warning that might have come with it. She wasn't sure if it was the tone, the language. It just didn't feel like it was written by a conference organiser. The virus scan software she used was government grade and she was regularly notified of attempted attacks, but from her own research on how political extremists were moving into cybercrime, Anna knew only too well that attacks could come in all sorts of guises. And they were constantly evolving.

She read it again. Was the virus warning linked to this particular email, or something that had come in at the same time and was in her spam folder? She knew one person who would be able to check that out very quickly. Her sixteen-year-old niece Hope had been building websites since she started high school. She could look and see if there was anything suspicious in the email's origin. Anna glanced at her watch; it was 9 a.m. but that was far too early to call Hope – she was a teenager who loved her sleep. Anna didn't want to forward the email until she'd spoken to Hope; if she texted her now, they could catch up later.

It was probably a completely reasonable request from a reputable conference programmer, but Hope would be able to tell her for sure.

And then there was the next email, from Xavier Ayari. She really didn't know what to make of that either.

Dear Professor Lockharte

I'm working on establishing a new international student society, focusing on free speech and essentially non-political. I was wondering if you would be free to discuss it? I would be honoured

if you would consider addressing our first meeting. Perhaps we
could chat over coffee?
   Kind Regards
   Xavier Ayari

It wasn't the request that was strange, it was his choice of communication – it seemed so formal. He was based in the science block on the opposite side of the campus but she often passed him as she cut through there on the way to the DART station on Pearse Street. Why couldn't he ask her in the canteen, or in the corridor?

Screwing up her face she read it again. What was this really about?

Anna took a deep breath and ran a hand over her forehead. She was overreacting. She was always overreacting, like her danger radar was permanently on. One day she'd learn how to get a grip on it, how to keep everything on the same level. One day. The psychiatrist had explained that she may read more into situations than was actually there, that she could feel distrustful; that in the early days after the attack, anything could trigger a panic attack – a sound, a smell – and that was quite apart from her anxiety about going into strange public buildings, or her inability to cope with a silent environment. She needed noise. Noise connected her with the outside world – no matter how mindless the radio DJs were, they were there, in real time. Music was a constant in her apartment, although she was sure the neighbours in her block preferred Beyoncé to Bach.

But why was Xavier emailing her? Perhaps it was because she was distant on the rare occasions that they'd spoken? She was sure he was used to women falling at his feet whenever he opened his mouth. He certainly had that confidence, something closer to arrogance, that suggested he was used to getting what he wanted. He couldn't know that every time she looked at a dark-skinned man with a French accent, she felt the hairs standing up on the back of her neck. She knew it was ridiculous, but her reaction wasn't something she could control. Like the panic attacks, and occasionally the absolute rage that she felt about the whole situation. She'd had counselling for both, had been genuinely worried in the early days that she'd fly off the handle and physically assault some random stranger. Her doctor had explained that it was a reaction to the powerlessness she'd felt as she'd lain on the floor of the bank, at the frustration at being unable to fight back. She could see how women in combat zones didn't hesitate to join the resistance after similar experiences, how picking up arms empowered them.

To be fair to him, Xavier had no idea of her issues, or of her background. She knew she was so much better than she had been two years before, but she still had moments. The other day she'd been thrown by someone dropping a tray, the explosive sound of china hitting the stone floor like automatic gunfire. It wasn't at all, of course, but something about the sound, the suddenness, had made her duck instinctively. She'd turned around and headed back to her office, praying no one had noticed that she'd almost hit the floor.

Anna sat forward in her chair and put her face in her hands as she reread the email. She'd seen Xavier looking at her as she passed him in the corridor, had been deliberately ignoring his slightly cloying attention – always materialising to hold doors open for her, somehow managing to bump into her whatever time she was heading home. Maybe Xavier was trying to make a move on her? Was that it? He was very good looking but absolutely not her type. She shivered; she hated that she couldn't disassociate other, completely innocent Frenchmen, from two specific ones. It was something she was working on, and like her panic attacks, she was sure it would improve with time.

Anna scanned the email again, her hand moving unconsciously to nervously twiddle with her diamond stud earring. *She was sure she was just overreacting*. Perhaps he really did just want her to talk to his society, and this wasn't about anything else at all.

How had she got so rusty? She'd had a few relationships after her husband, Brad. Divorce at twenty-five hadn't been part of her game plan, and every time she met a new guy she questioned herself. She'd fallen for Brad completely – he'd been her prom date, and then had signed up for the Navy, and she'd been all ready to be a Navy wife. She'd stuck by him through training, and his first deployment. She'd been at Cambridge University then, loving the strangeness of an ancient English city but also studying so hard she hadn't had time to sleep. It wasn't until she'd gone to London that it had gone bad. Much less intensive, her PhD years had been amazing – the theatre, the parties, which were so much fun after the Cambridge incubator unit – and she'd let her hair down and enjoyed it. Which hadn't been what he wanted to hear from the South Atlantic. It had been her European-ness that had attracted him to her in the first place, but actually being *in* Europe without him had all been too much.

She hadn't been ready for the possessiveness or the jealousy that had come with his being deployed while she studied – her emails met with questions from the moment he was online. If he loved her, he'd trust her, and he quite simply hadn't. And she'd realised all too quickly that the relationship she wanted wasn't about accounting for her nights out, or listing her friends. It was about mutual support and encouragement. He knew she wanted to get her doctorate, that she adored her subject, but being apart just hadn't worked and, as she'd discovered, some men just couldn't cope with an intellectual woman who knew her own mind. And the ones that could all seemed to be taken.

She looked back at her computer screen. Xavier had lots of opportunities to talk to her. She'd spotted him in the Arts building coffee shop again yesterday. She'd smiled at him politely as she'd got a Lucozade out of the vending machine. But then she'd felt his eyes on her, his gaze crawling over her back – and hadn't liked it one little bit. What was mad was that every woman within miles, both staff and pupils, melted when he looked at them – the accent, the Mediterranean looks, the worked-out body, his sheer confidence – just not her. She could hardly refuse his request to speak at the society, though, but she didn't need to have coffee with him to organise that.

Chapter 11

Saturday 9 a.m.

Cathy could hear the team before she saw them as she crossed the hall from O'Rourke's office to the incident room, the burble of chatter seeping out from the swing doors. When they'd got back the previous night, O'Rourke had brought Frank Gallagher, Dun Laoghaire's Detective Sergeant, up to speed. While they had been at the morgue and interviewing Anna Lockharte, he'd been getting house-to-house enquiries underway on both investigations. The machine was cranking into gear.

Dun Laoghaire's recreation room doubled as an incident room; ply boards had been pulled across the snooker table to create a conference table. As O'Rourke held the door open for her, Gallagher turned from the whiteboard, a dark blue marker in his hand. The room was full, members of the district detective unit and uniform, plus the lads from the traffic unit in Blackrock. Cathy nabbed a spare chair at the back and sat down as O'Rourke strode to the front, nodding his thanks to Gallagher.

'Bit of quiet please.' O'Rourke tapped his biro on the side of an empty coffee mug, looking for everyone's attention.

As she watched him from the back row, everyone fell silent. He'd grabbed his jacket as they'd left his office. He looked good. Too good.

Cathy pulled her necklace from under her sweater and ran the pendant along the chain. There were so many times like this, when she watched him from across the room, or when they were sitting in his car in the pouring rain, bags of chips open on their knees discussing a case, when she knew she was absolutely smitten by him. She'd been out on dates, had met guys she really fancied, but it was never the same, never the deep emotional connection that she felt with him.

Maybe the universe was trying to tell her something. Whenever she tried dating anyone else it never worked out, veered close to total disaster more often than not. Like the gorgeous Alexsy – she could still feel herself blushing at the thought of his beautiful blue eyes. That might have gone somewhere if things had been different. If he hadn't been a suspect in a case she'd been investigating.

O'Rourke began to run through the two cases – where they were with interviews, what they had already found out – but Cathy was only half-listening. She knew she couldn't spend her life praying that he felt the same as she did, and that one day they'd find a way to be together, but there were times when she just wanted it to happen so badly.

She was sure he *did* feel the same way about her, had witnessed a thousand clues over the years. They had a history, a shared past. In her first posting he'd been her sergeant and she'd ended up taking a bullet for him, the scar almost invisible now after the skin grafts she'd had following the explosion. He'd thought she was dying when he'd kissed her then, after the explosion, the sound of sirens intensifying as the emergency vehicles came closer, a member down their first priority. She had been, almost. But afterwards, although he was around loads and had supported her so much, being more of a friend than a colleague, it was like it had never happened. She knew he didn't do grey areas – that was the one and only time she'd known him to cross the line, any line. But it had been one of those moments that was suspended in time – her beautiful Mini exploding, the blast carrying her twenty feet across her neighbour's lawn. Caught in a moment that didn't feel real.

O'Rourke turned, putting his coffee cup down, slipping the pen into his top pocket, half-catching her eye. His smile was a flicker, but she caught it, and felt the warmth of his look as their eyes connected. For a split second she felt like they were the only people in the room.

Holy feck.

And then the moment was gone.

Cathy looked down at the floor, trying to gather her thoughts.

How did this keep happening? Would they ever move forwards? She wasn't getting any younger, and at thirteen years her senior he definitely wasn't.

Maybe the promotions list was a blessing in disguise. Maybe she needed to get away and get some distance.

Turning to the room again, O'Rourke pulled himself up to his full height and was fully focused. She envied his ability to switch like that, to think so fast. She reacted fast in the ring, but emotionally, especially after everything that had happened in the past couple of years, it took her longer to fully engage. Sometimes she wondered if she'd ever be able to.

O'Rourke was clear and precise as he summarised the situation in his soft Monaghan accent. Behind him, photographs of Lauren, blown up from her Facebook page, were taped to the incident board, the date, crime number and location detailed below in black marker. Beside them were photos of the park and the location of her body. On the other side of the board, a photo of Tom, also taken from his Facebook page, grinned down at them.

Beyond the closed concertina doors that separated the rec room from the kitchen Cathy could hear the sounds of crockery clinking. The early shift was having breakfast. Her stomach rumbled. She'd had some muesli before she'd headed for the gym but that felt like a very long time ago now. Straightening in her chair, Cathy stretched her back, concentrating on what was being said in an effort to distract herself from thoughts of her stomach.

O'Rourke began with Tom's accident.

'At seven on Friday morning, Tom Quinn was found on Ulverton Road, the victim of what appears to be a hit-and-run. Initial findings suggest that the vehicle was dark blue with metallic paint. And Saunders has confirmed he died from crush injuries.' He hesitated, glancing behind him at the board. 'Then, lunchtime Friday, a fisherman based in Bulloch Harbour, Michael McCarthy, spotted a girl's body on rocks below Dillon's Park.

'The District Detective Unit responded and secured the scene. Search and Rescue airlifted her off the rocks. Professor Saunders has confirmed her death was as a result of trauma sustained in the fall, coupled with extreme exposure.'

O'Rourke flicked on his laptop, and additional photos of the scene appeared on the wall behind him. Taken from the lifeboat, they clearly showed the height of the drop and the jagged rocks that subsided into the sea between Dillon's Park and Dalkey Island. In the middle of the shot Lauren O'Reilly lay like a discarded rag doll, gulls already scavenging.

O'Rourke continued, 'Next of kin have been notified. And she has been formally identified by her dental records. She had her student ID card in her coat pocket.' He flicked to a photo of a Trinity ID Card, an image of a pretty girl smiling from the right-hand side of the pale blue and white card.

Looking at Lauren O'Reilly's photo magnified on the screen behind O'Rourke, Cathy felt again the tragedy of her death. O'Rourke's voice cut into her thoughts.

'Lauren had registered her Leap card online and it indicates that she travelled from Pearse Street station to Dalkey on Thursday evening, arriving at 22:11. It's a twenty-six minute journey and it was the last trip she made. We know Tom was still alive at that time.' He stopped speaking for a moment, the room silent as they waited for him to continue. 'Tom and Lauren were in the same study group in Trinity and Lauren also interned at Tom's father's radio station over the summer at the end of their first year.' He turned to look at the room. 'Her death looks like suicide, but we have to be open to the possibility that these deaths are somehow connected. Perhaps Lauren was coming to Dalkey to meet Tom. Perhaps they had a row and he helped her over the edge at Dillon's Park. Perhaps a third party was involved in both tragedies. It's our job to find out.' He flicked to a screen showing their photographs side by side.

'We haven't found Lauren's phone. It's possible she had it in her hand when she went over the edge, but we've a request in for her records and identifying her this quickly is hugely in our favour. Significantly she had an envelope in her coat pocket with a note in it saying "I'm sorry" printed in block caps.' The screen changed again and the note appeared, crumpled and water-stained, a blank envelope beside it.

'Who types a suicide note, and then prints it out?' At the back of the room, Jamie Fanning was leaning against the wall, immaculate as always in a trendy casual tweed jacket and chinos, his blond fringe slicked back today.

Frank Gallagher leaned back in his chair. 'Perhaps she was planning to give it to whoever she was meeting, that's why it was in an envelope. You'd expect her to sign it, though.'

O'Rourke grimaced. 'You have a point there, Frank. It's with the technical bureau to see what they can lift from it. They'll be analysing the ink to see what it can tell us.'

The swing doors to the incident room opened and JP, Cathy's friend and housemate, came in, his navy uniform bomber jacket glistening with rain.

'Sorry, Cig, we were on a call.' Taking off his hat, he headed for a spare chair, the familiar Irish term for 'Inspector' rolling naturally off his tongue.

'You're grand, I'm just bringing everyone up to speed.' O'Rourke continued, 'The collision team from Blackrock are handling the technical investigation into Tom Quinn's death. They will have a 3-D reconstruction animation for us by Monday.' He looked at the two uniformed traffic officers. 'And we're pulling CCTV from the surrounding premises. I want every house visited on all and any of the routes these two took that night. Someone must have seen something.'

'Were they dating? Perhaps he dumped her and she jumps off the nearest cliff?' They all turned to look at Fanning, who shrugged theatrically. 'Just seems a bit co-incidental to me.'

O'Rourke shook his head. 'I think that's the point, Fanning. The co-incidence is why we're all here. There are times when I wonder how you got in to the detective unit.' A wave of laughter ran across the room.

Fanning took it as it was intended. 'Charm and wit.' He grinned, looking pointedly at O'Rourke. 'Obviously.'

'Yeah, right.' Cathy turned back to the board as Frank Gallagher leaned forward in his seat towards O'Rourke.

'And what about Tom Quinn? What does Saunders think about him?'

'Saunders found tyre impressions across his back, says he had major internal injuries. He's waiting for toxicology results on both victims but he won't have any conclusions for us for a while. He did, however, find some interesting bruising on Lauren's left shoulder.'

'Not both shoulders, like she'd been shoved?' Fanning asked.

'No, just on her left. He said he'll detail his opinion in the full report.' O'Rourke frowned. 'But I'm not at all happy with the location of Lauren O'Reilly's body, and quite what she was doing in this area in the first place, and I don't want to hang about while we wait to get his results.'

He turned to look at Lauren's smiling face. 'We need to find out if anyone saw Lauren enter the park and if they did, whether she was alone. Exact time of death is tricky because the body was so exposed; but some time Thursday evening is the earliest. Obviously that correlates with the time that she arrived in Dalkey.'

Nodding, Frank Gallagher said, 'Lauren was living in one of the Trinity College halls of residence in Pearse Street, about a three minute walk from the DART station – we're calling in all the CCTV. We'll also be working through the CCTV in Dalkey village itself.'

'What happened to her wallet?'

Everyone turned to look at Cathy. She was staring at Lauren's picture on the board, connections forming in her head. The student card had been in the lining of her coat – had she lost it and ordered another one that was still in her wallet? She'd used her Leap card to get to Dalkey but they hadn't found it yet. Cathy kept her Leap card in her wallet with her ID cards and her bank cards. So where was Lauren's?

'It could have fallen out of her pocket as a result of the fall, or perhaps she was holding it with her phone in one hand when she went over the edge. My wife walks around with her purse and her phone in her hand all the time.' Frank said it half to himself but they were all listening.

'Good point. Frank, can you get the park and the rocks checked today for it? If it went into the sea we may never find it, but she could have dropped it.'

'Will do.'

O'Rourke turned and gazed at the board for a moment like he was processing all the information.

'Frank, can you make up an interview list and work through all their friends? Cat, I want you and Fanning to go back and talk to Tom's parents this morning. See how well they knew Lauren, if at all, or if they had heard Tom talking about her. It's quite possible Conor Quinn has no idea who's interning with the station at any one time, but someone there must have known her other than Tom and might be able to give us a perspective on their relationship.' He paused. 'And then get over to Trinity. We need to take a look at her room, her computer, see if she was planning to meet anyone. Let's find out what happened here.'

Chapter 12

Saturday, noon.

Cathy would have much preferred to chat to Tom Quinn's parents with O'Rourke or Frank Gallagher, instead of Jamie Fanning, but she knew they had plenty to do. Everyone was a suspect until they'd been ruled out, which meant potentially hundreds of interviews, all of which had to be checked and cross-checked. Marie, the family liaison officer, was out sick and with so many lines of enquiry to manage it could be like herding cats, a task made more difficult with reduced manpower.

The second half of the morning briefing had been mainly about cameras and angles and timing. A huge map of the area had been blown up and pinned to the incident board showing where the CCTV cameras in Dalkey were located. Until they got the data they'd requested from the mobile phone providers, they had no idea where Tom had been when he'd sent the text to his mother, and it left a broad window to cover until the time he'd been found. That was a lot of videotape to watch. At least Lauren's Leap card had given them a clear time that she'd exited Dalkey DART Station. It was a fifteen minute walk to Dillon's Park – if she'd headed down the main street of the village she would have been picked up on camera in several locations.

After the briefing, O'Rourke had taken her to one side, muttering, 'Keep an eye on lover boy, make sure he keeps focused. We can catch up later.'

She'd nodded. Jamie Fanning wasn't all bad, he had had his moments in the past, and when he wasn't trying to get laid by every available female, he could be useful.

Walking up the granite steps to the Quinn house, Cathy glanced back at the view, taking in the panorama of the sea from the Pigeon House power station at Poolbeg to the brooding purple of the Wicklow mountains, thinking about Lauren O'Reilly, about the moment she hit the rocks. The sky was bright blue today, so different from the rain-heavy grey of the last few days.

They had been damn lucky to find her. As they'd stood at the edge of the park, waves breaking below them, the sound of the helicopter receding, the fisherman who had spotted the body had explained the tides to her, shaking his head.

'You're lucky we're in neaps, a spring tide would have taken her off the rocks and you may never have found her.' Cathy had looked perplexed as he'd continued. 'Neap tides are fairly high at this time of year, stay that way for about two weeks. Then they change to spring tides – the sea level is even higher at high tide and goes out further at low tide. Her body could easily have been lifted off the rocks and washed away.'

Cathy still hadn't quite got it until he'd explained to her that the tides had nothing to do with the seasons. The spring tide wasn't related to spring and neaps to summer – it was a lunar cycle, changing every two weeks. And the current through Dalkey Sound, between the land and the island, was very strong. If they'd had a high spring tide, Lauren O'Reilly would have been swept right out to sea.

On the Quinns' doorstep, Fanning pressed the round brass doorbell again and a moment later the door opened. Mira, the housekeeper, smiled politely at him. She was just as tidily dressed as the last time they had met her; her eyes red-rimmed. She ushered them into the hall, the scents of lilies still strong from the arrangement on the central table. The brightness of the flowers did nothing to lift the mood. The house felt still and silent.

'Come in. Mr and Mrs Quinn are inside.'

Fanning glanced at Cathy as Mira opened the living room door. The 'Mr and Mrs' sounded strange to Cathy's ear. Everyone used first names in Ireland, but then she didn't know anyone else who had a housekeeper.

Just like the last time they had been here, a fire was roaring in the grate. Orla Quinn was waiting for them, sitting on the sofa closest to it, her legs crossed, her mobile phone on the arm of the chair. At the far end of the room, Cathy got a better look at Conor Quinn than she had the last time she'd visited. He was standing staring out of the living room window, the tails of his jacket pushed back, his hands in his trouser pockets. He was broad shouldered, his dark hair immaculately cut and showing no signs of thinning, his jaw square, if a little soft. He had the type of looks that some women went mad for, but Cathy thought were just too pretty. His navy suit looked handmade but good clothes couldn't dress up a bad temper. The tension was almost palpable. She'd noticed it the last time she was here as well.

'Thank you for seeing us again. This is Detective Garda Jamie Fanning, he's part of the team working on finding out what happened to Tom.' Cathy addressed Orla, who started to stand. 'There's no need to get up, really.'

Orla fell back into the seat, as her husband Conor said, 'Have you found out what happened? Who did this?' It sounded more like a challenge than a question.

'We're making enquiries. We need to ask you both a few more questions if that's OK?'

Cathy kept her voice level. Often when relatives had lost a loved one they looked around for someone to blame, and very often that was the very people trying to help them find answers. Everyone dealt with grief in different ways and Conor Quinn was obviously and understandably angry.

'I don't see what more we can tell you.' His eyes narrowed as he scowled at Cathy, like she was the cause of the problem.

'Please, Conor, they're here to help.' Orla stood up. 'I'll ask Mira to get some tea. Please sit down.'

Jamie Fanning held up his hands. 'You sit down – I'll look after the tea.'

Somehow he made it sound perfectly natural that he would give orders to their housekeeper. Cathy didn't react. Orla was as pale as her cream silk shirt, obviously unable to focus on anything except the death of her son.

'Thank you, would you mind? Mira's just in the kitchen.'

As Fanning slipped out of the door, Conor Quinn turned around to look back out of the window again, rattling the change in his pocket.

'Will this take long?'

Hiding her own thoughts, Cathy sat down on the sofa opposite Orla and pulled out her notebook.

'I know how much of a shock this is for you both.' She sat forward in the chair. 'And I'm aware you were away, Mr Quinn. New York, was it?'

She'd been about to call him Conor but he was still scowling. He didn't turn to acknowledge that she'd spoken; instead he addressed his answer to the window.

'As I told you before. Washington and New York. I was only gone for five days and I come back to this . . .' He said it as if it was somehow his wife's fault.

'A business trip?' Cathy's direct tone made him look around.

'Yes, but I don't see what that's got to do with you. I was visiting a couple of radio stations. We're looking at expanding.'

'And when was the last time you saw Tom?'

'Before I left last Sunday. We had dinner the night before. Orla was out. She's always out, so it was just myself and Tom.'

'And how did he seem?'

Quinn looked at her like she was stupid. 'Exactly the same as normal, he was talking about college, about an assignment he was doing.'

'You've given us a list of his friends at college, thank you for that.' Cathy turned to Orla. 'Did he mention anyone in particular? We need to start by talking to his close friends.'

Cathy kept her face neutral. She wanted to see if Tom's parents mentioned Lauren O'Reilly.

Orla looked a little lost. 'I'm not sure, he had lots of friends . . . He talked about Olivier Ayari a lot, about him being very bright but a bit nerdy. Tom liked him. I think he was fascinated by him and his brother. I only met them briefly at the Ayari Building launch. Oliver seemed quite quiet compared to Xavier, they are completely different.' She turned to her husband. 'Do you remember, Conor, you were talking to Xavier for ages?' She turned back to Cathy. 'Their family paid for the building. I think

Tom said that they'd bought a property on the Vico Road as well. They must be planning to spend time here at some point.'

Anna Lockharte had told Cathy that they had a house in Killiney as well. 'Anyone else? Girlfriends?'

Orla shrugged, her eyes filling. 'I'm sorry, I can't think of anyone.' She seemed genuinely at a loss.

'Would the name Lauren O'Reilly sound familiar to you at all?'

Orla frowned, thinking hard. 'It does actually . . . Isn't she the girl who interned with you, Conor, at Life Talk. I'm sure it is?' Orla looked around at her husband. 'Conor? Lauren O'Reilly? I'm sure that was her.'

As if he'd only just heard her, Quinn turned and shrugged. 'I've no idea. I don't keep track of the interns. I'll have to ask the station manager to check—'

Orla interrupted him. 'The pretty girl. You must remember her. Blonde. It was when Tom was working there too – she's doing the same course as Tom at Trinity.'

Cathy looked over at Conor Quinn. 'Mr Quinn? Did Tom talk about her to you?'

'I don't think so – maybe. I don't know. What's she got to do with Tom anyway?'

'We don't know at this stage. Could they have been in a relationship?' Cathy looked at Orla.

'I think he'd have mentioned her if they were. I mean he did mention her occasionally, but in a more general context, I think they hung around together in a group.' Orla reached down beside the sofa and pulled a tissue from a box on the floor, dabbing her eyes. 'He was just enjoying his time in college so much, he had a lot of friends.'

'Do you think he could have been meeting Lauren in the village on Thursday night? Could she have been the reason he went out?'

For the first time since Cathy had arrived, Conor Quinn seemed to engage with the conversation, interrupting her.

'I do remember her now, I think. She was dating some thug from the inner city when she was working with us. Real gurrier. Used to pick her up in a four-wheel drive after work. Could he have something to do with this? Have you asked her?'

'I'm afraid we can't ask her, Mr Quinn. Her body was found on rocks below Dillon's Park yesterday.'

'Oh my God.' Orla's gasp was one of pure shock.

Outside in the car, Fanning fired up the engine as Cathy buckled her seat belt.

'That went well.' Fanning glanced up at the house as he turned the car around.

'There's a lot of tension there between Orla and Conor Quinn, whatever's going on. But what the hell happened to you? How does it take twenty minutes to make tea?'

Fanning glanced over to her, a sly look on his face. 'I was chatting to Mira about the inner workings of the Quinn household.' He raised his eyebrows and threw her a knowing look – a bloody irritating knowing look. 'Let's get out of here and I'll tell you.'

He pulled the car down the gravelled drive, glancing in the rear-view mirror as he rounded the corner to the gates. They were already sliding open as they approached.

Cathy sat back in her seat. 'So . . .?'

'So, reading between the lines, it sounds like Mira does everything, basically keeps the wheels moving on the Quinn household machine. She does all the cooking and the washing and virtually brought Tom up. She books all Conor's trips and makes sure his shirts are laundered. Orla works from an office upstairs but even when she's in the house, they rarely see her.'

Pulling out of the gates and swinging left, he headed back to the station as he continued.

'She said Conor Quinn works really hard, that the radio station is starting to do really well. Both parents are a bit work obsessed but I suppose it pays the bills. They wanted Tom to go into one of the companies, Mira says, except Tom wasn't keen.'

'Was that a source of tension?'

He shrugged. 'Long time till he'd have to worry about a real job. Amazing house, private education, housekeeper. Takes the pressure off a bit.'

Cathy corrected him. 'Young attractive housekeeper.'

Fanning raised his eyebrows but kept his eyes on the road. 'Yes, I noticed that too.'

'So ...' She rolled her hands theatrically. 'Is Conor Quinn usually that bad tempered?'

Fanning shrugged, chewing his lip. 'She said his plane was delayed so when he got home he was already in a foul temper. He gets terrible jet lag apparently. She said he didn't take the news about Tom well at all, but how could you?'

'What about Tom, what did she have to say about him?'

Fanning changed gear. 'She said she thought Tom was very happy. She corroborated what his mum said about him going for walks sometimes at night, that she thought it was because he was studying too hard and needed the air. No particular pattern to them although he seemed to go out between eight and nine quite often, sometimes later. She didn't think he was dating anyone. She's absolutely shocked to be honest, she was shaking while I was talking to her. She seems to be very close to them all.'

'How long has she worked for them?'

'Since Tom was small, she came as a nanny but she went to college here, did night classes. I get the impression she's very bright. She said she left Sarajevo when she was about fifteen.'

'During the war?'

Fanning indicated to pull into the yard behind the Garda station, pausing while the security gates opened for a van coming out.

'Yes, she clammed up a bit about that. Her family were refugees. It sounded tough.'

'Did she recognise Lauren's name?'

'She didn't know her specifically, said Tom had lots of friends, of both sexes. But he didn't really bring people home.'

'I'm interested in these walks he seemed to take at night. When I spoke to her originally Mira said she thought she'd heard him go out a bit before eight. But Orla thought he was home by eleven. So he needed to have left the house again in order for the accident to have happened. Could he have gone out twice?'

'I suppose it depends where he went the first time.' Fanning flicked on his indicator. 'If he did meet Lauren and she ended up falling off the cliff for whatever reason, he could have panicked and come home, and then got worried he might have left something behind and gone out again to check? Wouldn't be the first time a killer has gone back to the crime scene.'

Chapter 13

As Anna Lockharte pushed open the front door to her apartment her phone pipped with a text: *Send on. What do?*

Her niece had a mastery of text speak that never failed to make her laugh. But perhaps it wasn't classic text speakery but rather Hope's take on it. With a Mensa level IQ and a whole bundle of anxiety issues that matched Anna's own, Hope was a very special girl. And she had such a dry wicked sense of humour that she could keep Anna entertained for hours just with a description of her day. Which was probably what Anna needed today. Her plan to take her mind off Tom and Lauren, to get out of the apartment and focus on her marking, had been a total failure this morning. By twelve o'clock she'd decided she might as well be miserable somewhere more comfortable than her office, somewhere where she could eat ice cream and watch an old movie and try and work through her grief.

But 'What do?' was a good question. What do indeed? Anna dropped her handbag and papers in the hall and looked at her screen again. Clicking through to her email, she forwarded the message about the conference to Hope with the details of the virus warning her system had flashed up, asking if she could check it out. If there really was something weird about the email she'd received, Anna was sure Hope would spot it.

As she waited for the email to land and Hope's reply, Anna went into the kitchen and flicked on the kettle, heading back to her bedroom and changing into her oversized New York Yankees sweatshirt. She pulled her hair into a ponytail and wrapped it deftly into a messy knot, copper curls trying to escape like springs. Being at home was a much better idea than trying to distract herself in her office.

In the living room, she put her tea and laptop down beside her and sat back on the sofa, flexing her shoulders. A shaft of rare winter sun fell on Hope's silver-grey cat, Minou, who was stretched out to her fullest capacity right in the middle of the floor. Anna took a moment to turn her face into the rays. The apartment was all glass and steel, low maintenance, and with only two bedrooms it was small but airy and bright. And the living room was her favourite room – on the end of the block, two of its walls were glass, with electric curtains that ensured her privacy, and a recessed gas fire that meant she was never cold. One thing she missed about New York, Paris and London was the sunshine. Dublin was wonderful in many ways, but it really wasn't very warm. And when you got a day like today, the sky azure blue, the sun streaming in, Ireland was the most amazing place to be on earth, and you just needed to enjoy the moment.

Closing her eyes, Anna suddenly felt her sadness manifesting in a physical lump in her chest. It might be a beautiful day but two of her students wouldn't ever be able to enjoy the sunshine again. Her eyes filled with tears.

Tom's face – his laughing blue eyes and thick ink-black hair – jumped into her mind. What had he been involved in that Lauren had got caught up in, that could lead her to contemplate, let alone commit, suicide?

Had she been pregnant? Had she and Tom had a relationship and she'd gone to tell him, and he'd dumped her that night? Anna knew about the Magdalene laundries, about the shame of unplanned pregnancy that had left an indelible stain on Irish history, that even today some families found it hard to cope with. Had she been so frightened of her parents' response that Tom's reaction had literally sent her over the edge? That seemed utterly ridiculous in this day and age, but perhaps Lauren thought that getting pregnant was truly catastrophic for her?

Anna didn't know if the Guards would be able to tell her, but if pregnancy was the cause of all this, surely it would have shown up in the post-mortem? Perhaps it had, and that's why they had asked her about Lauren's relationships?

She took a long slow breath, focusing on her mug of green tea. *Focus. Breathe.* In for the count of five, out for the count of seven. She could feel the physical symptoms of anxiety building in her stomach, a feeling that she knew would make her feel physically sick and unable to eat if she didn't get on top of it. *Focus. Breathe.* She put her tea down again and put her face in her hands as she leaned forward, her elbows resting on her thighs.

So many things suddenly seemed unimportant – like Xavier's message, also waiting to be dealt with in her inbox. *Focus. Breathe.*

This worked, she knew it worked, she just had to breathe.

The beautiful little book about mindfulness and breathing that Rob had given her was on her bedside table. His face appeared in her mind as she thought about it. Rob Power, who understood her totally and whom she loved passionately, but whom she could never admit to loving. His position in the security services made any hope of them developing a proper relationship impossible; that, and the fact that he was married, however unhappily.

It was at moments like this that she wished so hard that he could be here to hold her.

She'd learned to live with their distance but Anna knew she would have moved continents to be a part of his life. Perhaps they would kill each other if they ever had more than a few hours together but until they tried they would never know, and in the back of her mind she'd always wanted to try. They were a perfect fit in so many ways but the constraints of his situation prevented him from connecting with her properly. He was part of her past, but Anna secretly hoped that he was also a possibility for her future.

It was all so complicated. From the moment they'd met at her sister Jennifer's wedding she had been pulled towards him. And the pull had grown stronger whenever they'd met at a family gathering. And all the times they'd found to catch up for lunch when Rob happened to be in her part of the world. After the Skype chats and the phone calls – all supposedly work related, of course. But falling in love with your new brother-in-law's sister's *husband* wasn't a good game plan. And if Charles's sister Rebecca had any idea that her husband might have found someone else – well, Anna didn't want to think about that. They didn't have children but that didn't make the situation any better. That first night, the night they'd met at Charles and Jennifer's wedding in the Hamptons, she and Rob had ended up sitting out the dancing at the same table, talking into the small hours, discovering common ground between his job and her PhD thesis, before they'd even realised they loved the same films, had the same favourite book.

She sighed deeply, listening to Minou's rhythmic purring, the sound magnified by the hardwood floor. The cat had rolled over closer to the sofa, her soft belly like grey velvet. Perhaps one day Rob would be free. Until then the book he'd given her, with its pale blue cover and charming Victorian engravings, calmed her whenever she looked at it, and whenever she felt really stretched or overwhelmed she reached for it, absorbing the author's advice word for word. It had been a gift at a time in her life when she had felt that everything was falling apart, and that little book had felt like a lifebuoy.

But it couldn't solve her current worries – the tragic loss of two young lives.

And then, on top of everything, there was Xavier's email. *He really gave her the creeps.* But why was she worrying about that? In the grand scheme of things how important was it? Tom's and Lauren's families were grieving and she was worrying about getting hit on by a student. *Let's get real here.* She was sure she could delay answering until she was ready and Xavier would just think she was busy. Instinctively she always responded to her inbox immediately, but this could definitely wait.

The Internet made you feel like you were on call 24–7. Anna knew Hope had a lot of difficulty regulating her online life; the imagined need to be available day and night was a constant drain. Hope had met the most amazing people over the Internet, other teens all over the world who shared her love of music and science, who understood her intense desire to learn. Anna smiled. Jennifer would have been so proud of her, of how she was adapting to life in Ireland, of the friends she had made, of what a beautiful young woman she was turning into. She shared their red hair – Anna's was curly, Jennifer's straight, Hope's something in between, thick and wavy and the most incredible blend of colours. Titian would have gone mad for her.

Minou shifted, grumbling to herself in her sleep, and Anna smiled, reaching over to rub the cat's belly with the toe of her Converse. Hope couldn't keep a cat at boarding school, so Anna had ended up minding her. It wasn't a problem; Minou was great company, kept her sane, and she'd always been an indoor cat so she hadn't noticed particularly that she wasn't in Rome or Paris. The nomadic lifestyle of a diplomat meant that since Hope had been born she'd lived in more countries than most people visited in a lifetime. And so had Minou. Anna felt that dull nauseous feeling of anxiety build again. Little knowing what the future held, Jennifer had given Hope the Russian Blue when Paris had been first mentioned as a possible posting, when Minou was not much more than a silver ball of fluff.

Anna loved her brother-in-law Charles Montgomery dearly, but the posting in Paris had been difficult from the start. Jennifer had never really taken to the Parisians, and then they'd all found themselves in the bank.

Since that day, the day Jennifer had died, Anna's points of reference had changed. She didn't have her big sister any more, instead she'd become like Hope's big sister, had tried to be there for her all she could. Anna knew that when *she* was sixteen, she hadn't had a care in the world. For Hope, life was very different.

Anna was about to get up to boil the kettle again when an email pinged into her inbox from Hope. From one of her many anonymous personal accounts, 'John Smith'. Anna picked up her laptop, open on the sofa beside her.

You're right. This email is weird. The warning is about a Trojan worm which could be someone trying to hack your computer. Forward everything that came in today to Uncle Rob to check out properly – his antivirus software should have isolated it, but if it's new code, it might not have.

Anna typed back:

Thank you, will do.

Hope replied:

Coolio. See you next Thursday morning, don't forget you need to sign me out. Excited!

Anna sent back a smiley face emoji.

She smiled at Hope's excitement. She was taking her to London the following weekend and she wasn't sure which of them was looking forward to it more. Anna couldn't wait to show her around the city – the plan was that they'd fly over on Thursday afternoon and once Anna had got her lecture out of the way on Friday they'd have the rest of the weekend to themselves. Hope would find plenty to do while Anna was tied up, she was sure. They both needed a break and her speaking engagement there had been the perfect excuse for a sightseeing trip.

But Hope was right, Rob always said she should check with him about anything she was worried about. It had been clear that ISIS had had very clear targets that day in Paris, and in the ensuing investigation, backtracking through her correspondence with Jen, the fact that they needed to call at the bank had been mentioned. There was a strongly held belief in intelligence circles that their email had been hacked, and the fact that the American ambassador's wife and daughter would be in the bank on the way to their lunch appointment in the restaurant next door was a factor in the timing of the attack. They could easily have hit the restaurant instead but there was significance in attacking a pillar of western capitalism. It made Anna shudder to think of it. Her trip to Paris had been the reason they'd been in the bank, she'd wanted to get cash out for Hope's birthday. She was the reason Jen was dead. She wasn't sure if she'd ever learn to live with that.

It had been Rob's team who had gone over her and Jen's laptops forensically, to try and detect if they had been compromised – not always easy, as Rob had explained, malicious viruses were often coded to self-destruct after they had served their purpose. Privately Rob had assured her that it wasn't her fault; in this instance it was extremely unlikely to have been her emails that created the situation. More likely one of the embassy staff who had overheard Jen and Hope chatting, or heard Jen on the phone to her, had passed on the information. He knew what he was talking about – he'd been approached by the US government before he had even graduated with his Master's from MIT. He led a team that focused on cyber threats, and Anna knew that Rob was increasingly worried, as she was, that ISIS in particular were engaging with rogue hackers to broaden their terror campaigns. The Anonymous hacker group had declared war on ISIS but there were other groups, Anonymous' rivals, who were solely focused on cyber dominance and destabilising democracy, who didn't care who their paymasters were and only wanted to go down in history for orchestrating the most devastating cyberattack. Anna was developing a whole section of her course in international terrorism to reflect the developments in cybercrime. She knew there was a bigger picture, but a part of her would always feel that Jen's death had been all her fault.

Chapter 14

Saturday, 2 p.m.

'You sure you want to do this now, Cat? You've been up since dawn and you're due off at six.'

O'Rourke turned around from his office window, his hands in his pockets. He'd abandoned his tie and had his sleeves rolled up. It was only early afternoon but he looked like he'd done a week's work already.

Cathy came into the office properly and leaned on the back of the guest chair. She was tired. After the gym in the morning and then the briefing, interviewing Orla and Conor Quinn again had been pretty intense, but she wanted to get this bit done, and if she was honest with herself, over with.

'It's a two hour drive to Longford and Lauren's parents' place is this side of the town, we won't be there more than an hour. And it's Sunday tomorrow. They're farmers, it'll be their only day off and there's a good chance they'll be in church in the morning. The last thing they'll want is us bowling in and asking loads of questions. We can be there and back by this evening.' She straightened up. 'I want to find out what sort of girl Lauren was. Everyone's saying she was very shy. I want to know if that's just because she was up here in a strange environment, or if she was normally quiet. Perhaps she was the life and soul of the party out of uni and we're completely missing a trick.'

O'Rourke held her eye for a moment than nodded curtly. 'I've got overtime authorised – we're running two enquiries simultaneously here, one of which is clearly murder. Reaction times are crucial.'

He didn't need to tell her. Before she could reply, Fanning stuck his head around the office door.

'I've got an unmarked car from DDU in Cabinteely. It's a bit of a junker but it should get us there.'

'Grand so, let me grab a coffee and we'll get on the road.' Cathy turned to follow Fanning out of the office.

'Eh, Cat?'

She paused at the door. 'Yeah?'

'Make sure Fanning stays inside the speed limit? You're a valuable asset, we don't want any accidents.'

Her face cracked into a grin. 'Don't worry, I think self-preservation is pretty high on his list of priorities.'

The drive to Longford was long, slow and marked mainly by the number of tractors they had to overtake. Also by Fanning's taste in music, which had surprised Cathy. She'd expected chart music but it appeared he was more into Shania Twain than Taylor Swift. Ever since she'd first gone to Pearse Street as a newbie and O'Rourke had been her sergeant, she'd never forgotten his advice:

'Welcome to Pearse Street. There's Templemore and there's the real world. This is where your training really starts. No smoking in the car, no country music and you'll do grand.'

It still made her smile. And she could imagine O'Rourke's humour if he had to spend two hours in a car with 007. To make it worse, as they'd hit a clear bit of the N4 close to Kinnegad he'd started singing.

Garth Brooks didn't have anything to worry about. 007 might have earned his nickname from his gorgeous dates and his conviction that he was devastatingly attractive, but he was never going to make it on *The X-Factor*.

The O'Reilly farm was signposted from the main road, down a deep, dark, narrow winding lane that seemed to go on for miles. Between breaks in the hedges, Cathy could see endless empty fields, the occasional whitethorn tree lonely in the middle, silhouetted in the gathering darkness. Single whitethorns were said to be the places where the fairies gathered and were considered sacred. Roads had even been diverted to avoid felling them lest bad luck fall on the builders and the road users. She shivered.

Bad luck had definitely fallen here, but Cathy was quite sure that it wasn't down to the fairies.

With the chill of the evening already setting in, the cattle now snug in their barn, Cathy could see how such powerful folklore could evolve around these ancient lonely trees. She was sure she'd read that some were four hundred years old, and stories were told of people seeing lights dancing around them at night.

Cathy was very happy with the lights of the city any day, and as they rounded a bend she was relieved to see a yard and a substantial Georgian two-storey farmhouse ahead of them, its windows lit to the encroaching darkness.

'Looks like we're here.'

Fanning slowed and glanced across at her. 'This is going to be fun, isn't it?'

She nodded silently. Nothing was going to be easy about the next hour. As soon as Saunders was able to release her body, the undertakers would bring Lauren home, but Cathy had no idea when that would be. She knew Lauren's parents would want to come up to Dublin to collect her things from college, but her room had been sealed until it could be searched. And Cathy wasn't sure when they would be able to release it.

When their whole world was falling apart, people needed definite answers, and the only thing they knew for sure right now was that Lauren O'Reilly was dead.

Cathy had called ahead and the O'Reillys were expecting them. As Fanning pulled up outside the five-bar gate in the granite wall surrounding the house the porch light came on and the front door opened. Silhouetted against the light from the hall, Cathy could see a thin woman in jeans and a chunky roll neck sweater, her arms crossed, waiting for them. A dog appeared beside her, looking out silently into the night.

Hopping out of the car, Fanning lifted the latch on the gate and pushed it open. It swung easily, well oiled. Everything about the place seemed to be well oiled, from the tidy path that swept to the house to the gleaming red front door. Cathy's boots crunched on the gravel. She'd pulled on her black jacket before she'd left the station, the one she kept in her locker for court, had tied her hair back in a low ponytail. But looking smart didn't make her feel any better.

'Mrs O'Reilly. I'm Detective Garda Cathy Connolly. Thank you for seeing us. We're very sorry for your loss, we know this is a terrible time.'

With the light behind her, Cathy couldn't see Eileen O'Reilly's face clearly, but from the picture she'd seen on Lauren's student pass, she recognised the same bone structure, the same high cheekbones.

'Come inside; it's cold out.'

Turning abruptly, Eileen walked along a black and white tiled hall. It was warm inside, cosy. The type of home that featured in interior magazines. Fanning pushed the front door closed behind them and Cathy followed Lauren's mother down the hall. She stopped to show them into the living room.

'Himself's inside. Cows need to be done at five. You've just caught him. I'll get the tea.'

'Himself' was obviously Lauren's father, a fit weather-beaten man in his early fifties, his red and navy check shirt emphasising a face flushed by the flames from a huge open fire. As Cathy put her hand out to greet him, a log shifted, sending sparks up the chimney.

'Tadgh, I'm Lauren's dad.'

'Thank you for seeing us.'

'Sit down. Excuse me if I wish we'd never had occasion to meet.'

Cathy nodded; she seconded that. Before she could say more Eileen appeared with a huge tray laden with a teapot and cups, home-baked scones crowded on a plate. Moments like this always gave Cathy a physical pain. How people could find the ability to be hospitable when they were in so much pain themselves, she would never understand.

As Eileen began to pour the tea, Cathy sat forward on the sofa.

'I believe the local Gardaí spoke to you yesterday? I'm afraid at this stage I don't have much more to add, but we need to establish exactly what happened to Lauren on the cliff, and how she got there.' Lauren's father nodded curtly. Cathy continued, the silence filled with grief. 'Can you tell me a bit about Lauren – did she enjoy going to Trinity?'

Eileen sat down beside her husband. 'She loved it – well, this term she did. We hardly heard from her. At the start it was a big change, she was on the phone every day and she came home at weekends whenever she could. She'd been excited about going. She had her heart set on this international politics course, but living up in Dublin was a big change, to be sure.'

'Did she have many friends that she talked about?' Beside Cathy, Fanning had slipped his notebook out of his pocket. They'd agreed that she'd ask the questions.

'She found it hard to make friends at the start. She met a lovely Spanish girl, Paula, early on. I think they were both a bit like fish out of water.' Lauren's mother's voice broke. Her husband put his arm around her, pulling her close. 'And then she got herself a job in the radio over the summer and she met the Quinn lad, Tom. He seemed to be a nice fella, he looked out for her. I think she'd seen him in lectures but didn't feel she could talk to him up to then, like – but she got to know him a bit at the radio station.'

Cathy nodded slowly. 'When you say she wasn't in touch much this term, you felt that was because she was happier?'

'I don't know. Really I don't. She sounded happy. I thought she wasn't in touch so much because she'd settled in. Lots of the second years move out of the halls into rented flats, but she volunteered for something so she got a place in the student accommodation for another year. It all seemed grand, I really thought she'd settled. And then . . .'

As she trailed off, a small ginger cat pushed open the living room door and jumped up onto the sofa between the O'Reillys. It sat looking at Cathy, its eyes an accusing shade of green.

'There are a lot of questions, and we're looking for as many answers as we can.'

Cathy paused, glancing at the cat. It was wearing a lilac collar with diamanté studs that flashed in the light of the fire. She had the hardest question to ask now.

'Had Lauren ever given you any indication that she might take her own life?'

Eileen O'Reilly looked at Cathy, incredulous. 'She didn't take her own life.' She couldn't have been more definite.

'You seem very sure.'

'I am. The Guards told us she was found on rocks below a cliff. There's no way she would have jumped. Just no way. Laurie was terrified of water. She never learned to swim, it caused huge problems at school when the class had lessons.' Eileen looked from Cathy to Fanning keenly. 'She almost drowned in the trough when she was five. She wouldn't have gone anywhere near that cliff edge unless there was someone else there. She just wouldn't. If she'd wanted to commit suicide she'd have taken a load of pills so she could go to sleep and not wake up. There's no way she would have jumped voluntarily. Not a chance.'

Chapter 15

Saturday, 6 p.m.

The cafe was quiet, even though it was a Saturday evening. It was hardly surprising though; the coffee was terrible, bitter, and hardly hot enough to call itself coffee. But the Internet was open access. It wasn't quite as secure as the library, but it wasn't far off. He turned the screen to face him. He was sitting right at the back wall, facing the door, so no one could see what he was looking at.

His fingers flying over the keys, he logged in to the admin area of the Discovery Quay site. This was where he saved the links to the camera feeds he didn't make public; usually it was because there wasn't enough happening, or someone had gone on holiday. Site visitors liked variety so it helped to have some streams in reserve. Although since he'd set up that link on the beauty website he'd had a constant supply of new feeds that were building into an interesting library. Soon it wouldn't matter if some of them were inactive. It was amazing how few women had virus protection and who didn't cover their laptop cameras. And that seemed to be the case all over the world – for his visitors, language wasn't an issue.

He clicked into a live window on the feed he'd been waiting for. The whole webcam thing was all about timing, and a little bit of luck. Not everyone used their laptop in the bedroom or the bathroom, although he'd discovered a lot of women watched Netflix in the bath. A fact that was keeping a large number of his visitors very satisfied.

Mobile phone cameras were his next target. He was going to have some real fun with them. Wait till he showed Karim. His mind went back to the empty office in Shepherd's Bush. He'd only been in Dublin a few months, and Karim had called to tell him that the group were relocating from Frankfurt to London, the excitement in his voice barely concealed. He wanted them all to meet up face to face.

The building Karim had found was ideal: a disused office block, loose papers scattered over the grey carpet in the entrance hall, a pile of cellophane covered telephone directories propping open the door to the stairs. On the way up he'd glanced through the glass landing doors to see odd chairs and desks abandoned at strange angles, a desiccated potted plant, trailing wires where computers had been disconnected. When they'd got to the fourth floor, he'd followed Karim across the landing and into what would have been a huge open-plan room, empty now. As the door sucked closed behind them Karim had beckoned him over to a group of ten guys of different nationalities sitting in a circle on the thin corded carpet, their laptops on their knees. They were all dressed in jeans or combats, sneakers and hoodies. Lots of layers as the building was freezing.

'Hey, guys, he's here.' The group had hardly raised their eyes. Karim had turned to him. 'We're using the bank next door's Wi-Fi. It's sweet.'

'What's everyone working on?'

Karim had turned to him, his smile slow. 'Maximum disruption. We're getting into the mainline station and underground computer systems. The signalling is a closed network but if we can get a worm in we can have some fun. That's what everyone's doing at the moment, trying to find a weakness and perfecting the assault code.'

'Like Stuxnet, man!' Without raising his eyes from the screen, one of the hackers lifted his hand in a victory signal.

'Yeah, if we can get the code we're developing onto an employee laptop we can get in. If we're lucky we can use a stick to get the worm in, but the boys are experimenting with email too. If we're fast enough we can develop an intelligent worm that won't be recognised by virus protection.'

He'd known Karim had been working on something interesting, had been teasing him about the size of the project for months, but Karim had wanted to save the big reveal until they could all meet in London. His curiosity piqued, he'd sat down beside the two guys nearest him, both bundled in fur hooded parkas and baseball caps.

'Why not go for something bigger if you've got a Stuxnet type worm? Not nuclear power plants like that one maybe, but the power grid, electricity supply companies? Think of the power you'd have then.'

Karim laughed at the pun, then smiled that slow smile, his thin moustache curving on his top lip.

'We want this worm to self-destruct twenty-four hours after the attack. We're working on making it responsive so it will send us back as much info as possible so we can develop the next generation, and then . . . Well, the power supply would be a natural escalation. Maximum disruption. Maximum kudos. And a nice big pay packet into the bargain.'

He'd nodded to himself then; it was perfect. Karim and his mates knew what they were about, and they were wired. He had good stuff going on now, a steady income stream, but it wasn't *exactly exciting. Money didn't turn him on like this sort of challenge did. He'd agreed straight away to join the crew. They called themselves Unanimous for a reason – they were in total agreement that they were awesome, and they were going to prove it to the world, whatever it took.*

A movement on the screen in front of him drew his eye and his mind left the Unanimous squad in London. He tuned back into the empty cafe and his laptop screen. On the web page he had a perfect image from the camera on the laptop he'd hacked. It looked like it was resting on a gold velour sofa in a modern apartment, floorboards pale, walls white or cream. A large widescreen TV dominated the shot. The angle was a bit off, like it was tilted on a cushion, but someone was moving around in the periphery of the camera's vision. He almost jumped back as a shape loomed large on the screen, blurred as the camera refocused. A large grey cat settled down in front of the keyboard and began washing its paws. He smiled. The camera shot was clear and crisp. It was only a matter of time before the image became a lot more interesting.

Chapter 16

Saturday, 8 p.m.

Cathy's house was in darkness when she got home, her windscreen wipers on full on the short drive from the station to the house she shared in Shankill with three other Guards. It had started raining as they'd headed back from Longford, but the roads were clear so they had made good time. Fanning had dropped her off to collect her own car and gone straight to the pub.

Pulling up outside the neat semi she was half-surprised to see the place empty, but then remembered that Decko was on nights. JP was out with Frank Gallagher, waiting for 007 to join them, and Eamon was on his long weekend. He'd gone home to Galway for a few days with an enormous bag of washing, to be pampered by his mother. Which meant she had the place to herself, and right now she needed it.

She pipped the central locking on her Mini; the car flashed its indicators to show it had responded, making her smile as she dashed to the shelter of the half roof over the front door, her keys ready in her hand. It was ridiculous but she always felt like the car was talking to her when it flashed, saying good morning and goodnight. But she had a special bond with this car – it had taken a lot for her to get back out on the road after her first gorgeous laser blue Mini had been blown up. The Garda advanced driving course had helped hugely, giving her back her nerve and rebuilding her confidence, teaching her skills that had come in very useful since. She'd taken her time in the showroom choosing another car. She still felt like the compensation she'd received was dirty money somehow and had stashed most of it in the bank for a rainy day, but her new Mini had been her one indulgence and she loved it.

Pushing the front door closed behind her, hearing the rain hammering on the roof, Cathy switched the hall light on. Despite the rain and the chill outside, the heating was on, and the house was warm and welcoming. She always felt safe here; she had done before the explosion, but now she valued her home even more. When you never knew what each day might bring, having that security was vital.

Cathy leaned back on the cold glass of the hall door, thoughts of safety taking her straight to Tom Quinn and Lauren O'Reilly. What had really been going on that night?

Scooping up the post that was scattered on the mat by her feet, Cathy headed for the black granite kitchen, the overhead spots bouncing off the polished surfaces as she switched them on. She threw the pile of letters, bills and circulars onto the gleaming counter and opened the fridge, pulling out a half bottle of white wine. Her training and diet regime was strict but one glass tonight wouldn't hurt. And with everyone out nobody would know. She smiled to herself as she sloshed the wine into a glass. Some days you just needed something to help you relax.

And right now she needed to be nice to herself. It had been a very, very long day.

She'd parked the promotions list firmly in a dark place in her head until now, but she knew she needed to have a really long think about it. Calmly and rationally.

O'Rourke's face flashed into her head. There suddenly seemed to be so many uncertainties in her life. She'd been so sure she knew where she was going, what her next move was, but now this. She still couldn't work out if O'Rourke wanted their relationship to go further. He either wanted to be with her or he didn't, but she knew it was complicated. She certainly wanted to try, though.

But she was getting ahead of herself. Again. Way ahead.

Sometimes she felt that anything between them was something that was going to stay firmly in her head, but then there were times when she'd catch a look, like today in the incident room, or they'd have a moment, and she'd see something in him – something he was trying to hold back. Right before the explosion he'd been about to take her to dinner, and she'd really felt like he cared – was about to step in and be her knight in shining armour. She'd certainly needed one then, with the mess she'd been in.

Cathy leaned on the counter nursing the cold glass in her hand. She shivered. *Christ, what was happening to her?* She'd thought she was getting on top of everything, that life had returned to normal. Well, maybe not everyone's normal, but her normal. She was on fire in the gym, was going to get her title back in April at the national finals, and based on her assessed coursework to date, she was guaranteed to get a first in her Master's when she handed in her final assignment in May. She'd astounded her tutors in college with the speed she'd flown through the course. *It had all been going so well.*

And then that fecking promotions list had come out.

What else did she have to do to prove she was a damn good officer and should be stepping into the profiler job? She knew she was young, but she'd had more experience than some officers would see in their whole careers. Surely that gave her an edge, and her age gave her insight into younger offenders.

Cathy took a sip of her wine. One thing she knew about herself was that she always needed a plan, an overall picture of where she was going, to make sure that she got there. Without one she felt rudderless, insecure. But now her master plan was in the manure pile of political favours that paralysed the country, that meant the best people for the job didn't always get it.

Deliberately, she took a deep breath. *She was getting cross again.* But it was hard not to be cross, to see what was good about not getting the job she wanted. More so, in making the application, Cathy had made the decision in her head that it was time to move on from Dun Laoghaire, that it was time to spread her wings to further her career. She'd started to look forward to new challenges, had begun to see how she could get stale staying in the same station, in the same unit for too long. And O'Rourke wouldn't be there for ever. That was for sure. She chewed her lip. She needed a change, and she needed it soon.

There was another option. An option that would get her out of Dun Laoghaire and right into the middle of the action. She'd been half-joking when she'd mentioned joining the Emergency Response Unit before, but it had been in the back of her mind for a long time and it was one she was very curious about. When Sarah Jane had disappeared back in October, she'd seen the ERU in action up close, had been wowed by their technology as well as their firepower.

Cathy topped up her glass again, taking another sip and savouring it. She so rarely had any alcohol when she was training that she could feel it hitting the mark.

She needed to keep positive. She needed to hold on to the good. She was going to get a first in her Master's, she'd got her fitness back and she was holding it together – mainly. And when she wasn't, nobody could see.

Was that what had happened to Lauren? Her mind shot back to meeting Lauren's parents.

Lauren's mother's revelation about her fear of water put a very different slant on things, that was for sure. If Lauren was terrified of water, it made no sense that she would have gone to the cliff edge to jump. Had she been drunk? Had it been too dark for her to see the drop? Or had she not intended to jump at all, but had slipped? Maybe she'd been meeting someone right at the end of the path and had lost her footing and fallen over the edge?

Or, maybe she'd been pushed.

Cathy tapped her glass on her teeth. She was sure there were techs who were better at physics than she was and could work out from the photographs the exact angle at which Lauren had gone off the cliff, and how much force was required for her to end up where they found her. But who dived onto rocks?

Her body had been found facing the sea. Surely if she *had* jumped, she'd be the other way up. In Cathy's experience few suicides wanted to see their fate coming at them.

Cathy had tried O'Rourke several times on the way back from Longford to tell him about Lauren's fear of water but he'd been constantly engaged, so she'd ended up emailing him. She pulled her phone out of her pocket to see if he'd replied, just as it pipped with a text.

O'Rourke. There were times when she thought he was psychic.

Have you eaten?

She texted back: *No.*

The doorbell rang.

Chapter 17

It took Cathy a moment to react to the sound of the doorbell. It took her another moment to get to the front door, opening it wide to a gust of cold air and O'Rourke sheltering under the half roof over the front door, rain falling solidly behind him like a curtain. Backlit by the street lights he looked like something out of a black and white movie.

She stood back to let him in, closing the door quickly to keep the heat in. Huge in the narrow hallway, cloaked in cold air, he stood with his back to her and shook his head and shoulders like a dog, raindrops scattering like icy shards of glass.

'Bloody hell, it's wet.'

'You don't say.'

He turned around, his face serious. 'Fish and chips all right? There was a queue a mile long in the Chinese.'

'The Boss will kill me.'

He grinned. 'Don't worry, I'll make sure you're on starvation rations for the rest of the week.'

Like hell, and he knew fish and chips were her favourite.

'Did you get onion rings?'

'Of course.'

Five minutes later they were sitting in the kitchen, brown paper bags torn open in the middle of the table. The Boss really was going to kill her. It wasn't time to increase her calories just yet, but it was one night and it had been as shit a week as she'd had in a long time.

O'Rourke had thrown his coat over the banister on the way in, dumping the bag on the table, before slipping his suit jacket over the back of the chair. Then he'd gone straight to the fridge to find a beer. He'd been here often enough before to know where everything was.

He took a long swig. 'God, I needed that.'

Not nearly as much as she needed fish and chips. And he'd remembered the salt and vinegar.

'Where is everyone? This house is normally like the Mad Cow at rush hour.'

He sat down opposite her at the round table and tore a strip off the fresh cod he'd bought for them to share, the flesh breaking away in chunks.

'Decko's on nights, JP's out on the batter with 007 and Eamon's on his long weekend home, will be back Monday night.'

'So you're all alone?'

'And enjoying every minute of it, thanks.'

He picked up his beer as she picked up her glass of wine. She'd added some sparkling water and ice to make a spritzer.

'So . . .' They said it together. O'Rourke grinned. 'You go first.'

She picked up a chip, frowning as she spoke. 'You got my email? Lauren's mum said there was no way she would have jumped, she was terrified of water. She had a near drowning accident when she was a child.' She hesitated but before he could say anything, continued: 'And the way she fell isn't right for someone who jumped. The way her body landed was all wrong. And like you said, there are much better places to jump, assuming she did.'

'But you don't think she did?'

Cathy shook her head emphatically.

He leaned forward on the table, his shirt rolled back at the cuffs. The battered diver's watch he always wore looked all wrong with his crisply starched shirt. He reached for another chip.

'I've got a team from the technical bureau in the Park looking at how she fell. They're calculating the angle from the height and the distance. Their early thoughts correlate with yours.'

Cathy pulled out an onion ring. 'I think she was pushed. That mark Saunders found on the back of her shoulder – I know he said it wasn't conclusive. You'd sort of expect to see a bruise on both shoulders if some had pushed her hard, but that would assume they were standing behind her . . .'

He nodded slowly. 'Maybe whoever it was, was facing her and twisted her around before they pushed. But the sixty-million-dollar question is: if that's the case, who pushed her, and why there?'

Cathy screwed up her face, thinking. 'Because it was close to Tom's house? Maybe she tried to call in on Tom but was too late? Or maybe she saw who hit him and challenged them? We don't know that he wasn't hit first. Perhaps she was in the car?'

'Or maybe she was in Dalkey to meet him, and they had a row. If he'd just pushed her off a cliff, you'd expect him to be a bit stressed. Maybe he was so distracted when the vehicle came around the corner that he walked right out?'

Cathy took a sip of her wine, shaking her head. 'Skid marks and tyre imprints indicate it was deliberate. The car went *up* onto the pavement to hit him. Then they reversed so they could finish the job.' She thought for a moment. 'Perhaps there were three of them meeting and there was a row that ended with Lauren going over the cliff. Then that other person needed to take Tom out of the picture because he'd seen what happened?'

'Definitely possible. I think Frank's right – putting that note in her pocket into an envelope suggests that she was expecting to give it to someone. Forensics are still looking at it, but it appears to be clean, doesn't even have her prints on it.'

'That's a bit weird. She'd have no reason to wipe it if she wrote it herself.'

'I thought that.'

'And if she didn't,' she picked up a chip, 'it suggests that someone else did, someone who doesn't want to be identified, which could lead us to think that she was pushed deliberately and whoever did it knew exactly what they were doing and wanted to make it look like suicide.'

'We'll know more when we get the full forensics report.'

She grimaced. 'We could speculate forever. Will we have their phone records in the morning? I really want to see who called or texted who and where from. See if she was trying to meet Tom.'

'I hope so. Both warrants have been filed, we're just waiting for the companies to produce them. They're usually very fast. Reckon Tom was seeing her on the sly?'

Cathy chewed a chip thoughtfully. 'Why on the sly, though? He had nothing to hide. She was a friend from college. Perhaps he invited her over to study or something and she met someone on the DART who led her astray?'

'We'll know more when we can see their phone traffic.' O'Rourke hesitated. 'How are you feeling?'

She looked up at him sharply. *So that's what this is about – the promotions list. She should have guessed.*

'Pissed off. Angry. Feeling like I've wasted a year of my life working for a Master's that's going to be completely useless. Apart from that, just great. I'm supposed to be focusing on the next fight but . . .' She opened her hands to indicate the chips and the wine.

'Everyone needs a night off once in a while.'

'Not if they want to win they don't.' Her tone was blunter than she'd intended. 'Sorry, I'm having a bad day.'

'That's not like you.' He reached out and rubbed the back of her hand, his fingers lingering there for a moment before he picked up his can of beer and took another swig.

She kept her eyes on the table. *What was that about?*

He continued as if he hadn't noticed her reaction. 'And you know you haven't wasted a year. It's vital experience that you'll have over the next man. It's experience and training you'll be able to use every day out on the job.'

'True.'

It was but it didn't make her feel any better. She looked up and found him looking directly at her. He looked away quickly, picking up his beer again. For a moment she felt the room go very quiet, could hear the clock ticking. She cleared her throat.

'I was thinking. I need to work out what my next move is, if it's not going into profiling. I'd prepared myself to move on mentally and now it's not happening and I'm already feeling a bit . . .' She paused. 'Sort of trapped. I need a change.'

That was the real problem here – that feeling that she'd seen outside the gate but now it had closed on her. She felt a bit like she'd been caught on the ropes in a fight – it could end there or she could forget about tactics, forget about saving energy, and fight her way out, go for the kill.

She'd had to do that before and one thing was for sure, she wouldn't be dictated to by circumstances. It wasn't in her nature.

He pursed his lips. 'I think you're right. Have you any ideas? Maybe see if there are any openings in Crime and Security or the Criminal Assets Bureau?'

She weighed the thought for a moment. Crime and Security's remit was far reaching – it was like the secret service wing of An Garda Síochána, covering everything from close protection to undercover units. It was a possibility for sure, but since she'd found herself in a lonely field in the Dublin Mountains with a unit of heavily armed highly trained police officers, she'd been wondering if she could make the cut.

'I was thinking of the Emergency Response Unit actually.'

She said it tentatively. Whenever it had come up before, he'd been very frosty about the whole idea. The ERU was an elite team based in Harcourt Square in Dublin city centre, but they were on alert to scramble to anywhere in the country in two hours. Heavily armed, they were the premier tactical operations unit. And they were part of the European ATLAS Network task force that could be called on to deal with major terrorist incidents anywhere in Europe. Every job they went on was potentially life threatening.

O'Rourke's frowned. 'The ERU? You sure? I didn't think you were serious when you mentioned it before. It's not exactly a walk in the park . . .' He stopped, thinking about it. 'But it's an ideal fit for you. And they are crying out for women.'

'I think the two-week army assault selection course puts a few people off a bit. To say nothing of the balaclavas.' Confused, he looked at her quizzically. She smiled. 'Hat hair. Not a good look.'

O'Rourke rolled his eyes. 'Jesus, Cat . . . But seriously, though, are you thinking about applying? They *are* recruiting at the moment. The closing date is pretty soon.'

Maybe it was the way he said it, sort of believing but not quite. And in that moment she made up her mind. She needed a change, she need to keep on top of her fitness, and she thrived on adrenaline. And let's face it, she'd already been shot once – and blown up. How many times could that happen in a lifetime? By the law of averages, she should be as safe as houses. And she looked great in black.

'Yes.'

She surprised herself with how definite she sounded. Her mum was going to kill her but she suddenly realised it was exactly what she wanted to do. If she was absolutely honest with herself she'd been a tiny bit worried about how she'd fare in a desk job, that the paperwork side of the profiler role could actually be the equivalent of a long, slow death for her. She was totally fascinated by the process, by the psychology, by getting deep into criminal motivation, and with everything a detailed knowledge of forensic psychology brought, but she needed action in her life. Maybe chasing armed gunmen across fields in the middle of the night wasn't everyone's cup of tea, but it was at moments like those that she felt absolutely alive, when she was using all her skills and she knew exactly what she was doing. It was moments like those that made her love her job.

Perhaps it was all about danger, about living on the edge. Maybe that's why she boxed, why she was at the top of her sport. And there certainly wouldn't be any danger flying a desk in headquarters. A profiler was never going to be on the front line unless there was a hostage negotiation, and then they would only be there in an advisory capacity. In a truck about as far from the front line as you could get.

O'Rourke picked up the last few chip ends and stuck them in his mouth, rolling up the brown paper bags ready to throw in the bin.

'Honestly, I think you're mad. A lot of people are going to worry themselves stupid about you. But I can see that it's the right decision. You're too young to get trapped behind a desk, you can do that at the end of your career.' He grimaced. 'Not wanting to tempt fate, but when you're missing a limb, then it's time to find a nice quiet number in headquarters.'

She half-smiled. There were times when she thought that he knew her better than she knew herself. He was making a very good point. One she hadn't thought of. When she was closer to her thirty years' service – *that* was the time to start thinking about taking it easy. Why did he always come up with the sensible stuff? Why hadn't she thought of that? But perhaps that's why they got on so well – their differences kept things interesting.

O'Rourke crumpled his beer can in one hand and wrapped it neatly into the brown paper parcel, pausing for a moment, the package tidy in the middle of the table. He cleared his throat.

'I've got some news too.'

Her eyebrows shot up. 'What?'

'I applied for Super.'

She'd known it had to come but it was still a shock. How long had he been the DI in Dun Laoghaire? A couple of years? Superintendent was the next rank up, and he'd always been on the fast track. But for once Cathy was stuck for words.

'It'll be on the next promotions list.' He hesitated. 'That's why I had to go up to headquarters. The Commissioner has asked me to take over as Detective Superintendent in Limerick, there's been a vacancy there for a while.'

'Limerick?' Bandit country. She wasn't surprised there was a vacancy. There were families there who put the Krays into the shade. And Limerick was at the other end of the country. Cathy felt her stomach go into free fall.

This was obviously her week for good news. Not.

Perhaps he was pretending that he hadn't noticed her face pale, but O'Rourke kept talking.

'The gang situation is hotting up again and the position has been vacant too long. There are going to be questions in the Dáil about it – the press, anyway. The Commissioner wants to be ready . . . I wanted . . .' He hesitated again. 'I wanted to tell you first.'

'When?' It came out more abruptly than she'd intended, the silences in the gaps so loud she felt like they might overwhelm her.

'A couple of weeks, I think. Before there are any more shootings.'

'That's soon.' She tried to hide the crack in her voice. Unsuccessfully.

'I'll write your recommendation for the ERU first. You'll need to be quick, though, I think the closing date is early next week. With me gone, Frank Gallagher should be made DI, he's a good man, dependable. He must have been pretty pissed off when I got the post – he'd applied too.'

Frank had managed to keep it quiet but Cathy had always suspected that might be the case. A couple of weeks, though. That was fast.

'I'll miss you.' It was out before she knew what she'd said.

His smile was sad. He stood up, wrapping the brown bags into a tighter ball.

'We'll have the phone. And I'll be in Dublin for meetings, I'm sure. And Limerick's not that far. You could come down on your long weekend?' His voice was quiet, hopeful.

Cathy smiled at him. 'I'll take that as an invitation. You won't be able to get rid of me that easily.'

He smiled back at her, his eyes meeting hers. 'Good. That's good.' O'Rourke turned like he had forgotten what he was doing. 'Right . . . I better be going, we've an early start tomorrow.'

She stood up as he crossed the kitchen to put the chip wrappers into the concealed bin under the sink. The cabinet door closed with a clunk.

'I better be going,' he said again. He stood awkwardly in the middle of the kitchen, half-looking at her.

Sensing his tension, Cathy pretended nothing was wrong, went around the table to pull his jacket off the back of his chair, passing it to him.

'What time are we meeting in the morning?'

He shouldered it on. 'I told the lads nine.'

'Grand, that'll give me time to go to the gym first, work off these chips.' He still didn't move. 'Your coat should be dry by now.'

Glancing at him, paralysed in the middle of her kitchen, Cathy just wanted to close the gap between them and hug him. He looked so lost, so lonely . . . but mention of his coat seemed to bring him back. He stuck his hands into the pockets of his trousers. Cathy went out to the hall to get his coat. He followed her. Turning in the narrow hall, she handed it to him and he slipped it on.

'We should have the bus CCTV by the morning too.' Back to the case with a bump. He hesitated. 'I better go.' He said it with zero enthusiasm.

'You need your beauty sleep.'

O'Rourke looked at her hard and grinned. 'Yeah, right. And you need yours . . . So I'll see you in the morning, then?'

'You sure will.' Pulling the front door open, she looked out into the night. It had stopped raining.

'Will you be OK?' He was right next to her in the narrow hall, looking out into the night.

She shrugged; of course she would.

'Good.'

He turned to her and sort of hovered for a moment, his eyes holding her face. Holy God, was he going to kiss her? Cathy felt a surge of emotion and her knees suddenly went shaky. If they had been in a movie she was sure there would have been a crescendo of violins.

And with that he was gone, jogging towards his car with the collar of his coat turned up.

Cathy watched him go, leaning on the door frame for support. She waited while he got into the car, until the interior light began to fade, then he started the engine and put his foot to the floor, roaring off down the road.

She closed the door gently. Things were changing. For both of them.

Chapter 18

Sunday, 7 a.m.

Cathy got to the gym in thirty minutes, the M50 virtually empty. She'd hardly slept, thoughts of O'Rourke moving to Limerick and the ERU careering around her head.

McIntyre was in his office behind the plate glass window engraved with a rising phoenix. He waved as she pushed open the door to the gym. It was empty, just the way she liked it. Pop music was blaring but McIntyre had changed the station to an Irish language channel; he must have been sick of the same ten songs playing on Spin all day. Cathy's Irish wasn't great – it had been good enough to get her into the job but was starting to fade now. Technically she was supposed to be able to conduct an arrest and prosecute a case in Irish. Fortunately, she'd never had to, although there was always the odd smart-arse who challenged a traffic stop *as Gaeilge*. Cathy threw her gloves onto the bench that ran around the brick-built gym and grabbed a skipping rope to start her warm-ups. As the rope whistled through the air, her feet rhythmic on the rubber matting, she let her mind drift. This was when she did her best thinking – when her mind wasn't cluttered with distractions. Fitness training was repetitive work and required none of the quick thinking and total concentration she needed in the ring, which gave her space to evaluate the interviews she'd been conducting and the data they had gathered so far.

Tom Quinn's night walks were bothering her a lot. It had been a clear night on Thursday, one of the few days they'd had recently without constant rain, but clear skies meant that it had been absolutely freezing. Admittedly close to the sea the ground temperature was higher than in other parts of the country, but she'd checked the records and there had been a stiff onshore breeze. Which made you think that anyone going for a walk in the dark would need a good reason for venturing out. It definitely wasn't the type of evening when you popped out for a stroll. Had he been meeting Lauren? It was looking more and more likely. Why else would she have been in Dalkey the same night? Maybe she'd had something to tell him they couldn't discuss at his house, where the ever watchful Mira might take too much interest, and maybe they hadn't wanted to go to a pub. The post-mortem hadn't found any evidence of a pregnancy, so it hadn't been that, but there had to be a reason they were both out that night.

They'd both had a couple of drinks at some stage that evening, they had alcohol in their blood. But the footage they had of Lauren leaving the DART station suggested she'd headed straight for Dillon's Park, which meant she must have had a drink before she arrived in Dalkey. She'd been picked up by the Allied Irish Bank cameras heading down towards Coliemore Road, had passed Paddy Power the bookmakers and the Club pub and then the cameras ran out. The one line that had always stuck in Cathy's head from her training at the Templemore Training Academy was 'Absence of evidence isn't evidence of absence.' Just because they couldn't see her didn't mean Lauren hadn't been there. Though quite whether she'd met someone on the way or not remained a mystery.

And despite scrolling through hours of CCTV, they were still no closer to identifying the time Tom was run down. There was no sign of him on the village CCTV, or at the petrol station, but as Frank had pointed out, he could have cut up the back way to the Queens pub, or continued walking down the back streets to meet Lauren. They were checking the car park footage from the Queens in case it had caught him in the periphery.

Cathy suddenly realised she was soaked in sweat. Throwing down the skipping rope, she switched to alternating star jumps and press-ups. It took her a few minutes to get a rhythm going.

'Hey there, miss, how are you doing? Sarah Jane on her way?' McIntyre's voice beside her made her jump. He had a way of floating around the gym; Muhammad Ali would have been proud of him. Stopping, she turned to grin at him.

'I'm good, Boss.' She bumped her fist against his. 'She said she'd be here soon.'

'Still mad about that job?'

Cathy took a moment to answer. She'd been mad as hell the last time she'd been in here and had virtually kicked the punch-bag off its chains, but now she was feeling remarkably zen.

'Actually I had a think about it and I'm not ready for a desk yet. I thought that's what I wanted but fate has a funny way of intervening, doesn't it?'

'So have you got another plan?'

'I have actually . . .' She looked at McIntyre sideways. 'I'm going to apply to the ERU.'

She wasn't sure what sort of reaction she'd expected – him trying to talk her out of it probably – but McIntyre just pursed his lips and scowled while he thought for a moment. Then he nodded slowly.

'You'll be good at that. I trained special ops for long enough – you've definitely got the full skill set. And it'll be easier to maintain your training programme, you'll need to stay at peak fitness.' He shook his head. 'I was always a bit worried about you getting stuck in an office. I reckoned you'd last about two minutes and end up banging your wings against the window trying to get out.'

'What does O'Rourke think?'

Cathy swung around at the voice behind her. Over the music playing in the gym she hadn't heard Sarah Jane come in. Her best friend had tied her long blonde hair up in a knot, was wearing her black lycra gym gear. Grinning, Cathy turned to give her a hug but Sarah Jane put up her hands playfully.

'Back off there, lady, you're drenched.'

Cathy glanced down at her sweat-soaked vest. 'You're right. What have you been up to this week? Every time I tried your phone I got voicemail.'

'You got voicemail? I've been leaving messages with *you* all week. I was starting to think you'd left the country after that promotions list nonsense.'

Cathy punched her playfully on the arm. 'Sorry. It's been mad the last few days. We've a double case on. I saw the missed calls but you know what it's like, I'm not dossing around DCU any more.'

'Really?' Sarah Jane glared at her playfully. 'Dossing? I've been in the library all week.' She reached for a skipping rope hanging from the wall, checking it was long enough for her, then said, 'I'm on a deadline for a *paid* article.'

Cathy threw her a teasing look of amazement, but Sarah Jane wasn't letting her win that round.

'Shut up. It's a good one. About how Facebook Analytics are being used to influence consumer decisions, but I ended up finding loads of stuff on how your personal info is mined and hackers use it to get your bank and credit card info. It's . . .'

'Here, less chat, ladies, more action. You can talk all you like after you're done. Make sure you take it easy, SJ.'

Sarah Jane flicked the rope behind her and grinned at McIntyre. 'Yes, Boss.'

It was like being back at school but they loved it.

An hour later, they were both exhausted. McIntyre gave Cathy the signal that she could finish up, do her stretches and then head for the shower. The two sparring partners he'd found to fight her looked just as relieved as the girls were. They'd come in looking a lot more awake than Cathy had expected for a Sunday morning and were, she'd quickly realised, as dedicated to success as she was, but McIntyre had pushed them all hard. The lads high-fived them as they headed back into the men's locker room.

In the women's changing room Sarah Jane flopped down on to the slatted bench that ran around the walls opposite a huge bank of steel grey lockers.

'My God, I'm shattered. What part of me thought getting up this early to train on a *Sunday* morning was a good idea?' She put her hand on her shoulder and rotated it carefully, her face taut. 'The things I do for you, Cat Connolly . . .'

'How does it feel?' Cathy indicated Sarah Jane's shoulder as she hauled a fresh towel out of her locker, running it over her face and neck. She sat down beside Sarah Jane and leaned her back against the cool plaster wall.

'Much better. Less stiff, but I need to keep moving it and doing all the exercises. The doc thinks I should be able to get back to proper sparring *very* soon.'

Sarah Jane had had a good session with McIntyre on the pads while Cathy was in the ring with each of the boys, but Cathy knew she was desperate to get back in the ring properly. Sarah Jane interrupted her thoughts.

'So what's this about the ERU? You going to transfer there instead?'

Cathy's text to Sarah Jane about the promotions list had been a long one. She knew precisely how mad Cathy had been, and why.

'If I can get in, what do you think?'

Sarah Jane laughed. 'I've think I've got a lot to thank the ERU for, so I'd say that it's a brilliant idea. So, what does O'Rourke say?'

Cathy pursed her lips, pausing for a moment. 'He thinks it's a good idea.'

'Did he actually say that or are you trying to read his mind again?'

Cathy grinned sheepishly; Sarah Jane knew all about her obsession with O'Rourke, and exactly how difficult it was to know what he was thinking at any given moment.

'He said it. Really. Actually did.'

'He'll miss you.'

'He said that too.' Cathy glanced sideways at Sarah Jane under her eyelashes. 'He's transferring to Limerick.'

'*What?*' Her hand still on her shoulder, Sarah Jane leaned forwards and looked around at Cathy, her face incredulous. 'And how do you feel about that?'

Cathy shrugged. 'Not great, obviously, but he said I should go down to visit him . . .' She said it deliberately innocently, not quite looking Sarah Jane in the eye.

'Really? You *have* had a busy week. I'm going to need to know every detail of *that* conversation.'

Cathy laughed and for a moment she was back on her doorstep, seeing O'Rourke out. She could feel herself starting to blush. She'd have to fill Sarah Jane in for sure, but that was a conversation for somewhere more private than the gym changing room, even if they were the only people there.

She needed to change the subject. 'Tell me what you're working on, it sounds interesting.'

Sarah Jane took a slug of water from the bottle beside her. 'Well, I started looking at the whole way the Trump campaign had mined data from Facebook and how they'd crafted their election messages to tick boxes for the broadest number of people. It's one of the theories behind why he kept changing tack every time he spoke to a different group.'

'I thought that was because he was nuts.'

Sarah Jane grimaced. 'So did I, but it's a bit more sinister than that. So that led me on to a whole load of interesting stuff about personal data and how much information people give away without realising it, how we all leave this online footprint and how easy it is for someone to hack your bank account or get your credit card details with just a few pieces of information.'

'That's refreshing. As if there isn't enough crime in the real world.' Cathy bent over to undo the laces on her trainers. 'I was reading something the other day about Bluetooth devices in people's houses getting hacked. Some guy did an experiment and got this animal toy that talks to the child who owns it, to say all sorts of random stuff. It was a cat toy, and then he gets it talking to an Amazon Echo in the same room and it gets Alexa to buy cat food from Amazon.'

Sarah Jane burst out laughing. 'My God, but that's actually terrible, being able to speak directly to a child from outside the house?' She shook her head. 'We've really no idea of the level of exposure we have, my dad keeps going on about it.'

Sarah Jane's father, Ted Hansen, was a Pulitzer prize-winning war reporter; he understood a huge amount more about threats, online and offline, than most people. He was one of CNN's top correspondents, his face familiar with viewers all over the world. It suddenly clicked in Cathy's head that there was a very good chance Ted Hansen knew Anna Lockharte.

'He's dead right. By the way, has he ever mentioned a professor at Trinity to you? She's originally from New York, but she's an expert in international terrorism—'

Sarah Jane interrupted Cathy before she could continue. 'Anna Lockharte? She's amazing. And gorgeous. I think my dad has a crush on her. He reads all her papers. I think they met originally at some convention somewhere. She's one of his go-to sources when he needs to fact-check. How do you know her?'

Cathy unlaced the other trainer and kicked her shoes off. She really didn't have the energy to get into the shower, and suddenly realised that sitting down had been a very bad idea. But she hadn't seen Sarah Jane in what felt like ages. They had a lot of catching up to do.

'We're working on this case – two actually, like I said. A student from Trinity was killed in a hit-and-run and a friend of his apparently committed suicide the same night jumping off Dillon's Park.'

Sarah Jane raised her eyebrows in surprise. 'Dillon's Park? Seriously?'

Cathy sighed. 'I know. It wouldn't be my first choice, but then I don't think it was suicide. Nor does O'Rourke.'

Sarah Jane had known Cathy long enough to understand what she could and couldn't say. She didn't probe more.

'Wait till I tell my dad you know Anna Lockharte. He's always talking about her. He's got this theory that terrorism is going to move into cyberspace. The likes of ISIS will still orchestrate real world atrocities, but they could paralyse a whole country if they attacked it online.'

'That's a pretty scary thought.'

Sarah Jane pulled a face. 'It looks like Russia's doing it already. There was an attack in the Ukraine that looks like it emanated from an Internet provider whose technical facilities were being serviced by a company linked to the Russian intelligence agency. The attack was a ransomware one, but the virus encrypted all of the files on the computers it infected and some got completely wiped or their files got rewritten. It was a bit like the WannaCry ransomware attack on the NHS in the

UK, but there was no kill switch.' She paused. 'That UK attack seemed to be a rogue event, but what if it had been perpetrated by a terrorist organisation? Think of the chaos, the lives that could have been lost.'

Punching in her pass code, Cathy let the inner door of Dun Laoghaire Garda station's public office fall closed behind her and trotted up the stairs. She could feel the muscles in her thighs and calves burning. Soon she'd be training twice a day – in the gym down the road from the station in the mornings, and over in Ballymun every evening. She couldn't afford not to win back her title this year.

O'Rourke was already in his office when she rounded the top of the stairs; she could see his light on over the door. She knocked gently.

'Come in.'

Sitting at his desk, his shirtsleeves already rolled back, he didn't look up as she entered but seemed to already know it was her.

'Team will be in shortly and I'll brief everyone but we've got both sets of phone records.' He rifled through a pile of printouts next to his desk. 'Sit. You need to concentrate on this.'

She didn't need to be told twice. She sat down in the chair on the other side of his desk and leaned forward, trying to get a look at the records. He pulled them out of her view, a twinkle in his eye.

'Hold your horses.'

She glared at him. 'Come on, tell me, don't make me wait. That's cruel.'

He raised his eyebrows playfully like he was considering making her wait even longer, then cleared his throat.

'So Lauren first.' He swung the call record around to face her. 'She called a pay-as-you-go mobile at 3 p.m., 3:10 p.m. and 3:30 p.m. and then sent a text: *NEED TO TALK. V URGENT*.

'That was followed by several calls to the same number that look like they hit the message box, until she tried again at eight that evening. That call was answered, the conversation lasted eleven minutes.

'That was followed by a text twenty minutes later: *Sorry. V tierd*. That was spelled wrong. *Meet me at Dillon's Park at 10:30. We can talk there xxxxx*.

'Lauren replied, *Where's Dillon's Park?* Plus a series of emoji hearts and kisses. The response was, *Dalkey. Get the Dart, go through the village turn right onto Coliemore Road. Keep walking to the end*.'

It took Cathy a moment to process this. She could suddenly see Lauren walking anxiously through the darkness along the road.

'That works with the time she got off the train and the times we have her on CCTV. She must have gone straight there.'

'It certainly seems that way. She also called Tom's own mobile at nine, but doesn't appear to have left a message – call lasted less than a second.'

'Like she got his message minder and hung up.'

'That may be so.'

'So do you think she was meeting him? That it was his pay-as-you-go she called the first time, and then she mixed up the numbers with his regular mobile? Whatever she needed to talk about seems fairly urgent.'

'He was a student. Why would he have needed a second phone?' He frowned. 'Do you think he used it for Tinder or something?'

Cathy shook her head, smiling. 'People don't use a second phone for dating sites, they use their Instagram or Snapchat user accounts to connect with people. If teenagers have a second phone it's to contact their drug dealers.'

'So perhaps he was dealing? We need to explore that.' He paused. 'OK, on to Tom's mobile. He called Lauren mid-afternoon and they had a long chat. Then he called another number almost immediately, one he calls regularly – we're checking that. The call lasted just a few seconds, looks like he got voicemail, he then texted that number: *You around? Need to talk to u. No more email.* Sounds like he's as sick of his inbox as I am.' Cathy smirked as he continued. 'Then it appears Tom also texted a pay-as-you-go number at 7:30 that evening, with *?xx.*'

'The same one as Lauren?' Cathy couldn't keep the surprise out of her voice.

'I wish.' He scowled. 'A different one, but that's not to say he and Lauren didn't have some complex reason for having several untraceable phones. If she needed to talk, his question mark makes sense.'

Cathy looked at him, shaking her head. 'They were students. None of it makes sense – why all the cloak and dagger stuff?'

'Maybe one of them was blackmailing the other? Maybe someone was blackmailing them both? Maybe it made things more fun – I don't know, all I've got are the facts.' He tapped the printout with his forefinger.

'Keep going.'

'So Tom receives a reply from the same pay-as-you-go – that could be Lauren's, we don't know – saying *usual time xxx.* Then at eleven there's the text from his mother, and his reply that we know about.'

'So what was he doing between eight and eleven? Meeting Lauren at the park when she got off the DART?'

'Possibly. The timing seems to fit, assuming he went somewhere else first before he went to the park. Perhaps he needed a drink? There was alcohol in his blood, according to Saunders.'

Cathy pulled her necklace from the neck of her sweater as she pursed her lips, her brow furrowed.

'It was freezing, though, why meet so far from the house, why not meet *in* one of the pubs in Dalkey?'

'Maybe they didn't want to be seen together.'

Maybe – there was that word again. Sometimes she felt like it haunted her. As she was always saying to 007, 'maybe' didn't stand up in court. End of. This wasn't about maybe, although granted they had to speculate sometimes to understand all the possibilities, to see where to take an investigation next, but ultimately a successful case had to be about the facts.

'I'm going to get all the calls to these numbers checked for the last month and we can see if we can piece together more from their previous texts. They are probably all to college friends about homework and who's dating who, but we'll see.'

Cathy ran her necklace over her nose. 'Have house-to-house turned anything up on Lauren going into Dillon's Park? Did anyone see her?'

He frowned. 'A lad who lives opposite saw a woman with a dog at around 10.30. There were a couple of joggers earlier. No one seems to have seen anyone who looked like Lauren accompanied by anyone else. The dog walker may have seen or heard something, though. I'm thinking of putting out a call on the news for information, I'm sure she'll come forward if she knows we're looking for her. It's looking like we might have to appeal for witnesses to Tom's accident too, but . . .' He stopped for a moment. 'First, forensics . . .'

Cathy raised her eyebrows and looked at him. 'You sound more like you're in *CSI* every day.'

'Fuck off. Forensics is what they do – the technical bureau, if you want to be correct . . .'

'Always.'

She stifled a smile, catching his eye. The twinkle was there again. It was like he'd been incredibly tense for the past few days and now he'd told her about Limerick he was back to his old self. She still found the thought of not seeing him every day a tiny bit heartbreaking, but he'd invited her down to Limerick, and she was sure that he'd been thinking about kissing her the night before. Of course she was famous for getting things like that wrong, but something had definitely changed. It was like he was more relaxed or something – happier for sure. She knew he was hungry for promotion, that that would inevitably mean that they'd end up working in different places, but maybe that's what he wanted.

Cathy mentally shook herself. *Where had that thought even come from?* Right now she needed to keep focused on the case and her training and on her own next move. There was no room in her schedule to start getting miserable.

There'd be time enough for that when he'd gone.

'So the technical bureau. . .' O'Rourke hesitated, 'aren't finished yet but they're collating the data from the collision team.'

Cathy leaned back in her chair, stretching, her abs sore. 'When will they have an idea of the vehicle involved?'

'It's going to be a few more days at least. As soon as they have a make and model we'll put out a call to see if any of those vehicles have been repaired recently. We've got all the local garages on alert already, looking for a vehicle with blue metallic paint and recent damage.'

Cathy looked thoughtful. 'The thing is, how did the person who hit him know he was going to be there, and at that time, when no one seems to be able to tell us where he went for these walks? Tom must have told them, or arranged to meet them.'

'That,' O'Rourke scowled, 'is a very good point.'

Chapter 19

Sunday, 10 a.m.

It was starting to rain as he waited for the lights to change so he could cross the road. High up to his left a train rattled over the bridge. He glanced up at its green carriages as it slid along the line like some sort of giant snake, empty this early on a Sunday morning. It was quiet at ground level too, no sign of the usual coagulating traffic of the morning rush hour. It was usually crazy here, the diesel engines of buses drowning the cars, the roar punctuated by sirens. He didn't know how people coped with all the noise.

He'd never get used to the cold either. He winced as needle-like darts of rain bit at his skull through his close-cropped dark hair. For now, Dublin served its purpose. It was close to London, but far enough away for him to feel secure. He thrust his hands into the pockets of his dark navy jacket, the shoulder emblazoned with the Superdry logo. It made him invisible in the city crowd, his jeans and Nikes like a uniform, the backpack containing his laptop slung over one shoulder.

He watched a girl across the road hitch her own backpack, a patchwork of button badges, onto her shoulder, the strap pulling her denim jacket open awkwardly, revealing her neat breast, thinly covered by a cheap T-shirt. Even from here he could see the lines of her bra. He watched as she glanced up at the lights, shivering, her long wispy chestnut hair blowing across her face, the ends of it a dark blonde like it had been dip-dyed. She pulled it away from her mouth and the light changed. Head down, she hurried towards him.

As he reached the damp, dark grey paving stones on the opposite side of the street a smile twitched across his face. Girls were always incredibly grateful for his help when their webcams were compromised, and if they weren't, he made sure that they understood the consequences of what was happening to them, subtly, explaining how badly wrong some of these situations could go. He didn't need to explain often. They let him into their private spaces to show him the emails on their laptops, and he listened to how their lives would fall apart if the images were made public, how they couldn't possibly afford to pay the blackmailers, whoever they were.

How they could never tell anyone that this had happened.

He'd nod, warming his hands on the mug of tea they had brought him, telling them in his soft voice how he could solve their problems: that it was better to use their own computer; that it might take a couple of tries but he could usually block the accounts, remove the images remotely from the hacker's system. Cyberspace was different from the real world; there were walls online but every wall could be breached, and whoever did this wouldn't be expecting a cyberattack, had usually left the back door open. He built their trust, speaking ardently in a language they didn't understand.

Then he'd work hard, focused on the screen, apparently hardly noticing them as he whizzed around the Web, the screen dark, showing rows and rows of scrolling code. But he noticed everything. The colours of the nail polishes lined up on the windowsill, the photos pinned to the noticeboard above their desks. The smell *of the room: layers of body lotion, deodorant, perfume, hairspray. He took the top Post-it note off the pad so later he could hold it up to the light and see what it said. From the moment he had identified them as a possible target he'd been building a picture, checking their social media sites for information. By the time he arrived he knew the names of everyone in her family, their brother's best friend, where they had been to school, what their home address was. He knew they'd worn the purple nail polish to the college ball, but their favourite was the black. Getting into their rooms or apartments – being inside their space – was the next part of the challenge, one of the bits he enjoyed most.*

It would always take a while to solve their problem, but he'd tell them just to ignore him – if they needed to go out or study, that was no problem, he'd just keep going. They trusted him. He wasn't the type to go through their underwear drawers, their laundry basket, to hold their lacy knickers to his face and breathe in their scent. He was quiet and safe and trustworthy.

And he'd secure their systems, assuring them he'd be back to check, that it should all be OK but he just needed to be sure. And then they'd throw their arms around him, so relieved that he could help, or they'd collapse sobbing and he'd be there to put his arm around them, to kiss the top of their heads, to assure them that nobody need ever know. If he passed them in the street there would be a silent exchange of looks, never acknowledging that he knew them, that they had a shared secret.

Then he'd come again to check if everything was working – it took up to thirty-six hours for something to propagate across the Web, he'd explain. And as he ran his checks, he'd slip a tablet into their tea, one that made their gratitude overwhelm them, that relaxed them and made them happy.

And then he fucked them.

He knew he didn't need the pills; he knew they wanted him at that stage, that he'd become a god in their eyes, but there was no point in taking risks. The pills made the exact series of events a bit blurry, made them more compliant. Made them forget that their laptops were open on the desk. That the webcam was picking up all the action. He didn't broadcast that footage, though; that was for his private use. And it was his guarantee if anything went wrong that everything was entirely consensual; he made quite sure it appeared that way.

He just wished he was able to film the special ones. There weren't too many of those. Couldn't be. The circumstances had to be perfect, there were so many variables that needed to fall into place to ensure that he was totally safe. That he could get what he wanted and vanish. He could feel himself hardening at the thought.

Memories swirled in his head as he walked swiftly down the road, his head down against the rain. The others were almost as good as the special ones. Part of the joy was in the chase, in choosing the subjects, finding out everything about them, then hooking them and reeling them in. It was all about control. He thought of them now, each one of them, as a slow smile twitched at the corners of his mouth.

His glasses steamed up as he pushed open the cafe door, the warmth spilling out and surrounding him like a caress. He smiled at the waitress, ordered a double espresso and, seeing his table in the corner was free, headed over.

Pulling his laptop from his bag, he fired it up and checked his email. The anonymous account he'd set up was untraceable, his emails arriving in carefully chosen inboxes. He smiled to himself; his targets had no idea that as soon as they opened a particular email, or clicked to visit a site, a worm was unleashed that burrowed its way into their hard drive and gave him complete access to their webcam and microphone. He loved the tingle of anticipation when he first activated a new camera – what would he see? What would he hear? Would any of them be right for him to choose to keep for himself? If they were a day or so later he'd send another email with some stills, this one explaining what he wanted, what would happen if they didn't comply. He had it all worked out now: the wording; how to escalate revealing the images; how to increase the pressure until his target was terrified.

It was foolproof. Everything was hidden in the depths of the Dark Web.

But for the special ones, the conditions had to be just right.

The first one hadn't been planned at all, but it had shown him the possibilities, and then he'd known he needed more, needed that utterly intoxicating high again. He'd only been sixteen then, but sensible enough to know it couldn't happen like that too often. It was too dangerous to take risks. After that first one in Paris he'd learned so much and, despite the furore, everything had worked out in the end. And in that one moment he and Karim had become connected for life.

The bracelet had been Karim's idea – a true masterstroke. It was a shame it hadn't gone quite the way they had expected, but the evidence was still there, waiting like a sleeper. He smiled – a sleeper that was about to be woken up.

Karim hadn't been there for the next one, the American, Serena del Guardo. He liked the sound of her name. Rolling it around his head brought back all sorts of pleasant memories.

It felt like a long time ago now – it had been the summer he'd left school. The Youth Study programme in Long Island had been *the perfect opportunity for him to test his hacking skills away from home, and when he'd sent the second photograph she'd walked right into his arms.*

Her email address had been easy to get, her laptop almost permanently open on her desk in her bedroom. He'd spent the evenings watching her, felt like he was part of her world. As she stood at the edge of their crowd in her skintight jeans and white hoody, her dark wavy hair pulled back off her face in a ponytail, he knew that she was wearing a lacy lilac bra and thong, that she had a birthmark on her back just below her shoulder blade.

From the moment he'd sent the first email, she'd become more attentive, listening to the others talking about him building gaming sites, showing off that they knew someone who could hack into the White House. And he'd seen her looking at him, wondering if he could help.

He'd kept it low-key as always, not confirming or denying, just keeping quiet. He knew she wanted to ask him, but she must have been too shy, and, if he was honest, he'd got a bit impatient. She was beautiful, Latina, with those small firm rounded tits he liked and a narrow waist, thick dark hair. And she liked to walk around her bedroom naked.

Almost as soon as he'd sent the second image she had come to him, waiting for him on the way back from the chess championships at the school one evening, waiting in the shadows at the edge of the woods that butted onto the quiet suburban street. He'd been heading back to his host's family home. She'd taken him by surprise.

It had been a sticky, sultry night and she'd been wearing a low-cut T-shirt. She had been so desperate not to let anyone see her, so desperate that nobody knew about the emails, that she'd taken him into the dense woodland to talk. And then she'd started to explain, haltingly, the tears beginning to fall. She'd held his arm tightly, imploring him to keep her secret, terrified that someone would find out, begging him to help, how he was the only one who could. How her father would go mad, how they'd think she was doing it for money.

And then she'd begun to really sob so he'd put his arm around her, his hand brushing her nipple, erect in the chill of the shadows, and it had set off that feeling he just couldn't control. It had been her fault. He'd sought her lips in the darkness and she'd kissed him back, but as he'd rolled on top of her, his erection painful in his jeans, she'd started to struggle and he knew he couldn't risk anyone finding out. If they connected him to the email, it could lead them to the site and then he'd be in even bigger trouble.

And he couldn't fuck her now she knew that's what he wanted. Couldn't fuck her in case she said it was rape and his DNA was all over the place.

That's what had made him angry.

He'd been patiently working to bring her to him, dreaming about the moment he would push her back on her soft patchwork eiderdown and get his cock in deep between her legs. But it was all ruined. He hadn't had any choice.

As they lay there, the dry leaves and twigs cracking beneath them, the scent of loam strong, she'd tried to scream. He'd pulled up her T-shirt, shoving it in her mouth, holding his hand over her face until her eyes looked like they were going to pop out of their sockets.

And her fear had been intoxicating, just like the first time in France. He'd been so high on the power, on her terror, on the need to fuck her, he'd felt like he was going to explode. It had taken longer than he'd expected for her to lie quiet, but eventually she'd passed out and the pulse in her beautiful honey-coloured neck had subsided. He'd waited a moment to be sure, then he'd jumped off her and, running as far into the woods as he could bear, he'd fallen against the nearest tree and undone his jeans. Closing his eyes, he'd imagined ejaculating over her tits, over her lifeless face, and he'd finally come.

When the cops had come to question everyone the next morning he'd explained he'd been playing chess, had walked home through the woods. He'd heard sounds like animals, like maybe someone having sex, but he'd had no idea that's what it was.

He'd got away with it, but only just. He was blessed no one had seen them, that the woods were so close to the school's back entrance and not overlooked. The road didn't even have street lights. They'd found the anonymous emails with the images, but everyone had reckoned that she'd been meeting someone that night whom she'd met online, that she'd asked for it.

He'd learned two things that night. The first: to be more careful. The second: how fucking amazing it felt to be in total control.

Sitting down at the back of the cafe, the rich aroma of coffee rising above the sound of gentle Sunday morning chatter and clattering china, he smiled to himself. He needed control – control of his life and total control of the sites. Being here in Dublin had confirmed that more than ever. But everything was working out – he wouldn't have to wait much longer. Everything had gone to plan from the beginning. The blonde had texted him to meet her at her room last Thursday afternoon, said that she needed help with her computer. She'd been nervy and upset, kept checking her phone constantly, but he'd only got inside the door and one of her friends had arrived and she hadn't been able to explain. She'd gone out *of the room to try and get rid of the girl, which had given him his chance to look around, and he'd had just enough time, before someone else had arrived, to take the next step in the master plan that Karim had set in motion back in Paris, to lay the next part of the trail that would lead the authorities to a multiple international killer. There wasn't room for two of them. It was time to take over running everything and to be his own boss, and to do that, he needed to remove the one person who was blocking his progress. It was long overdue. He couldn't remember a time when he hadn't hated being told what to do. It was hilarious really, how easily someone else could be convicted for his crimes – a win-win in every possible way.*

He almost laughed out loud.

It was such a perfect plan. Like all his plans.

And it was all falling into place.

Chapter 20

It was raining again. Even with the windscreen wipers going full tilt, Cathy couldn't see out. A motorbike crossed in front of her and nipped up the inside of a bus. She often wondered how more of them weren't killed.

It was her turn to drive. Fanning was sitting beside her on his mobile, sorting out some fiasco from last night that wasn't a relationship overlap at all apparently, despite circumstances that suggested the exact opposite. She ignored his frantic texting, concentrating instead on the road, her mind alternately wandering to the case, then pulling her back to her next fight. She'd had a tough session this morning, sparring with the two lads, but she'd landed some incredible punches, had even sent one of them across the ring with an awesome back kick. Sarah Jane and McIntyre were a demon combination. Between them they pushed her hard, but it was worth all the aches. It had been good to catch up with Sarah Jane; there was so much news and Cathy missed seeing her in the DCU canteen. Between sharing lifts to college and training together when Cathy was off work recovering from the explosion, they'd seen each other almost every day. Now that Cathy was back at work full time and only had a couple more assignments to finish her course, the only time they were sure to meet was at their sparring sessions in the gym, and those got a bit messed up if Cathy was involved in a big case.

She flicked on the indicator, shifting in her seat, her abs still sore. With the National Kick-Boxing Championships in April – only about twelve weeks away, as McIntyre kept reminding her – from next week she was going to be in the gym pretty much every minute she wasn't in work. It was a good place to be, though; she did her best thinking when she was bashing a punchbag.

And this case was baffling her. Cathy was really hoping that Lauren's room in Trinity's halls of residence might give them some clues.

Lauren's parents had understood that they needed to search her room, but had asked that one of her friends and her tutor Anna Lockharte be present. Cathy didn't need them, had thought twice about agreeing, but having them there could save her time if the room threw up any questions they might be able to help with.

The halls of residence where Lauren had been living were on Pearse Street beside the DART station. Someone had once told Cathy that if she was ever buying a house not to buy it next to a train line, and she was quite sure every student came out with that same thought. A 1970s style building, all glass and concrete, the residence had a large open-plan cafe on the ground floor, lifts and stairs leading up several floors to the maze of small single rooms that had shared bathrooms and kitchens on each landing.

Cathy met Anna and Lauren's friend Paula Garcia at the porter's desk; Jamie Fanning trailed in behind her, still on the phone. He put it away quickly the moment he saw Anna Lockharte. She was wearing wide-legged black pants and a starched white shirt with bell-shaped cuffs. Cathy smirked to herself, she was sure he didn't have a hope with Anna Lockharte. Not that that would stop him from trying, of course. He meant well but he could be a right dope – although, as O'Rourke often said, if everyone was busy being Einstein there'd be no one to open the post.

Lauren's friend Paula was a quiet girl. She had a slight Spanish accent but her English had obviously been learned in Dublin, probably at one of the many language schools in the city. She looked pale and drawn and, despite long dark hair she could almost sit on, looked like every other student in the building in sneakers, jeans and an oversized dark sweatshirt, friendship bracelets plaited around her wrists.

She looked to Anna for reassurance as the porter accompanied them upstairs, jangling his master keys.

Outside Lauren's door Paula stood back, her eyes red-rimmed. 'I can't go in there, all her things . . .'

'Don't worry, you don't need to.' Cathy smiled at her reassuringly. 'Please wait outside. We won't be long. Then we can have a chat downstairs if that's OK?'

Fanning for once had the sense to keep quiet, smiling at Paula sympathetically as she leaned against the corridor wall opposite the door, her arms tightly crossed in front of her, her mobile phone in one hand. It pipped, distracting her, and a moment later she was absorbed in the screen.

The porter, his navy uniform sweater straining over a generous stomach, unlocked the door and for a second he looked poised to come into the room with them. Cathy smiled at him.

'Thanks so much, we can take it from here.'

He stood back. 'If you need anything, give me a shout, I'll just be downstairs.' He hovered as if reluctant to go.

Cathy pulled a pair of latex gloves out of the pocket of her combats and pulled them on. The porter took the hint and headed back down the corridor.

'Will I wait out here too? It's very small.' Anna's voice was steady but Cathy could tell from the frown on her face that she wasn't relishing being involved in this part of the process. Searching a deceased person's personal space wasn't easy no matter how long you were in the job, but it was essential to get over the sense of violation and invasion and to focus on finding out the facts if justice was to be served.

'That would be great, thanks.' Cathy pushed the door open.

The room was dim, the curtains drawn. Even with the lack of light Cathy could see there was hardly space to get a cat in, let alone swing it. She reached for the light switch.

Whoever had decorated the Arts building with its interesting colour scheme had been at work here too, although at least the red corded carpet was cheerful, even if it clashed with the green cushions on the desk chair and an easy chair positioned under the window. A door led into a compact bathroom and beyond it a narrow single bed was crowded with cuddly toys and bright satin cushions. Fitted cupboards and a wide modern desk dominated the room. The desk was piled with textbooks, a heart-emblazoned mug beside them. It was certainly a compact space but Lauren had made it her own with a fluffy fur throw over the end of the bed, the cream block walls covered in posters of kittens. Beside the bed a pair of fluffy purple slippers lay where they had been kicked off.

On the desk Lauren's laptop was open, its screen asleep.

Cathy stepped carefully into the room, checking the floor in case anything had been dropped. It looked clean. In fact, the whole room looked clean and tidy, as if Lauren could come back at any minute.

Cathy said over her shoulder to Fanning, 'I'll check the laptop and desk. You do the bathroom and the wardrobe. Check her pockets.'

Fanning pulled on his own gloves, grinning. 'On it like a car bonnet.'

Cathy rolled her eyes. She caught Anna's puzzled expression behind him. He didn't notice; he was already checking the bottles and pots around the built-in washbasin. He could be a twat but he was thorough, Cathy had to give him that.

At the desk she touched the scratchpad and Lauren's laptop woke up. She turned to Anna, who hovered beside the doorway, her arms folded.

'Would Paula know Lauren's password by any chance?'

'I'll find out.' Paula had moved further down the corridor, out of sight of the door. Anna was back in a moment. 'It's the name of her cat, Sparkles. Are you OK here for a minute? I'm just going to make sure Paula's all right, she's very upset.'

Cathy gave Anna a reassuring smile. 'Of course.'

Turning back to the computer, she tapped in the password and the computer came to life. Lauren had left several Internet windows open. One of them was her Gmail.

'Handy.' Cathy spoke half to herself, and leaning forwards, ran her eye down the emails in Lauren's inbox. YouTube clips, what looked like a few photo attachments, some college assignments. Not as much as she had expected.

From the other end of the room, Fanning looked over her shoulder at the screen, and as if reading her mind said, 'Everyone uses Snapchat and WhatsApp these days as well. Once we've got her WhatsApp username we can recover her password, assuming she's used her email as the backup, see who she was talking to.'

'I'm not sure that's entirely legal, Fanning, although I appreciate your motives.' Cathy glanced behind her; Anna was still out in the corridor.

Cathy checked the other tabs that were open: Tumblr, Facebook. The last one was an image. Cathy clicked on it.

'Holy feck.'

A photograph of Lauren filled the screen: Lauren in her underwear, getting dressed, apparently unaware that the shot was being taken. Cathy looked at it carefully. It was at a strange angle – part of the top of Lauren's head was out of shot. Cathy swung around to look at the room. In the photo Lauren was standing next to the bed, a towel tossed on it like she'd just come back from the shower.

'I think this has been taken from here. From her laptop.'

Chapter 21

Sunday, 12.30 p.m.

Sticking her head out of Lauren's door, Cathy looked for Anna. She had her arm around Paula's shoulder, comforting her. Cathy stepped into the corridor, keeping her voice low.

'Have you got a second?'

Anna looked up and, nodding, gave Paula a hug. She followed Cathy back into Lauren's room. But before either of them had got a foot inside the door, Jamie Fanning straightened up from where he was bending over in Lauren's wardrobe. His hand was full of white prescription drugs boxes.

'What have we got here, then?'

Cathy's tone belied her surprise. 'What *have* we got here?'

'Good God.' Anna spoke slowly, looked at the boxes, shaking her head.

Cathy glanced back at her, nodding towards the corridor and raising her finger to her lips. She hardly needed to say it but they didn't need gossip circulating around the college; Cathy was sure there was plenty already. Slipping behind Anna, she stuck her head outside the door.

'Are you OK there for a minute? We just need to close the door to check something behind it.'

From further down the corridor a forlorn Paula looked up from her phone and nodded. For a moment Cathy wondered if she was surgically attached to social media, that somehow disconnecting from the Internet would damage her. Cathy was sure she was filling all her friends in on their search of Lauren's room.

Cathy smiled and retreated back inside gently closing the door.

'Don't move for a minute, stay exactly as you are.' Fanning looked at her, puzzled. 'Won't be a sec.'

In three strides she was at the other side of the room and had closed Lauren's laptop lid. They could get to that problem in a moment.

'Let me guess – is that Modafinil?' Anna crossed her arms tightly.

Fanning inspected the boxes carefully. 'It certainly is. How did you know?'

'A lot of students are taking it to get through their exams. We're always warning against it.' Anna shook her head. 'But how many boxes are there?' She looked at the four he had in his hand. 'That's several months' supply at least. It's not something you take every day.'

'Perhaps she was selling it to her friends. Did she seem the type that needed money?'

An investigation Cathy had been involved in at Trinity previously had involved the sale of prescription drugs, but it had been a long time ago, before Lauren had even started at the university. Anna shrugged, her face creased in a frown.

'She was a student, they never have enough money, but she was so shy, she wasn't the type to deal in drugs. I mean really, she wasn't.'

'Unless someone else had put her up to it.'

Anna wrinkled her nose as she thought about it, her face serious. 'Maybe.'

Whatever Lauren's motivations were and however she had got hold of the drugs, one thing Cathy knew for sure was that this find put a whole new angle on the investigation. Thoughts flew around her head. Had Lauren upset whoever was supplying her enough for them to kill her? Did she owe the dealers money? And why Dalkey? Why had she gone there? Was Tom involved too?

Cathy pulled out her phone. 'We need to get Thirsty to process the room. He can see if anyone else has handled those boxes.'

Fanning pulled out a clear evidence bag from the back pocket of his jeans and slipped the boxes inside.

'I really can't believe it.' Anna was still shaking her head, her face serious.

'I've got something else to show you.' Cathy moved to the end of the room. 'When you said Lauren was shy, how shy did you mean?'

'Extremely. She was very nervous. I wasn't sure if it was because she'd come from a country town and found the city and university daunting, or if it was just the way she was.'

Cathy lifted the lid on Lauren's laptop, but before she re-entered the password, she looked around the desk. Spotting a pad of fluorescent pink Post-its she tore one off, tearing the corner of it and sticking it over the camera on the computer. 'That's better.'

She could feel Anna watching her.

Cathy clicked on the image tab. 'I found this image open – it must have arrived just before she left and she forgot to close it.'

She stepped back to show Anna the still of Lauren getting dressed. Jamie Fanning leaned forward to look at it.

'That looks like a still grabbed from a video – see, it's a bit blurred around the edges.'

Anna was shaking her head, her face even more puzzled. 'Why would she have filmed that? You can see her face. It doesn't make sense – she was so shy she could hardly speak in tutorials. She certainly didn't like drawing attention to herself.'

'Perhaps she had a hidden life online?'

Cathy bent down over the laptop and opened Lauren's email. She was about to look through the emails with attachments when the system updated and a new email arrived:

Thank you for your registration with Discovery Quay . . .

Cathy stopped and looked at it. This was an autoreply message, the type you received seconds after you registered with a site. *How exactly could Lauren have registered with a website if she was in the morgue?*

She clicked on the incoming mail.

Thank you for registering with Discovery Quay, click on the link below to visit your account. Videos will be uploaded within 48 hours. Click on the screenshot to see your profile page if the site does not load in 5 seconds.

Cathy tucked a corkscrew of hair that had sprung loose from her ponytail behind her ear and leaned forward.

'Let's just see what this is all about, shall we?'

She clicked the link in the email and a blank screen appeared with text in the centre:

This site can't be reached.
extt7tdjoddiud.onion's server IP could not be found
Search Google for onion.

Fanning looked over Cathy's shoulder. 'That's a site on the Dark Web, all dot onion sites are unindexed. She doesn't have the right browser installed for you to access it. You need Tor.' He paused. 'Which means she couldn't have registered from this computer. Just click back to that email.' Cathy took the screen back to Lauren's Gmail. 'Click on the screenshot that's attached.'

Cathy clicked and the screenshot opened. She raised her eyebrows.

It was a dark red web page with white text, Discovery Quay written across the top. Some sort of profile page; Sexy Sparkles was entered as the username. Cathy frowned. *Why would she use part of her password as a username?* A photo of Lauren top-less looked out of the screen at them. She was brushing her hair in the picture, standing apparently naked in her room. *Had she taken it herself?* It didn't look like she was aware it was being taken. It was a raw photo, obviously without any filters – would she have uploaded that herself? *Unlikely.* Below the photo Cathy could see a video box. The frozen image of Lauren was different from the still above it – she was lying on her bed wearing some sexy black lingerie. Cathy glanced back at Anna and 007.

'Look, there's the dot onion address at the top.' Fanning leaned forwards. 'And see those images down the side? Those look like they are on the same site, they look like webcams.'

Cathy scrolled down a bit further and another ad appeared in the sidebar. Another site – Merchant's Quay – this time with images of drugs and heavy duty weaponry.

'Do you think she got the drugs from there? From that site?' Fanning was still frowning.

'When I was working on that undercover op here before, it turned out that students were ordering drugs online. So it's a distinct possibility. Perhaps she was saving on postage by ordering for her friends?' Cathy hesitated, thinking out loud. 'Something or someone obviously connects her to Discovery Quay and that seems to be linked to Merchant's Quay, who have special offers on . . .' She scrolled down a bit further, 'AK47s and Viagra . . .'

Fanning scowled again. 'They've probably got weapons grade plutonium if you look hard enough.'

Anna had been quiet, her face troubled as Cathy had revealed the image. Cathy glanced at her now.

'The image grab from the video was emailed to her. Have you heard anything about students getting their webcams hacked?'

Standing in the middle of the room, Anna paled about three shades. She shook her head.

'No, not students. But I got a strange email the other day about speaking at a conference. I sent it over to a friend of mine in the States, he works for the security services.' Anna pulled out her phone and flipped it open. 'Let me find his email.' She scanned the screen. 'I only got his reply this morning. I scanned it, but I haven't read it properly yet.' She paused. 'Here it is. He says the email contained a spyware virus that was designed to enable someone to access the webcam on my computer remotely. Apparently this virus contains a rootkit designed to hide all the malicious files, preventing it from being detected. It came in at the same time as some other emails. I got a virus warning on one of them – it happens all the time – but this email stood out because of the way it was phrased, it didn't read right. My laptop's at home so I haven't done anything about it yet. When I get back tonight my friend wants me to give one of his tech guys remote access so they can clean the system and see if they can track where the worm originated from.'

'But you know who sent the email.'

Anna grimaced. 'Not exactly. It was a general info address for a conference. Which was what made it look a bit odd, to be honest. I get asked to speak at things all the time but it's usually more direct, more personal – an email from the conference organiser. I was going to let Rob, my friend, see what he could find out. His people specialise in cybersecurity.'

'You need to cover the camera on your laptop first off. You know there is a roaring trade on the Internet with websites featuring hacked footage.' Fanning sounded like he knew what he was talking about for once.

Anna nodded. 'I know – my niece Hope told me. She's very techy, she suggested sending the email to Rob in the first place.' She shook her head. 'I have to say it's not something I've ever needed to search for.'

'I wish you were alone in that.' Cathy looked back at the screen. 'It seems someone felt the need to inform Lauren that her images had been or were about to be shared. Which might suggest she was being pressured into doing something or was being blackmailed. From everything you've told us about her she certainly wasn't the exhibitionist type.'

Anna shook her head again. 'The poor girl. She must have been terrified. Do you think she jumped off the cliff because she couldn't cope with the images being made public?'

Cathy shrugged. They were pretty sure that Lauren hadn't jumped off the cliff, but no matter how much she liked Anna

Lockharte, there was only so much information that was safe to share.

'We'll get our tech people to look at this – would your friend be able to share his findings?'

Anna hesitated. 'I'm not sure. But I'm sure if he can track the email to the source he can share that. He works in a highly classified area and he's doing me a favour, so I don't know how much he can tell you.'

'Anything he can do would be much appreciated.'

'He works for the US Government. It's a powerful thing.'

Anna's tone was very definite, and made Cathy stop for a moment. Had she had something to do with the US Government? Was that why O'Rourke was familiar with her name, why he'd clammed up when Cathy had asked him about her? Intrigued, Cathy knew better than to ask outright. She'd tackle O'Rourke first and see what he had to say for himself. If that failed she'd have a word with Sarah Jane and see if she could find out anything from her dad.

Downstairs in the common room-cum-cafe, they found space to sit in a corner at the back. Cathy nursed a coffee. Paula, obviously still very upset by their visit, was looking paler by the minute. Cathy knew it was tough enough for her to deal with the death of her friend without then having to cope with the Guards asking questions, a full investigation, and a post-mortem. At her age it was quite likely that this was the first time she had lost someone close, and possibly someone her own age as well. Anna had bought her some hot chocolate and as she sat on the sofa nursing the cup, Cathy prayed she wasn't going to pass out or get hysterical. She leaned forward and started with the easy questions. Beside her, Fanning had his notebook out.

'Were you and Lauren good friends?'

Paula shrugged, her eyes filling with tears. 'We were really close last year. But this year, when we came back after the summer holiday, she wasn't around so much, to come out with us I mean. She said she was studying but I'm pretty sure she wasn't all the time. I don't know if she just didn't want to come out or if it was something else.'

'Did she ever talk about taking drugs to help her concentrate?'

A flash of fear ran across Paula's face; her voice became defensive. 'Why are you asking that? Lots of people use them, they're not illegal.'

Cathy kept her face open and friendly. 'I know – we just need to get some background on what Lauren was like. Did she talk to you about drugs?'

'Once. She asked where she could get some Adderall. She was looking really tired. I think she was worried about something, she seemed really preoccupied. She said she wasn't sleeping but she needed to concentrate on her college stuff. I told her most people order them online.'

Cathy took this in. Perhaps Lauren had tried a few different brands to see which one suited her, but that still didn't feel right. Students usually didn't have the money to experiment.

'Tell me what she was like.'

Paula shrugged. 'Pretty, really shy.'

'Was she seeing anyone?'

Paula shook her head. 'I don't think so. Lots of guys liked her, like I said, she was really pretty, but she didn't seem interested in any of them.'

'How about Tom Quinn. How well did she know him?'

Paula shrugged again. 'They knew each other quite well, I suppose – they'd both worked at his dad's radio station last summer. I think they might have had a bit of a thing, they were a bit awkward at the start of term, didn't hang out much. There are different groups here. Tom got on really well with the tech nerds, hung out with them a good bit.'

'Was he popular?'

'Well, he was gorgeous and loaded so, yes.'

Paula said it like Cathy was a total idiot. Nice. Cathy ignored the attitude, she'd heard worse. What was much more interesting was the tension Paula had picked up between Tom and Lauren – what had that been about?

Chapter 22

Heading back to the station, Cathy drove again. Fanning already had a browser called Orfox downloaded on his phone that gave him access to the Dark Web – Cathy wasn't even going to ask him why. He'd made a note of the web address of the Discovery Quay site from the address bar in the screenshot, and was having a look around.

As they'd guessed, Discovery Quay was a video site, the discovery apparently being the video cams of a very large number of young women. The lights ahead of them changed to red and Cathy glanced over at his screen. She could tell immediately that the cameras had been hacked. When girls made porn videos they wore make-up, fancy underwear. The majority of the girls in the videos on this site were getting undressed, or were in the bath, very obviously unaware that they were being filmed. Ads to other webcams and porn sites updated in the sidebar as Fanning clicked through the site, then a pop-up advert appeared: 'Prescription drugs fast, total discretion guaranteed.'

The lights changed and her attention was back on the road. Beside her Fanning clicked on the ad.

'This takes you to Merchant's Quay again. Looks like it sells everything you could possibly need across every conceivable family of narcotic. And plenty of other stuff too.'

'Discovery Quay and Merchant's Quay. Sounds like they might be vaguely related.'

He grunted in response, then said, 'Jesus, you really can get anything on this Merchant's Quay site, and I mean anything.'

'Like what?'

He scrolled down. 'It's like a marketplace, loads of different vendors. It looks like they pay a hefty fee for space and then give a percentage of their profit to the site owner, who . . .' he paused, 'is predictably anonymous.'

'But there must be a bank account that can be traced.'

Fanning shook his head. 'All payments are in Bitcoins.'

'Which are what exactly? I keep hearing about them on the news.'

'It's basically a row of code, it's not a thing.'

'OK, so don't even start to explain that, I don't have the head-space. They work like real money, though?'

'When the FBI closed down that Silk Road site, they seized about 25,000 Bitcoins they reckoned were worth over $3 million.'

'Holy feck . . . Argh, Jesus, indicate, you idiot!' Cathy flashed the car that had cut across in front of her. The driver raised his middle finger. She flashed the blue lights concealed in the head-lights and he braked hard.

'Do we have to stop him? It's raining.'

Cathy shot him a withering look. 'No, we don't, Fanning, unfor-tunately there's no law against being an arsehole and us giving him grief isn't going to earn us any brownie points. We'll end up creating a traffic jam here that will cause gridlock on the quays.'

She could hear O'Rourke in her head now. And the AA traffic report. *It's Sunday afternoon, where's everyone going?*

The driver pulled off, indicating. At least he'd got the point. Cathy always found it mildly hilarious how people slowed down the moment they spotted a patrol car on the motorway – it was like some sort of Mexican wave. As if the patrol hadn't noticed they were exceeding the speed limit twenty miles previously.

'So tell me more about Merchant's Quay? What do they sell? What's everything?'

'What do you need? Fake driver's licences? Weapons, assassinations – there's a rocket launcher here – but they don't do child porn.'

'That's good to know.'

Cathy checked her mirror and indicated to change lanes, her focus on the traffic. The point was that if the site was anything like Silk Road, it was generating massive money and presumably trading all over the world. Which meant they weren't likely to be the only branch of law enforcement interested. Cathy was quite sure Anna Lockharte's friend – who, she'd explained as they'd left Lauren's room, was in the CIA – was likely to already be familiar with Merchant's Quay; particularly if it had taken up the slack in the online drugs trade when Silk Road was shut down.

But how did Discovery Quay fit into the picture? It sounded like it was a sub-site, perhaps run by the same people. Had Lauren's drug order brought the webcam hacker to her? Maybe the owners of the site had realised that she had access to other students when they saw her university email address, and figured she could be a valuable asset in their drugs supply network.

What sort of a mess had she got herself tangled up in? From everything Cathy had learned about Lauren O'Reilly, she came across as a gentle country girl. Perhaps seeing herself on camera really had pushed her over the edge? Literally. Maybe her suicide *had* been real?

Fanning cut into her thoughts. 'Here, this is what was in the FBI documentation from the Silk Road trial. From February 6, 2011 to July 23, 2013 there were "approximately",' Cathy was focusing on the road but out of the corner of her eye she saw him glance at her, '"1,229,465 transactions completed on the site" – holy fuck. That's on Silk Road. They reckon the total revenue generated was over *nine million* Bitcoins, and the total commissions collected by Silk Road from the sales amounted to over half a million Bitcoins. Back then, that was the equivalent of almost eighty million dollars in commission. That's a lot of fucking money.'

'Sure is.' Cathy flipped her indicator again, glancing in her rear-view mirror.

'I think Lauren was small time – she'd need a lot more stock than she had if she was dealing properly. We should get an idea from her texts if she was buying and selling.'

Fanning said it like it was a given. Cathy wasn't so sure.

'Perhaps she was waiting for a new delivery, and that's why she only had a few boxes. I mean, it was a lot if it was for personal use, but if she was passing it on, four boxes really wouldn't go far.' She paused. 'All these sites work by delivering plain packages through the post. We need to check with the porter to see if she'd previously had a lot of boxes delivered from foreign places. I can't see Merchant's Quay being run from Ireland – if you've got that sort of money you hole up in Nice or Antigua. Somewhere where the sun shines. Even the big crooks here spend half their life on the Costa del Sol. I can see why they'd target universities, though, so that bit makes sense.'

O'Rourke was in his office when they arrived back. As soon as Cathy stuck her head around the door he stood up.

'Incident room – I want you to brief everyone at the same time.'

She withdrew and headed across the corridor to the rec room. It was already starting to fill up; he must have told the team that they were on their way.

O'Rourke kicked off.

'So first, Tom Quinn – we've an approximate time frame and a list of vehicles that were in the area that we need to check.'

O'Rourke waved at the board behind him. It was a long list. That was going to keep someone busy.

'There's a good bit of traffic to both victims' phones, mainly student banter about essay deadlines and potential dates. Tom and Lauren *were* in touch that afternoon, but perhaps more significantly it seems that both of them were in pretty much constant contact with two different pay-as-you-go mobiles. Their texts to these numbers would suggest they were in a sexual relationship with the recipients. We're requesting the call records and the signals are being triangulated to find out where those phones were being used.

'This morning Cat and Fanning went out to Lauren O'Reilly's room in Trinity and have found some interesting stuff. Over to you, Cat.'

Cathy stood up. It only took her a minute to summarise the findings on Lauren's laptop and the drug discovery.

'So we've sealed Lauren O'Reilly's room and a full foren-sic examination is underway. Anna Lockharte, her year tutor, is contacting a friend of hers in the US security services – in the CIA, to be exact – who is a computer specialist and who recognised that an email *she* had been sent contained a worm designed to give the sender remote access to the video camera on her laptop. It's possible this is a wider problem in Trinity but we'll only know for sure when we have a look through the videos on Discovery Quay. Then we'll see if we can recognise anyone or the locations.' Jamie Fanning cleared his throat loudly. Cathy looked at him pointedly. 'And I think we have a volunteer.'

A chorus of catcalls erupted across the room. Cathy shook her head, rolling her eyes. *What was he like?*

O'Rourke interrupted. 'Traffic cams first, Fanning, don't get too carried away.' He nodded for Cathy to continue.

'We'll see what Lauren's email traffic can tell us.' She paused. 'Lauren's friend felt there was tension between Lauren and Tom when they came back to uni after the summer. She also felt that Lauren had been moody and preoccupied, as if she was worried about something.

'There's one guy we still need to talk to, an international stu-dent called Olivier Ayari. It's clear from Tom's phone and email traffic that they knew each other well. He's not answering his phone but I've left a message.'

'Good.' O'Rourke stepped forward as Cathy went back to her chair. 'When you find him, see if Tom told him more about his personal life than Lauren shared about hers.'

Chapter 23

Sunday, 2.30 p.m.

Anna Lockharte pulled her shaggy scarf out of the sleeve of the jacket the porter had been minding for her and wrapped it twice around her neck before slipping her coat on. The sunshine of the other morning had been short-lived; now sleet-like rain was falling. Anna shivered, not relishing the walk back to her office through the university grounds. It was only about ten minutes, but in this weather . . . But if she walked quickly she'd keep warm and get there faster. Anna glanced back into the cafe area. Paula had eventually calmed down enough for her to leave her. She was now sitting at a table with several of her girlfriends, her dark head bowed. Anna felt relieved that she had close friends, that the whole year group had seemed to gel. They would help each other through this nightmare. You didn't expect your friends to die at nineteen or twenty.

At that age you didn't expect your friends to die at all. Or your family. The thought made her start, made her ache for Hope, for all that she had lost. Anna closed her eyes and focused on centring herself for a minute. There was too much happening right now; she couldn't let herself slip back into the dark place that paralysed her, that kept her behind closed doors. It hadn't happened for ages, not now she was here in Dublin, so far away from a terrorist threat, but every now and again something unexpected triggered it and she found herself overcome.

But not today, not now. She had students that needed her, and if Cathy Connolly was right, there could be more students in Trinity whose computers had been compromised. It was something she was going to have to discuss with the head of Trinity and make students aware of. Anna felt her temper rising. It was so wrong – there was every chance other vulnerable young students had been targeted and that made her really mad. As soon as she got back to her office she'd call Rob and see how he could help. Perhaps his team would be able to find something in her computer that could help guide the Garda investigation. The photos, the drugs – they had to be factors in Lauren's death. Rob would do everything he could, she knew. She trusted him absolutely.

She stuck her hands deep in the pockets of her coat, turning everything over in her mind as she hurried along the wide pavement, rounding the corner before she waited at the lights to cross the road. These deaths didn't make any sense whichever way you looked at them. First Tom and now Lauren, two deaths in such close proximity, two people who knew each other. How could they not be related?

The green man appeared and Anna hurried across the road, heading for the entrance to the university beside the science blocks. She glanced into the gym as she passed, the glass wall opening into Pearse Street like a stage, the fittest, keenest students lapping up the attention. The ridiculousness of having a gym with a glass wall level with a busy public street always made Anna smile. There should have been a sign on the door: 'exhibitionists only'.

Anna was quite sure that Lauren O'Reilly hadn't been an exhibitionist, that the video they had seen had been filmed without her permission. Anna cringed inside, feeling Lauren's embarrassment as she opened that first email, her shock at the image. Because Anna was completely sure that's what it had been – shock. If Lauren had wanted those shots to be made public she would have worn make-up, would have stood more provocatively, like the girls on Instagram mimicking the models they saw in magazines. Her stomach twisted at the thought of Lauren's reaction to the contents of those emails, the intrusion into her personal space. The unspoken threat that came with it. Anna would rather be facing a guy with a knife any day.

Turning into the gate, Anna hurried on, weaving through knots of students. There was rarely a time when Trinity College was quiet.

'Professor Lockharte?'

Lost in her thoughts, Anna started, turning to whoever had spoken, and her heart almost stopped. Xavier Ayari. All six foot of him looking just as devastating as ever in a thick, navy blue padded ski jacket, a purple tubular scarf at the neck. Very French. His smile was disarming, a flash of white in olive skin, his jet-black hair cropped short.

'Xavier, how are you?' Anna couldn't think of anything else to say, was aware that the few students milling in the science block had noticed them, were looking their way. Suddenly she felt like she was the centre of attention. This was all she needed.

'I'm good, thank you, Professor. I wondered if you had got my email, about speaking to the society?' Xavier smiled at her, his hands thrust in his pockets.

His inner confidence disarmed Anna slightly. She suddenly remembered one of the other female tutors commenting that it was his nonchalant sophistication that made women swoon. He was also quite brilliant intellectually, according to her colleagues. He was wealthy, good looking, he had it all. He reminded Anna for a split second of Rob; he had that same blend of charm and talent.

But the combination of Xavier's accent and looks made her mouth go dry. She tried to mentally focus on the sound of the chatter around them, on the cold, on everything that wasn't Paris in the spring. Everything that wasn't the sound of another dark-skinned Frenchman, his voice echoing out across the hushed lobby of the Banque Nationale de Paris, a voice followed seconds later by automatic gunfire.

'I did, I'm sorry I haven't had a chance to reply. Of course I'll speak to your society. Let me know when you've got it organised.'

Anna flicked him a smile and turned to hurry on, deliberately dismissing him. It seemed to work. She held her breath, hoping he wouldn't call her back. Leaving him standing there, Anna focused on the sound of her boots on the concrete, on getting to her office before the memories closed in on her.

But it was too late. She could feel her heart rate increasing, feel the cold sweat running down her back. In her mind she could see the figure dressed in black standing over them, gripping his Heckler & Koch MP5. From where she lay on the floor, out of the corner of her eye she had watched him scanning the huge, ornate entrance hall. Every muscle in her body had tensed as he'd sent out another spray of bullets at what had been, until his arrival, an unexceptional line of business people and tourists waiting for service in one of Paris's busiest central banks: native French, Algerians, a couple of Polish students, an American and an elderly German couple. Suits, smart pinstripe pencil skirts, stiletto heels, backpacks and Birkenstocks.

The images fighting for her attention, Anna put her head down and headed straight for her office, praying she wouldn't be stopped on the way. Her mouth dry, her heart thumping, just like that day . . .

It had only been May but the sun had been hot, creating shadows on the broad pavements behind them as they left the Hôtel de Pontalba on the rue du Faubourg Saint-Honoré, the US Ambassador's residence in the 8th arrondissement, heading for Paris's main shopping area. They shrugged off suggestions that they should take a car, walking instead along the sun-dappled pavements, cherry trees heavy with blossom, Jennifer's secret service minder following at a discreet distance. The plan had been to have lunch and then to find a dress for Hope for an embassy event. The three of them out on the town. Together. Simple.

But then suddenly, not so.

Anna's overpowering memory was the confusion and the smell of blood.

As they'd entered the bank, Jennifer had seen someone she knew, someone who had insisted on introducing the ambassador's wife to her mother. Jen's secret service minder hovering in the background, Anna had slipped around the group, urging Hope into the queue before it got any longer. Hope had rolled her blue eyes, not needing to be asked twice.

And then behind them a heavily accented voice had announced that infidels would be punished . . . and the shooting had started and they'd hit the floor. Anna was sure that the gunman closest to her had been muttering a prayer. Her

Arabic wasn't good but she recognised the phrases from the videos she used for students on her course. There were two of them, dressed in black military combats, their automatic weapons trained on the people who now lay injured and dying on the cold, hard, tiled floor of the bank. Anna reckoned the whole episode had taken less than sixty seconds. Sixty seconds that had lasted a lifetime.

She'd known the men were likely to be on a suicide mission. The most dangerous sort of terrorists were those who didn't give a damn about their personal safety. If they hadn't been completely dedicated before, six months in an ISIS training camp would have turned them into killing machines. For the first time in her life Anna wished she knew a bit less about terrorism. Living her PhD thesis hadn't been part of the master plan for this trip.

'Play dead,' she'd whispered into Hope's hair, so quietly Anna had wondered if the girl could hear her. But Anna had felt Hope relax, felt her slow her breathing. Having something – anything – to focus on, would help get them through this.

If getting through was an option.

And then Anna had suddenly caught the sound of sirens, distant but getting louder.

From where she lay, Anna couldn't see if the terrorists were padded up with explosives. She'd prayed not. If these men were valuable operatives perhaps they had been instructed to cause maximum damage and then get out.

The sirens had grown louder. If she'd had space in her head, Anna would have imagined the pandemonium in the broad elegant street outside. But she didn't. She was focused on only one thing. On getting Hope out of this alive.

And suddenly the men were shouting, and there had been another hail of bullets, this time sprayed across the entire hall, the high-pitched whimpers of those left alive, and then another round of gunfire, absorbed by wood. Anna wasn't about to turn her head to look. The sound of a door banging shut.

Then silence.

Striding into the Arts block, Anna punched the call button on the lift to her office, her heart beating so loudly she thought it would explode. She could feel her breathing accelerate, panic nipping at the edges of her conscious mind. But she couldn't panic. Everything the counsellors had taught her was coming into play right now. It was anxiety, she knew, her fight or flight mechanism kicking in. She just needed to hold it all together long enough to get into her office so she could lock the door and fight the images in her head, to breathe.

Anna punched the call button again. *Why was this the most godawful slowest lift? Why?*

She closed her eyes and focused on her physical reaction to the memories. She couldn't stop them coming but she could try and regulate her response. And she was getting there. It was slow but she was getting there.

Chapter 24

Sunday, 4 p.m.

Cathy was relieved to see that the kitchen in Dun Laoghaire station was empty as she headed in to it. She went straight to the kettle, the form she needed to fill in stuck under her arm, a biro behind her ear. She literally had about ten minutes free. The partition doors were partially folded back between the kitchen and the incident room, but everyone was either out on enquiries or in the detective office.

Thirsty had found more drugs in Lauren's washbag – a single box of Adderall this time – and was tracking the batch numbers on all the boxes as well as dusting them for fingerprints. Cathy had stuck her head into O'Rourke's office on the way past but he'd been on the phone. On top of these investigations, a series of thefts from the marina had escalated over the weekend and had boat owners bombarding the station with calls. The armed robbery in Cornelscourt had turned into a massive job, with the raiders traced back to one of the major Dublin gangs. They'd shot and injured a member of the public when they'd abandoned their car in the city centre and the press were going mad. Pearse Street were managing that investigation but keeping him in the loop. It would prepare him well for Limerick.

The thought gave her an unpleasant jolt, made her previously positive mood – buoyed up by the feeling that they were finally getting somewhere with the case – evaporate. Everything was changing, but she wasn't going to sit around and get left behind. She knew she was young to be in the detective unit, that some older members saw her in a role that they felt they should be doing. But she'd proven herself time and time again. And now she was ready for the next move. In a weird way, the timing couldn't actually be better. She was almost at peak fitness, was ready to take on the world right now and McIntyre's training was as much psychological as physical.

The kettle boiled and Cathy stuck a spoonful of instant coffee in a mug, sniffed the milk carton left on the counter, and sloshed some in, stirring it as she headed to a table tucked in the corner. As she sat down her phone pipped with a text: *Dad says to say hello to Anna Lockharte from him.* Followed by a row of hearts and winking eye emoji. Cathy smiled, and texted Sarah Jane back: *Will do!* Cathy hadn't mentioned Ted Hansen to Anna this morning when she'd met her; it hadn't been appropriate with everything else going on. And she wanted to get closer to some answers about Anna Lockharte's background first. But Sarah Jane's constant matchmaking for her dad was hilarious. Sarah Jane reckoned he was never going to find love in a war zone, and he was never at home in his apartment overlooking Central Park long enough to get involved in the New York social scene, so he needed all the help he could get. Cathy shook her head. *They could all do with all the help they could get.*

Cathy smoothed out the application form she'd brought with her onto the table and pulled the pen out from behind her ear. The pre-selection course for the Emergency Response Unit was the toughest in the job – two weeks in a military style training camp. Assault courses, overnight treks. Helicopter drills. It tested every particle of your being, your ability to function in a team, your ability to make life and death decisions when you were exhausted and broken. It was pure hell.

She knew she was going to love it.

Assuming she got to that stage. She had to be selected for interview first and she knew the competition for what would be only a handful of posts would be fierce. There were plenty of other officers just as fit and determined as she was.

Sometimes she wondered if she was an adrenaline junkie, but there was nothing more exhilarating than hitting the wall and powering through it. It was completely and absolutely mind over matter. As your muscles screamed you had to keep on going, knowing that when you got past the pain, the going got easier and you'd have done it.

When she thought back to the moments when she'd really been up against it – like when she'd got shot the first time – it had been adrenaline that had got her through. Cathy took a sip of her coffee, glancing over the front page of the form. Some officers never even saw a dead body in their entire career, let alone drew a weapon, but she was getting a reputation for getting shot at. She was up to three near misses now.

The second time it had happened, in the car park beside Blessington Lakes, she'd been much more on top of the situation than that first time with O'Rourke. She'd had the benefit of surprise but, as she'd learned subsequently, the man she was pursuing, Dave Givens, had been one of the British Army's most decorated soldiers, and his aim was sure. She'd sort of guessed that going in, but there had been too much at stake to start arsing about getting cold feet. It had been all about adrenaline that night as well – sometimes you just had to act. Like later, in Keane's Field in Ballymun, when she'd come face to face with the barrel of a gun once again.

That had been a horrible night. Dark and wet and bloody freezing, although she hadn't felt the cold until later. She'd stayed with Sarah Jane, not daring to move her jacket from the wound in her shoulder in case she bled out. Backup and medical support had come fast, getting straight to work on Sarah Jane. Cathy had gone to Jazz, a lost and lonely fifteen-year-old boy who was sobbing beside the one thing he really loved, his beautiful, enormous and badly injured piebald horse. Then the air ambulance had landed at the top of the hill and Krypton, the animal they both thought was dead, had snorted and lifted his head, rolling his eyes so Cathy could see the whites, baring his teeth. She and Jazz had scrambled back in the mud as fast as they could, giving him the space to try and stand. It had taken a few attempts, his hooves digging into the mud, his flank bleeding from a deep wound as he staggered to his feet, tossing his head. He'd stood still for a moment and then had come over to nuzzle Jazz. Cathy had given them plenty of space, sliding back further up the hill, but it had been one of those moments she would never forget. Watching them, boy and horse, mesmerised, she'd felt O'Rourke materialise beside her. She'd reached for his hand so he could pull her up and then for a few precious moments she'd leaned against him, her head on his shoulder, his chin resting on the top of her head.

Cathy looked at the ERU application form in front of her, the Garda badge at the top, and filled in her full name and registered number, below it her station. This was it. She took a hasty swig of her coffee and looked over the form. With a bit of luck, she'd have time to get most of it filled in before she was called back to the office.

'Competencies' seemed to be the buzzword in the various boxes she had to complete. At least she had plenty of those.

'Cat, you busy?'

Cathy looked up to see O'Rourke's head around the partition door between the incident room and the kitchen. She almost had the form complete, and was very glad she was used to writing essays for college – some of the answers required were long ones.

'What's up?'

'The mobile companies have come back with locations. Both those pay-as-you-go mobiles were being used close to each other in Dalkey, they were all bouncing off the same masts.'

'Even the one Lauren was calling?'

O'Rourke nodded. 'Maybe she *was* calling Tom. We've got a map with the triangulated signals marked but it's looking like they were in the same area very close to where he lived. The call records aren't giving us any clues unfortunately.'

'So our main focus is on Dalkey? At least that narrows things down a bit.'

'Looks like it. Can you give 007 a hand getting an interview list together from the CCTV in Ulverton Road? I want to get house to house out again around both locations. See if anyone can remember anything. I'm feeling like we're missing something.'

'No problem.' She slid her chair back and picked up her coffee cup and the form.

'What's that?'

She took another sip of her coffee and pulled a face as she realised it was cold.

'Application for ERU.'

He looked at her hard, didn't say anything for a moment, like he was thinking about it.

'Apart from the increased likelihood of you getting yourself killed, I still think it's probably a good move.'

'I can get myself killed here. I don't need to be in ERU. When your number's up . . .'

He gave her a withering look; he'd never believed any of her superstitious 'nonsense' as he called it. He endured her reading out his horoscope when they were stuck on a job in the middle of the night, but that was more out of sheer boredom than interest. They both knew she didn't fully believe in it either but it gave her something to needle him with.

'You know I'm right.' She glared at him, half in jest.

'Get moving. 007's in the office. You'll be faster at checking the info on the system than him. He can only type with one finger.'

She threw a salute and followed him out.

In the cramped detective office, Jamie Fanning turned around from the desk he was sitting at, looking very pleased to see her.

'Where've you been? I hate doing this stuff. You're way faster than I am.'

'What have you got?' She stood behind him, bending to look over his shoulder at the screen. He hadn't got very far.

'Traffic have lifted all the plates off the CCTV they can find covering both ends of Ulverton Road – right down to Sandycove. There was a good bit of traffic.'

'Right, budge over.'

Her fingers moving quickly over the keys of the computer, Cathy created a follow-up list of the names and addresses of every vehicle owner. Any one of the drivers could easily have seen something they didn't realise was important. Had Tom been with someone when the accident had occurred? Had he been on his own?

'Whoa.' Her hands poised above the keyboard, Cathy stopped and reread the data on the screen.

Behind her Fanning looked up from the printout in his hand. 'What have you found?'

'Ronan Delaney. He's that DJ that works for Life Talk FM and was MC at Orla Quinn's charity thing. Married to Karen Delaney. Bit of a shit, from what I gathered when I spoke to her.'

'What about him?'

Cathy scrolled down the page. 'He lives in Ulverton Road. This address can't be more than a couple of hundred yards from where Tom was found.' She thought for a moment. 'I guess Karen thought I already knew that when I spoke to her at her salon.'

'Think he could have seen something?'

'I do – I think we need to have a chat to him.' She leaned over to double-check the time from the CCTV listed beside the registration plate. 'From the time Delaney was passing this camera in Sandycove, it looks like he would have passed the place that Tom was hit about five minutes after his mum had called him. And he obviously didn't feel the need to share that fact with his wife, or his good friends the Quinns.'

Chapter 25

Sunday, 4 p.m.

It had taken a good ten minutes for Anna to steady her breathing. She'd locked the door to her office as she came in. Someone had knocked but she'd ignored it, had instead grabbed the edge of the desk with both hands, braced herself and closed her eyes, playing the psychologist's words through her head over the soundtrack of gunshots and people dying. She'd focused on her favourite page in the book Rob had given her. It was a beautiful woodcut illustration, black on white, showing how to breathe consciously. Step by step she felt her anxiety receding.

Success. And immense relief.

A year ago she would have curled up under her desk, safe in its dark confines, but she had come on so much in the last twelve months. She needed to find another counsellor here she could talk to, though. The first doctor she'd gone to had been brilliant but was now on an extended study trip in the States, and stupidly Anna hadn't found someone else immediately. The doctor had trained in trauma counselling in Belfast, had been so good that she'd come on in leaps and bounds. It had been a good nine months since she'd had a panic attack like this, which just proved it. But she needed to keep it up, needed to keep working through her issues. And she needed to keep the little book Rob had given her closer to hand. It was her talisman, a reminder that there was a safety net out there, that she didn't have to do this on her own.

Running her hands over her face and tucking her hair behind her ears, Anna sat down and powered up her desktop computer, trying to concentrate on her work, on anything that would occupy her mind.

It was a struggle, but it was an hour later when she heard her mobile ring, the sound muffled. It was in her coat pocket. She turned around, realising she was still sitting on her coat, and rooted for it in the folds of the fabric. She got there before it stopped ringing, smiling as she saw the name that flashed across the screen.

'Hello, stranger.'

'And how are *you*, Professor Lockharte?'

It was Rob, his gorgeous velvety voice with its all-American accent sounding stronger when she couldn't hear similar ones all around her. Anna found herself smiling. They didn't talk nearly often enough on the phone; they emailed and texted but it wasn't the same. He was exactly what she needed right now.

'I'm at the office, but I'm good, always pleased to hear from you.'

She could hear him chuckling as he replied. 'Always good to hear. Why are you working on a Sunday? I thought that was my prerogative? I wanted to touch base – I'm really sorry I haven't sorted this out sooner and I don't have much time now. I'm going to call back later so we can sort out this email issue.'

'I know you're busy, really, thank you. Hope said you'd know what to do.'

'How is my beautiful niece?'

'Doing great, loving school. I'm whisking her over to London next weekend to see the sights and a show. I'm speaking at a training seminar on Friday and we live so close, but she's never been.'

'I like the sound of being whisked away by you.'

Anna smiled, her voice low. 'I'd whisk you away tomorrow if I could, you know that.'

She heard him sigh, then in the background another voice – someone had come into his office.

'I'm sorry, honey, I gotta go. Your laptop's at home?'

'Yes, it's back at my apartment.'

'What time will you be back?'

'Just after six?'

'I'll call you then, don't turn it on until you talk to me. I'll have a team ready to work on it.'

'Thank you.' She meant every letter of it.

'I'm always here for you, you know that. We'll get this fixed.'

The line went dead and Anna hung up, smiling. He always made her happy. She adored that he took the time to write her the longest emails, telling her about the silly stuff that happened to him. He could never talk about his job specifically, they both understood that, but they had developed their own code when they needed to say something sensitive.

Anna sighed, shaking her head half to herself. She was a bit old for this, knew she needed to find someone else eventually, but knowing that he felt the same about her made her want to hang on, just to see. He wasn't available right now; would he ever be? She knew he wasn't happy at home but separating was a big thing. And even then, their getting together would be complicated. He was Hope's uncle by marriage. She shook her head. It was all very messy, whichever way you looked at it.

Still, he was going to call back tonight so they'd get a chance to chat properly as well as sort out her laptop. She hoped her webcam hadn't been hacked – she kept her laptop in the living room and closed it when she wasn't using it, but she still didn't like the idea that someone could be watching her. Was that what had happened to Lauren? It certainly looked like it.

Another knock on her door interrupted her thoughts. Anna was about to say 'come in' when she realised that it was still locked. Rolling her chair backwards, she put her mobile down and stood up to open the door.

But it wasn't one of her students as she'd expected – it was Olivier Ayari, Xavier's younger brother. Anna drew in her breath, not sure she was ready for a conversation with him in the confines of her office after the day she'd had, however irrational her fears might be.

'Hello, Olivier, how can I help you?' She thought fast. 'I was just about to go out.'

The boy outside her door cleared his throat. 'I was wondering . . .' He cleared his throat again. 'I was wondering if I could talk to you. About . . . about Tom.'

Anna winced inwardly. Even though it was quiet down in the cafe today, they could hardly go down there to have that conversation, but she didn't feel comfortable about inviting him in. Olivier didn't have any of his brother's good looks; he looked lost and a little forlorn standing out in the corridor, his backpack heavy with books, slung over his shoulder, his hands in the pockets of his jeans. What was it with these brothers? Anna took a deep breath, slowing her heart. She was being ridiculous, they were Tunisian, weren't even the same nationality as the men in the bank. Olivier had obviously been in college today, probably visiting the library. That's what students did. She really needed to get a grip. Maybe this was the time to start.

'Come in.'

He looked at her hard for a moment and then nodded. 'Thank you.'

Heading for the chair opposite her desk, he sat down half-reluctantly, lowering his backpack to the floor.

She sat down. 'What can I do to help?'

Olivier shifted in his seat. 'It's about Tom. I don't know who else to ask. There are all these rumours going around about him, about what happened to him.' He frowned. 'Do you know anything?'

Anna hid her surprise. It seemed a strange question to ask her. He'd been Tom's friend; surely he knew Tom's parents, or the rest of his close friends who had spoken to the Gardaí. But then perhaps he didn't. Olivier may never have had a reason to go to the Quinns' house. And he wasn't the most sociable student on the campus. In fact, he was the polar opposite of his good-looking, popular brother. She'd always felt there was a tension between them whenever she'd seen them together, as if Xavier resented having a nerdy brother hanging about him. Or Olivier resented having a good-looking, popular one.

He'd been friends with Tom, though. She chose her words carefully. When she'd seen them together the previous week, which felt like a lifetime ago now, they had been chatting and messing with their phones.

'It was a car accident. The Guards don't know what happened yet, they're investigating. Have you spoken to them?'

Olivier shook his head. 'Not yet.'

'They want to talk to all his friends, to build a picture of what he was doing in college. Have they been trying to get hold of you?'

'I've had some missed calls . . . I thought they were sales calls or something, I haven't picked up my messages. Perhaps it was them.'

'I'll give you the number of the detective I spoke to, she's very nice. I know she'll want to talk to you.' Anna pulled out her drawer and fished out a pad of Post-it notes and a pen. She looked for her phone, flipping open the leather case, scrolling down for Cathy Connolly's number.

'Here you go. Give her a call.' She wrote the number down and he took the proffered Post-it.

'So they've no idea what happened?'

Putting the lid back on her pen, Anna shook her head. 'Not at the moment as far as I understand it.'

She slipped the pen and Post-it pad back in her desk drawer as he said slowly, 'Thank you.' He hesitated, then said, 'When will they know?'

'I'm afraid I don't know. I'm sure the Guards can tell you more.'

Anna tried to hide her irritation, then regretted being irritated at all. She shouldn't be cross with Olivier, he wasn't the problem here; he was asking about the rumours about his friend, a friend he had lost. He wasn't being mean or creating malicious gossip. And he hadn't asked about Lauren, although Anna was sure by Monday word would have spread across the university and there would inevitably be connections drawn to Tom.

He nodded rather mournfully. 'Thank you. I'd better go.'

Anna stood up to show him out.

'If you're worried about Tom, about what's been happening – there are people you can talk to, you know. People here. It's very private. The university offer a counselling service.'

'Thank you.' Not meeting her eye, he slung his backpack over his shoulder.

Then he turned and smiled at her and Anna look a step back. Her own smile polite, she closed the door quickly. She was sure it was her imagination, but something about the way he looked at her made her feel very uncomfortable. When he smiled she could see the family resemblance to Xavier. She shivered. This was ridiculous; she really needed to get her life on track.

But at least her life hadn't gone as far off track as Orla's. Heading back to her desk Anna reached for the phone. She'd tried to call several times, had left messages on Orla's mobile and messages with her housekeeper, Mira, but she understood completely that Orla might still not be ready to talk. She'd probably switched her phone off.

Expecting to leave another message Anna was surprised when, this time, Orla answered.

'I'm so sorry I didn't return your calls.' Orla's voice sounded different, agitated, a little on edge for a woman normally so in command. But perhaps she'd just grabbed the phone before it rang off. Anna knew that feeling.

'Don't be at all. I just wanted to see how you were doing, to let you know if you need anything . . .' Anna stopped herself. It was something people had said to her so often after Jen had been killed, but what could they do? The only thing she'd needed was Jen back and they couldn't help with that. Orla must be feeling exactly the same.

'I know, you're so good. Really. Have you spoken to the Guards?'

'Yes, I've told them all I can—'

Orla cut Anna off, 'I don't know what they are doing, it's taking so long to get any information. I thought the first forty-eight hours in an investigation were supposed to be crucial. It's *Sunday* today, that's *four* days.' She paused, and Anna heard her let out a sharp breath. 'I'm sorry, I just need to do something. I'm not very good at just sitting back and letting things happen. I keep thinking of all our conversations, of what Tom was doing over the last few weeks. Going over and over everything. This can't have been totally random.'

'I know the Guards are questioning everyone.'

As if Orla hadn't heard her she continued, 'I've decided if they haven't got any solid information in the next few days, I'm going to have to hire a private investigator. I have to do something, I have to find out who did this and why.'

Anna could hear the pain and frustration in Orla's voice, could sense her helplessness. This was so devastating and Orla was so used to being in charge of her world, having to wait for news was making it all worse, if that was possible.

Anna knew that feeling, she'd been there too. Orla needed closure before she could grieve for her son.

Chapter 26

Sunday, 5.30 p.m.

Pulling up on the narrow pavement outside Ronan Delaney's house, Cathy checked the wing mirror before she jumped out of the passenger seat of the District Detective Unit's silver Opel. Ulverton Road wound down from the picturesque village of Dalkey to Sandycove, running parallel with the sea, but many of its bends were blind. It might only be early Sunday evening but it was dark now. And she didn't want to end up like Tom Quinn.

Standing on the pavement waiting for her, Fanning flicked his blond fringe out of his eyes and rattled the car keys, looking up at the house where Ronan Delaney's dark blue Range Rover was registered. Like much of Dalkey, the houses here were big and well kept, set back from the road. Delaney's was on the end of the terrace, a narrow ornate iron gate opening onto the pavement. Further down the high red brick wall that surrounded it, another wider gate opened into the garden; behind it a white jeep was parked, partially illuminated by the weak street lamp on the other side of the road.

'Nice place.' Fanning indicated the house. 'That must be her car – very sporty. She used to work in TV, you know, did that fashion show on RTE.'

'Yep, she runs the beauty salon in the village now.' As Cathy spoke her phone rang. 'Just give me a minute.'

Answering it, she listened to the caller then signalled to Fanning that she needed a pen and paper.

'Thanks for calling. I can't give you any details at this stage I'm afraid, but I need to arrange a time for myself or one of my colleagues to meet you for a chat about Tom. Tomorrow morning?' She listened to the answer. 'Yes, eleven is great. I think we need to be somewhere more private than a restaurant. What's your address?'

Fanning passed her his open notebook. Leaning on the garden wall, Cathy scribbled it down.

'Great, we'll see you then.' She ended the call.

'Who was that?'

'Olivier Ayari, that friend of Tom's that I've been trying to track down. Very apologetic, he thought my missed calls were sales calls. I'll get over and talk to him in the morning. He said he hadn't seen Tom since last week. The last contact he had was a text about a strategy they were working on for Dark Souls Three. It's a computer game apparently.' She handed Fanning back his notebook. 'I'll copy that address down later. Right, let's see who's in, shall we?'

A security light flashed on as they walked up the path, throwing cold white light over an immaculate front garden. It took a few minutes after they rang the bell for the front door to be opened. Despite a huge creeper that grew around the front door and blocked the security light, Karen Delaney looked just as good as she had done the last time Cathy had met her – her long dark hair pulled back off her face, her make-up so subtle it didn't look like she was wearing any, despite her luxurious eyelashes and polished red nails. Dressed in a black high neck T-shirt, skintight black leather trousers and high-heeled boots, she had a fabulous figure. Fanning had noticed too, of course. Cathy could feel his radar bleeping behind her, but she held her ground in front of him on the doorstep. He'd have plenty of time to ogle later.

Opening the door wider, Karen Delaney recognised Cathy immediately.

'Hello again, is everything all right?'

Cathy smiled warmly. 'We're sorry to call so late. We've got a few more questions about Tom and the accident.'

Karen hid it well, but a shadow passed across her eyes. She took a deep breath before speaking. 'How can I help?'

'We were hoping to chat to your husband, actually. Is he at home?'

'He's at work, but he's due back shortly.' Karen forced a smile.

'Would you mind if we waited for him?'

Karen hesitated for a split second, then stood back from the door. 'Of course, please come in.'

Cathy could almost feel Fanning smiling behind her; she couldn't see it, but she was quite sure he had his full beam on. She shook her head inwardly. One day they would need to have a serious chat about his approach to women.

Karen opened the door wide to a softly lit narrow hallway, the walls dark green below the dado rail, cream above it, the passageway floored in period black and white tiles. An elegant flight of stairs with an ornate banister rose to the right. To their left, a credenza with a mirror above it was flush to the wall, letters and keys tossed on its white marble top. At the end of the corridor Cathy could see bright lights radiating from the back of the house.

'Come in, please, go straight though, the kitchen's at the back.'

Cathy smiled her thanks and, passing Karen, headed down the hall, followed by Fanning. Behind her she heard the door close, and a few seconds later Karen's heels clicking on the tiled floor.

At the back of the house a huge kitchen-cum-living room ran the entire width of the building. Obviously a later addition, it was mainly glass, a beautiful half conservatory, half family room, a huge scrubbed pine table in the glazed section, a comfortable sofa arrangement to the far right, soft sidelights casting relaxing pools of light from square occasional tables at the corners of each of the three sofas arranged facing the garden. The kitchen was state of the art, pale granite worktops and a spotless Siemens cooker, a white marble island in the centre with a huge butler sink in the middle. It didn't look like a kitchen that was used all that much, if Cathy was honest. With the bright downlighters under the cabinets, it looked like it belonged in a show house. But maybe that's what this was – more show house than home. It felt too perfect somehow. And from what Cathy had already seen of the Delaneys' relationship, there seemed to be a lot of plaster covering the cracks.

'Sit down, I'll put the kettle on. Ronan shouldn't be long.' Karen indicated the sofa area and went over to the island, flipping a tap to noisily fill the kettle.

'Thank you.'

As Cathy sat down, she watched Karen fussing in the kitchen, took in the designer coffee machine, the American fridge. Fanning opened his mouth to say something, but Cathy silenced him with a raised eyebrow. She wanted to keep him focused and he could be less than tactful. What he was good at was watching and listening, giving her his angle on an interview. She needed him to be wallpaper right now, to use all his skills to read the hidden messages while Karen Delaney was speaking, not start a conversation about celebrity gossip.

Cathy and Fanning sat down at right angles to each other on the oatmeal sofas. Cathy's look had done the job; she could see that he was busy taking in his surroundings, looking at the original pictures on the wall, at the accessories artfully placed in the room.

'Have you any idea when Orla will be able to organise the funeral?' Karen had finished filling the kettle, busying herself getting cups and saucers out of the cupboards, setting them on a wooden tray on the island. 'She's still so shocked, and the delay is making it all worse. She's used to getting answers and right now she doesn't even know when he's coming home . . .' Her eyes filled with tears as she bit her lip, obviously fighting with her emotions. She took a ragged breath. 'Do you know what happened yet?'

'We're still making enquiries at this stage.'

Fanning chimed in, acting the innocent. 'You know the Quinns well, then?'

Karen stopped in the middle of the kitchen and crossed her arms. 'We're good friends with Conor and Orla. Tom worked for Ronan, as you know.' She turned around, her back to them, looking at the kettle as it came to the boil. Cathy could see her shoulders shaking like she was trying hard not to cry.

'Would you like to sit down?' Cathy watched her carefully. 'I'm sorry, I know how difficult this is.'

'But . . .' Karen turned back to them and waved her hand in the direction of the kettle, not quite focusing on it, like she knew she was standing there for a reason but had suddenly forgotten what it was.

'Don't worry. Detective Fanning makes great tea.' Cathy turned to 007 and raised her eyebrows.

'Totally, master tea maker. Please sit down.' Fanning stood up and headed into the kitchen area.

Karen looked at him blankly for a moment, then, realising what he was saying, snapped back to the room. 'Thank you. There's sugar . . .'

'I'll find it, don't worry.' He blazed his full-on smile, all eyes and dripping with charm. Cathy had seen girls go weak at the knees when he did that, but it was wasted on Karen Delaney. As if she was in a daze, she came to sit beside Cathy on the edge of the sofa, her hands flat on her leather-covered knees like she was trying to control herself. Cathy could feel the tension radiating off her.

'Tell me about Tom.'

Cathy leaned forward in her seat, her voice soft. If her instincts were correct, there was more going on here than the death of an employee. She was suddenly getting the feeling that Karen had been very guarded the last time they'd met, had left out some important details. Being friends with Orla, it had seemed logical that Karen would have been invited to the charity event that her husband was MC-ing – famous faces added the gloss at those types of events – but now Cathy was beginning to wonder if that was the case. Ronan's call to Karen while Cathy had been talking to her the last time had been quite a surprise. It had rattled Karen so much that Cathy was now sure that their relationship was far from perfect. As if to confirm Cathy's thoughts, at the mention of Tom's name, Karen paled, her lip trembling again.

'He . . .' She faltered, then continued almost too fast. 'Tom was great. He needed a part-time job – he was in Trinity.' She bit her lip. 'Sorry, you know that . . . Well, he picked everything up really fast. It was a favour to Conor to start with, but it all . . . worked out.'

'So he came here a lot?'

Cathy watched her carefully. Beyond Karen, in the kitchen, she could see Fanning quietly sliding drawers open, looking for teaspoons. He was picking up on it too, kept glancing at Karen.

She shrugged. 'Most weekends.' Her lip trembled again as she hesitated. 'Some evenings. Sometimes.'

'Thursday evening?'

Staring at the glass-topped coffee table in the middle of the sofas, at the magazines artfully arranged on its spotless polished surface, she answered slowly. 'Yes, Thursday evening.'

Cathy took this in. Karen had said he often worked evenings but if he was coming here on Thursday evening, why hadn't he told anyone? His mum and Mira had assumed he'd gone for a walk – but why hadn't he told them he was coming to work, why the secrecy? Cathy was suddenly sure there wasn't much walking being done during Tom's nocturnal excursions.

'And Ronan was out on Thursday, at Orla's charity event?'

Karen nodded miserably. 'I was invited too, but I had a migraine.'

Cathy looked at her – *a migraine? Yeah, right.*

'And what time did Tom get here?'

'Just after eight I think.'

'You mentioned before that he had his own key to the studio?' Cathy said it innocently.

Fanning had loaded a tray with a teapot, cups, the milk jug and sugar bowl, and now brought it over to the coffee table. Cathy slid the magazines away from the middle to give him space.

Karen stared at the tray as if she wasn't seeing it. 'Yes, yes, he had his own key.'

'Quite late to be working?'

Fanning's tone was just as innocent as Cathy's as he lifted the teapot, but she could tell that he was thinking exactly the same thing as she was. Tom's mysterious walks had been visits to see Karen; she was sure of it. The real question was, did her husband know?

'He . . .' Karen faltered. 'Yes, he came late sometimes.'

Still staring at the tea tray, it was like Karen had dried up, couldn't say any more. Cathy tried a different tack.

'And what time did Ronan get back?'

Direct questions always helped get the wheels moving, helped witnesses focus on the facts.

Karen shrugged. 'After eleven, I'm not sure.'

'Was Tom still here then?'

'No, no, he'd just left.'

'Could Ronan have passed him on the road?'

Cathy kept her voice low. Was this what Karen was thinking, a further reason for her distress? Did she think Delaney had seen Tom leave and perhaps had his suspicions confirmed that his wife was having an affair? Had it been enough to push him over the edge and cause him to deliberately drive into him? Karen's reaction when he had telephoned her, and his demeanour towards his wife, had rung alarm bells with Cathy.

And from the time stamp on the CCTV and the time Orla had received the last text from her son, it seemed extremely likely that Delaney had been passing at the right time. Was that what his wife thought?

Before Karen could answer, a mobile phone started ringing in the kitchen. She didn't move.

Cathy said, 'Do you want to get that?'

'Err, yes, it's in my bag.'

She looked around blankly but Fanning jumped up and retrieved a black leather handbag from a chair at the head of the pine table. He'd obviously been paying attention as he made the tea. The bag was big, looked expensive, all tassels and studs, no doubt a designer brand. Like the red handbag she'd had at her salon.

Fanning handed it to her and Karen reached into it and found her phone, checked the screen.

'That was Ronan.'

'Ring him back, if you need to.'

She flicked the keys, held the phone to her ear, her voice hesitant, her anxiety clearly written on her face.

'Sorry I missed your call. I'm sorry, I know. Yes. The Guards are here. To ask about Tom. Are you on your way?' *At least he hadn't put her on speaker this time.* Cathy hid her thoughts as Karen continued, 'OK. OK. I'll tell them.'

Clicking off the phone, she turned to Cathy. 'He's still in town, he's going to do the late night show.' It seemed very final. 'He said he can talk to you tomorrow. He's on air until nine and needs to prep for the morning show. He won't be finished until after ten so he's going to be back late.'

Really? Cathy would be talking to Ronan Delaney when it suited her, not when it suited him. Masking her thoughts, she said, 'That would be great. He could be an important witness. Is the car in the drive his?'

Cathy knew it wasn't, but watched for her reaction.

'No, that's mine. He's getting something fixed on his. He got the DART in to work. He said he was going to get a cab home.' And then, as if she needed to justify why she needed her car and hadn't let him use it for work, 'I had to go the wholesaler today to get stuff for the shop. I couldn't leave it any longer and the girls were fully booked.'

'That's grand. I think we might need to talk to Ronan fairly urgently.'

Karen turned to her, and then, her voice hoarse, said, 'Do you think it could have been him? Ronan? Could he have hit Tom?'

Cathy wasn't about to share what she was thinking; instead she asked her own question.

'Do you?'

Tears began to fall. 'I . . . We . . .'

Cathy put her hand on Karen's arm. 'Take your time.'

Karen sobbed. 'Tom and I, were, we were having an affair. He was – oh my God . . .' her words were lost in her tears.

Over her head, Cathy exchanged a look with Fanning. They were going to be here some time.

Chapter 27

Sunday, 5.30 p.m.

Sitting down, he put his coffee on the floor beside the arm of the low sofa, pulling his laptop out of his backpack and flipping it open. The communal areas in the Arts building with its bizarre drainpipe sculpture was fairly well lit from a weird tile pattern of fluorescent lights recessed in the ceiling. Predominantly raw concrete, it was probably supposed to look industrial but everything about it was grim – and the shiny brown floor did little to lift it.

He didn't know how students could come in here every day. Between the miserableness of the place and the malicious gossip he'd already heard since he'd been sitting here, everyone prying into other people's business, he could see how some students couldn't handle university life. He felt his anger rising.

He didn't like situations he couldn't control either. But he was good at bringing things into line.

He typed his password into his laptop. The sofa was pushed back behind a pillar where he could easily watch all three exit doors. He couldn't see the door to the stairs, but that meant that anyone coming downstairs wouldn't see him either, so it was a good payoff. The hallway was huge, but he had a good clear view.

Or would do soon, he hoped.

There was some event on in one of the lecture theatres downstairs, some American author speaking. Which meant there were plenty of people milling about. Which was good. Very good. He lifted his coffee onto the arm of the sofa and, clicking on the camera on his phone, he leaned it against his cup, angling it so he could film the steel and glass doors leading into the Tunnel. She probably wouldn't go towards Grafton Street, unless she had shopping to do on the way home, but he knew she'd definitely use one of the exits he could see. When he'd followed her before she'd always left the college through the science block, heading for Pearse Street. He still didn't know how she managed to give him the slip every time. The first time it had been on the DART. They'd even been in the same carriage, but she'd literally vanished when they pulled into a station, melting into the crowd of incoming commuters. He'd realised late and jumped off at the last moment but she hadn't been on the platform. It was weird. The next time, he'd followed her off the DART but lost her in a supermarket. It was like she was trained to give people the slip. But how did she even know he was there? He knew he blended in well, was good at being invisible.

He smiled to himself. So many elements of his life were about being invisible. Karim had been on the phone last night. He'd helped the project along a lot remotely, but Karim wanted him to come over when they actioned it, wanted him to be a part of the awesome chaos they were going to cause. And the plan had grown since he'd last been in London. Grown big time. Karim had assured him he'd be safe, that their part was completely untraceable; they would be able to do it all remotely, and then vanish like mist. He wasn't sure how much fun there would be in not seeing the action at first hand but he was thinking about it.

Karim wanted to hole up in Dublin afterwards, where no one would think to look for him, which made a lot of sense. It paid to be careful, never to assume they were safe. They weren't going to make any rookie mistakes. If that prick Dread Pirate Roberts hadn't used his own fucking email address to register a fake ID right at the start of Silk Road, he'd still be trading. But that was what happened when you didn't plan ahead, when you didn't think about the details. Human error was always the problem. But Dread Pirate Roberts was in jail now and his loss had been their gain, so it wasn't all bad. Silk Road had been started to sell magic mushrooms but had grown exponentially. And that's what was happening with Merchant's Quay. He chuckled to himself. When they'd started the site they had had no idea there actually was a Merchant's Quay in downtown Dublin. He liked it when things connected.

Although Karim kept asking him, he still wasn't totally sure about going to London; the timing was wrong. He had other things on his mind at the moment; there was stuff keeping him here. He had plans.

He was in that place mentally now, was thinking about that moment when it would all come together, couldn't get the feeling out of his head. Paris, Long Island, London and now Dublin. The thought of it was intoxicating. And the dreams . . . He needed to make it happen soon but he didn't want to rush things and make a mistake. He'd already taken a stupid risk that had complicated things, but that was dealt with now.

Karim's gig in London was just so tempting. It would be so fucking big. He'd known Karim for so long. They were interested in a lot of the same things, had grown together, pooling their skills. And now Karim and his friends had created a masterpiece that would go down in cyber history; it would make them all famous, and they'd be the most highly demanded hackers in cyberspace. They'd be the best. They were the best, he knew that. He and Karim had developed hundreds of projects together; he knew exactly how good Karim was.

And it would show everyone who was really in control. He might not have the business brains but nothing could happen without his coding skills, the sites wouldn't exist without him. But now with Karim's plan the balance was changing. In many ways. He glanced up at the door to the stairs. No sign yet. What was she doing? It was time she left. She'd been in her office all afternoon. He needed to find out where she lived. Knowing where she lived was important. Holding his phone in place, he picked up his coffee and looked around at the mass of students heading down the stairs to the lecture theatre. She wouldn't be long now; he was sure of it.

He replaced the coffee cup carefully, adjusting the camera on the phone, and opened his browser. He'd have a quick look at the screen on her office desktop to see what she was doing . . . It only took a second to load. It had no camera, wasn't nearly as interesting as her personal laptop, but the Trinity College virus protection was easy to bypass, especially from inside. Right now she was shopping, apparently. He could see her cursor flying over the screen, clicking on a black cocktail dress. Size ten. He watched as she went through to the delivery window selecting 'collection'. Damn, and her credit card was registered to her office address. Nice dress though, it would suit her.

He still didn't understand why he couldn't find her address online – he'd looked everywhere. He hadn't been able to find out nearly as much as he'd like, and everything he had found had been on the Trinity College site – all very professional. Nothing on

Facebook or LinkedIn. He'd thought it was a given for someone like her to have a profile page at least – but she wasn't there, or on any of the other social media sites. It was like she had no history, no interactions at all. Maybe she wasn't into social media but it was strange no one else had posted anything tagging her, a photo of a school basketball team or someone's twenty-first.

It was like she didn't exist.

Then it struck him. Perhaps she didn't; perhaps she wasn't who she said she was at all.

Chapter 28

Sunday, 6.15 p.m.

Anna Lockharte's mobile phone started to ring as she pushed open her apartment door. Dropping her handbag in the darkened hall, she pulled it out of her coat pocket and looked at the screen.

It was Rob calling from New York, and she had never felt happier to see his number flashing on her screen. Her encounter with Xavier Ayari earlier today had creeped her out a bit. And then she'd seen him in the cafe as she'd come out of the lift to go home, and part of her had wondered if actually she wasn't being paranoid at all, but that she should be concerned. She knew there was some sort of event on in the Edmund Burke Theatre, so perhaps he'd been heading in to that, but still . . .

'Hello, handsome.' She heard Rob's wonderful deep laugh at the other end as she answered the phone, slipping her coat off and throwing it over the back of one of the high stools at the kitchen counter. 'How's your day been?'

'Good, always great to spend the weekend at the office. I've got the guys here ready to go on your laptop.'

Anna glanced at the kitchen clock. It was after six, would be lunchtime in New York. And probably a crisp, clear blue sky day.

She'd spent so many years in Europe at school and university, but New York would always be home and there were times when she really missed it.

'Give me five, I've just come in. What do I need to do?'

'Just open up your laptop and click the link I sent you. The boys can then access it from here.'

Anna went through into the living room, flicking on the side-lights as she went. Her laptop was on the sofa where she'd left it, Minou curled up at the end. The cat looked up as Anna sat down beside her.

'Almost there. Cathy, the Garda detective, said that I should cover the camera,' she said into the phone as she flipped open the lid and typed in her password. The home screen came alive and she opened her email. Rob's email was right at the top. 'OK, all done.'

'Cathy's dead right, but we're going to take over now. Don't touch anything.'

'Good God, is that you?'

Anna's cursor had started to fly around the screen on its own, opening up windows. Dialogue boxes appeared and disappeared, screens with rows of code.

'Yes, they are going to be a few minutes. You can put the kettle on, isn't that what the Irish do?'

He was teasing her, she knew. 'They do and the tea's very good—'

Before she could finish a gust of wind hit the apartment windows, carrying a squall of rain. The water hitting the windows sounded like an explosion.

'Christ, what was that?'

'Rain. It's very Irish too.'

'Sounds like a tornado . . . So how have you been?' It sounded like he'd gone somewhere quieter, probably into his own office. A moment later she heard a door close, confirming it.

'I'm good, the junior freshmen are keeping me on my toes.' She sighed. 'And some big stuff with the senior freshmen too. Which could be linked to this email thing.'

She hadn't wanted to email to tell him about Tom and Lauren, it was all too raw and there were some things she didn't want to put into print. Particularly if there had been some sort of Internet security breach. Who knew who was watching?

Rob's voice cut into her thoughts, immediately calming. 'Tell me.'

She took a deep breath, heading back to the kitchen. She did need a cup of tea.

'So one of my students was knocked down in a hit-and-run on Thursday night . . .' Anna recounted what she knew of the circumstances of Tom's death. She could tell that he could hear the sadness in her tone as he responded. 'Jeez, that's awful.'

'Oh, Rob, he was such a lovely guy, it's absolutely tragic. His parents are devastated.'

'I can imagine.'

'That's not all, though. The next day one of his friends was found at the bottom of some cliffs near when Tom lives. She was on my course too. It looks like she jumped.'

'Holy moly. Not good. Was she seeing Tom?'

'No, that's the weird bit. They knew each other, but I don't think they were dating or anything. The Gardaí are investigating. The thing is, I had to go with them to search Lauren's room this morning. And . . .' Anna hesitated; where did she start with this one?

'Go on, I'm sitting down, explain.'

'OK, so first the detective finds a load of prescription drugs – uppers – which is just really strange. She couldn't be a more unlikely pusher.'

'Hmmm. Go on, what else?'

She knew what he was thinking: that you could never tell what was going on behind closed doors. People's lives on the outside were often very different from what went on in private. Look at her. 'So the next bit is the bit that worries me and I'm hoping you can help with . . .'

'I'm here, you know that, whatever you need, honey.'

'I know, Rob.' Her voice was soft. She knew he was there for her, and if things were different he could be there for her in so many more ways. She cleared her throat; this wasn't the time to get emotional. 'It's just that when the other detective, Cathy Connolly, opened Lauren's email, someone had sent her photos of her getting dressed.'

'Her webcam was hacked?'

'It looks a lot like that. But then while we were looking at her computer this email came in from a website called Discovery Quay . . .'

'Really? Interesting.'

She continued, 'It was one of those instant auto-response things – it said something about registering with them . . . But she couldn't have, unless she managed it from beyond the grave.'

'I'd imagine that would be tricky. Sounds like someone was putting pressure on her. Was there anything in the emails that the images were attached to?'

'I don't know – I didn't get to read them. The Guards have taken her laptop to examine it. But the Discovery Quay registration email came with a screenshot of what was supposedly her account page. It looked like a really compromising video and these photos were about to go live online.'

'OK.' Anna heard his tone of voice change. It sounded like he was sitting forward at the desk. 'Can you hook me up to the detective working the case? My colleagues at the FBI have been very interested in Discovery Quay, and its parent site Merchant's Quay, for some time. Both sites are being run by someone who really understands the Dark Web, who has every possible way in firmly sealed. They have their eyes on a couple of hackers that they think would have the ability to keep them out. They move about a lot but I think they are based in London at the moment, which isn't a million miles away from you.'

'But how would they find Lauren – why her?'

'It can be quite random, there are loads of normal sites that are infected with malware. The hackers get access to your webcam and start recording or simply pushing a live feed out to the web. Sites like Discovery Quay have tens of thousands of visitors a day.'

'Nice.'

'And if she was very shy, or even if she wasn't, something like this would be a real shock. Do they think it could have been a factor in her suicide?'

'I'm not sure they think it *is* suicide at the moment, reading between the lines. There's a lot of stuff that doesn't add up. But she must have been distraught. It's just so evil. You wonder why people do it.'

Rob's voice was hard. 'Discovery Quay makes a lot of money and all it does is live feed video cam footage. Zero effort, zero sales force needed, no overheads. There's a membership model as well as advertising. It's very lucrative. Not nearly as rich as Merchant's Quay though – that's making millions.'

'Merchant's Quay was advertised on the Discovery Quay screenshot that was sent to Lauren. The detective was wondering if she had ordered the drugs from there.'

'Certainly possible.'

What had Lauren got mixed up in? 'The detective here – she's so nice, one of those people you feel is really capable – anyway, she was wondering if other students at Trinity have been targeted, might have had their webcams hacked, I mean.'

'Quite possible also. The worm in your system is a classic type, delivered by email. They had your email address, but then it's all over the Trinity College website so it's not exactly private. We'll know more when we track its path and take a look at how it's made. Some coders have distinct signatures.'

Anna shuddered. 'Do you think someone's been watching me?'

'It's very likely someone got access to it, but not for very long as that email's only just arrived. And they can only see what's in front of the laptop when it's open through the webcam. If you keep it closed when you're not using it then the camera's not operational. But it's always worth covering the camera anyway. No point tempting fate.'

'I'll be doing that as soon as your guys are done. How long will it take before they know anything?'

'A couple of hours. They'll clean your system so you'll be good to go again, and download all the data they can about the attack. Then see what they can find out.'

'Thanks, Rob. I can't imagine anything worse than ending up as a live feed on a site like that.' Her voice softened. 'So how have you been?'

At the other end she heard him sigh. 'Super busy. Some people just don't seem to understand how vulnerable they are online or on the phone. They do stupid stuff and then wonder how they get compromised. I mean really stupid.'

She knew he was letting off steam, could hear the tension in his voice, also knew that he couldn't be specific about anything.

'I'm guessing the problem is that it's not only themselves that they're compromising?'

'That's for damn sure.' She could almost hear him shaking his head.

Ironically, cybercrime formed part of the talk she was giving in London at the end of the week. And even with all her knowledge she'd still had to call Hope to confirm her suspicions about that email. But perhaps youth was the key, that ability to think outside the box that teenagers had. Most of Rob's department were recent graduates, but he had a couple of guys working for him who hadn't ever graduated school, guys who had dropped out when they were the same age as Hope and for whom code was their native language. With ransomware attacks on the increase and the Dark Web completely unregulated, Rob's job was one of constant change. He'd had to go to the highest level to persuade his superiors that two unqualified teens from immigrant families could be their strongest line of defence, but they'd proven their worth within days. The one thing they could all be absolutely sure of was that there was a whole lot of stuff going on, so well hidden that it only came to the surface when an attack was in progress. And then it was all about reaction time.

'So where are you taking Hope when you get to London?'

'The Science Museum . . .'

He burst out laughing before she could continue. 'I should have guessed.'

Anna laughed with him. 'And she wants to check out Imperial College. It won't be long before she has to start thinking about university.'

'With her grades she should be looking at MIT.'

'It's top of her list, but she'd been googling Imperial and discovered it's right next to the Royal Albert Hall, she'd have music on her doorstep – literally. And it's a beautiful part of London.'

'It certainly is.' He paused. 'I'm going to have to go, honey, all my lights are flashing here. I'll call you back when the boys are done.'

'Thanks, Rob.'

Anna held on for a second after he had hung up, suddenly wondering what she would do when Hope went to university. Hope would be eighteen, wouldn't need a guardian any more, and whether she ended up studying in London or Massachusetts, she definitely wouldn't be in Ireland. It was the first time Anna had thought about it properly; perhaps it would be time for her to move back to the US.

Chapter 29

Cathy could see why Karen Delaney was so upset. If her husband had murdered her lover in a hit-and-run, Cathy would be pretty upset too. She sat forward on the sofa and glanced at Jamie Fanning, who was sitting at right angles to them, notebook out. Outside it had begun to rain again, the sound of raindrops on the glazed roof of the house suddenly loud.

'I just need you to backtrack a bit here. Did Ronan know you were having a relationship with Tom?'

Who had to be at least twenty years her junior, but Cathy wasn't about to say that. Karen was a very attractive woman in a less than happy marriage and from the pictures she'd seen of Tom, he was pretty devastating looking. These things happened. Perhaps Tom had listened to her, knew what her husband was really like, and one thing had led to another. Although quite what his mum would make of it, Cathy wasn't sure. But right now that wasn't her problem.

Finding out precisely what the events were that had led up to Tom's death, was.

Karen shook her head in answer to Cathy's question as Fanning passed her a tissue. Karen took it gratefully, smiling her thanks.

She dabbed her eyes and wiped her nose before shaking her head again, wringing the tissue in her hands as she spoke.

'I really didn't think he did. We were so careful. Ronan's out a lot and Tom always had a reason to be here, to be working in the studio. When Ronan was here Tom would sometimes come up to the house for a cup of tea and to talk about whatever they were working on, so him being here wasn't odd. Tom never called or texted my mobile unless it was something practical about the studio. Ronan can be quite dominating, I'm sure he checks my texts. Tom knew that. He was so careful.'

Cathy glanced at 007 again, who was listening intently, his notebook open. He wagged the end of his pen to indicate he was taking it all down.

'Can you take me through what happened that night? Ronan was at the fundraiser? What time did he leave?'

Karen took a deep breath. 'He was supposed to be there at seven, the events people called to see if he was on the way. They always get worried, but he's done this type of thing so many times. He just wants to arrive as late as possible so he doesn't have to do all the pre-dinner schmoozing. All he's interested in are the press shots, getting paid and getting out.'

'So what time did he leave home?'

'About 7.15, I think. He drove into town – he knew he wouldn't be drinking. He had to do the early show the next morning.'

Cathy's ears twitched. 'So what time would he have left the next day?'

Karen shrugged. 'About six-ish. He can easily get into town that early. His show starts at seven.'

Cathy shifted on the soft sofa. Ronan Delaney seemed to have a lot of explaining to do. Tom hadn't been found until 7 a.m. by the dog walker, so it looked like Delaney could have driven past him twice. Unless he'd gone the other way – up to the village to get a coffee or something before heading into town – and therefore had taken a different route. But there was a state-of-the-art coffee machine on the counter in the kitchen, one of those super-expensive ones that looked like it had enough technology to take it to the moon, so collecting takeout seemed a little illogical. The CCTV from Friday morning would help them, though. If he had gone up to the village, driving away from where Tom had been lying, he'd be all over the CCTV; at the very least he'd have had to drive past the petrol station and the post office. Unless he'd deliberately taken a more circuitous route. Cathy made a mental note to check it out.

'So on Thursday evening you were here alone?'

'Yes. Tom knew Ronan was doing his mum's charity thing and I wasn't going, so he was waiting for me to text. One of the girls from the salon rang and I couldn't get her off the phone. He texted me about seven, and came over just before eight.'

'And he walked?'

'Yes, he's got a car but he doesn't . . .' She corrected herself. 'Didn't . . . normally use it to come over in case someone saw him leaving late, we had to be so careful. It was easier for him to slip away on foot. I wish he'd driven on Thursday now.' Karen's voice caught.

'His mum said he often went for late night walks. He was coming here then too?'

Karen nodded. 'Ronan often phones after the show to say he's going out for a few drinks or to a party. I'd text Tom then, to let him know it was safe to come over.'

They seemed to have it all worked out.

'And when Tom left that evening, what sort of mood was he in?'

'Good. He was a bit hurried because Orla texted him and we realised the event must have finished early, that Ronan was probably on the way. We should have been watching it – Orla was live streaming it to the Internet so we would have known when it ended, but well, I didn't think of it. I panicked a bit when she texted, but Tom was really quick leaving. We'd had a glass of wine, so I rinsed the glasses and ran down to the studio and left the light on there just in case anyone saw him leave. I should have done it earlier but I totally forgot. Then I texted him to say goodnight but he didn't answer.'

'And what time was that?'

'About 11.10, I think, maybe 11.15.'

'And what time did Ronan come in?'

'Just a few minutes later. I'm sorry, I wasn't looking at the clock, but it felt like he could almost have met him at the gate. I was terrified he'd seen him. We had a plan worked out if any-one did see him, but Ronan ... I was frightened he wouldn't believe me. He gets so angry. Sometimes when he's got an idea in his head, it doesn't matter what I say.'

'But he didn't see him?'

Karen shrugged. 'He might have done – I wasn't going to ask. It was really dark and Tom had put the hood on his jacket up before he left, so he might not have realised it was Tom if he did.'

'How did Ronan appear when he came in?'

'I don't know. I ran up to bed as soon as I'd put the studio light on – if he asked I was going to pretend I'd been reading in bed and hadn't realised Tom was there. I heard him come in but he didn't come upstairs. I think he got himself a drink. I heard him on the phone down here. I don't know who he was talking to, though.'

Cathy's mind was working fast. 'And where's his car now?'

'In the garage, I think. I can't remember what he said. I'm sorry, I've been so upset it's been hard to concentrate.' Tears began to fall again. 'Oh, God, I want to leave him, but the publicity would destroy my business, he'd make sure of that, and he'd spread enough lies about my sanity to make sure I never worked in the media again. I'm just totally trapped.' Cathy glanced at Fanning. Really you could never guess what went on behind closed doors, what secrets people were hiding. It took Karen a moment to recover. 'I'm sorry.'

'Don't worry, we appreciate this is very hard. Does the name Lauren O'Reilly mean anything to you?'

Karen sniffed and dabbed her eyes, thinking for a moment. 'There's a Lauren who worked at the station last summer who was in college with Tom. I don't know her surname. Ronan liked her. Tom mentioned her last time he was here, if it was the same girl.'

'Really? In what context?' Cathy kept her voice level, as if it wasn't important.

Karen frowned. 'Something about a video. Someone filmed her or something. Someone showed him the video, he said, but he hadn't realised it was her to start with. Then, when he did, he was pretty upset. He was worried about her because he said she's really shy. I'm sorry, I don't really remember – I think he said he was going to help her, he said he'd called her about it and he was going to stop the video going onto Facebook. I'm not sure. It sounded like one of those revenge porn things. He was just telling me when Orla texted, and we never got a chance to finish the conversation.'

Cathy smiled, her mind whirring. 'That's really helpful. If you remember anything else that he might have said about it, can you let us know?'

So Tom had known about the video? Did he know who had filmed it? More questions jumped into Cathy's head. *Had Lauren wanted to meet him to talk about the video?* Both the pay-as-you-go phones had been connected to this area. But . . . Cathy suddenly realised there was an obvious explanation for one of them.

'How did Tom contact you if he couldn't text your mobile?' Cathy had a feeling she knew the answer.

'I got a cheap mobile, one of those pay-as-you-go ones.' Karen hesitated. 'But someone must know, someone else has the number. After . . .' She faltered. 'After the accident someone was trying to call.' She sobbed again. 'I didn't answer, I was terrified Ronan had got hold of the number and had someone call it to confirm it was mine.'

Chapter 30

Sunday, 7.45 p.m.

Even from the road, Cathy could see the yard behind Dun Laoghaire station was packed, members' cars parked in every available inch right up to the pale blue security gate. Fanning slid down the window and punched in the entry code. The gates rattled and began to grind open slowly. Always impatient, he nudged forward as the gap widened, squeezing through, swinging around the side of the station. O'Rourke's BMW was parked in his spot in the corner. There was one empty space and as Fanning pulled into it, Cathy glanced up. O'Rourke's light was on in his office.

'You get the coffee, I'll update O'Rourke and see if he wants us to bring Delaney in after his show tonight or question him at home.'

She checked her watch; it was almost eight. There didn't look like much chance of her getting over to Phoenix – it was just as well she'd got there this morning. The championships were getting closer by the day and Cathy wasn't quite ready to admit to herself that she was nervous, but she was. Coming back after so much had happened in the past year felt like an uphill struggle.

But she was good at climbing, and as McIntyre always said, she just needed to keep her eyes on the prize.

Pulling open the back door to the station, Fanning was following her when his phone rang. Turning to look at him, he answered it and gestured for her to go ahead. It was probably one of his harem. She headed inside taking the stairs two at a time, knocking gently on O'Rourke's door.

'Come.'

O'Rourke was at his desk, looking tired. He was wearing his pink shirt, the cuffs rolled back and a pink silk tie loose at his neck. He had a pile of printouts in front of him, the gold Cross pen she'd given him a hundred Christmases ago in his hand.

'You busy?'

He looked at her and half-smiled, a sort of tired smile that admitted he was close to the edge – the type of smile that he only let her see. In his role it didn't do to be too honest, but Cathy knew he let her in more. He ran his hand over his forehead.

'I'm always busy, unfortunately the gurriers out there don't take weekends off. Sit down.' He waved the top page on his pile in the direction of the guest chair on the other side of the desk. 'How did you get on with Ronan Delaney?'

Cathy came in, and closing the door gently behind her, sat down, leaning forward on the desk.

'Haven't talked to Delaney yet, he's at work, but we had a very interesting chat with his wife.'

'Go on.'

'So it turns out Tom wasn't going to the pub or for an evening ramble that night.' She paused for dramatic effect. He gave her a withering look.

'And?'

'Sorry.' He obviously wasn't in the mood for teasing. 'He was visiting Karen Delaney. They were having an affair, had been for about six months.'

O'Rourke's eyebrows shot up, and he suddenly looked more alert.

'Really? And does her husband know about this?'

'Well, she thought he didn't, but looking at the timing, there's a distinct possibility that he might have done. Tom worked for them so he sort of had a reason to be coming out of their house at eleven at night. But equally, if Ronan Delaney saw him he might have thought it was a bit odd. Or it might have confirmed his suspicions if he wasn't sure before.'

O'Rourke raised his eyebrows again and shook his head. 'I think I'd be wondering what he was doing there at that time all right, whether he worked for me or not.'

'There's more. Tom told Karen Delaney that someone had made a video of Lauren and he was worried about her.'

'Did he know who?'

'He didn't say, just that he was going to help her with it.' She pursed her lips, thinking. 'But there's a chance Ronan saw Tom leaving and doubled back. The timing works. According to Karen, they realised the event was over when Orla texted Tom, sounds like it was a close thing Delaney didn't walk in on them.'

He put down his pen slowly, thinking, then steepled his fingers. 'And where is Delaney now?'

'On air until nine.' She checked her phone. 'Someone called in sick. He's on live.'

'And does he know we're looking for him?'

'He knows we were at his house enquiring about Tom, but nothing more.'

'What sort of man is he?'

Cathy shifted in the chair, pulling her necklace from under her sweater. 'Controlling. I get the impression Karen is quite frightened of him.'

She ran her dog tag along its chain, could feel the nicks in it where it had been dented in the explosion. She'd never met Ronan Delaney but she didn't like the sound of him one little bit. Domestic abuse was constantly on their radar; in her experience it took a long time for women to report an assault, and then about twelve reports before they were prepared to press charges. By then the violence had usually escalated significantly and they were often in fear of their lives. Karen hadn't reported anything, but everything about their relationship rang alarm bells for Cathy. And Karen had the added problem of media interest in everything she did. It never ceased to amaze Cathy how otherwise brilliant, intelligent, independent women got caught up in abusive relationships. But she still had more to tell him.

'The other interesting thing is that Delaney's car's in for repairs.'

'Really?' His eyes on her necklace, O'Rourke watched her fiddle with it. 'And he knew Lauren, didn't he? She worked at the radio station?' Cathy nodded as he continued. 'I'd imagine with the hours he keeps that he'd be quite familiar with some of those drugs that Lauren had in her room.'

'True. Reckon he was having an affair with her? Maybe he had something to do with the video? Karen thought it was revenge porn. Perhaps Lauren wanted him to leave his wife, was saying she'd go to the press if he didn't and he was using it to stop her.'

'Everything is a possibility. He's in the media, she's young and impressionable. I can see how she could get drawn into something.'

As he spoke, Fanning stuck his head around the office door. 'Will you be needing me, Cig?'

'I thought you were bringing the coffee?' Cathy looked at him questioningly.

Fanning grimaced. 'Bit of a domestic to sort out.'

O'Rourke shook his head. 'Go, you were due off at seven. Cat and I can chat with this Delaney character. If he's on live radio I'm guessing he's not a flight risk. I'll just get finished up and we'll head into town. That suit you, Cat?'

'Yep, the sooner we can speak to Ronan Delaney, the better.'

'Thanks, Cig. I'll see you in the morning. Keep me posted?'

Cathy gave Fanning a thumbs up as he disappeared around the door. She could hear his shoes on the hard treads as he ran down the stairs. The details of his domestic had sounded hilarious as they'd unfolded this afternoon. He'd earned his nickname for getting involved with too many women, too close together, not for anything useful, like driving speedboats or saving the world.

She stood up, stretching, went over to look out of the window at the car park behind the station, leaning on the windowsill while O'Rourke sorted out his paperwork. As if he could feel her watching, as Fanning appeared out of the back door, skirting the base of the radio mast that towered above the station, he looked up at the office, and threw her a mock salute. She watched him stride across the car park to his own car, some sort of low-slung red sports car – a Honda NSX, someone had said it was. Probably one of the most ridiculous looking cars

Cathy had ever seen, with its side yokes and gleaming spoked wheels, the go faster spoiler. But Fanning was into cars in a big way and thought he was the business in it. He revved it up and flashed her as he roared out of the yard.

'Right, we'll head into town in thirty minutes. Write up your interview and I'll finish up here, and then we'll go and have a chat with him, will we? Give him a call and tell him we're on the way.'

Chapter 31

Ronan Delaney hadn't been at all impressed that they were coming to talk to him at work. He had blustered a lot when the producer had put her through to him, had deliberately kept the call short, saying he only had another two minutes of ads to run before he was back on. He'd tried to make a point about the press blowing the story up, but it was late and Cathy was pretty sure he wasn't a big enough noise to have the paparazzi hanging about outside his door on a Sunday night. They'd agreed to be discreet when they came into reception. Cathy had smirked to herself as she put the phone down. While she might not look like your classic detective, there was no taking O'Rourke out of the job. Even in a suit he was unmistakable. It was something to do with the way he walked into a room and comanded the space. He did the same in the interview room. Ronan wouldn't know what had hit him.

O'Rourke pulled his overcoat around himself as he strode out of the back door of Dun Laoghaire station. It was always roasting inside and the contrast with the January night was shocking. Cathy zipped her leather jacket up firmly to the neck, walking briskly behind him, the indicators on his sleek navy

BMW 7 Series flashing as he approached. He turned the heating up full the minute she closed the door.

'Jesus, it's cold. Right, where is this place?' Reversing rapidly, he skirted the side of the station and rolled up to the electric gates waiting for them to open.

'On the Quays beside the O_2 or O_3 or whatever it's called now.'

'The Point?'

She smiled. 'Yep, that's it.'

The Point Depot had been built as a train depot in the 1870s, but redesigned as a music venue in the 1980s. Now its utilitarian red brick exterior hid several sound stages – and it had been rebranded several times, creating more confusion than clear message. It was like the Burlington Hotel in Donnybrook; it had been a Hilton and something else, but everyone still called it the Burlo. Dubliners weren't good with change.

'You still sure about the ERU?'

O'Rourke's voice cut through her thoughts and Cathy realised that she had drifted off slightly, lulled by the soft leather of the seat and the smooth drive. It had been a busy day with a tough start in the gym.

'Yes, sent in the application as soon as I finished it.'

'You really want it?'

There was something in his tone that made her glance at him. His jaw was tight as he watched the vehicles braking in front of him, their tail lights flashing. If he could feel her looking at him, he didn't acknowledge it.

'I need a change, a bit of action. I think it'll be fun.'

Cathy glanced at him again, smiling, trying to sound light. He was in a funny mood. Sort of tetchy.

'I'm not sure "fun" is the word I'd choose.'

She shrugged. 'I can't stay in Dun Laoghaire all my life, and I need to expand my skills base. This makes perfect sense – it builds on what I'm already good at. That ERU inspector said—'

He cut her off. 'That they were looking for more women.' He glanced at her. 'He called me as soon as your application arrived. He wants you in for interview.'

Cathy looked at him, stunned. She'd thought it would be weeks before she heard anything.

'Really?'

She couldn't think of anything else to say. O'Rourke braked at a red light and turned to look at her.

'Why are you surprised? He wanted you to apply, especially after that whole thing in Wicklow.'

The 'thing' in Wicklow had had the makings of a major incident, but he was right. The ERU Inspector had phoned her for a chat afterwards, had made it clear he wanted her on his team. But the timing hadn't been right. With O'Rourke on the move, though, it was now. Cathy felt the stirrings of excitement. She loved a new challenge, was always the first in the queue to try new things – whether it was a Taser or a new stab vest. And, assuming she got through the interview, moving to the ERU would keep her very busy. It was definitely better than feeling miserable about O'Rourke moving to Limerick. It wasn't like they hadn't worked in different divisions before, but since the explosion things had changed between them. Maybe not working together would be the thing they needed to get closer still. She could hope.

She realised she hadn't answered him, cleared her throat.

'I know, but I didn't think they were *that* keen for me to join.'

He looked at her again as the traffic light changed to green, half-amused.

'You're young, you've huge energy and enthusiasm, you're a national kick-boxing champion, you're on course for a first in your Master's. What's not to want?'

There was something in the way he said it – the last word loaded with . . . She wasn't sure what. Something that made her stomach flip and her heart beat faster. She looked across at him but his concentration was back on the road. That was perhaps just as well. She had no idea what to say in response.

Her phone started to ring. A moment later her ringtone was drowned out by O'Rourke's phone ringing through the car's internal system. She pulled hers out. It was Anna Lockharte.

'You first.'

She flicked hers to voicemail as he depressed the button on the steering wheel to answer. It was the fingerprint expert calling from the Technical Bureau in Garda Headquarters in the Phoenix Park.

'O'Rourke.'

'Evening, Cig, we've got something interesting for you on the Lauren O'Reilly case.'

Still focused on the traffic, O'Rourke said, 'Got you on speaker, go on.'

'We found several sets of prints on the boxes of Modafinil in her room, none of which were hers, notably. We've several unidentified but one's come up with a hit on the Interpol database.'

Cathy looked across at him, her eyebrows raised. *What was that about?*

'Go on.' He was still concentrating on the traffic.

'No ID unfortunately, but there was a murder in France a few years ago, a sixteen-year-old schoolgirl was suffocated in a park near where she lived. She was wearing a gold bracelet, there was a partial unidentified latent lifted from it. We just got a match.'

'Any suspects in their investigation?'

'Not looking like it. We've got calls in to follow up, we're waiting for the files.'

'Good job, keep me posted.'

He clicked the phone off.

'So we could be looking for someone with links to France?'

'Sounds like it.'

Cathy thought for a moment; where had she heard France mentioned recently? Then she got it.

'You know Tom's family have a place in the south of France.'

'Really? I think we're going to need to have a chat with them again.'

Cathy's phone pipped to indicate she had a message. She was so caught up in the implications of the fingerprint on a bracelet, the sound made her jump.

'Who wants you on a Sunday night?'

'Anna Lockharte.' Cathy hit the redial on her phone and waited for Anna to pick up.

'Professor Lockharte? Cathy Connolly, sorry I missed your call.'

'Thanks so much for coming back to me.' At the other end Cathy heard her pause, take a breath. 'My friend in the US security services has been in touch about the email I received.'

Cathy glanced across at O'Rourke. 'What did he find out?'

'He wants to speak to you directly. His team have gone into my laptop remotely. That email contained a virus that gave the sender access to my webcam, as we suspected.'

'Like Lauren's?'

'Apparently yes. Very like Lauren's.' Cathy heard Anna clear her throat. 'The thing is, Rob's team found a similarity in the code emailed to me to an open case in the US. I told him about

Lauren and he did a check to look for any cases that involved webcam footage. There was a murder in Long Island a few years ago. The girl had images on her computer that the local detectives thought at the time she'd filmed herself, but someone was suspicious that she might have been hacked. The detective tagged the case but it was never properly followed up. Well, like Rob said, even if they had realised that she'd been hacked, the origin of the virus is untraceable. But the thing is, the Discovery Quay site was mentioned in emails sent to her too. He wants to check Lauren's computer to see if it's the same virus.'

'He thinks that this case in Long Island could be linked to Lauren's?'

'Yes, he's positive it is. He's having every case where webcams were an element checked. But one of his guys was able to look at that girl's computer, the one in Long Island. It was in storage but they were able to fire it up for him to look at remotely. There's some sort of data fingerprint in the code it was infected with. His team say it's linked to the worm that was used to access my computer. They are moving really fast because there's an ongoing investigation into these websites, a really big one.'

Cathy caught her breath. Suddenly this case was taking on a whole new angle.

'How did the girl in Long Island die?'

'She was found in woods close to where she lived.' Cathy thought she heard Anna's voice catch. 'She was assaulted and suffocated with her own clothing.'

Chapter 32

Sunday, 9 p.m.

Cathy hung up and looked at her phone for a moment. While she had been speaking they'd crossed the East-Link Bridge and slipped down the Quays, turning into the maze of narrow streets that spread like veins up from the river. O'Rourke had pulled the car to a halt.

He turned off the ignition. 'That sounded interesting.'

'You could say that.' Frowning, Cathy unclipped her seat belt and twisted in her seat to face him. 'Remember I told you Anna Lockharte has this friend in US Security who was looking at her computer?' Cathy told him what Anna had just related to her. O'Rourke took the information in, his face expressionless, but Cathy knew his mind was in fifth gear, processing the information.

'He's suggesting the same hacker could have been involved with a murder in the US?'

'Yes, he's sure of it. Lauren's stuff hadn't been broadcast yet, but the threat was there. He'll know for sure when his guys access her computer and take a look.'

'OK. And we've also got forensics linking the drugs in her room to a murder in France.'

'Yes, and both girls, the one in Long Island and the one in France, were suffocated. Both found in wooded parks.'

O'Rourke pulled his key out of the ignition. 'We need to look at the files but the two MOs sound remarkably similar, which would suggest we have a very mobile killer.'

'And somehow he knew Lauren, gave her the drugs and then hacked her webcam.'

'Which means he must be here, on Irish soil.' O'Rourke rolled his keyring through his fingers. 'The hacker who wrote the code may have had nothing to do with the murders, it could be circumstantial. We have to be open to all possibilities, but I think we need to connect all these agencies, schedule a Skype meeting. Going after Lauren could have been his big mistake.'

'But she wasn't suffocated.'

'No, but she was in a park. It's possible he was planning to murder her and she jumped to escape him.'

'What about the note in her pocket?'

'Perhaps he meant he was sorry, perhaps he's had enough and wants help. He obviously infiltrated Lauren's life – perhaps more than he did with the others.' O'Rourke paused. 'Let's see how Ronan Delaney fits into all this, shall we?'

The offices of Life Talk FM were in a nondescript office building with no external branding. The road outside was cobbled, bisected by the Luas track. A few parked cars were scattered along its length but it was otherwise empty. Life Talk was on the third floor on the other side of a door entry system. A gust of freezing air blew up the road from the river Liffey, bringing with it the tang of salt. Cathy shivered as the door swung open.

O'Rourke strode ahead of her and, not bothering to look for the lift, took the stairs two at a time. She followed him. She knew from his posture that he was on a mission. She didn't fancy Ronan Delaney's chances if he was thinking he'd be able to hide the truth from them.

As he reached the top of the stairs, the huge Life Talk logo greeted them. O'Rourke pushed open the door into reception. Cathy was surprised to see that even at this time of night there was a girl behind the main desk, but then as the phone rang, Cathy realised that of course they needed staff on whenever a live show was going out. It was the interaction with the listener that was the success of this particular station.

The girl lifted her head and smiled. Her hair was chopped in a severe pixie cut that emphasised her high cheekbones and big brown eyes. Delaney had obviously told her to look out for them.

'Ronan's expecting you, would you like to come into the conference room? He's just coming off-air now. Can I get you a tea or coffee?'

She looked at O'Rourke slightly strangely, like she wanted to ask who he was but didn't dare.

'Thank you, that would be great. Coffee for me, black, Detective Connolly has hers white, one sugar.'

The girl's eyebrows shot up.

Behind her, Ronan Delaney appeared from a side office, his hand held out. *Too late if he was planning on keeping their identities quiet.*

'Great to see you, come in, come in.'

Reaching for O'Rourke's hand, Delaney clapped him on the arm with his other hand like he was an old friend, trying to sweep him into the conference room at the same time. It was a pantomime that wasn't lost on O'Rourke. Cathy followed them, watching Delaney, wondering what he had to hide.

As soon as the conference room door was closed, Delaney's tone changed.

'I really don't know how I can help you. Tom worked for me. My wife and I are good friends of his parents. We were devastated when we heard about the accident.'

There was a pause that was slightly longer than was comfortable before O'Rourke spoke.

'We're aware that Tom worked for you, that he was regularly at your house. And that he worked here at the station last summer. We're interested in talking to you about the night that he was killed. Perhaps we can sit down and you can take us through your movements that evening.'

O'Rourke pulled out a chair as pixie haircut came in behind them. She slipped a tray onto the table and hovered for a moment.

'Thanks, Tamsin.' Delaney was smiling but his tone was dismissive.

Cathy pulled out a chair and slipped her notebook out of the leg pocket of her combats. Unhooking the elastic, she flipped open the grainy black cover and slid out her pen.

She looked at Delaney expectantly as O'Rourke remained standing, his arms folded. Delaney got the point and, pulling out a chair, sat down, casually throwing one ankle over his knee, putting one elbow on the table like he didn't have a care in the world.

'Of course, I want to help as much as I can. I don't know what I can tell you, but where would you like me to start?'

'You were at Orla Quinn's charity event at the Intercontinental Hotel last Thursday night?'

'In Ballsbridge, yes, there all evening from about seven forty-ish. Usual thing, introducing the speakers, telling a few jokes, getting people to put their hands in their pockets for the raffle. It was a great night. I left just after Orla. Drove home. Back by about 11:15, I think.'

'And on the way home did you see anyone walking down Ulverton Road?'

Delaney shrugged. 'I really can't remember, it was a long day, I just wanted to get home.'

'We've CCTV that places you in Sandycove within the time frame you describe, which also means that there's a strong likelihood that you drove past Tom.'

Delaney looked surprised. 'I'm sure I didn't. I would have noticed him.'

'He could have been lying on the pavement at that point.' Cathy's tone was blunt.

Delaney shook his head, thoughtfully, like he was trying to remember. 'I'm sorry, I really didn't see anything. I don't think I would have missed him if he'd been hit and was lying there. I was tired and it was dark, but you couldn't miss that, could you?'

Cathy thought not.

'And the next morning? When you went to work? I believe you came in for an early show?' O'Rourke looked at him sharply.

Delaney grimaced. 'I wish I'd driven that way and I might have seen him, but I turned up into the village. From what Conor said, the accident was further down the road, around the bend?'

O'Rourke nodded curtly. 'It was. Now tell me about Lauren O'Reilly. I believe she had a job here over the summer?'

Delaney ran his hand over his face. 'Nice girl, bit shy for media. She ended up making the tea most of the time. She was here for about six weeks over the holidays.'

'Did she make friends with anyone?'

'Well, she knew Tom, they were on the same course in college. She met Conor at some event in Trinity, the opening of that new science block, I think. She was one of the student helpers. Conor got chatting to her and organised the internship.'

'Did she want to work in radio?'

'She must have done. Intern jobs are hard to come by in our industry. I'm not sure it was exactly what she thought it would be. Conor was great, though, kept her busy so she wasn't in the way.'

O'Rourke took this in, then said, 'I believe your car is in for repairs? Can you give us the name of the garage, please? We need to examine it.'

'It's JB Motors, but why?'

Delaney did a good job of trying to sound innocent, but his body language was telling Cathy something different. The leg thrown across his knee, the crossed arms – all closed signals that showed he was feeling uncomfortable. And he kept glancing to the right, like he was trying to remember what had happened. She'd done a whole module on body language and the behaviour of liars. She didn't believe him for a minute. She could tell from O'Rourke's tone that he didn't either.

'For any damage consistent with a hit-and-run.'

'That's ridiculous.' Delaney uncrossed his legs and leaned forward, his face flushed red. 'You think *I* hit Tom? That's just . . . ridiculous! I didn't even see him. I had nothing to do with it. And what possible reason would I have for driving into him?' He ran his hand across his chin, and then, pointing his finger at them, said slowly, 'You're just looking to close this case before the media get hold of it. We're always hearing about the Guards fitting people up for stuff . . .' He shook his head in disgust. 'I need to speak to my lawyer.'

Cathy kept her face impassive. Delaney's acting skills were good, but they were wasted on her. There was definitely something he wasn't telling them. His unconscious body language was giving her all the clues that he had something to hide.

Chapter 33

O'Rourke was silent as they left the building. He reached for his phone as they headed back to his car. He dialled, glancing at Cathy to make sure she was still with him as he waited for it to be answered.

A moment later it was.

'Sorry to disturb your Sunday night, Fanning, but first thing in the morning I want you to get down to JB Motors in Sallynoggin and check out Ronan Delaney's car. He's having it repaired. Find out what's been done and stop them doing any more for the moment. Then come in and we'll compare notes. Good. Thanks.'

O'Rourke clicked off his phone. 'Our friend Delaney wasn't very helpful, was he?'

'I sort of expected that. I think we need to keep an eye on him now, though. Have forensics come back with anything more on the vehicle involved?'

'Nothing more than the paint being blue metallic – this isn't the movies unfortunately. Analysis takes time. They need to find the manufacturer now. At least it's not silver. Every car on the road seems to be silver these days.'

'See what 007 turns up tomorrow. He's good on cars. One of his areas of expertise.'

'He has one, apart from women? You do surprise me.'

They reached his car and O'Rourke pipped the central locking, pausing for a moment before he started the engine. The windscreen was covered in raindrops which caught the orange glow from the street lamps. With the movement of them closing the doors, several scudded down the glass, gathering others as they travelled. Cathy watched them, her thoughts with Ronan Delaney and how things connected – how one thing, an action or a statement, could have an effect on so many others. It was like the butterfly effect or ripples on a pond. O'Rourke's voice brought her back.

'France is only an hour ahead of us, isn't it? Professor Lockharte's friend in New York will be in his office around lunchtime our time, so if we schedule a meeting then, it'll give us time to get the details from the French and get over to the Quinns' for another chat. The one person who could possibly be linking all these events at the moment is Tom Quinn. He's obviously got the money to get to the States, was there a few weeks ago—'

Cathy interrupted him. 'And he speaks excellent French – both Anna and his mum told me that.'

'And you said the parents have a summer house in France?'

'Yes.' Cathy clicked her seat belt into place. 'In the south somewhere, I think she said. He'd be fairly computer savvy too, especially if he was a sound engineer in his spare time. Could he be behind all this?'

O'Rourke switched on the engine and put on his headlights. The rain had started falling in solid lines now, like rods cutting through the headlights' beam.

'I really don't know. My God, what a lovely night. Roll on June, I need some sun.'

O'Rourke checked his mirrors. Cathy didn't answer. Instead she tapped her phone on her teeth; there was still something puzzling her.

'So tell me how Anna Lockharte has access to someone so senior in the US security services that she can get an investigation moving this fast. What's her story?'

'Why do you think she has a story?'

His voice was deliberately neutral, making her about a hundred times more curious. He was trying to hide something from her, she was sure of it. She knew him too well. He pulled the car into a three-point turn.

'Because of the way you reacted the first time I mentioned her name.'

He glanced at her and pulled over on the other side of the road, letting the engine idle, obviously thinking.

Then he said, 'This is need to know only.'

Cathy rolled her eyes. 'I think you can trust me.'

He turned the engine off and swung around to face her, his face amused.

'I think so.' He hesitated. 'So briefly, Anna Lockharte's brother-in-law is the current US Ambassador to Moscow. He's on a high risk list with the US agencies for many reasons.' O'Rourke summarised the situation, pausing before he said, 'Anna Lockharte's computer being hacked would have the highest priority.'

Cathy took it in. 'That's a fair amount to have to deal with. She seems so together.'

'From what I can gather she's quite a remarkable lady. Obviously she's very intelligent, you don't get to be a professor at her age without being fairly sharp. But in the aftermath of the ISIS attack she saved several people's lives at the scene.' He paused. 'And despite everything that was happening around her, she remembered some crucial details about the terrorists that helped hugely in identifying them. There was a pan-European alert and they were tracked to Amsterdam. It was her info that made that happen. They were all killed in the ensuing gun battle but there was irrefutable evidence in the apartment they had rented that they had a very specific brief.'

As he spoke Cathy remembered the news stories. There had been international outrage over the attack; civilians from seven different countries had been killed. And then the chase had ended in two Dutch police officers being shot. It had been all over the press for ages, days of national mourning called all over the world.

'I remember,' Cathy said, half to herself. 'The question is, how do Tom and Lauren – and Ronan Delaney – fit into all of this?'

He turned the engine back on. 'That's the million-dollar question. We better get moving – we're going to have a busy day tomorrow and you need your beauty sleep.'

'Thanks for that.'

'Any time.' He grinned. 'Just as well you can get away without too much, isn't it?'

It took a moment for Cathy to work out that it was some sort of backhanded compliment. She blushed, didn't quite know what to say in response.

'So will you come and visit me in Limerick?'

'If I'm invited. I'd guess the ERU are needed down there quite a bit with these gangland feuds, so you might be seeing me sooner than you think. If I get in, that is.'

Her tone had been half-joking but his reply wasn't. 'I'd like that. I'd like that a lot.'

She looked at him sideways. His eyes were on the road but he was smiling.

Before Cathy could think of anything to say, her phone pipped with a text. She looked at the screen blindly, unable to quite focus. Had he just said he wanted to see her in a not so professional voice?

She took a steadying breath, trying to slow her heart. Why did he have this effect on her? That was a stupid question – she knew why. But she also knew how ambitious he was, and getting involved with someone in his unit – quite apart from their age difference – the fact that he was her brother's friend only made things more complicated.

'Who's that?' He indicated to pull around the roundabout and on to the East-Link Bridge.

'Anna Lockharte again. She's texted me her friend's contact details and says she's given him mine.'

'Excellent, we'll organise that meeting for tomorrow. She's very well favoured with the CIA, she's done all sorts of training courses with them – covert counter-surveillance type stuff. The original briefing was ages ago now, but I'm pretty sure she's fire-arms trained and has done their hand-to-hand combat courses.'

'Really?' Cathy couldn't hide the surprise in her tone – there she'd been thinking Anna Lockharte was just a very nice, albeit super-intelligent woman, and now it turned out that she had a whole hidden side that was utterly fascinating.

As if he read her mind he said, 'But you don't know any of that, remember. She's just a teacher at Trinity as far as we're concerned.'

'A professor.'

'Well, yes, but you know what I mean. I did wonder if the CIA had recruited her but she'd hardly be here if they had. Ireland isn't exactly a hotbed of international political intrigue. But with her family connections she's certainly within the fold, ticks all the boxes from a security point of view.'

'Maybe she's a sleeper. How old is the niece?'

'Sixteen, maybe seventeen. She must be heading for Leaving Cert.'

'And when she goes to university she won't need her aunt to mind her.'

'That's true. But I don't get the impression she's a sleeper. I think her connections would be too hard to hide.'

'Sometimes it's easier to hide in plain sight. But I bet if we google her we'll hit a brick wall. Actually . . .' She pulled out her phone and opened Google.

'There she is on the Trinity website. But . . .' Cathy scrolled down the page with her thumb, 'nothing else. I think she's a covert CIA operative.'

O'Rourke chuckled. 'You should write books, you know. You've an overactive imagination. Why would the CIA tell us she was here if she was one of their own? Our alert is for a civilian. Very different story.'

Overactive imagination. He had that right. In every story in her imagination he had the lead role.

Chapter 34

Monday, 8 a.m.

The next morning Cathy walked into O'Rourke's office, her body aching from thirty minutes of weights, followed by a very hard swim.

O'Rourke had dropped her back to the station the night before so she could collect her car. As she'd pulled out of her space in the car park, she'd seen the light go on in his office.

Did he ever go home? The station was operational twenty-four hours a day but no one else worked the hours he did. Perhaps that was the only way he could keep on top of all the various investigations he had running at any one time?

She knew he had an apartment somewhere in the south of the city, had moved from the city centre when he'd got the Dun Laoghaire posting. She didn't even know if he owned it or rented, like she did. She knew from things he'd said that it wasn't shared; he liked his own space. But she got the distinct impression that he didn't like going home all that much. He certainly spent a lot of time here. And he never talked about his apartment, never talked about the drains, or needing to redecorate, or the sort of stuff you chatted about when you had your own place. She knew he had no pets, so perhaps it was going home to an empty space that was the problem. Cathy realised she'd never thought about it much before, but in all the time she'd known him he'd always almost lived at the station. And he never mentioned his family – he was from Monaghan, from a farming family somewhere along the border. She knew that from McIntyre, knew the Troubles had affected his childhood, but she didn't know much else.

As she'd headed home last night, she'd wondered if he was lonely. You didn't get to the top in any job by making friends, but now she thought about it, she was the only person he really talked to, relaxed with. They had shared a lot of crap over the years, had a history. Not entirely the sort of history she wanted but it was still a history, and it didn't matter about the moments when she despaired about her feelings towards him. The laughter they shared, even out on the job, the special moments, made it all worth it. He'd always be more than a friend – a very special friend – and for that she was grateful.

Now Cathy hovered in the doorway to his office, watching him for a moment before he glanced up. She let his door close behind her. He must have been home at some stage unless he kept all his clothes in his locker – he was wearing a crisp pale blue shirt in a soft heavy cotton, a pink and baby blue striped tie. He'd stuck his navy jacket on the back of his chair, was looking at his laptop screen, checking his email she guessed.

He smiled, his look warm and welcoming, was about to speak when his mobile began to ring. He indicated he wouldn't be a minute. A moment later his eyebrows shot up.

'Well done, Fanning, I didn't know you functioned this well at this time in the morning. Good job. Call Traffic, will you, and get them to send in a technical team. Keep me posted by phone? I'll be very interested in their take on that.' He paused. 'JB bloody Motors better have a damn good reason for not reporting it.'

He hung up, looked at the phone for a moment. '*That* was 007.' He said it with emphasis.

'You sound impressed . . .'

Cathy couldn't hide the amusement in her voice as she headed over to her perch on the windowsill. The radiator ran under the window and she was feeling chilly, the early morning mist not agreeing with her damp hair on the walk up to the station.

'I am – he must have been down at that garage waiting for them to open up.'

'He has his moments.'

'He certainly does, and this is most definitely one of them.'

She settled herself on the windowsill, her hands in her pockets; she could feel the heat of the radiator through the fabric of her khaki combats.

'Did he find Delaney's car?'

'He certainly did. And he found something else too.'

She stared at him meaningfully. 'Well, tell me . . .'

'You were right about him knowing about cars. Delaney's jeep was there. Being serviced – it had some problem with the electrics, a light coming on, on the dash or something.'

'He could have saved us a lot of bother if he'd shared that with us last night.'

O'Rourke rolled his eyes. 'I think his whole world would be looking better if he shared a bit more than his bad temper. But guess who else's car is in for repair?'

Cathy jumped off the windowsill. 'Who? Tell me.'

He looked at her cheekily. 'Guess.'

'How the heck am I supposed to do that?' He was teasing her but she liked it, played up to him. 'Someone who knows Delaney, who uses the same garage, maybe recommended it to him or vice versa, so probably someone who lives in the area. Someone who is connected to the case?'

The answer was obvious before she even finished the sentence, but he interrupted her.

'Someone who has, according to Fanning, a very distinctive collection of classic cars.'

'See, told you he knows his cars. And he knows all the celebs. He must have dated half of TV3 at this stage.'

O'Rourke held up his hands like he was stopping traffic. 'Spare me the details. So who do you think?'

'Conor Quinn.' She said it with absolute certainty. He looked disappointed that she'd guessed so fast.

'You're right . . .' He stopped, like he was waiting for a drum roll. 'According to Fanning's findings at JB Motors this morning, he has a collection of BMWs, all different models and different years, but all a very distinctive metallic blue. It's some sort of special colour that's top of the range, not too many of them in this state.'

'Jesus Christ, *Conor Quinn* hit Tom? How could that be?'

'We can't draw any conclusions yet but there's a blue BMW jeep with Life Talk FM stickers in the back window that's in to get the brakes, among other things, repaired. There are some scratches and a dent below the bumper on the passenger side. But we'll only know if they are consistent with an impact when the Traffic team takes a look.'

'He'd only come back from New York that night but he said something about having to go to a meeting that was rescheduled.'

'He was jet-lagged – who knows, perhaps he never even realised he'd hit anyone.' Cathy looked at him, incredulous, as he continued, 'Maybe he was drinking on the flight?'

Cathy shook her head in disbelief. 'Will we bring him in?'

'I think we need to speak to him on his own, that's for sure.'

Chapter 35

Conor Quinn was perplexed when they'd called at his house. He had looked in disbelief at Cathy when she'd explained that they needed to have a chat about his cars and the night of Tom's death. He'd shrugged, shaking his head like going down to the station was all a waste of time, but, as he'd assured them, he didn't have anything to hide. Cathy had been banking on his arrogance to carry them through. They didn't have enough to arrest him but O'Rourke was right that they needed to explain to him what they did have, while he was on tape. They needed to see his reaction.

Mira had looked on anxiously as he'd reached for his jacket and accompanied Cathy down his front steps to the detective unit's Mondeo. Orla Quinn had been at a breakfast meeting, but Cathy was sure Mira would be straight on the phone. And no doubt Orla would be on to his solicitor. They might not have much time.

The interview room was lit by a harsh fluorescent light that bounced off the cream walls and neutral flooring. Dressed in a casual check shirt and a navy V-neck sweater and jeans, his thick dark hair gelled, Conor Quinn had tried to move the chair closer into the table as he'd sat down, had been slightly surprised to find that it was bolted to the floor. Now he sat back in the chair, his arms folded.

O'Rourke sat opposite him, his jacket on, a notepad in front of him. Despite his assertions that he had nothing to hide, Cathy could feel the tension radiating off Quinn as she unsealed the discs for the tower recording unit on the wall beside them. She kept her face friendly, smiling warmly as she noted the numbers on each disc and handed them silently to O'Rourke, who loaded them.

O'Rourke glanced up to check the video camera was functioning as he began.

'For the tape, those present are Conor Quinn, DI Dawson O'Rourke, and Detective Garda Cathy Connolly. Mr Quinn, you've agreed to come and have a chat with us voluntarily about events on the night your son Tom was killed in a traffic accident. Can you confirm your full name and home address for us, please?'

'Is this really necessary? My son is the victim here. I . . .'

'Please state your name and address for the tape.'

'Conor Quinn, St Gabriel's House, Sandycove, County Dublin.'

'You are aware that you are not under arrest but that this interview is being recorded and that you are not obliged to say anything unless you wish to do so, but anything you do say will be taken down in writing and may be given in evidence?'

Quinn pursed his lips as he thought about it, then said, 'This is ridiculous.'

He shifted in his seat as if he was suddenly realising that this was a significantly more serious 'chat' than he'd expected. But from what she'd seen, Cathy was sure he wasn't the type of man to lose face and show his fear. Arrogance was a dangerous thing.

'For the tape, please.'

'Yes.'

'Thank you.'

Out of the corner of her eye, Cathy could see O'Rourke smile. It was the smile he reserved for suspects. It lifted the corners of his mouth but didn't hit his eyes.

'Now, Conor, can you take us through your movements on Thursday evening last please? The night that your son Tom was killed in a hit-and-run incident in Ulverton Road in Dalkey?'

Quinn paled, a sheen of sweat appearing on his forehead, but then, Cathy reasoned, being reminded of what had happened under these circumstances would make anyone go pale – it was all still very raw. But O'Rourke didn't like Conor Quinn and he could be a total bastard.

'You know all this.' Quinn sighed theatrically, shaking his head. 'I was in New York. I flew home on Thursday. The plane was delayed.'

'How did you get home from the airport?' Cathy kept her voice light.

Quinn stared at her impatiently, like they were wasting his time.

'I caught the air coach in the end. I was going to get a cab but the coach almost delivers me to the door. No point in shelling out for parking or a taxi when it was sitting there when I walked out of arrivals.'

'So you got off the air coach in Sandycove and made your way home?'

'Glasthule, but yes, exactly.'

'And what time was this?' O'Rourke was holding his pen, making the occasional note in the form of hieroglyphics he used in front of suspects.

'I got home just after eight, I think.'

'And who was in the house when you arrived?'

'Well, Mira, obviously. She told me Tom had just gone out. Orla was at her charity thing.'

Cathy leaned forward in her chair, her elbows on the table. 'What did you do when you arrived?'

Conor Quinn looked at her like she was stupid. 'I unpacked, had a quick shower, got changed.'

'And then, Conor?' The way O'Rourke said his name made him sound like a child in school.

Quinn looked at O'Rourke, objecting to his tone, but biting his tongue.

'I told you before. I went to a meeting, with an investor actually. It was rescheduled when we left New York late. I wanted to get to it.'

O'Rourke raised his eyebrows. 'Where did that meeting take place?'

'At a house on the Vico Road. I met with a guy called Xavier Ayari.'

Cathy pushed a stray curl behind her ear. She'd arranged to meet Olivier Ayari, Tom's friend, at twelve today. Now that suddenly everything had started moving fast, she doubted she'd make it. It was in the job book, though, so Frank Gallagher would have it covered.

'That's the Xavier Ayari whose family funded the new science wing at Trinity College?'

Quinn nodded. O'Rourke cut in, his tone clipped. 'For the tape, please.'

'Yes, one and the same.'

'Do you normally have meetings at people's homes that late at night?'

Quinn looked at O'Rourke like it was none of his business. 'It was a private conversation. This is Dublin, Inspector, you can't do anything or have a conversation without people seeing you or overhearing. We needed to be somewhere discreet and Xavier had to do something to his boat so he was going to be in Dun Laoghaire. The timing just worked out.' He shrugged. 'Well, apart from the flight delay, that is.'

Cathy wondered what they had been discussing. Karen Delaney had said something about Quinn's US trip being related to expanding the station – was Quinn looking for investment in Life Talk? And if he was, why had he organised a meeting when his wife – who presumably was the other shareholder – was tied up at an event? Cathy was sure Orla Quinn had been busy all day bringing her fundraiser together. Did she even know about it? Cathy was desperate to ask, but right now they had more important issues to get to the bottom of first.

'How did you get to that meeting, Conor?'

Cathy could see where O'Rourke was going, and he wasn't messing about with preliminary chat, was going straight for the truth. Although what Quinn's version of the truth might be remained to be seen.

'I drove, obviously.'

Cathy watched him closely. Had he been drinking on the flight? Was he even capable of driving?

'And what car did you drive?'

Quinn shook his head like the question was unnecessary. 'My Z3. It's the car I use most often.'

'You're quite sure?' O'Rourke looked at him hard.

'Of course I am.'

'How many cars do you have?'

'Five. All Beemers. Different models.'

'But all the same colour?'

'Yes, estoril blue. To match my eyes.'

Ick. Cathy kept her face impassive.

'Where do you keep them?' O'Rourke straightened the pad in front of him, said it like it wasn't important.

'In the garage at the back of the house. I use the Z3 most of the time, sometimes the jeep. The others I usually only bring out to classic car events, rallies, that sort of thing.'

'And when did you last use the jeep?'

Quinn shrugged. 'Before I went to the States. I'm not sure. It's not something I keep in my diary.'

'And where's your jeep now?'

'In the garage at home, I expect. Where else would it be?'

O'Rourke shifted in the chair. 'Actually it's at JB Motors in Sallynoggin, getting some repairs done. Do you have any explanation for that?'

'There was something adrift with the brakes. I asked Mira to call the garage and get it serviced – it was due one. It usually takes them ages to collect it. If one of those bloody mechanics has damaged it . . .'

'We have reason to believe that the car involved in Tom's accident was metallic blue.'

Quinn's mouth opened and closed again. No sound came out. He at least had the decency to look shocked. O'Rourke changed tack.

'Did the meeting with Xavier Ayari go well?'

Cathy smiled inwardly. O'Rourke was going for state of mind – exactly what she'd been thinking a moment previously. What sort of mood had Conor Quinn been in heading back home? Had he been driving recklessly? She'd been in a BMW jeep once, and knew from O'Rourke's car that BMWs were very solid; you felt safe and invincible inside one. If he had been jet-lagged, would he have noticed hitting someone? It had been very dark and Karen Delaney had said Tom was wearing dark clothing. Maybe Quinn had fallen asleep at the wheel and mounted the pavement, clipping Tom. Then reversed to get back onto the road but, groggy and maybe confused, had changed his mind, and decided to drive forwards along the pavement instead. Surely he'd have felt a big jolt as he drove over Tom's body. But that would be one good reason why he could be lying about the vehicle he'd used that night.

Quinn licked his lips, then he finally found his words. 'I don't know yet if it was successful. I want to expand Life Talk. Orla's not so keen. I want Xavier Ayari to invest so she doesn't have to worry about the company any more and we can develop it into new areas. She has enough going on in her own companies.'

Cathy was quite sure Orla Quinn wouldn't be impressed with that.

'But isn't your wife Orla the majority shareholder?' As usual, O'Rourke had done his homework. 'Surely she'd need to be involved in that discussion?'

Quinn shrugged. 'She's very busy with her various roles. I know what direction I want to take Life Talk in – we need to shake things up a bit to increase our market share.'

'And she's happy with this, is she?'

'We haven't had much time to discuss it since I got back. A lot has been happening.'

O'Rourke nodded curtly. 'So tell me about Lauren O'Reilly.'

A flash of shock crossed Quinn's face but he hid it so fast, he thought they hadn't seen it. Cathy felt O'Rourke shift in the chair beside her. He hadn't missed it either. He didn't miss anything.

'What about her?'

Belligerent. He'd seemed genuinely surprised about the car – either that or he was a very good actor, but now his mask was starting to slip. He leaned forward and started to fiddle with his wedding ring.

And several things collided in Cathy's head.

Quinn had organised the work experience for Lauren at Life Talk after meeting her at the Trinity event. But she was shy and Ronan Delaney had felt that she wasn't cut out for the media. Cathy knew hundreds of students would give their eye teeth for that type of work experience, yet Quinn had brought someone in who wasn't suited to it. And she hadn't been friends with Tom at that point, so it wasn't like Tom had put pressure on his dad to give her a job. Cathy suddenly had a very strong feeling that Conor Quinn had other reasons for getting to know Lauren O'Reilly. Hadn't her friends said she'd dropped off the radar a bit when this term had started, that she'd become secretive and reluctant to come out with them? Cathy could think of one very good reason for that. She had been a very attractive girl.

'How well did you know her, Conor?'

Her voice was low, but the way Cathy said it was loaded with innuendo. O'Rourke picked up on her meaning immediately. Quinn did too, his cheeks flushing red.

'She worked for Life Talk last summer, she's one of Tom's friends . . .'

'But she wasn't one of Tom's friends then, Conor.'

He pursed his lips.

Cathy looked at him hard. 'She was coming to see you that evening, wasn't she? Did she call you? We've got a pile of calls to a pay-as-you-go mobile in her phone records. Texts sent to the same number that would indicate that she was in a relationship with the recipient. A pay-as-you-go phone, Conor. Isn't that what people use when they are having an affair?'

Quinn licked his lips like they'd gone dry. His hand went to his wedding ring again as he looked from one of them to the other.

'Look, Orla can't know about this, and I had nothing to do with Lauren's death. Nothing, do you hear me, I wasn't even there.'

Before O'Rourke could speak, there was a knock on the door. Fanning stuck his head in.

'Solicitor's here asking to see Conor Quinn.'

Chapter 36

Taking Quinn to his solicitor, O'Rourke kept his face straight until they got down the corridor and around the corner from the interview room.

'Damn his solicitor arriving, but how the hell did you guess that one, Miss Marple?' His face cracked into a grin as she leaned back on the wall beside him.

'No guesswork, pure deduction. And brilliance, obviously. As soon as you mentioned Lauren's name he started twisting his wedding ring.'

O'Rourke interrupted her. 'Lots of people do that.'

'True, but when my little brother is playing poker, he always looks for the tell, a movement or a twitch that says the other player is concealing something.' She hesitated. 'And he's damn good at poker.'

'He has you well trained. But you needed more than a twitch to get that one.'

'Just a few things people have said suddenly made sense. Paula Garcia, Lauren's friend in college, said her behaviour had changed after the summer. Ronan Delaney said that Conor had organised the job for her but she wasn't a media type. Anna

Lockharte said she was incredibly shy – she's not the type who would want to work in radio, you need to be confident and outgoing for that. I think Quinn fancied her as soon as he met her at that Trinity thing and got her the job so he could see more of her. I thought Ronan Delaney could have been seeing her on the sly, but Quinn's a much bigger fish – he *owns* the station. She has to have been flattered by his attention.'

O'Rourke looked thoughtful. 'And when that photo arrived in her inbox she panicked, and who does she call?'

'Her friend with the pay-as-you-go mobile. Exactly.' She could see from O'Rourke's face that it was all fitting into place for him too. 'There were a few days between the first email arriving and her calling the pay-as-you-go that threw me a bit. But we can safely say she was a bit shocked when she saw it the first time, must have spent a couple of days frantically trying to work out what to do about it. Perhaps she thought she could sort it out herself. She must have been terrified of telling him too, that their relationship could be compromised and about to go public – who's to know he's not on one of the videos too? And she must have known Quinn was flying back from New York, knew what time he was due to land. There was no point trying to call him earlier.'

'That would be grounds for panic all right. Imagine if the media got hold of this, they'd destroy him.' O'Rourke tapped his fingers on the wall, his face creased in thought.

'I can't imagine his wife would be too impressed either.'

O'Rourke rolled his eyes. 'We've got him on tape admitting the affair. Think he killed her?'

Cathy screwed up her face. 'Maybe it was the only way he could think of to get rid of the evidence. It's not an entirely logical reaction, though, is it? It doesn't solve anything, just makes a heap more trouble.'

O'Rourke turned to look at her, his blue eyes full of mirth. 'Cat, when is murder ever logical? I mean, what are you like?'

She nudged him hard in the ribs. 'Don't you laugh at me. You know what I mean. People kill because they think it will solve their problems. If Quinn was filmed in a compromising position with Lauren O'Reilly, he's hardly going to think that getting rid of her will solve the problem – the video is still out there.'

'Maybe he thought, if she wasn't around, then any links to him would be impossible to prove? That the only person who could say that he hadn't been photoshopped into the video was Lauren. But I take your point. Well played on the connection between them. I love your intuition, Cat Connolly, it's like you can see inside people's heads.'

Cathy could feel herself blushing. *Christ, she wished she could see inside his head.* She kept talking, trying to hide her reaction.

'Maybe he *did* arrange to meet her in the park and she slipped. Maybe the "I'm Sorry" was part of a note to him?' Cathy hesitated, her mind suddenly at the edge of the cliff, gorse and brambles behind her, jagged rocks reaching up from the sea below, the wind freezing her face. 'It's just with this hacker being involved and connections between this case and those other cases – it's like he has a preferred location. I'm wondering if she was going to meet him – the hacker, I mean – and maybe expected Quinn to come and help her?' She hadn't put it quite as clearly as she would have liked, but she could see from his face that O'Rourke knew what she meant.

'You could be right.' He looked at his watch. 'It's after eleven now, we've got this conference call scheduled for 1 p.m. Quinn could clam up on us but forensics should be quick enough now they've got a sample to compare to the paint chips that were found on Tom's body. We need to get someone over to Quinn's house to look at that Z3. Although I can't imagine how you'd not realise you'd hit someone in one of those. They are tiny and so low to the ground that if you hit a pedestrian at speed they'd go sailing over the top, and would be more likely to land in the road than on the pavement.'

'I arranged to speak to Olivier Ayari at twelve to get the scoop on Tom.'

'I think we've pretty much got the scoop at this stage, don't you? The scoop and the sprinkles and raspberry sauce. Check in with Frank and get him to reassign it. We need to stick with this one, Cat. That Master's you're slaving for has its uses, you know.'

Cathy fought a smile, then frowned. 'Do you think Tom knew about his dad and Lauren? Maybe that's why they were a bit awkward at the start of the semester?'

'It's possible, but we don't know who was awkward with who. He could have been blissfully unaware but she found the whole situation a bit difficult.'

'As you might.' Cathy studied the floor for a moment while she thought about it.

'Indeed. Fanning's with the Traffic technical team down in Sallynoggin examining those vehicles. They're sending the photos over so we'll be able to see the scratches and damage repairs for ourselves fairly soon.'

O'Rourke pulled out his phone as if he was about to make a call. Leaning on the wall, Cathy shifted to face him, at the same time realising how close they were standing to each other. This wasn't the moment to react or comment on it. She stayed where she was.

'Do you reckon he really did meet Lauren? Tried to set himself up with an alibi by meeting Xavier Ayari first? Whatever happened to land her on the rocks had to be pretty bad. He's jet-lagged, he leaves the scene and comes whizzing down Ulverton Road, sees someone on the pavement, tries to brake but hits whoever it is. He doesn't want to stop because he might have to say where he's been, that he's just witnessed a girl fall to her death . . .'

'And he couldn't call it in because he'd have to explain why he was there? You could be on to something there. Let's ask him, shall we?'

Chapter 37

When Anna Lockharte finally got back into the security of her office, she leaned against the firmly closed door, her heart racing. Had she been followed? Her head swam, diminishing her ability to rationalise. *Surveillance helped to quantify the target, to note possible weaknesses and to begin to identify potential attack methods.* Her CIA trainer's words came back to her, cold, clinical. Factual.

She took a few deep breaths, focusing on the china blue carpet tiles, summoning images of Rob's face and his little blue book with its woodblock prints into her mind. She imagined him putting his arms around her and holding her, breathing in his aftershave, feeling the crisp cotton of his shirt as he encircled her in a protective embrace. It took a few moments, but gradually her heart rate began coming down, slowly. *Thank God.* Breathing deeply, she counted each inward and outward breath.

Was she imagining things or was this a real threat? Or was she so rattled by the events of the week, of the memories they bought back, that her imagination was in overdrive? The past few days had been terrible and just proved that she needed to find a new counsellor; she couldn't function with the threat of a panic attack looming over her every time she got worried.

But the feeling that she'd been followed from her office into Grafton Street had been overwhelming. She hadn't wanted to turn around but she'd had that instinctive sixth sense that someone was watching her as she left the Arts block, had ignored it – to start with – walking briskly down the Tunnel out of the university. And then, as she'd crossed the road beside House of Ireland, she'd done what she'd been trained to do and scanned the crowds behind her in the reflections in the shop window. Tourists and students, many on their phones, not even looking her way. *Nothing out of the ordinary.* She'd tried to shake it off, but the feeling of being watched had persisted.

Disrupt the take-away. She could hear the CIA counter-surveillance expert's voice in her ear. She had started to walk towards Grafton Street, but doubled back, instead headed down Nassau Street, dipping in behind the printer's, skirting a car park and circling back to cut across Dawson Street to get to Dublin's main shopping area.

It had been hard to take the security training seriously at first, but as it had progressed and she'd heard more examples of simple but effective ways that operatives could lose a tail – and ways to know that you were being tailed in the first place – the more it had made sense to listen. Now she incorporated the techniques she'd learned into her life without thinking, varying her routes to and from the university, shopping in different supermarkets, never sticking to the same routine. She'd been trained to analyse her route, to look for 'choke spots' – she hated that phrase – places where she could be ambushed.

Surveillance was about information gathering; anyone watching was doing it for a reason. If she felt she was being watched or followed, her trainer had explained that it was an early warning, that she should be ready for what might come next. And surveillance could come in so many forms, at any time. Keeping alert was crucial.

Rob hadn't said it, but Anna had wondered whether the webcam worm might have been part of something more sinister than a voyeur's website. But she knew he'd check, and she'd be the first person to know if he believed she was in any sort of danger.

This morning, as she'd looked out of her office window over the grassy quadrangle that connected the ancient university buildings with the concrete Arts block and library, the sun had peeked through steel-grey clouds and she'd realised how confined she felt inside, how she really needed to get some air before her tutor group arrived. She knew the guys would have lots of questions. Their focus would be on Tom and Lauren, and she needed to be in the right mood to help steer them through. It was going to be a heavy day.

To deal with it, Anna knew she needed to shut off completely and relax for a few moments. What did they say about shopping being therapy?

She'd ordered a gorgeous dress from L.K.Bennett online the previous night – one that wasn't stocked in Dublin – and had arranged to collect it when she got to London. But she really wanted a smart top that she could wear with her jeans and boots on Saturday when she went out with Hope. It had only taken her a moment to make up her mind. She'd seen a fabulous blouse in Karen Millen's online store, had checked to find that they had it in their concession in Brown Thomas, and she had an hour free before her students arrived.

She knew shopping wasn't really the answer but it made her feel better, however temporarily. There were times, like today, when she wondered if she really was just going mad? This weekend would be good for her. She really did need to get away, to put some distance between herself and everything that was happening here at the moment. On top of the feeling that she was being followed, the webcam hack had really spooked her, and all in all, the last few days had been devastating. Now she was looking forward to getting away with Hope so much it was almost irrational. It was ages since she'd been back to London and she had so much to show Hope: she wanted to take her to Greenwich on the river taxi, to show her the London Eye and see a show. To show her the beautiful station at St Pancras and take her on the Underground, to show her the Shard. She knew Hope would love the city.

It hadn't taken her long to decide. Even if it was only a quick distraction for this morning, she knew it was high time she spruced up her wardrobe. Since she'd moved to Dublin she hadn't been out that much, only for drinks with her teaching colleagues, the occasional dinner, so she hadn't really needed anything new. But London was a great excuse, and in all honesty, she'd wanted to cheer herself up after the grimness of the past few days. When she'd split up with Brad she'd bought loads of new clothes; she was sure it had been an effort to reinvent herself, to move on to the next stage in her life. She needed to do something similar now.

Which had seemed like a great idea until she'd got the feeling that someone was following her. It was like she could feel a shadow behind her, eyes boring into her back.

Disrupt the take-away. Doubling back on herself, winding through the back alleys, looking around her as if she was taking in the architecture, checking in every reflective surface, she'd been pretty sure she'd lost whoever it was. And then getting to Brown Thomas, heading upstairs on the escalator, she'd looked down, checking again. And her heart had almost stopped. Xavier Ayari was on the escalator coming up from the floor below her, heading in the same direction. And a black hole of anxiety had opened in her stomach.

Was he following her?

Brown Thomas was Dublin's most prestigious department store; it was a totally obvious, understandably normal place for Xavier to shop. He was a postgrad student in Trinity. He came from a wealthy family. It was perfectly plausible on a Monday morning when the sun was shining that he might want to come into Grafton Street. It was total coincidence that he was there at the exact same moment that she was.

Hurrying on, she'd headed towards the women's fashion floor. Karen Millen was tucked away at the far end of the designer brands room. He'd have absolutely no reason to head that way. Grabbing the blouse she wanted off the rail, she'd slipped into the changing area and closed the door of the luxurious grey carpeted booth. There was no way she was in the mood to try the blouse on now, but she was safe here, and when the wobble had gone from her legs she'd go and pay for it and leave via the couture floor, slipping down the spiral staircase and out of the shop's side entrance.

Feeling her heart slow at last, Anna put her bags down beside her desk, shouldered off her coat, draping it over the back of her office chair, and, sitting down heavily, ran her hand over her eyes. She'd looked everywhere for Xavier as she'd left Brown Thomas, had been relieved that he had apparently disappeared.

It didn't matter; the feeling of being followed had passed, leaving behind it the stirrings of a panic attack that she was determined not to succumb to.

She glanced at the clock. It was too early to call Rob and her students were due any moment anyway. She'd call him later, tell him all about Xavier Ayari and his email, and see what he could find out about his history. Anna let out another deep breath. Having a plan was vital, even if it was only a plan for the next hour. It made her feel like she was in control. And right now, that was what was going to get her through the rest for the day.

Chapter 38

Monday, 11.45 a.m.

Conor Quinn looked distinctly rattled when he sat back down at the table in Interview Room 4. He ran his hand over his gelled hair and licked his lips, the bright overhead lights catching the silver bracelet of his Rolex as he put one hand apparently nonchalantly in his jeans pocket. It didn't fool Cathy. He was anxious; good looks and designer clothes weren't enough to hide it.

O'Rourke set up the tapes again, waiting for the dull buzz to indicate the machine had started recording. From his outward appearance, the visit with his solicitor didn't seem to have calmed Quinn's nerves.

O'Rourke went through the preliminaries for the tape again. Name, rank and number. Cathy watched Quinn carefully as he answered the statutory questions. She just knew they were on to something here. She was sure his solicitor had told him not to answer their questions, but there was a good chance he'd let something slip if they were lucky.

'So, Conor, where were we? You've told us you got back from New York last Thursday night, arrived home just after eight in the evening, and then went out again to meet with Xavier Ayari.

This was the evening that your son Tom was killed in a hit-and-run incident in Ulverton Road, close to your home,' O'Rourke paused, 'and a fellow classmate of Tom's, Lauren O'Reilly, met with a very nasty accident off Dillon's Park. Perhaps you can elaborate on your relationship with Lauren O'Reilly?'

Quinn shifted uncomfortably in his seat. Whatever his solicitor had said, he couldn't contradict himself now. It took a moment for him to find the words.

'We were having an affair. Since she started working with Life Talk in the summer.'

Cathy could feel her jaw stiffen She wasn't seeing contrition or loss in the man sitting in front of her, and that made her angry.

'So take me through the events of Thursday evening again. This time with all the details.'

O'Rourke's tone made it very clear that they knew more than Quinn was letting on, was designed to spook him. Bluff and double bluff, that was what poker was all about. Cathy could hear her brother's voice in her ear. He was in Australia now, playing poker on some TV channel that also broadcast to the Internet. She'd taken a look but it had mainly been shots of his hands and scantily clad croupiers dominating the screen.

Quinn cleared his throat. 'She called. Lauren did. We had a phone we used so she could contact me privately, but I'd told her never to call, just to text. So I got home on Thursday night and I checked the phone.' He took a shaky breath, pulled his hand out of his pocket and crossed his arms, pushing his shoulders back. 'We'd been emailing a bit while I was away but there were all these missed calls and a voice message when I got back and then the phone rang again. She was hysterical. She said someone had been filming her in her room, getting dressed . . .' He flushed as he hesitated but didn't elaborate. 'She didn't know how, but they'd sent her photos and a video and were threating to publish the whole lot online.' He hesitated. 'I'd only been to her room in Trinity once, we usually met at a hotel . . ' He trailed off.

Cathy prompted him gently. 'For sex?'

Quinn nodded. There was so much she could say about that statement, like asking how a shy, impressionable young girl really felt about that. Did she feel used, or was she in love with him – what had he promised her? Part of Cathy felt utter despair at the situation Lauren had found herself in. Whatever she had thought the eventual outcome might be, the reality was something very different.

'And how did Lauren feel about that?' She kept her voice low, unthreatening.

Quinn took a deep breath and looked at the ceiling. For a moment Cathy thought his eyes had filled. Touching.

'She wanted me to leave Orla, for us to live somewhere together.'

'And had you given her the impression that that was a possibility?' *You dumb fuck.* Cathy would have loved to have said it.

He shifted uncomfortably. 'Actually, Orla and I haven't got on well for years. She's totally focused on her business. Lauren was a lovely girl.'

'Young and pliable?'

'No, she was very intelligent. She wasn't cut out for all the crap in media, she was a thinker, she had plans to build her own company.'

'So on Thursday. She called you?' O'Rourke bought it back to the business at hand.

'Yes, I was just out of the shower. I was in the bedroom. She was just sobbing down the phone. I couldn't get any sense out of her.'

'And what did you say to her?'

'I just told her that I loved her and that everything would be fine, that it would all work out. I needed time to think. She wanted to meet but I said I couldn't meet that night, that I'd work something out. She had this idea about us living together in the future. I said something about that, I can't remember what, I was trying to calm her down. She just wouldn't stop crying.'

'But she turned up in Dalkey anyway. Did she call at your house?'

'No.' He looked shocked. 'I told her I couldn't see her. I didn't see her. To be honest I was panicking a bit. I needed to talk to someone who understood this type of thing. I mean if the media got hold of it . . .' a look of terror passed across his face, 'it would be a total disaster. From what she'd said it sounded like someone had hacked the camera on her laptop – I mean it was the only way they could have taken the shots – she always had her computer open on her desk.' He cleared his throat. 'I needed time to think, to get Lauren to calm down so she could work out when it was filmed and if I was in any of the shots.' He shook his head. 'She said she knew a guy in college who was really good with computers, that she'd already asked him to come over and see what he could do but people kept calling on her and interrupting and he hadn't had a chance to look properly.' Quinn almost rolled his eyes, his face clearly showing his horror at that idea. 'She said I wasn't in any of the images that had been sent but, Jesus . . . I told her not to call him again, that I'd look after it.'

'And then you went to see Xavier Ayari?'

'Yes, I had to go straight out to the meeting, I'd arranged to meet him at ten. After I met Ayari I headed up the Vico for a bit. I wanted some peace and quiet to think, to work out what was the best thing to do. Then I came home. That's it. I was wrecked, I'd been in the air half the day, and then with Lauren getting hysterical . . .'

'And you sent the texts before your meeting, just after you'd left the house?' O'Rourke had his patient voice on, the one he used when they were only getting half the story.

Frowning, Quinn shook his head. 'What texts?'

Cathy leaned forwards. 'The texts sent organising to meet Lauren at Dillon's Park.'

She had to give Quinn full marks for his acting ability; he looked stunned for a moment.

'I didn't send any texts.'

Cathy opened the manila file in front of her and flipped the pages to find Lauren O'Reilly's phone records. She ran her finger down to the night in question.

'You admit that Lauren tried to call you several times on a pay-as-you-go mobile during the course of the afternoon, but got no answer because you were still on the flight from New York at that point. She then called the same number at 8.58 when you had the conversation you've just described. There are a series of texts from the same number starting at 9.30. The first one says "*Sorry. V. tierd. Meet me at Dillon's Park at 10.30. We can talk there xxxxx.*" She replied, and you gave her directions.'

'I didn't send those. I never met her, I told you. I left Ayari's house about half ten, I think, I don't know, I wasn't looking at the time. I wasn't there long. I went up to the Vico for about half an hour, maybe longer, I had a lot to think about. Then I came home.'

'Which route did you take home?'

Quinn shrugged. 'Down Sorrento Road I suppose, through the village. I had so much on my mind I can't remember.'

'Really? We'll check the CCTV.' Cathy paused. 'So who do you think sent those texts, Conor?' Her voice was dripping with sarcasm.

'I've no idea, honestly, but it wasn't me. I didn't even have that phone with me.'

Chapter 39

'Do you think he's telling the truth?' O'Rourke sat back in his office chair, his arms crossed, scowling.

Sitting opposite him, Cathy ran her fingers into the roots of her hair. She'd been thinking about Lauren walking into the park, her state of mind – she'd been heading there thinking she was meeting someone who would solve her problems. Cathy suddenly felt hugely protective towards her. And she knew that she had to find out exactly what happened that night and ensure the perpetrator felt the full weight of the law.

'Who, Conor Quinn?' Cathy snapped back to O'Rourke's brightly lit office, the sun making a rare appearance through the cloud outside and shining straight in through the picture window that filled the entire end wall. Despite its heat, Cathy still felt chilled by this case; there seemed to be so many strands and so many secrets. 'I think he has his own version of the truth. If he had a phone that he used for communicating with her secretly – regularly, if her phone records are anything to go by – what are the chances of it *not* being him sending those texts? I mean, who else knew about it? I think he sent them, then when he left Xavier Ayari's house, he met her and it all went horribly wrong. He's saying he went up to the Vico to account for the time lapse between leaving Ayari's and arriving home.' She frowned. 'You'd think he'd need to see those images to be sure he wasn't in them. I don't know why he didn't ask her to send them.'

'Perhaps he was worried about creating an email trail with something like that.'

'Or perhaps he sent them. There could be a much bigger picture here if he was involved in those cases in Long Island and in France. It's a possibility. We already know he has a holiday home in France and travels frequently to the States. Maybe Tom wasn't involved – maybe it was his dad. Quinn's got the money to set up sites like Merchant's Quay and Discovery Quay and the connections to make sure the profits stay hidden. And he obviously likes teenage girls.'

'We need to check Quinn's whereabouts at the time of those murders in Paris and Long Island.' O'Rourke checked his watch. 'Right – we can log in now.'

O'Rourke put his desk phone on speaker so Cathy could hear and dialled into the conference call, punching in the call's ID pin code. An automated voice said 'Caller two has joined the conversation.'

'Hello, this is DI Dawson O'Rourke in Dublin. With me is Detective Garda Cathy Connolly.'

'Bonjour, Inspector, Pierre Beaussoleil here in Paris.' Cathy raised her eyebrows at the velvety tones of the French officer's accent. 'We're just waiting for—'

A voice interrupted: 'Caller three has joined the conversation.'

'Hi, guys. Rob Power, Central Intelligence Agency. Good to be talking.'

O'Rourke's face was serious as he replied. 'Thanks for this, gentlemen. If I can just outline our situation here.' It took O'Rourke a moment to summarise. 'And Rob, you've found a connection to a similar case where a webcam was hacked?'

'Indeed, my guys are checking the FBI and the Interpol databases to see if there are any more too. As you know we've got a cold case here on Long Island. Hacked computer images are a common feature and there are similarities in the code to a worm that infiltrated Professor Anna Lockharte's computer, one of Lauren O'Reilly's lecturers at Trinity College.'

O'Rourke pursed his lips. 'We're giving your team access to Lauren O'Reilly's laptop today.' He paused. 'And you have a latent print in your case, Pierre, that's a match to a print we lifted from drugs boxes in Lauren O'Reilly's room.'

'We do – it was taken from a piece of jewellery worn by a student who was murdered in a park near her home in Paris. She too was suffocated.' Pierre's English was perfect.

In the office, O'Rourke was nodding. 'So there's a similar MO in both cases. Lauren wasn't suffocated but she was in a wooded park. She appears to have fallen or been pushed off a cliff, but equally if she feared for her life she could have jumped.'

Rob voiced all their thoughts. 'It's looking a lot like the same perp, isn't it?' His accent was cultured but very American, if that was a thing. Cathy imagined he looked a bit like a young Robert Redford. 'We certainly have a lot of common denominators.'

'Here in Paris we are now running all our data through the Interpol computers. It looks like our friends in the Metropolitan Police have two cases that show startling similarities – murders in public parks or woodland. Both were in central London, again young female students who were suffocated with clothing. We are checking with them to see if there is any record of the girls having issues with their computers.'

Cathy pulled her pendant from under her sweater and ran it along its chain, listening intently. If there were two more cases in London perhaps they'd throw up another piece of evidence, however tiny, that could be added to the puzzle. This case was suddenly looking huge.

O'Rourke's voice was serious. 'Sounds like we need to talk to our colleagues in London as well. Obviously we've got a very mobile perpetrator who has cash to travel. What's the next step?'

Rob came back on. 'I think we need to combine our data to search cold cases – at this end we've only been looking for unlawful killings with links to video images but we need to check everything with a similar MO.' He paused. 'To put this into context, we also have another major investigation going on here into the Merchant's Quay and Discovery Quay websites, Operation Honey Bee. We can tell from the site architecture that they've been built by the same person, so they are definitely linked. What we need now is for someone in the real world to make a mistake that will open the back door. You've found a link between your girl and Discovery Quay – we're teaming up with the techs here working Honey Bee to see if any of the other victims appeared on the site. This could be the breakthrough we all need. If we can identify that fingerprint and the origin of the narcotics, we could be a step closer to finding a very dangerous individual.'

'I think we need to keep in touch, gentlemen. It's looking like this character is here in Dublin somewhere, and I want to stop him before he leaves our island.'

They said their goodbyes and O'Rourke clicked his phone off.

'Sounds like there's something much bigger going on here than just our suspicious deaths. It wouldn't be the first time Dublin has been used as a headquarters for international criminal activity.' O'Rourke pursed his lips. 'Do you think Conor Quinn could be capable of this?'

Cathy pulled at her necklace again. 'I'm not sure he'd have the tech know-how, but you can hire anyone these days. Who's to say he didn't get a developer to build the sites and write those viruses for him? He likes young girls – maybe watching them is part of that too. That's the whole reason Discovery Quay exists, for people like that. He's very media savvy, it would make sense that he's got an investment interest in websites too.'

'And a personal interest in suffocating young women in woodland?'

Any sympathy Cathy had for Quinn at the death of his son was rapidly evaporating.

'I don't understand why he would have sent the images to Lauren, though. What did he need her to do that she needed to be blackmailed for?'

'Maybe he wanted to break it off with her but didn't know how? He needed to control the situation – like you said before, those images would give him power, would make sure she didn't tell anyone about their relationship.'

'Or maybe he gets off on their fear, on the control it gives him. It's like a game. Lauren's death brings it very close to home but perhaps he's getting overconfident. It sounds like there could be four other cases, and they've not even been connected before, so there could be more. At this stage, even if he's only involved in the ones we know about, he probably thinks he's invincible.'

'I'll buzz Thirsty, we need to get Quinn's prints taken and cross-checked.' As he spoke, O'Rourke's phone rang. He shot her a look as he answered. 'Fanning, how are you getting on?' Listening to 007, his eyes met Cathy's and his face cracked into a smile. 'Good work. Let's see what happens when we notch this up a gear.'

He hung up. 'The blue metallic paint *is* made by BMW. There's no sign of major damage to the vehicle but if the Traffic lads are right and he was knocked down first and then run over to finish the job, that would be consistent. It's a jeep, it doesn't take much to knock someone over with a vehicle of that weight.'

'Ouch.' Cathy winced. 'It's looking a lot like he hit Tom, isn't it?'

O'Rourke shrugged. 'If he'd just murdered Lauren O'Reilly, it's possible. We'll question him again, but I want to see those files and get the dates when those girls were killed in Paris and Long Island first. We need to check his whereabouts.'

Something was niggling Cathy about this whole thing. 'While we're waiting for the info I'm going to go back over the house-to-house reports from the premises overlooking the park. See if there's any reference to Quinn's vehicle or one like it in the area around the time Lauren arrived.'

'Good stuff. And we need to get onto the Met in London.' O'Rourke looked at his watch again. 'Meet you downstairs in an hour and we'll regroup and see if Quinn's ready to talk?'

Chapter 40

Cathy collected the bulging house-to-house files and went into the incident room with them. There was no one in there, thankfully – she needed to spread everything out and she didn't have time to explain what she was doing. She needed to concentrate.

There was something here that had been mentioned before, she was sure of it, but exactly what was eluding her. Every report was catalogued and numbered and recorded in a job book, so she knew exactly which of the manila files to pull from the stack in the detective office. Although stack was an understatement. They had only found Tom's and Lauren's bodies on Friday, with the two investigations running concurrently the number of statements that had been taken was colossal. There were a lot of bits of paper to collate.

Cathy started with the statements from the houses over-looking the park. It had been late on a cold January night so it was understandable that most people had their curtains firmly closed. And it was a residential area, so there was no commercial CCTV. Several of the houses had highly advanced security systems, being in one of Dublin's most sought after locations.

Thinking back to a house she'd been in recently, with its indoor swimming pool and marble floors, she could imagine what some of the interiors of the houses that overlooked the park looked like. The residents were highly security conscious but so far the team hadn't found a property where the cameras had an uninterrupted view of the road itself. Within their perimeters everything was state of the art, but none of the systems were monitoring traffic conditions.

Cathy looked at the house numbers recorded on the statements and glanced up at the huge map pinned to the incident board. *If Conor Quinn had visited Xavier Ayari on the Vico Road, the most logical route home to Sandycove would have been along Coliemore Road, driving right past Dillon's Park, even though he claimed to have gone through the village.*

She stood up, walking over to the board to look more closely at the map. If Conor Quinn had left the park, continued along Coliemore Road and driven down past Bulloch Harbour, he would have come out onto Ulverton Road a bit below where Tom was hit. Logically he'd have turned right to go home at that point. But what if he'd turned left and gone up towards Ronan Delaney's house for some reason? They were good friends – they worked and holidayed together, and Delaney knew Lauren O'Reilly.

Cathy wondered if Ronan Delaney knew Conor Quinn was having an affair with her. *What if Quinn had been heading to Delaney's house in the hope of establishing a better alibi but had remembered too late that he was at Orla's event?* Perhaps he'd done a U-turn, had been in even more of a mess mentally then, and had accelerated around the corner and hit Tom as he tried to cross the road?

That was an awful lot of *ifs*. Cathy shook her head and looked at the map again. They needed to check Quinn's phone records to see if he'd called Delaney that evening.

She put her finger on the map and traced the route from Dillon's Park to Convent Road. *Surely he would have wanted to avoid the village; any fool would know there were lots of CCTV between the pubs and the banks. So . . .* She ran her finger on. *If he'd turned left off Convent Road down Carysfort Road, which would be a more direct route home, his right turn onto Ulverton Road would have placed him in exactly the right location to hit Tom as he stepped off the footpath, according to Traffic's three-dimensional reconstruction.* They knew the vehicle had to be travelling down the road and had the point of impact mapped. *And* if he'd taken that route, he'd have just missed the CCTV cameras at the Topaz petrol station at the top of Ulverton Road. *But,* Cathy tapped the map with her finger, *the camera at Paddy Power at the junction of Coliemore and Convent Road should have picked him up.*

Maybe he'd got home, swapped cars and retraced the route through the village he claimed to have driven in the Z3, to try and strengthen his alibi? It was a possibility.

Cathy went back to the table and picked up her phone. They needed to look at the tape from the bookmakers before they spoke to Quinn again.

O'Rourke answered on the first ring. 'Why are you ringing me? I'm downstairs.'

'I know, but listen, I think Conor Quinn must have driven past Paddy Power's that night. If he was coming from Dillon's Park, he would have had to have done or we would have seen him on the CCTV from the Topaz garage. That route would have been his quickest way home and would have still brought him down Ulverton Road to hit Tom.'

As usual, O'Rourke didn't need her to draw him a picture. 'I'll get Traffic to check. They've already been looking at those tapes for Lauren walking up the road to see if she was followed. Good work, Cat.'

Cathy clicked off the phone and went back to the files. The CCTV was exactly what they needed – it would be irrefutable. The problem with witness statements was that they were notoriously unreliable. People often remembered what they *thought* they had seen, not what they had actually seen.

She skim read the top one, taken at a house overlooking Dillon's Park. They'd had their curtains closed all evening. Turning to the next one, she saw a more detailed statement. Seventeen-year-old Michael Caffrey was supposed to be studying applied maths for his Leaving Cert, but had spent most of the evening either staring out of the window or on his phone. Cathy pursed her lips, reading further. Several cars had gone past, he said, but he didn't mention a jeep parking. There was no way that a seventeen-year-old boy would have missed the BMW Z3 that Quinn had claimed he'd been driving, if it had parked within his view. But the Z3 could have been a smokescreen if the jeep *had* hit Tom – perhaps he'd parked it further up the road?

Cathy read on – young Caffrey hadn't seen a lone female going into the park; the only person he could remember seeing was a woman with a fairly big dog. Marvellous. They knew for sure Lauren had been there but if he hadn't seen her, he could have easily missed Quinn entering the park as well. Helpful.

Cathy closed the file. The CCTV from the bookmakers should clinch it. She just hoped the cameras were pointing in the right direction. They'd already pieced together Lauren's route to Dillon's Park passing that point, but would the camera angle be wide enough to pick up a car across the road?

Downstairs, O'Rourke was on the phone. As Cathy rounded the end of the staircase he held up his hand.

'That's great. Send what you have as soon as possible.' He clicked the phone off and slipped it into the inside pocket of his jacket as he turned to speak to her. 'I've been on to London – they're checking their records. We really need to speak to the original investigating officers, which might take a day or so – they might not be working in the city any more.' He paused. 'Blackrock should have stills from Paddy Power's CCTV in about half an hour. They'll email them as soon as they have them. Let's grab lunch and then we can chat to Quinn again when we have all the facts.'

Chapter 41

Monday, 2 p.m.

After the morning session in the interview room they both needed some air and coffee as well as food, so they grabbed their coats and headed to the cafe nearest the station. It was grey and damp outside, one of those days where a sea mist made it feel like there was rain suspended in the air. The broad pavement in front of the station and the next-door courthouse made everything feel greyer. Cathy flipped the collar of her jacket up and huddled inside it. She hated January. For nearly a thousand years the first of February had been considered the first day of spring in Ireland. Cathy had always been convinced it was a psychological trick invented by the druids to stop people going mad, to give them hope that the darkness might end some time soon.

Inside the cafe it was roasting and the scent of food was mouth-watering. It was run by a Polish husband and wife and renowned locally for its fabulous soups and generous sandwiches. Which meant there was always a queue. Today the various people waiting at the counter were steadily unpeeling their layers as they warmed up. The floor to ceiling windows that overlooked the street corner had all steamed up and it felt incredibly cosy. A stark contrast to the clinical interview room they would be heading back into shortly.

A table for two became free at the back and O'Rourke nudged her.

'Go grab that table. What are you having?'

'Has to be a chicken salad, no dressing. Lots of salad.'

'And coffee?'

Cathy looked longingly at the coffee machine. 'A skinny latte, please.'

She made her way to the back of the cafe, nodding to Starsky and Hutch, who were sitting opposite each other nursing coffee and large chunks of cake. They grinned at her – they both looked far too big for the small table, bomber jackets slung around the backs of their chairs. The whole station had been keenly following the events in this case. After notifying the Quinns in the first instance, Starsky had been popping in to the incident room regularly to follow developments. Not that there had been a huge number of those until now.

Cathy squeezed between the chair and the table and sat down facing the wall. O'Rourke always insisted on sitting with his back to the wall so he could see what was going on. It made her smile. If anything happened, she'd be about twenty times faster than him to react, but she wasn't going to bruise his ego by pointing that out.

She pulled out her phone and flicked through Instagram, not really looking at it. Sarah Jane had posted a picture of the ring at the Phoenix Gym and Cathy immediately felt nervous. Despite her swim and weight training this morning she was going to have to work really hard to catch up with the training time she knew she was going to lose this week. Fanning had put up a picture of a sleek yellow Maserati. Not much chance of him ever owning one of those unless he married into some serious money. She scrolled down the images, thinking about cars, about what Conor Quinn had told them this morning. Thinking about the map on the incident board.

Dillon's Park really was an isolated spot to meet someone at night and the trees completely blocked the far end of the park, where they'd found Lauren, from view. Quinn must know the park well to think of it as a place to meet. That thought jarred with her. He really didn't look the type to be taking long walks. Not when he had a choice of five cars to use.

But he had been just around the corner that evening, and there was a possibility that his car had hit Tom. Cathy flicked open her email. Traffic had sent through a copy of the video from Paddy Power's CCTV. She could see a second email with the stills attached. She felt her heartbeat quicken as she clicked on the first attachment to download it. She glanced over her shoulder; O'Rourke was just at the counter making his order. The girl taking it was stunning and was smiling at him like he'd just beamed down from Planet Hollywood, but she could tell by his body language he'd hardly noticed. He was as preoccupied with this case as she was.

A moment later the video opened on her phone. She hit play. It was grainy and dark. The camera angle took in the Corner Note coffee shop opposite the bookies where it straddled the junction of Coliemore and Convent Road. At 23:07 a blue BMW jeep swung around the corner, its headlights dazzling as the camera caught it head-on, and then, the road clear, it headed straight down Convent Road, staying in shot for another few seconds. She hoped if they kept looking they'd find a clearer shot of the registration plate, but there wasn't any question in her mind that it was Conor Quinn's.

O'Rourke materialised beside her with a glass of water and a cup of coffee in his hands.

'The video came through. It's definitely his jeep. Look.'

O'Rourke quickly slipped off his overcoat, slung it over the back of the chair and sat down, taking the phone.

'Here.' She leaned forward and swiped it to start the video playing. He looked at her witheringly.

'Do I look so old that I don't know how a phone works?'

'No, silly.' She shook her head despairingly. 'But my phone's different to yours. Just look at it, will you?'

A moment later he was nodding. 'Looks like his vehicle. We'll get them to keep looking for a shot that shows the reg plate.'

'I'm just not sure we'll be able to see him driving – the light's very bad.'

O'Rourke pulled his phone out from the inside pocket of his jacket. 'Let's see what they can do.'

As he spoke, at the nearby table, Starsky's phone rang. Cathy looked across – he scowled and indicated to Hutch that they needed to move. They both stood up and Cathy caught his eye.

'What's up?'

'Another yacht broken into at the marina.' Starsky shook his head. 'They've got the most sophisticated security system I've ever seen – their CCTV is as clear as Sky News and they've got a biometric entry system, but this is . . . what?' He glanced back at Hutch. 'The fifth yacht in the last month?'

'Yep, second this week. And a bunch of tools were stolen over the weekend as well.'

Starsky pulled his jacket off the back of the chair and, glancing around the restaurant to make sure no one could hear him, said, 'I was wondering if it's one of their own, someone who owns a boat down there and can just breeze in and out. Or maybe one of the local scrotes who's conned someone into registering their fingerprint on the system. If we can run their biometric data through AFIS we can see if anyone we know comes up.'

O'Rourke glanced up from Cathy's phone. 'It would be a good starting point if we had a match on our database. I'll organise a warrant, you talk to the marina manager?'

Starsky gave him a thumbs up. 'Will do, Cig, be nice to get this one tidied up. I get seasick just looking at a bloody boat.'

As Starsky and Hutch left, Cathy looked at the image again, replaying the video. She didn't know what it was but something was wrong with the whole picture. Quinn had claimed he was in the Z3. Why say that when there was CCTV all over the place? Why drive one of the most distinctive cars available to meet your girlfriend in a secluded spot? It rather defeated the object of being invisible.

She opened her mouth to speak just as the waitress arrived with their food. O'Rourke had ordered a club sandwich that looked like it would feed about three people. She smiled as he picked it up; she often wondered if he ate properly at home. Not that he was ever at home, of course.

Picking up her fork, Cathy ran the video again.

And the pieces began to fall into place.

She wasn't sure how her brain worked but when it did, it was like the domino effect. As soon as she got the first bit right everything else just followed suit. And she was sure she'd got it right this time.

Quinn had taken the call from Lauren at home.

That's what had started this. He'd said himself he'd had to raise his voice to get her to calm down. Then he'd left the house. What if someone had heard him? If he hadn't taken the phone with him, had someone found it, someone angered by the fact he was talking to his girlfriend? Had Tom sent the texts or . . . a woman walking a dog. The one thing their witness from across the road *had* seen. Anyone who regularly walked a dog would be very familiar with Dillon's Park. And the Quinns had a dog. A big golden retriever.

Orla had been out that night, so that left one other person.

'It was Mira. It had to be.'

O'Rourke looked up from his sandwich, confusion written all over his face.

'What had to be?'

'Mira overheard Conor on the phone. He left the phone in the house when he went to Xavier Ayari's. She must have found it and sent the texts.' Cathy looked at him, her salad forgotten. '*That's* why there was no follow-up call to Lauren's phone. Lauren assumed Conor was sending the texts so she followed them to the letter. But he said he needed time to process what Lauren had told him. He went off to his meeting and I bet he did go up to the Vico afterwards to try and work out the mess Lauren had presented him with. He was terrified someone would expose their affair and he'd lose everything.' She hesitated. 'Maybe he was looking to Xavier Ayari for investment because he was thinking about leaving Orla but couldn't afford to. This is a man who likes his comforts.'

O'Rourke looked at her, astounded, the sandwich poised between the plate and his mouth. Before he could say anything, she continued.

'She took the dog with her. Mira knew Quinn used the jeep as his second car, the keys would have been in the house. She took the jeep and the dog so if anyone saw her going into the park it looked completely natural.' Cathy shook her head. 'I can't believe I didn't see it before.'

O'Rourke took a bite of his sandwich and chewed thoughtfully. Her fork still poised above her salad, Cathy waited for his response. A moment later it came.

'This is why you are amazing, Cat Connolly – because you just get it. Eat that salad and we'll get Conor Quinn back in the interview room.'

Chapter 42

The interview room was exactly as they had left it, but after the bracing air outside it felt comfortably warm. 'Bracing' had been O'Rourke's phrase as he'd urged her to get a move on. Fecking freezing was closer to the mark.

Quinn looked paler and more drawn than he had done during their first session. As Cathy sat opposite him she could see how Lauren O'Reilly had been swept off her feet, how she'd lapped up his attention, how she'd slipped so easily into his bed. He had looks, power, money. Everything she didn't have. The villa near Nice. That was something the cows on her family farm down in Longford didn't see very often. Christ, he was the lowest form of life in Cathy's mind. She could understand why relationships didn't work, that people had affairs – she saw it every day in this job – but getting Lauren into the radio station so he could get to know her, giving her the impression he was going to leave his wife? That wasn't a good place to be.

But perhaps Conor Quinn would prove her suspicions wrong.

Whatever her personal feelings were, this job was about being impartial, in finding the truth, no matter how unsavoury that might be. And unfortunately it usually was.

Quinn shifted in the chair in front of them and cleared his throat.

O'Rourke repeated the statutory requirements for the recording. Sometimes Cathy felt like it sounded like that safety message you got every time you boarded an aircraft: 'You will find the emergency exits on the left and on the right.' But there was no emergency exit for Quinn and the preliminaries meant that the tape stood up in law. There was no room for a mistake that the defence counsel could take and wave about the court room. They'd all seen cases where the guilty got off on a technicality generated by sloppiness. O'Rourke didn't do sloppy. It just wasn't his thing. But he didn't arse about either. His first question got straight to the heart of it.

'Tell me about your housekeeper, Conor.'

Quinn had looked like he was about to say that his solicitor had told him to keep quiet, but he hadn't been expecting that question. He looked utterly perplexed.

'Mira?'

'Indeed – when did she join your household?'

'Christ, I can't remember, she started as Tom's nanny. She's from Sarajevo, she was there during the siege. It was very tough. She lost half her family in the war.'

'But she came to Ireland?'

'Yes, she escaped with her brother. She had to leave her parents behind and he was shot somewhere on the border. She spent the night hiding under a hedge in the snow and then managed to get across. She doesn't like talking about it. I can't imagine it was pleasant.'

'How did she end up here?'

Quinn's brow furrowed. 'She had an aunt here – her English was good so she was able to talk to the authorities. She was under eighteen and a refugee. The Red Cross were able to make contact with her aunt and she's been here ever since.'

'And she came to work for you?'

'Yes, Orla found her, she'd done well in school. She was looking for a job so she could work through college. She was exactly what we needed. She'd come from a big family – she was the oldest girl – so she was well able to look after Tom.'

'And her role grew?'

'Yes, I suppose so. She's very organised and reliable, she looks after the whole household now.'

'So take us back to Thursday night. Where was Mira when you arrived home?'

Quinn flushed. Only slightly, but Cathy spotted it. She nudged O'Rourke gently with her knee under the table.

It took a moment for Quinn to answer. 'I think she was in the kitchen.'

It was so obviously a total barefaced lie that Cathy almost laughed. And she could tell from O'Rourke's reaction that he thought so too. Whether it was the way Quinn said it so matter-of-factly, or the total change in his tone coupled with the rub of his nose, she wasn't sure. But one thing she was quite sure of was that Mira hadn't been in the kitchen. As Cathy watched him she remembered Fanning's reaction to Mira. She was a very attractive lady.

'Will we try that one again?' O'Rourke frowned. 'Were you in a relationship with Mira as well?'

Phew! Cathy hadn't expected him to go in that fast. But Quinn blushed bright red.

'No, of course not.'

'She's young, she lives in your house. Your wife's out a lot . . . It must have been tempting . . .' O'Rourke's tone changed. 'It really would be a good idea for you to be frank with us, Conor. You're looking at a murder charge as well as a manslaughter charge for the death of your son at the moment . . .'

Quinn went white. 'But I didn't kill anyone, you have to believe me, I never even saw Lauren that night. And Tom? How can you think I killed Tom?'

'But someone met Lauren that night, Conor, someone who had access to your phone. And the only other person in your house at the time you took that call was Mira, so please answer my question truthfully. Are you now or have you ever been in a relationship with your housekeeper, Mira?'

Quinn licked his lips and shifted in the chair. 'Look. OK, we have a thing. She wanted me to leave Orla, set up with her. I couldn't do that financially, and Tom was too young . . .'

'So you strung her along a bit, made a few promises about the future?'

'*No!*' His reaction was sudden, but then he calmed down. 'Well . . . maybe.'

Cathy cut in. 'So Mira, who had survived escaping from Bosnia during the war, seeing her brother shot, who had arrived in Ireland with nothing, who has built a life here, was pinning her hopes on a future with you?'

Quinn had the decency to look uncomfortable. 'Maybe.'

'And did she know about Lauren, Conor?'

Cathy was starting to see the bigger picture now. The hopes dashed, the burning pain of betrayal, the blind anger. No one Cathy knew who had served with the UN in Bosnia after the war had come back quite the same; it had scarred them all. She could only imagine the effect it had had on a young teenager.

And Cathy understood post-traumatic stress disorder like no one else, understood the see-sawing emotions.

Surviving the siege in Sarajevo would have hardened Mira to death. It was a different world with a value system that was about survival. And if Mira had seen Lauren as a challenge to her survival, how might she have reacted?

'No, of course she didn't know about Lauren, I wouldn't have done that to her.'

Cathy wanted to ask if he loved either of them, but now wasn't the time. She quite wanted to send him across the floor with a right hook too, but she knew O'Rourke might have something to say about that. She drew in a deep breath, focusing on calming her own anger.

'So let me ask you again: where was Mira when you arrived home?' O'Rourke was using his patient tone. It usually meant he was really mad.

Quinn had obviously forgotten his solicitor's advice to keep quiet. 'She was waiting for me. Everyone was out, that doesn't happen very often.'

Cathy arched an eyebrow. What he was leaving unsaid was painting a very clear picture.

'Is it possible that she overheard your conversation with Lauren? You told us that you told Lauren that you loved her. Is it possible that Mira overheard that?' O'Rourke sounded like he was speaking to a child.

Quinn looked like he was about to vomit. It was a pretty much instantaneous reaction. Cathy mentally shook her head; *he was some prat.*

'Err, she . . . She was in the bedroom. I had a shower, but she'd gone downstairs to get coffee when the phone rang. I was tired, I had a meeting . . . She . . . I . . .' He stumbled. 'I thought she was downstairs. I told Lauren never to ring, the stupid little bitch. I told her.'

'I don't really think it's Lauren's fault that your conversation was overheard by your other girlfriend, do you?' O'Rourke's tone was sharp. 'So tell me what happened after the call ended.'

Quinn shook his head. 'I finished getting dressed. Mira didn't come up with the coffee, so I went downstairs. She was in the kitchen.'

'Did she say anything to you?'

Cathy could only imagine what was going through Mira's head; he was lucky she hadn't thrown the coffee at him. But maybe that would have been a better outcome. Cathy had a feeling Quinn wasn't quite giving them all the detail on the call with Lauren. What had he said to her? *It'll all be fine, darling, you know I'll always look after you.* She could almost hear the words coming out of his mouth. How many years had Mira been patiently waiting for him, running the household, living in the same house as his wife? When they entertained she was the one who made it all happen; when Tom needed picking up from school, she was the one who did it. And she was the one who was in love with Conor Quinn.

Cathy couldn't imagine what her mental state was like after escaping a war zone and then finding herself in this situation. Thinking it was all fine, and that night, looking forward, no doubt, to Quinn coming back from New York, realising they'd have some time on their own, making love to him in his wife's bed, only to have all her dreams shattered by one overheard phone call.

She could see how that could push someone over the edge.

Quinn looked confused, like he'd forgotten Cathy's question. She repeated it.

'Did she say anything to you when you saw her in the kitchen? How was she?'

'I don't think she said anything, I was rushing, I needed to get to the meeting. I wanted to get Xavier to invest so I could divorce Orla, she knew that, she knew it was an important meeting.'

'And where did you leave the phone, Conor? The one Lauren had called you on.'

'Upstairs. I hid it in the bedroom.'

Cathy pursed her lips. Mira knew that house inside out. If she'd found the phone before, perhaps she'd originally thought it was Orla's or an old one? Quinn probably had the sense to delete the messages off it as they came in. But once Mira had realised what it was for, and Quinn was out of the house, she'd come up with her own plan. Had she printed the note to make it look like Lauren committed suicide? She couldn't have known that Lauren was terrified of water, that jumping off a cliff was the last thing she'd do.

Cathy was sure the note was part of an elaborate hoax. A desperate attempt by the killer to hide their tracks. They'd know for sure as soon as they checked the printers in the Quinn house; each one had its own unique set of characteristics. And the envelope was being tested for DNA – someone had licked the flap. DNA results took ages to come through. They were still waiting to see if Lauren had been the person who sealed it – but now they had someone else to check, and if Cathy was right, it would be very hard evidence to try to explain away.

'And your cars, Conor – does Mira look after those?'

Quinn looked confused. 'Of course, she does all the insurance stuff and the tax, makes sure all our cars are serviced.'

'And the jeep?'

He sighed. 'Yes, yes, like I've already told you, I'd asked her to organise for the garage to collect it for a service, it was overdue. The garage is very efficient. Ronan – Ronan Delaney – recommended them.'

'Did you mention the brake problem to her?'

Quinn took a moment to think. 'I don't think so. It's one of those intermittent things. I reckoned the garage would pick it up in a service, it was probably low brake fluid or something.'

'And did Mira ever drive your cars?' O'Rourke made the question sound offhand.

'Yes.' He drew out the word, realising its implications. 'She has one of her own but she used the jeep more often, for the shopping and taking the dog out.' He hesitated. 'And one of the reasons I went up to the Vico was because she called. She said to hold off coming back for about fifteen minutes because she had a surprise for me. I lost track of the time . . . When I finally got home Orla had arrived, so I assumed the surprise would wait. Then the next morning we got the news about Tom.' He put his head in his hands. 'Was it her? Was she driving the jeep? She met Lauren and pushed her off the cliff? Oh my God, the stupid, stupid bitch.'

Cathy did a mental double take. Quinn seemed to be missing the fact that he was the catalyst for all this. *What sort of an arrogant bastard was he?*

'It appears that Lauren's death might not have been the only incident Mira was involved in that night.' O'Rourke spoke slowly, taking his time. 'As we explained, the paint chips we've recovered from the scene of Tom's accident are metallic blue.'

Quinn looked at them aghast, his mouth open. He tried to speak but nothing came out.

'There's apparently no damage to the headlight casing on your jeep consistent with the glass fragment we've found, but there are scratches to the paintwork. We believe whoever hit Tom knocked him down, and then reversed to run over his body as he lay on the ground. That initial impact might not have caused huge damage to a vehicle as solid as your jeep. Our forensics team are looking at it now.'

Finally, Quinn found his voice, but it was little more than a whisper. 'You think she hit Tom?'

O'Rourke's tone was matter-of-fact. 'We think there's a strong possibility that she'd just pushed Lauren O'Reilly off a cliff, and it's fair to say that she might not have been in a clear state of mind when she was driving home. Perhaps Tom witnessed something and she couldn't risk him telling someone. We don't know at this stage. What we do know is that the timing and initial forensics suggest that we need to consider it a strong possibility.'

Conor Quinn shook his head slowly from side to side, his eyes unfocused. 'The stupid, stupid bitch.'

Chapter 43

'We've done it.' *Karim's voice was low on the phone. He strained to hear him over the sounds of the traffic outside. It was only four o'clock in the afternoon but the Dublin traffic was already starting to snarl. His phone pressed to his ear, he pushed through the apartment building's sleek rotating glass door and headed for the lift. He was so excited by Karim's news that he'd already pushed the lift call button before he realised he'd lose the phone signal inside. Instead he strode to the far end of the glazed lobby and sat down on a leather chair overlooking a pond trapped outside between the angles of the building. Huge orange carp swam like sharks just below the surface. He pushed away the fronds of a potted palm as he leaned forward, listening intently to Karim.*

'Start at the beginning . . .' *He cut across him, couldn't help the smile slipping onto his face. He was sure Karim could hear that same smile in his voice. But then Karim was his best friend, like a brother.*

Better than a brother.

'We're in, we have full access. That little piece of code worked like a dream.' *He could hear the suppressed excitement in Karim's voice.*

'I know, I developed it, obviously it's awesome.'

At the other end Karim laughed, his voice echoing slightly. He sounded like he was in one of the empty offices he and his compatriots used. Unanimous, soon to be the world's most notorious hackers. He couldn't hear any other sounds in the background, guessed Karim was on his own. He'd probably sent everyone home to get rested well in advance. The type of disruption he was planning would require accurate timing and total concentration.

They'd discussed it, strategising, looking at every scenario. A core team would deliver the final plan that would work like a domino effect in different branches of the rail network, all creating maximum chaos. The rest of the team would already be out of the country, monitoring progress remotely. They would pick trains that were heading into stations where the speed was reduced – this wasn't about casualties, it was about orchestrating a crash where it would cause the biggest problem and block up the network. The emergency services would be responding to one incident as another occurred on the other side of the city. It was like poetry. One team could deliver each blow and the chaos would grow. He felt a thrill deep down, but this was a different thrill from the one he got with the webcams. That was about total control. This was about world domination.

He could feel his smile taking over. His teeth clamped together, he sucked in, trying to stifle the need to laugh. This was his moment. His and Karim's. They'd waited a long time, but now it had arrived. Everything was coming together.

His voice low, he spoke into the phone. 'So what's the plan?'

'We need to move fast now – we might not have much time before it's spotted. We're going for Thursday evening, rush hour.'

'That's only three days away.'

'I know, but moving fast has worked before. We're the dream team.'

Karim chuckled and he knew exactly what he was talking about. It felt like years ago now, when they'd first met – Karim had come to stay as part of his school's language exchange programme. They'd become inseparable, hanging out in the park in the evenings with the rest of the year group.

It had been the final goodbye party when it had all happened – more accurately, the hours after it when everyone had gone home and it had just been them and the girl . . . they'd all got a bit carried away. Well, maybe he had got a lot more carried away. It had all been going great until he'd tried to lift her skirt, to get between her legs.

But Karim was a fast thinker and the bracelet he'd bought to take home for his sister had been a stroke of sheer genius. A slim gold-coloured chain with a gold disc charm dangling from it, the Eiffel Tower stamped on it. There were hundreds, probably thousands of them in Paris, impossible to trace. But it had done its job. Everyone had thought she was meeting some secret boyfriend who'd given it to her. They'd all been interviewed, but no one had seen anything. The whole investigation had focused on a missing stranger. A stranger who had left his fingerprints on the Eiffel Tower charm.

But they weren't his fingerprints, or Karim's. That was the best bit. That was the genius.

That night had sealed their friendship. But that was then; now they had business to do.

'So how did you manage it? How did you get my beautiful code into the mainframe?'

'On a USB stick. So easy. We've been monitoring a couple of employee's computers for a few weeks, checking their searches. Just watching, you know, looking for leverage – got plenty of that – but in the end it was so simple . . .'

'Tell me.'

'So the guy we're watching is searching for a memory stick on Amazon. He was looking for one with a big memory but they must have been all too expensive – he searched for cheap ones but they didn't have the storage he needed. It was like giving candy to a baby. One of our guys gets on the tube with him and follows him. He goes to this coffee stand every morning on the way to work, takes milk and sugar. While he's ordering the coffee, our guy's over by the sugar and stuff. The minute he's heading over, our man leaves a memory stick behind. The dude comes over, sees it, slips it in his pocket. Bingo.'

He laughed out loud. Human nature was a wonderful thing. 'So he sticks it into his laptop?'

'Better – he goes to work and sticks it straight into one of their computers to see if there's anything on it. Sweet.'

He shook his head. 'Unbelievable.'

'So it's all good but I need you here, man, will you come?'

He almost laughed. He'd been hesitant about going over before, everything he needed to do could be done remotely, but Karim wanted him there, wanted them to be together when it went down. And now the timing was perfect. Absolutely perfect. He knew exactly where he needed to be, to literally kill two birds with one stone.

He thought fast. The chaos couldn't be a better cover. It wasn't his preferred location but he didn't have much time left to make this happen and he could be adaptable. He'd thought that it would have to happen around the university somewhere; he'd been looking at the architectural drawings to understand every nook and crevice.

How fucking sweet was this, though? Everything was coming together. This was totally his payday for the other fuck-up.

'One proviso.'

'What, man? Tell me.'

'We do it from inside a station. Then we can see what's happening in real time. And I've got another little bit of business to take care of.'

Karim didn't speak for a moment. 'OK.' He drew the word out, obviously thinking about it. 'Nobody's going to be looking at two students on laptops. We'll be hiding in plain sight. I like it.'

'So it's a deal?'

'Deal.'

'I'll book a flight now.'

'Let me know your movements, dude.' He could hear the relief and excitement in Karim's voice as he continued. 'This is going to be the biggest cyberattack Britain's ever seen. Never mind the NHS, those twats fucked up big time not registering the site for their kill switch. We've got everything worked out.'

He clicked off the phone, shaking his head. It was pure poetry.

Chapter 44

Tuesday, 8 a.m.

Totally absorbed in her own world, Cathy didn't look at who else was hanging about in the lobby of the station as she headed in the next morning. They were bringing in Mira today; they had a full day of interviews ahead of them. She was making straight for the internal door, her kitbag thrown over her shoulder, when the desk sergeant stuck his head out of the hatch.

'Cat, you got a minute?'

Her hand on the keypad, she turned to look at him, still not completely tuned in.

'What's up?'

'You've got a visitor.'

The desk sergeant indicated the pine bench on the opposite side of the tiled lobby. She turned just as Ronan Delaney stood up. His mobile phone and a bunch of car keys were in one hand, he had the other deep inside his jeans pocket. He was wearing a pale blue shirt and navy V-neck sweater, a thick leather jacket looped over his arm. He looked decidedly uncomfortable.

'Detective Connolly? I was wondering if I could have a chat. About the night Tom died. I think I have some information for you.'

Interview Room 4 was exactly as she had left it yesterday, only this time she had Frank Gallagher beside her instead of O'Rourke. The moment Delaney had spoken, her brain had kicked into gear and she'd called up to O'Rourke's office, his line diverting to Frank's desk. O'Rourke been called to a meeting in the Phoenix Park, and had told Frank he'd be back by ten to bring Mira in for questioning. They needed to get as much forensic evidence together as they could first, and Conor Quinn had made it very clear the night before that he never wanted to see Mira again. He was going to spend the night in the city so there was little danger that he'd tip her off. As soon as he heard she was out of his house, he planned to go back. Cathy wasn't sure what Orla would make of all that, but if she'd had any suspicions that he was having a relationship with the housekeeper at any stage, she probably didn't care whether he came home or not. She certainly wasn't a lady Cathy would want to mess with. She was warm and courteous, but right from their first meeting Cathy had sensed a steel edge, her focus on finding whoever had killed her son like a laser beam. The type you used to guide missiles. She hadn't been pushy but she'd been in constant contact with O'Rourke, looking for progress reports. Which was probably why she was so successful in business; you didn't get to where she was without dogged determination and creating your own opportunities. Orla Quinn was used to getting results.

In the interview room, Ronan Delaney looked distinctly uncomfortable. Gallagher loaded the discs into the grey steel tower unit on the wall and waited for the buzz to indicate everything was working.

'Present: Detective Sergeant Frank Gallagher and Detective Garda Cathy Connolly. Can you state your full name, please?'

'Ronan Patrick Delaney.'

On the other side of the small table, Delaney kept his eyes on his phone, lying idle beside a cardboard cup full of steaming coffee. He wasn't under arrest and Cathy had needed a few minutes to gather her thoughts so she'd got coffee for everyone. She needed it as much as Delaney looked like he did. He was decidedly pale. Cathy could see a hint of the movie star looks he was known for, but this morning his face was puffy. Perhaps it was working late nights on the radio that did it, but he looked like he needed a decent night's sleep. She could relate to that. He picked up his coffee and took a sip.

'You are here voluntarily, but you understand that this interview is being recorded and anything you say will be taken down in writing and may be given in evidence.' Frank's voice was clipped. O'Rourke had brought him up to date last night.

'Yes, I understand.'

'So, Ronan, you've something to tell us about the incident involving Tom Quinn on Ulverton Road last Thursday night?'

Delaney closed his eyes tight, rubbed his hand over them, and then opened them again.

'I saw her. I saw Mira driving Conor's jeep. She turned down Sandycove Avenue in front of me at the lights.'

'You are absolutely certain it was Mira?'

'Absolutely. I was the only car at the junction, she turned right across me.'

'Have you any idea what time this was?'

'About 11.05, maybe 11.10? I wasn't thinking about the time to be honest. I'd just done Orla's charity gig in town and I wanted to get home, I was hosting the breakfast show early the next morning.'

'And why are you only telling us now?'

Delaney shook his head, and shrugged. 'I didn't think it was important. I didn't connect the events until now, until Conor called last night. He told me you were going to arrest her for Lauren's murder. Then I remembered and I realised the timing . . . You seemed to think I'd hit Tom when you came to the radio station, that's all I could think about.'

Saving his own skin, that would be about right.

Cathy had a hard edge to her voice when she spoke. 'When you spoke with myself and Detective Inspector O'Rourke, we established that you drove past the scene within a few minutes of it happening but you claimed you didn't see Tom lying on the pavement.'

Cathy knew she had to be beyond professional in the interview room but she didn't like Ronan Delaney – hadn't from the moment she'd met him. He was far too full of his own importance for her liking. He talked shite on the radio for a living and somehow that made him better than other people? Cathy wasn't seeing it. It made him a prat in her book. She was starting to see why he and Conor Quinn were such good friends. They were quite a pair.

Cathy knew she wasn't alone in her opinion either. From what she'd seen of his behaviour with his wife, Ronan was a control freak who used subtle emotional abuse to grind her down. Cathy didn't have time for men like that. Unless they were confident enough to get into the ring with her – then she had all the time in the world.

Thankfully Karen Delaney was strong. She had her business and her own life, and she also knew she needed to move on, she just hadn't worked out how yet. Maybe this was the push she needed. Cathy really wasn't completely sure if Karen would be able to keep her affair with Tom a secret if the case came to court. If she was called to the stand she'd have to explain that he had popped in at 8 p.m. and why he was only popping out again at 11 p.m. Cathy could imagine the press speculation, the tabloid headlines.

But now here was Ronan Delaney with a crucial piece of information that he'd managed to forget until this point. Cathy's mind darted about as she evaluated the man in front of her. Either he was telling them he'd seen Mira because Conor Quinn had called him and explained that he could be in the frame for murder unless the Gardaí received evidence to the contrary – *or* he had genuinely seen Mira and not realised the significance. Cathy bit her lip. There was one way of knowing for sure, but she wasn't ready to ask that question quite yet.

'The last time we met,' Cathy kept her smile friendly, 'you told us that you hadn't seen Tom lying dying a few hundred yards from your house. Have you reconsidered that statement?'

Delaney had the decency to grimace, sucked in a breath between clenched teeth.

'I didn't know it was him. Really, I had no idea.' Cathy didn't respond. She just looked at him like he was the lowest form of life. He got the message as he stumbled on. 'You have to believe me. I was tired, it was dark, I was desperate to get home and I see this homeless drunk lying on the pavement—'

Cathy cut across him. 'You didn't think of calling us, or maybe an ambulance? I mean, it's January. It's an absolutely freezing night. There's this thing called hypothermia. If he hadn't been hit by a car he'd likely have been dead by the morning. As it was, he was barely alive when the ambulance crew got to him. A timelier intervention could have saved him.'

Delaney put his head in his hands. 'Look – I know. Don't you think that hasn't haunted me every single night since? He was a lovely lad – he was one of my best friend's kids. Conor's devastated. Orla's lashing out at everyone. And they can't even have a funeral yet because you lot haven't released his body.'

Oh, so it's our fault now, is it? Tom's family couldn't complete the grieving process because his death was under investigation. Delaney had totally missed the part where he could have saved Tom's life, where calling an ambulance might have made everything turn out very differently.

'So tell us how long you've known Mira Mandić.'

'Years. Conor and I were at school together. I've known her as long as she's worked for them.'

'And you are aware of her background?' Cathy straightened the manila file in front of her.

Delaney nodded. 'She doesn't talk much about it, never has done. I don't suppose it's any of our business really, but I know she lost her little brother in Sarajevo. That's why she was so good with Tom growing up. The Quinns became her family, she really loved him like her own.'

'And how did she get on with the rest of the family?'

Delaney glanced at her nervously and licked his lips. 'Well, she and Conor are very close.'

'As in having an affair? A long-term affair?' Cathy raised her eyebrows in question.

'Err, did he tell you that?'

'It doesn't matter what he told us, Ronan, I'm asking you.'

'Well, yes.'

'How long?'

Delaney shook his head and shrugged again. 'I'm not sure – years.'

'Did he give her the impression that he'd leave his wife for her? That they'd set up home together?' Cathy's voice was flat. She wasn't impressed with anything she was hearing.

'He might have done. I don't really know – I wasn't privy to their pillow talk.' His tone dripped sarcasm.

Like hell he didn't know. His best friend is having an affair with the housekeeper and he doesn't mention it. *Bastard.* Did Orla know? Cathy hoped not. Finding out now could push her right over the edge.

Cathy was liking him even less – if that was possible – but his description of their relationship confirmed in her mind how utterly devastating that overheard phone call must have been for Mira. Conor Quinn was all she had. She'd spent years virtually bringing up his son, waiting for the time when he'd be ready to leave, and then she'd discovered he was cheating on her. And whatever had happened on that cliff path, she wasn't in the mental state to be driving safely anywhere, let alone down a road infamous for its steep blind bend. Had she hit Tom on the way back and not realised?

'Did you speak to Conor Quinn that night?'

Delaney shook his head. 'No, the next day – he needed me and Karen to go to a sponsors' dinner instead of him and Orla. He said he'd had a meeting with Xavier Ayari but he was too upset to give me the details then. I spoke to him about the meeting the day after. He was looking for an investor to take over from Orla so he could divorce her. Life Talk FM is hers, all the businesses are hers. He's got a small shareholding, and he persuaded her to bring me in, we've got forty-nine per cent between us. Karen, my wife, has five per cent. Orla gave her that when the company first started before she brought Conor in to run it – she couldn't start it as a limited company without two directors then. Karen was just a name on a piece of paper, she was happy to do it. She wasn't involved and with only five per cent she has no say.'

'And Orla didn't want her husband to be a director when she started the company?'

Delaney shrugged. 'Obviously not at that stage.'

'So if the three of you got together, you could vote against her if she didn't agree with Xavier Ayari coming in.'

'That's about it.'

Cathy was fairly sure he'd seriously underestimated his wife. Karen Delaney knew her own mind. Would she vote against her friend, a friend who had trusted her enough to put her name down as a director of her company, no matter how small the shareholding might be?

'So take us back to that Thursday night. You drove home from the Intercontinental in Ballsbridge and you approached the traffic lights in Sandycove, and then what happens?'

'I'm sitting there waiting for the lights to change and I see this jeep coming down the road fairly fast.'

'Fairly?'

'Well, maybe pretty quick.'

'And?'

'Well, the lighting's pretty good around that junction. I knew it was Conor's jeep. I could see the reg plate, so I'm thinking it's him, so I'm getting ready to flash my headlights at him to say hello and I realise it's not him driving.' Delaney suddenly dried up.

'Was there any damage to the vehicle?'

Delaney shrugged. 'I don't remember, I was looking at the driver, wondering who it was.' He shook his head, half to himself. 'Conor's tall, when he's sitting behind the wheel he fills the space. I could see whoever was driving was much smaller. And then as she swings around the corner I can see straight into the car. It was Mira. She was focused, hunched over the wheel, but I knew it was her, no doubt. She had the dog in the back.'

Chapter 45

Cathy was supposed to be working lates for the next two days – four in the afternoon until two in the morning – but she wasn't about to let someone else interview Mira. And they couldn't wait until she clocked in at four; she needed to get it done now. Fortunately, O'Rourke had agreed with her. The current shift system meant the station was covered 24–7 but that created issues with continuity across a complex investigation like this. They worked six days on, in ten hour shifts, a mix of earlies, lates and nights, followed by four days off. But those four days sometimes meant handing over to a new team, which wasn't good for anyone.

Sitting on the windowsill of O'Rourke's office, Cathy looked up as Sean O'Shea stuck his head around the door.

'Car's downstairs. I'll be down in five.'

'Thanks, Starsky.' O'Rourke pushed the drawer of his filing cabinet closed and turned to look at her. 'You happy taking Fanning?'

Cathy threw him a smug grin. 'He's perfect for this one. And Starsky isn't exactly invisible. Think of it as a charm offensive. We haven't got grounds to arrest her until we get the results from forensics, so she has to come in voluntarily. A false sense of security might make her overconfident. Let's hope so.'

Cathy was crossing the office as he turned back to his laptop.

'Hang on a sec, the detective in that case in London has emailed. He wants to meet.' O'Rourke stopped speaking for a moment, reading his email. She could almost see the cogs turning in his head. 'He wants us to talk him through what we've got, show us what they've got.'

'Can he come here? We're in the middle of a murder investigation.'

'So is he apparently. But he can get everyone together in London on Thursday evening.'

She grimaced. 'I'm rostered to rest on Thursday.'

O'Rourke glanced up at her. 'My overtime budget is going to be shot to pieces with this case.' He clicked his tongue on the roof of his mouth. 'Skype just isn't the same as a face to face though, we can't see the files and maps and have a proper conversation. We could miss something.' He paused. 'If we went late afternoon we could get a flight back later in the evening. It's only an hour or so. You haven't got a break in the Canaries planned, I hope?'

Cathy shook her head. 'No such luck. Just lots of training.'

He half-smiled and scanned the email again. 'They've got DNA from one of their victims, she scratched her attacker.'

That could be a clincher. But before Cathy could comment, his words sank in properly. She felt her heart rate quicken, a blush rising.

'We?'

He didn't look up. 'It'll be good experience.'

He had a point and she wasn't about to turn down a trip to London. Even a short one. He didn't give her time to speak as he continued.

'We'll get flights into London City Airport, there's one at 15.30 gets in at 17.00. We can meet him at New Scotland Yard . . .'

The door suddenly moved under her hand and Cathy took a hurried step back as Sean O'Shea stuck his head in again.

'Sorry, didn't realise you were right there. I'm good to go when you are.'

'With you right now.'

She didn't dare look back in case O'Rourke saw her blush.

'Please state your full name for the tape.'

O'Rourke had his jacket back on, the sleeves slightly pulled up. He glanced at his watch as Mira answered, the casing even more battered now than it had been when Cathy had first met him all those years ago in Pearse Street.

'Mira Mandić.'

Cathy glanced across at the Quinns' housekeeper. Dressed in an obviously expensive red silk top and navy trousers, her blonde bobbed hair pulled back in a low ponytail, she looked less like a housekeeper than anyone Cathy had ever seen. She'd noticed it before, but Mira had an inner confidence about her. It was possible that came from having had a long-term affair with her boss, of course. That said, she looked tired. Cathy could see she had dark rings under her eyes, well hidden by make-up, but definitely there. But then you couldn't really expect to go around killing people and still sleep, could you?

'Mira, can you tell us your movements on the night Tom Quinn was killed, please, starting at perhaps six that evening?' O'Rourke sat with his pen poised above his pad.

'Of course. I don't know the exact times. But Tom was home from college early in the evening. He went out again just before

Conor came home, said he needed a walk. He was hoping to see him – his dad, I mean – but Conor's plane was delayed.'

'Did he call you from the airport to say he was on his way?'

'Yes, he always called.' Mira's voice was clear and confident.

'And what did you say to him when he called?'

'I told him everyone was out. He'd forgotten that Orla had her charity event on. He said he had to go out to a meeting a bit later – he'd rescheduled it from earlier in the day.'

'Did he expect you to have dinner ready for him?'

'He said he'd eaten on the plane. That he was fine.'

O'Rourke cleared his throat. 'So Tom went out for his walk, and Conor arrives back from the airport, and then what?'

Mira shrugged. 'Conor had a shower, then he went out for his meeting.'

'Then what did you do?'

'I took the dog for a walk.'

'Do you normally take him for walks in the middle of the night in January? Wasn't it freezing?' Cathy tried to keep the disbelief out of her voice.

'I like walking at night. I don't sleep very well; I find a walk helps. The dog's used to it, he's got a thick coat.'

'Do you know that there are CCTV cameras all over Dalkey, Mira? Not just on the banks, they cover the whole village.'

Mira didn't flinch, just shrugged like it wasn't a thing that was relevant. 'I didn't go through the village.'

O'Rourke kept his eyes on his notepad. 'There's a camera on the bookmakers too. Paddy Power's. The corner of Coliemore and Convent Road. Do you know it? There was a bad fire next door a few years ago.'

A glimmer of recognition crossed Mira's face. She shrugged again, like she didn't see why it should concern her.

'For the tape please.'

'Of course I know it, Inspector. Everyone in the village knows that corner.'

O'Rourke flicked her a smile. 'Great, we'll come back to that later. So where did you take the dog?'

'Up Coliemore Road to Coliemore Harbour. We usually walk that way.'

Cathy looked at her hard. She was one cool lady. She had this all worked out. O'Rourke was obviously holding back Ronan Delaney's statement about seeing her in the jeep. But she'd taken the dog. If someone had seen her on the way to the park, she had a reason for being there, had a reason for being out at that time of night.

'And did you see anyone else on your walk?'

Mira shook her head. 'I didn't see anyone. It was late. Cold. The Irish don't like the cold. I'm used to it. You don't know what cold is here.'

'You're sure you didn't see Lauren O'Reilly on the way?'

Mira shrugged. 'I don't know Lauren O'Reilly. I didn't see anyone.'

'So let's just roll back to earlier in the evening. I believe Conor took a telephone call when he got home?'

Mira shrugged again. 'He might have done, I didn't hear. I needed to walk the dog. I needed to get out of the house.'

Well, wasn't that the truth?

The only bit Mira had missed out was the fact that she had been driving the jeep. Ronan Delaney's statement put her at the scene, and Traffic in Blackrock were trying to improve the image they had in the hope that they could see who was driving. You could never have too much corroboration.

While Cathy had been at the Quinns' this morning bringing Mira in, Thirsty had arrived to collect a sample of the dog's hair, as well as all the Quinns' computer printers, of which there were many, apparently. If Lauren's clothing had matching dog hair on it, and if the note in her pocket was printed in the Quinns' house, their case would be much stronger. If Mira's DNA was on the envelope flap, they had a case for murder.

As if O'Rourke could feel Cathy's tension increase beside him, he shifted in his chair, his knee touching hers.

'So, Mira, tell me about the damage to Conor's jeep. I believe you dropped it up to the garage for repairs early on Friday morning?'

'He'd asked me to take it in while he was in New York, but I wasn't able to. I had shopping to collect and then flowers and signs to deliver for Orla's charity event. The garage was too busy to collect it, so I took it in as soon as I could.'

'Did he mention what was wrong with it?'

She shook her head. 'He just said it needed servicing.'

'There were some scratches on the wing – do you know anything about that?'

'It's not my car.' She shrugged. 'I just had to drop it in.'

'Where was it the night Tom was killed?'

'In the garage, as far as I know.' She said it like it was a stupid question.

'What car was Conor driving that night?'

'He usually drives his Z3, but I didn't see him leave. He could have taken the jeep, I didn't see. They are both at the front of the garage.'

'Thank you, Mira. It's almost ten to five, I think we should take a small break. I'll organise a coffee for you.'

Again the shrug, like she didn't care, didn't know why she was there.

O'Rourke didn't speak until they got into his office. He marched in, firmly closing the door behind him.

'My God.' He shook his head and tossed his notepad onto the desk, standing in the middle of the office and crossing his arms. 'She's one cool customer, isn't she?' He rolled his neck, scowling. 'And she's giving herself room for movement in case anyone saw the jeep.'

Cathy stuck her hands in her combat pockets and went to lean on the windowsill, a frown on her face as she contemplated her boots.

'She clearly didn't think about the CCTV cameras that night.'

'She had a lot on her mind.'

'For sure. I'm not seeing how she could be linked to the other cases, though, in Paris and Long Island. If we're right about her overhearing the phone call, this is a crime of passion, not something carefully orchestrated by a serial killer.' Cathy screwed up her face, thinking about the characteristics of the crimes. 'I think there's something else going on here that Mira's blundered into the middle of.'

O'Rourke frowned. 'We've got forensics linking those cases with ours, so there has to be a connection somewhere. It could be that Tom's the fulcrum here – he knew Lauren, he travelled a lot. We need to check out where Mira was at the time of the other attacks, though. None of those women were raped, so we can't assume their attacker was a man.' He paused. 'And we need to compare her fingerprints to the drugs boxes in Lauren's room.'

'Let's hope Thirsty hits gold on some sort of solid forensic link between her and Lauren at the scene. At least we'll have a solution to one part of the puzzle. We can tear that house apart looking for Quinn's missing secret phone, but you know what? I reckon she threw it into the sea after Lauren. She had to take it with her in case Lauren texted for directions or got lost.' Cathy puffed out her cheeks, blowing out a sigh.

Still standing in the middle of the office, O'Rourke looked out of the window over her shoulder. His face was set. He was cross. It wasn't hard to tell. He shook his head.

'We can't lose this one. We need an evidential link or an infallible eyewitness to prove she actually met Lauren. Even if we can prove she was there, she can still claim Lauren jumped, but . . .'

Cathy shook her head. 'If that note was printed on one of the Quinns' printers and she licked it closed, it'll make it a lot harder for her to claim it was all an accident or a deliberate suicide attempt. Lauren couldn't have printed it herself – it had to come from Mira, and that means premeditation.' She pursed her lips. 'We need to ask her about the affair with Quinn.'

'She'll just confirm it, won't she?' He stopped himself. 'Sorry – what she'll actually do is shrug like we're idiots. She's nothing to hide. There's no crime in having an affair. Not one we'd be worried about anyway.' O'Rourke uncrossed his arms and came over to to stand beside her, leaning both hands on the sill so he could see out directly below him. 'Maybe they did it together? Maybe Conor Quinn and Mira killed Lauren and then hit Tom on the way home by accident.'

Cathy closed her eyes and ran her fingers into the roots of her hair, thinking hard.

'We need to think about Lauren and Tom separately. The Traffic guys are absolutely sure it wasn't an accident. It could only have been someone who knew where Tom was that night and when he would be leaving.'

'But how would they know that? Karen is sure no one knew about their affair.'

'Maybe whoever it was saw him go in, knew he worked there. That wasn't a secret. But they must have parked up, watching, to know when he left. I'm not seeing Mira or Conor having the time to push Lauren off the cliff – bearing in mind she was supposed to be meeting the texter at 10:30 – and then getting back in time to lie in wait for Tom.'

She stopped, biting her lip as she thought. There was something else . . . She knew she was getting close . . . Then it hit her.

'Orla said the event was live streamed – supposing there is someone who knew where Tom would be that night, and why. They'd know he needed to leave the Delaneys' house at the end of the event, that Ronan Delaney would be heading home then. It's, what, twenty minutes from Ballsbridge to Dalkey at that time of night? Karen said they weren't watching the live stream, but if someone else was, they'd have a window.'

'Lot of *if*s, but I see where you're coming from. The timing is very tight for Mira or Conor to be involved – you don't shove someone off a cliff and calmly get back in the car. More to the point, I think Quinn might have had a quiet word with Karen before that night if he knew his son was having an affair with his best friend's wife.'

'I think we need to check the CCTV again at both ends of Ulverton Road from *before* Tom texted his mum, from when the charity gig finished – before that even, from when it started. If the driver of a metallic blue BMW knew the camera locations, it's logical they'd avoid them after they'd hit Tom. But perhaps they weren't so careful when they arrived.'

O'Rourke was heading for his desk phone before Cathy had finished speaking. Watching him punch in Thirsty's extension, Cathy screwed up her face. There was something else.

'And let's see how Mira spells tired, will we? I can't spell "separately" – I get it wrong every time. If she sent those texts she might not have realised there was a typo.'

Chapter 46

'Hey, honey, how are you doing? I got your message. Sorry I couldn't call last night. You know what Mondays are like. By the time I got free it was stupid o'clock with you.'

Anna could feel her spirits lift as she heard Rob's voice. She'd left a voicemail on his office line yesterday, had been hoping he'd call back, but he must have been tied up. The time difference didn't really help. She glanced at the clock – it was six in the morning in New York. She smiled; she couldn't complain that he didn't always prioritise her. For a moment she wondered where he was. Perhaps he was at home, making coffee in the kitchen, preparing for an early start at the office, but it was *so* early. Maybe he'd come downstairs specially to talk to her, his wife still asleep in bed. She sighed inwardly. She'd give anything to see him; it had been months since she'd been home. Last time she'd been in New York they'd had lunch and then dinner the next day, and then cocktails at the Rose Club in the Plaza before she left, snuggled into a corner of the pink velour banquette, surrounded by purple and gold tasselled cushions and the sound of jazz. Part of her ached to be nearer to him.

'You should be asleep, Rob Power, not calling me at this time in the morning.' She tried to sound like she was scolding him but it wasn't very convincing.

She heard him chuckle. 'And how can I sleep if I'm worried about you all the way over there? What's happening?'

She felt her breath catch, fought to steady her voice. She didn't want to panic him.

'I . . .' She stumbled, let out a sigh. 'I thought there was some-one following me yesterday. It's happened a few times going home from work over the last few weeks, but this time the feel-ing was so strong. I really don't know if I'm overreacting or if I should be worried.'

There was a pause at the other end, like Rob was thinking. 'You know the drill, honey, take no risks. Better to assume there's a problem than to ignore it.'

'I know. I've been varying my routes, I always do, and the couple of times it happened before, I went into a supermarket, or doubled back and caught the DART back a few stops so I could change trains.' She paused, remembering the creepy feeling that there was someone in the carriage watching her. 'Yesterday I was heading into Brown Thomas, I just got this feeling . . . So I took a really circuitous route, but then as I was going up the escalators—' She stopped; she could feel herself getting emotional.

'Take it easy, honey, I'm listening.'

She started again. 'So there's this postgrad, Xavier Ayari. When I got that email about the conference, the one with the worm in it, the same day I got one from him asking if I'd speak to a group he's setting up. It's just . . .' It sounded so crazy when she said it out loud. 'It felt like a really weird way to ask. I mean, why email when he could just stop and ask me in the corridor? Too formal somehow. And he keeps appearing in the Arts block, he's doing sciences, and the science students rarely come over to this side of the college. So anyway . . . When I got to Brown Thomas yesterday, there he is coming up the escalator behind me.'

'What do you know about his background?'

'Really not much. He's an international student doing a post-doc, something to do with nanotechnology. Trinity are world leaders in that field, it's a really progressive department. His younger brother is here too, doing computer science. Xavier's French Tunisian, his family sponsored the new science block, it's called the Ayari Building.'

'That takes some amount of cash.'

'I know – I think his family are in oil or something. I don't know. I feel really bad because he could be completely innocent, it's just that he's dark and French and every time I see him . . .'

'I know, honey, that's not your fault. It's PTS, you know that.'

'Exactly, so I can't tell if I'm overreacting, if he just gives me the creeps because of . . . or if I should really be worried.'

'Have you spoken to the detective there about this?'

'No, not yet. I probably should do but I've got absolutely no evidence. I don't think the Gardaí take gut feelings and coincidences very seriously. And if they do, I could bring a ton of trouble down on a completely innocent man because of my own prejudices.'

Rob thought about this for a minute. 'How about I check him out? Do you think he could have anything to do with the stuff that's going on there, with your students?'

Anna ran her hand into her hair. 'I don't know. He would have known Tom for sure. His brother hung out with him.'

'So there's a connection. And if he's doing a PhD in nano-technology he's a bright guy, understanding the Web isn't going to be a challenge. Let me see what I can find out. You know we've got that link between your two students and some cold cases. There are a couple in London too.'

'It's a pretty big case, then?'

'Involving a very mobile perp. The question is, could this guy have been involved? If he's following you because he can't watch you online now, you need to be very careful.' He paused. 'He shouldn't be hard to check out, leave it with me. Someone is behind Merchant's Quay and Discovery Quay and Lauren O'Reilly seems to link both sites, between the emails she received and the drugs found in her room. It's entirely possible that someone in her social circle could be involved. Maybe your instincts aren't way off at all.'

'Were the drugs in Lauren's room bought from Merchant's Quay?'

'We've tracked the batch numbers back to a vendor who has a shop on Merchant's Quay so it's looking very likely. The information we have keeps interconnecting – I'm pretty sure we're heading in the right direction.' He paused. 'So are you looking forward to taking Hope to London?'

Anna smiled. 'Yes, I am. I can't wait. I need to get away and there's so much to show her, she's so excited.'

'And is she really looking at London for university?'

'I don't know yet, she's also keen on MIT but she wants to look around.'

He hesitated. 'Will you come home, when she leaves Ireland, I mean?'

It was the way he said it, like he was asking her. But before she could answer there was a knock on her door. Her 11.30 tutorial.

'Oh my, I've got to go.' She paused, then said quietly, 'I hope so, I've been away a long time.' The knock came again, louder this time.

'Whoever that is really wants you, you'd better go. I'll call as soon as I have information on this Ayari character – might be a few days so don't engage and keep safe, honey.'

'I will. And I'll check out flights home for Easter, Hope needs to see more of her grandmother.'

She hung up and, swinging around, realised she was still sitting on her coat. She picked it up and went to open the door. Paula Garcia was standing with her back to it, her long glossy hair tied back in a low ponytail, her full attention on her phone.

'Come in, Paula, sit down.'

Leaving the door open, she crossed the office to hang her coat up just as her phone pipped with a text. As Paula settled herself, Anna could see it was from Rob: *smiling* xxx

Chapter 47

Back in the interview room Mira Mandić looked relaxed, inspecting her neatly cut nails as they came back in. She had a cardboard cup of coffee in front of her and looked distinctly bored. She hadn't asked for a solicitor; she was obviously confident enough to continue on her own.

O'Rourke ran through the preliminaries for the tape again and glanced behind him to make sure the red light was showing on the video camera high up on the wall. As Cathy watched her, Mira's eyes followed his, taking everything in. Conor Quinn had said she'd been to college when she'd arrived in Ireland, had done well. Sitting across the table from them, Mira reminded Cathy of a cat, her eyes intelligent and watchful.

'Now you told us in the last session that you are originally from Sarajevo. How long have you worked for the Quinns, Mira?' O'Rourke straightened the page of notes in front of him as he spoke.

Mira shrugged. 'Since Tom was about five. Fourteen, fifteen years? I was nineteen when I started.'

Nineteen, very attractive and intelligent. Cathy was starting to see a pattern emerging here. O'Rourke was straight on to it too.

'And when did your affair with Conor Quinn start, Mira?'

If she was surprised they knew, she didn't show it. She shrugged again. 'About when I started working for them.'

Cathy kept quiet, her notebook open in front of her. O'Rourke had been right: Mira couldn't give a damn that they knew, but she wasn't giving away any more than she absolutely had to, either.

'And did Conor at any stage suggest that there was a future in your relationship?'

The shrug again. 'We talked about it, about if he could divorce Orla and how that could happen.'

Watching her, Cathy suddenly felt sure that Mira would have considered lots of ways that she might get rid of Orla. One of the things that had been worrying her about the text messages, about the whole way Lauren had been duped into going to Dillon's Park, about the note, was the speed at which the plan had been formed. But perhaps Mira had been walking through Dillon's Park for years, ruminating on a life with Conor Quinn, and thinking about ways to get Orla out of their lives? Perhaps the plan was already half-formed when she overheard Quinn's telephone conversation? The note in the pocket, the perfect place to push someone off the path? She must have had it all worked out.

But while lots of people fantasised about what might change in their lives, very few of them actually acted on those thoughts.

And she hadn't bargained on Lauren's fear of water making the whole scenario deeply suspicious.

'Fifteen years is a long time to have an affair.' Cathy kept her voice sympathetic, unthreatening.

'We lived together. It wasn't really like an affair. We were careful and Orla is out a lot.'

Cathy raised her eyebrows, wondering if Mira had realised that their cosy arrangement meant that Quinn didn't really have an incentive to leave his wife at all. He had everything he needed under one roof. The phrase 'cake and eat it' jumped into her head.

Until Lauren came along.

Another young and impressionable nineteen-year-old, with the added excitement of clandestine meetings. And no doubt Lauren's attention flattered his ego – he wasn't getting any younger. He had his cake and now he was getting the cream with it.

'Do you know how to use a computer, Mira?'

Mira looked at O'Rourke like he was stupid. 'Of course, who doesn't know how to use a computer?'

'And a printer?'

'Of course.'

O'Rourke smiled before continuing slowly. 'There was a note found on Lauren O'Reilly's body, Mira, in an envelope in her pocket. It said "I'm Sorry" but unusually for a suicide note, if that's what we are to believe it is, it was typed and printed.' He looked straight at her. 'Do you have any thoughts on that?'

'You said this girl was a student. Students all use computers. What's surprising about a student using a computer?' Mira was totally unfazed.

O'Rourke smiled again, as if he was agreeing with her. 'Indeed, all students use computers. That is very true. But never in my career have I ever seen or heard of someone typing and printing a suicide note. It tends to be a more personal thing.' He said it like it was the understatement of the year.

'I'm sure somewhere in the whole world someone has typed a note.'

'I'm sure that's so. But this type of note is fairly special, wouldn't you say? The very last thing you write before you take the extreme measure to end your own life?'

'I don't know. I have never thought about ending my life. I'm afraid I cannot help you.'

Cathy leaned forward. 'Writing is a very personal thing, though, isn't it? Some people use particular phrases or punctuation, have their own way of saying things.'

'I'm sure they do.'

Cathy looked across the table at her. Mira's answers were curt and uncommunicative. Perhaps she was just that sort of person but she was definitely giving the impression that this was all a waste of her time. Cathy could live with that.

'Would you mind writing something for us?'

'Why? Do you need to analyse my handwriting now? You said this note was typed.'

Cathy smiled and, without elaborating, turned her notepad around, offering Mira her pen. Mira hesitated for a moment, then, as if it was a vaguely ridiculous request, sat up theatrically, the pen poised.

'What would you like me to write?'

'"I've dreamed a lot. I'm tired now from dreaming but not tired of dreaming." It's a quote.'

Beside her, Cathy felt O'Rourke glance at her sideways, but she didn't look at him. She kept her eyes instead on Mira, who raised her eyebrows like Cathy was mad, then wrote on the notepad. Her writing was fluid, rounded letters flowing into each other.

Putting in the final full stop, Mira pushed the notepad back towards Cathy.

'Thank you. Perhaps you could sign that for me and pop the date underneath?'

Mira pulled the pad back and did as she was asked, pushing it back across the table again.

Cathy swung the pad around. She'd spelled tired, *tierd*. Twice. O'Rourke scanned the page smiling at Mira, then continued.

'Thank you. We need to advise you that we're currently examining the printers in Orla Quinn's office and in the rest of the house, Mira. You may not be aware of this but all printers have a distinct pattern. Something to do with the way the ink heads become misaligned during use, I'm told. We believe that the note in Lauren's pocket could have been printed in the house.'

Mira shook her head like it wasn't important, shrugging theatrically again like it wasn't anything to do with her.

'Perhaps Tom gave it to her?'

She'd almost said 'prove it' but fell marginally short. And it was down to them to prove that she had given Lauren the note, but O'Rourke was saving the best till last.

The more Cathy watched her, the more she was sure Mira thought she had it all worked out. And she had, almost. But under pressure, she'd made one mistake. At least Cathy prayed she'd made one mistake.

'You could be right, Mira. But our forensic team in the technical bureau is analysing the envelope that was found in Lauren's pocket as well as the note itself. Rather surprisingly, as well as being typed, it appears to have been wiped clean of fingerprints.'

Mira stared at him like she didn't care, her face bored.

'But the bureau isn't just looking at the ink on the note, they are also looking at the flap on the envelope. Instead of slipping it inside, someone licked it closed. Which means there will be conclusive DNA evidence that will tell us who has handled that envelope.'

Mira's face froze. She was a good actress but very few people could mask extreme shock. And it looked to Cathy that that was exactly what she was feeling. As she realised the implications her smugness evaporated and she looked a lot like she was about to vomit.

They had her. It was just a question now of waiting for the forensic results.

Chapter 48

Cathy couldn't resist a grin as she leaned on the windowsill in O'Rourke's office the next morning. Yesterday had been a long intense day and she wasn't due in until four this afternoon, but O'Rourke had suggested she come in mid-morning instead and go home early while the rest of the team cross-checked the various statements they had gathered. Calling together everyone who had been in last night, O'Rourke had brought them up to speed on their interview with Mira, and word had travelled fast that they had made an arrest. When Cathy had come in, the whole mood of the station had gone up a notch.

A warrant had been granted for Mira's mobile phone records. Cathy had a feeling they'd make interesting reading.

O'Rourke sat down at this desk. 'So ...' He paused but he didn't need to continue.

She finished the sentence for him. 'Now we need to find out exactly what happened to Tom.'

'We certainly do.' O'Rourke pursed his lips. 'Orla Quinn is calling me at least twice a day about it. We're not the only ones who want to know.' He paused, 'I'd love to be a fly on the wall in that house at the moment, I'm sure the air is quite colourful.' He continued, 'So Traffic aren't convinced that it was Quinn's jeep that hit him. The damage isn't consistent with hitting a person – there's nothing significant enough to confirm that it has been involved in a hit-and-run.'

'But we do still have blue metallic paint from a BMW.'

He frowned. 'What did Quinn call the colour of his cars?'

'Estoril blue.' *To match my eyes* – how could she forget?

'Colour-wise it's definitely a match for his vehicles. The lads are going through the database to find all the metallic blue BMWs in this area, all models.'

'That *could* be a lot.' Cathy winced inwardly as she said it.

It would take hours to go through every single one. The only blue BMW they had on CCTV so far was Conor Quinn's jeep, although throwing the net wider in terms of time frame might produce another vehicle.

'You said it. Half of south County Dublin has a Beemer. Let's hope they aren't all blue.' He cleared his throat. 'The lab is cross-matching makes and models with the sample they have. There are a couple of layers of primer before the colour coat, then a clear coat on top, apparently. Different factories use different combinations. It'll take a while longer before they have enough info to help us narrow the search.'

'I hope you've got an alibi for Thursday evening, you drive a blue Beemer too.' She grinned as he shot her a withering look. Cathy looked at her boots, turning over the information they had in her mind. 'Karen said that Tom mentioned Lauren's video, that he was going to sort it out. Do you think he knew who made it? That his death could be linked to that?'

'Discovery Quay is the main thing connecting our case with the ones in London, and those cases in Paris and Long Island. Someone's out there killing people. If Tom had any inkling who it might have been, it could put him in a very dangerous place. I've had Tom's fingerprints sent over to the guys in London ahead of our meeting. They're going to liaise with the French and the Americans to check everything.'

'Do you think Tom was involved, that he could have been the killer?'

'Who knows. He comes from a media background, he could easily have been involved in the websites, and he travelled a lot. He had the money to invest in building that type of platform. When we get to London we can take a proper look at what they've got on their victims, see if we can spot any links to here.' O'Rourke picked up his pen. 'Can you get over to that lad who lives opposite Dillon's Park this afternoon and get a full statement from him about the woman he saw going into the park? I'm going to chase up the boys in the bureau and see how they are doing with the printer ink. Get back here when you're done and we'll see where we are on Tom.'

'Consider it done.'

'We need to check the dates those attacks took place abroad. I was going to get Marie to check with Orla during her liaison visit, but I think we can spare her our suspicions for now and cross check his passport instead.'

'He might not have told her he was going.'

O'Rourke looked up. 'Good point, it's not something you advertise, is it? And those murders appear to have been planned. The girls had their webcams hacked first and somehow the killer found out where they lived.'

'Stalked them.'

'Very likely.'

Cathy hadn't expected the lad who had seen the woman going into the park to be home when she called, but he was still struggling with his applied maths, had taken a day's study leave. And he'd turned out to be incredibly helpful; he had described Mira perfectly, as well as the golden retriever with her. Cathy had been very careful with her questions. There was a possibility they'd need him to come to an ID parade and she couldn't risk leading him in any way. She'd played it cool, couldn't show him how important his evidence was, but she'd wanted to punch the air as she'd left the house and headed for the patrol car that had swung past to pick her up.

It was late afternoon by the time Cathy pushed open the back door to the station, bumping straight into Starsky as she did so.

'Got a syndicate running on the Lotto, you in?'

Cathy didn't gamble as a rule, unless she was very, very sure of the results, but if a syndicate was running in the station there was no way she was going to miss it.

'You doing it now?'

He nodded. 'Shit could hit the fan later and if I don't get to the newsagents, then our numbers come up?' He rolled his eyes.

Cathy burst out laughing. That was one way of becoming the most popular guy in the station. She rooted in her jacket pocket for change, dropped it into his hand.

'Count me in.'

He vanished into the yard as she headed up the stairs. They were a good bunch in Dun Laoghaire; she'd miss them if she moved to the ERU. That wasn't an *if*. She was going somewhere – she just hoped to God it *was* the ERU.

O'Rourke was on the phone when she arrived in his office. He waved her in and held his fingers to his lips.

'Thanks, Rob, we'll check everything out this end. Keep in touch.' He put the phone down. 'How'd you do with the lad?'

'All done. I think he'll be good for an ID parade. We've got Ronan Delaney's statement as well that puts her in the jeep, and the CCTV, so we might not need it.'

'Good. I's dotted, T's crossed, that's what we need.' He paused. 'So that was Rob Power in New York.'

Cathy leaned forward in the chair, her eyebrows raised. 'Go on.'

'Anna Lockharte was on to him. He's very concerned about her. She thinks Xavier Ayari has been following her. Ayari's emailed her, keeps appearing. He's spooking her.'

'Why didn't she say anything?' Cathy had thought she had a good rapport with Anna Lockharte.

'She's worried she's overreacting. Her whole experience in Paris has left her badly scarred. Rob said she's really not good with French-speaking Muslim men.'

Cathy thought about it for a moment and could see Anna's problem. She didn't know if the Ayaris were Muslim but they looked like they might be.

'Do you think he's involved?' Cathy sat back in the chair, frowning. 'Xavier Ayari, I mean. The Ayaris keep popping up. I checked his brother Olivier's statement. He was a friend of Tom's, said Tom had talked a bit about Karen Delaney, about working for her, but he didn't say anything about them being in a relationship.' She tapped her fingers on the desk. 'According to his statement he was in the library all that Thursday evening.

They've a digital pass system so he would have been logged in and out.'

'I think we need to do some checking. Rob says he's drawn a blank so far on the Ayari family in Paris. He's still looking.'

'They must have come from somewhere. Maybe they've still got relatives in Tunisia, isn't that where Anna Lockharte said the family was from originally? It was a French colony, wasn't it?'

He nodded slowly, looking thoughtful. 'If they paid for that science block, they must be very wealthy, which means they could be anywhere. We'll put out all the feelers, see what we turn up.'

'Anna said their company is registered in the Caymans. They are probably domiciled there as well.'

'Very true. Let's see what Rob Power can turn up there.'

'I think we need to have another chat with Olivier, and his brother too, by the sounds of things.'

O'Rourke nodded. 'Give them a call. And check in with Frank on Mira, I think we've got all our ducks in a row but I don't want her to slip out of the frame because we missed something.'

Chapter 49

Wednesday, 6 p.m.

The gym was busy when Cathy got there. Even though she hadn't done a full shift, it had been a long day going over all the interviews, checking and rechecking. One of those days when everyone you needed to talk to had their phones switched off. She'd been up to O'Rourke about four times to see if she could just grab a car to go out to find the Ayari brothers, but driving around the city or wandering around Trinity wasn't a good use of her time. They needed to get the file on Mira ready for the Director of Public Prosecutions.

She felt like she'd left messages everywhere. Conor Quinn had vanished off the face of the planet, perhaps understandably given the circumstances. When she'd called Orla to see if he was at home, she'd never heard anyone so angry. Which was also understandable. It wasn't that she'd cried or shouted, Cathy had seen that many times. Orla was different, the exact opposite of the wronged wives or grieving parents she'd met before; she'd been so quiet, so focused, she'd been almost frightening. And Cathy didn't scare easily.

She didn't fancy Conor Quinn's chances right now.

She could understand it though. On top of Mira's arrest, Marie, their family liaison officer, had dropped Tom's effects out to Orla that morning, just as Karen Delaney had arrived to help her plan Tom's funeral, apparently. There was little more disturbing than being presented with a loved one's life in a cardboard box. Their phone, their jewellery, the contents of their pockets. Cathy could still hear Orla's words: '*You need to find out who did this. I won't rest until whoever it is pays. I'm going to make absolutely sure of that.*'

Cathy was quite sure she would. Whatever happened with the State's case, Cathy could see Orla Quinn hiring the best lawyer in the country and taking out a private prosecution. Cathy was starting to feel like Orla Quinn was somebody she really didn't want to cross.

She reminded Cathy of a mother grizzly who would do anything for her cubs.

But at least Orla had Karen to help her through it all though. Cathy had winced slightly at the thought of the two women together, but at least both of them had loved Tom, even if it was in different capacities. And more importantly, he'd loved them.

When Cathy had finally left the station, she'd felt dissatisfied and irritable.

And the gym was busy, which made her worse.

Six o'clock during the week was pretty much peak time at the Phoenix Gym for anyone who worked a normal nine to five sort of a job. She usually tried to avoid it, but Cathy knew if she didn't go now she wouldn't get a long enough session in. Through the glazed wired door from the changing rooms she could see McIntyre over in the corner running a children's class, tiny boys and girls in Phoenix T-shirts throwing punches at each other. It made Cathy smile. She'd started boxing when she was ten, had loved every minute of it. It taught you co-ordination, balance, and gave you confidence as well as keeping you fit.

McIntyre raised his hand as she pushed open the swing doors and grabbed a skipping rope from the wall. She'd hoped to meet Sarah Jane here, but after their session the other night, Sarah Jane's shoulder was still aching. She'd been studying all day in the library in Dublin City University and by the time Cathy had called, she was back at home and in the middle of taking her painkillers. A gym session really wasn't the best idea, much as she would have loved to have joined Cathy.

Cathy started skipping, the rope whistling through the air as she found her rhythm, running the case through her head. Thirsty had spent the day working through the forensic findings from the scene in Dillon's Park. With a strong suspect in Lauren's murder, the process was different. He was looking for matches, forensic evidence that confirmed contact with the victim.

And they still had a ton of CCTV to go through, looking at the many possible routes that a vehicle could have taken to reach the site of Tom's accident.

As Cathy's feet pounded on the polished boards of the gym, jumping rope, she began to feel better. From the moment Mira had passed back her notepad in the interview room, with the misspelling on it, Cathy had known that they'd found Lauren O'Reilly's killer.

Even without their physically having Lauren's phone, the typo in her text reduced the level of reasonable doubt significantly.

They still needed to put her at the scene, to connect Mira directly with Lauren. But Cathy was sure they would.

Locard's exchange principle stated that every person who entered or exited a location added or subtracted material from that scene. If Mira had been there, there would be trace evidence. The key would be proving that she was there at the crucial time. Whichever way you looked at it, this one was tough. Just because her footprints were on the path didn't mean she'd been there at the same time as Lauren. Just because there were dog hairs on Lauren's coat that matched the Quinns' dog – assuming they did – it didn't mean Mira had met Lauren at all, just that the dog had. But the more people who insisted Lauren had never been to the Quinns' house increased the likelihood that she had met them both in the park. And even if Mira claimed Tom had given Lauren the note, finding a plausible reason why she, Mira, had licked it closed would take some doing.

'How's it going, girl? You wearing a hole in my floor?'

McIntyre's voice brought Cathy back to the gym. She had been so preoccupied she had no idea how long she'd been skipping.

She stopped. 'Sorry, I was miles away.'

'Big case?'

'Complicated.'

McIntyre put his hand up for a high-five, the army tattoos covering his toned arms dark under the bright lights of the gym. He was in incredible shape despite his age. That's why everyone called him The Boss. You did what you were told when Niall McIntyre said it. He looked at her, a twinkle in his blue eye.

'You'll be grand. You can do anything, girl.'

Cathy knew he was talking about her upcoming fight. She had one chance to prove she was back on top and the National

Championships were it. It was a constant at the back of her mind. Everyone in the station knew how much she'd wanted the profiler job, how she was working her arse off to get a first in her Master's. There had been unified disbelief as the promotion list had been passed around. Now they were all rooting for her for this fight, had a sweepstake going on the QT. She wasn't supposed to know about it but Fanning had managed to let it slip.

Their support made all the difference, but you could never get complacent, never assume you were going to win, no matter who your opponent was. Anything could happen on the day. Kick-boxing was a bit like her day job – every piece of information gave her an edge. And in every free moment Cathy had been studying Jordan Paige's form, watching YouTube videos of her previous fights, looking for weaknesses. And Cathy was sure Paige was doing the same for her.

'So any news for me?'

McIntyre crossed his arms, watching her as she went over to the low wooden bench. She'd thrown her kitbag down there earlier. She pulled out a towel and a bottle of water, and took a swig. Despite her best efforts there was little she could hide from him.

'The ERU inspector called O'Rourke. They want me for interview.' His arms still crossed, McIntyre raised his eyebrows. 'And I have to go to London tomorrow afternoon, so I'll miss training, but I'll make it up.'

He took both pieces of information in his stride. 'You did a good job with the ERU before. They should want you, you're perfect for them.' He thought about it for a minute, grinned at her mischievously. 'And keeping on top of your fitness in that job is paramount. So when you win the Nationals you'll have more time to train for the Europeans.'

Typical McIntyre – and there she was thinking maybe she'd actually have time for a social life. Her mind flicked back to O'Rourke. They were going to London together and he wanted her to come down to see him when he was settled in Limerick. The London thing meant they'd be on their own, but they were still working together. If she went down to see him in Limerick they wouldn't be, and that was a different thing altogether. But she didn't have time to think about it now, McIntyre was already pulling out the pads.

He put her through her paces, circuit training, then more pad work until the sweat was running off her. Then he pulled on his own gloves and hopped into the ring. She didn't know how he had the energy.

By nine o'clock she could hardly stand.

'Good job, girl. Keep this up and . . .'

'I'll be dead, Boss. I'll definitely be dead.'

McIntyre laughed. 'Don't talk like that, you're a winner. Now some bar work and you can go.'

Balance was vitally important to success in the ring, but as Cathy looked across at the bar surrounded by crash mats she had no idea how she was going to find the energy to even get up onto it. On a good day she could dance across it, do cart-wheels along its length. She took a step towards it but McIntyre stopped her.

'I'm joking, girl, you get home and get some sleep. God, you're all fight, aren't you. That's how we like it.'

Cathy shook her head, smiling, a stray curl that had worked itself out of her ponytail falling across her eyes. Her gloves still on, she pushed it out of her face and spat out her mouth guard so she could speak properly. Not that she was really capable of forming words.

'Here, let me help you with those.' McIntyre pulled back the Velcro on her gloves and eased her hands out of them.

'Thanks, Boss.'

'Have a shower, early night, I'll see you when you get back from London.'

They fist-bumped and she headed for the changing room.

Chapter 50

Cathy had only got inside her front door when the doorbell rang behind her. Throwing her kitbag down at the bottom of the stairs, she turned around and opened it to find O'Rourke standing on the doorstep, his hands deep in the pockets of his overcoat. He had his back to her, turned around as he heard the door open. Cathy was really too tired to care what she looked like but she was fairly sure it was pretty shit. She hadn't had time to get her hair cut since she couldn't remember when, and even madly curly it reached almost to her elbows. She was pretty sure she looked like one of the Witches of Eastwick. But right now she really didn't care.

If she looked horrific, he didn't show it; instead he stepped up into the hall without being invited and headed for the kitchen.

'Where is everyone?'

'Out, I guess, I've no idea. I've only come in myself.' She almost added *it's not my job to keep tabs on them*, but didn't bother. He was looking annoyed.

'What's up?'

She followed him into the kitchen, where he'd helped himself to a beer. He flipped open the ring pull and went over to the sink to throw it in the bin in the cupboard underneath. She watched him, feeling slightly dazed, but realising she was thirsty, hauled open the fridge door and pulled out a bottle of water.

'Lounge?' He waved his can in the general direction of the living room.

'Be my guest.'

Standing back into the hall she watched, slightly mystified, as he stalked into the living room and, putting his beer down on the mantelpiece, slipped off his coat. The room was in shadow, the only light, soft and yellow, coming from a lamp at the other end of the sofa, but it didn't seem to bother him. He threw his coat onto the easy chair and, grabbing his beer, sat down on the edge of the sofa, his suit jacket sleeves pulled back, his elbows on his knees. He'd taken off his tie at some stage; knowing him, he had it neatly rolled up in his coat pocket.

'So?' She leaned on the door frame, exhaustion washing over her.

'Thirsty found a print, one of Lauren's, on the dog's collar.'

'Ooh.' She started to perk up. 'That's good.'

'The guys at the Park are checking the ink and print patterns on that note against the printers from the Quinn house, and I've put a rush on the DNA on the envelope now we've got a sample to compare it to. Now she knows we've got our sights on her, I'm concerned Mira could be a flight risk so we'll keep hold of her for the moment while we wait for the results.'

'Sounds good.'

Cathy had to sit down. Propelling herself across the living room, she flopped down onto the sofa beside him, and kicking off her Nikes, pulled her knees up, curling around to face him.

'You been to the gym?'

'Yup, The Boss nearly killed me.'

'What's he think about you applying for the ERU?'

'That it's good.' She didn't have the energy to repeat their conversation. 'Is there any more news from the Americans on the video hacking thing?'

'I had another chat to Rob Power after you left. Lauren O'Reilly is our link to these other cases and to the websites. Tom was the only one who seemed to know about the videos. I was wondering if he was actually running the sites and one of his minions hacked her webcam without realising he knew her.' O'Rourke sat back into the cushions, his head resting on the back of the sofa. He was obviously tired too. He put his can on the arm of the sofa and twirled it thoughtfully. 'What I don't get is why this creep is hacking webcams and then demanding money from the girls if he can make a fortune by putting it up on that Discovery Quay site.'

'I'm not sure it's all about money. I think whoever it is has a personal interest in the girls. It's about power, the need for dominance, and that's always a strong feature in the psychological profile of a sex offender.'

O'Rourke took a sip of his beer. 'Rob Power said Discovery Quay is definitely a part of that Merchant's Quay site – they use Discovery Quay as an advertising tool, pushing buyers to the multitude of vendors on Merchant's Quay. You can get anything there. But he's looked at the set-up and he thinks there's one hacker providing all the footage on Discovery Quay – there's no way for anyone to randomly upload video like there is on some other sites. It's all locked in.' He took another sip. 'You know he's had guys undercover for months trying to find out who is behind both sites. But as he said himself, he only needs one element of human error and he'll blow it open. He thinks that print on the drugs you found in Lauren's room could be key.'

'I didn't find it, Fanning did. It's just so weird that it's a match to that crime scene in Paris. Have they found out if that girl had her webcam hacked as well?' He shook his head, and she continued, 'Even if she didn't, the connections are starting to show, aren't they?'

'I've got feelers out on that Xavier Ayari guy that Anna Lockharte is worried about. He's squeaky clean, no previous here or in France. He's lived here about four years, pays tax outside the jurisdiction, bought his apartment for cash.'

Cathy pulled a face. 'These cases are all interconnected, like a spider's web, invisible when the sun's on it, but when the dew falls, clear as day.'

'That's very poetic, you should write a book.'

She stuck her elbow in his ribs and reached over to haul over the footstool so she could put her legs up. She was getting stiff.

'Here, move up there.' He kicked off his shoes and put his feet up next to hers.

'I wonder how she was targeted? Lauren, I mean. And then Anna. Why them?'

'Two very attractive women. But with these cases cropping up all over the world, it makes you wonder. Perhaps he travels a lot, finds the women randomly and, depending on the reaction he gets to his emails, goes to meet them?'

Cathy frowned. 'No, you wouldn't meet someone you knew was watching you in the bath, you really wouldn't, that makes no sense. It's more likely to be the other way around – someone the girls knew or had been in contact with previously got their email and hacked their cameras because he wanted to know more.' Cathy thought back to an essay she'd done at the start of her Master's. 'You know there's overwhelming evidence that assailants who start as peeping Toms don't stay that way. Their violence patterns escalate as their confidence grows and they need a bigger kick to get off. This hacking thing is the same – it's just like a peeping Tom online.'

'The evidence we've got, the fingerprint matches at the scenes, the similar MO, would suggest the same person is involved in the cold cases as well as ours, even if he does get about a bit. Maybe it's someone who travels with their job?'

Cathy took a sip of her water and pursed her lips, thinking. 'Or a lecturer? Anna Lockharte told me she'd studied all over the place – in the UK, in London and Cambridge – and now she's teaching here. Perhaps it's someone like that? Someone in a position of trust the girls would go to for help. The girl in Paris was a student – well, a schoolgirl – and it was students that were targeted in London too.'

'We'll find out where the two girls in London were studying, get info on their backgrounds when we go over tomorrow. See if there's any connection with anyone at Trinity.'

Cathy ran her finger down the edge of her water bottle, her brain trying to process the information.

'It's awful to say it, but if Lauren hadn't been killed we might never have made any of these connections.'

He rotated his beer can again thoughtfully. 'That is very true. And the guys up at the Park have worked out all sorts of models to prove she didn't jump, so that's something.'

'I was absolutely sure her body was at the wrong angle. But after seeing her in action, Mira doesn't strike me as the type to break down in the interview room and confess all. She's more likely to claim Lauren *did* jump to get herself off the hook, so that evidence could be vital.'

O'Rourke sipped his beer. 'She's a tough one all right.'

'The war in Bosnia was pretty . . .' Cathy was about to say *pretty shit*, but an enormous yawn escaped before she could stop it.

'You need to get some sleep.'

'I do, but I'm quite cosy here. I'm not sure I've got the energy to move.'

'Here.' O'Rourke leaned one arm behind her and dragged the rug off the back of the sofa. She leaned back on his arm and pulled it over her knees. 'Curl up.'

It was more of an order than a request and as she snuggled into his shoulder, he put his arm around her shoulders. She could smell his aftershave, feel the heat of his body through his shirt. Why was this happening when she was completely exhausted?

'You definitely coming down to see me in Limerick?' He smoothed her hair with his hand, playing with the ends.

'Yup.'

'I might be going sooner than we think. They want me to go as soon as we've got this case wrapped up.'

Shocked, she leaned back and looked at him. 'That could be next week if the DNA results come back quickly.'

He didn't answer, but his eyes locked on hers. Cathy felt like the air had gone out of the room and they were suspended in a vacuum. He put his hand to the side of her face, pushing her hair back, and before she knew it he had leaned forward and was kissing her – or perhaps she was kissing him, she wasn't sure. What she was sure about was that it was a very long kiss. She moved closer to him, twisting to face him, putting her arm around his back between his shirt and his jacket. She could feel the powerful muscles there as he ran his fingers into her hair, cradling her head. Feeling his lips on hers, she was back there again for a moment – lying on her neighbour's lawn after the explosion, her emotions whirling inside her, overriding the pain. But this was so much better. She slipped her hand up to his shoulder, the cotton of his shirt soft on her palm, felt him move to hold her tighter.

And then they heard a key in the door.

Breaking apart, he smiled at her. 'I had better go.'

He kissed her again, a quick kiss, a let's do this again kiss, and she sat back on the sofa, pulling the rug around her as he stood up to slip his shoes on.

Had that really just happened?

He reached for his coat and pulled it on. 'I'll see you in the morning. Nine sharp?'

She smiled at him. Whoever had come in had gone straight into the kitchen, was crashing about taking crockery out of the cupboards.

'I'll let myself out.' He started to go out of the door and then, as if he'd forgotten something, turned around and in two strides came back to the sofa and kissed her again, his lips soft on hers. 'Get some sleep. We've a long day tomorrow.'

And with that he was gone. Cathy heard the front door close behind him, followed by her housemate Eamon's voice.

'Who's that?' The next minute he stuck his head around the living room door. 'Oh, you in here? Why are you sitting in the dark? Who was that?'

'O'Rourke.' It didn't quite come out as she'd expected. She cleared her throat. 'O'Rourke.' She smiled at Eamon, praying he couldn't see her blush in the dim light. 'We've made an arrest in the O'Reilly case. I haven't seen you since you got back, how was Galway?'

Chapter 51

Thursday, 9 a.m.

Cathy could feel her nerves dancing the tango in her stomach as she pushed open the back door to the station the next morning. She'd been for a swim. A hard swim. She'd been so exhausted the night before she'd fallen into bed as soon as she'd been able to get away from Eamon. She normally adored hearing his crazy stories from his family's farm, but her mind had been too busy to concentrate on anything. Too busy to let her sleep. Eventually she'd had to get up and go in search of the remainder of the tablets she'd been given by the doctor after she'd struggled with her last bout of insomnia. She'd broken one in half, praying it wouldn't knock her out so badly that she'd be groggy in the morning. It had worked quickly, but now, even with sleep, her heart was pounding and her mouth dry as she headed into the station.

O'Rourke had kissed her. And he hadn't left her in any doubt that he'd wanted to keep kissing her. Perhaps it was as well Eamon had come in. Who knew what could have happened?

And now she had to behave like everything was normal, like nothing had happened, when deep down her emotions were whirling like the tornado that had taken Dorothy out of Kansas. If she clicked the heels on her ruby slippers, would she discover that it was all a dream, that he'd changed his mind?

She didn't think she could cope with that.

But she needn't have worried.

When she got up to the detective office, humming now with activity, Frank was on his way out of the door heading for the cells.

'Morning, Cat. O'Rourke's been called into the Park, he said he'd emailed you details of the flights and he'll see you at the gate in the airport. Someone can give you a lift there at 1.30, should give you loads of time.'

'Cool, what's the scoop now?'

'A follow-up with the lovely Mira, you and me in Five. Starsky and Hutch have a gang of shoplifters in, have taken over half the place. When we're done, you can shoot off.'

'I'm right behind you.'

She threw her kitbag into the corner of the office. Her swimming togs and towel were wet but they could stay there for the moment; she'd hang them up in the shower later.

1.30 came far faster than she expected.

Mira had definitely wobbled a bit when Frank had brought up Ronan Delaney's statement about seeing her in the jeep. On top of their news yesterday about the envelope, her perfect exterior was starting to show signs of cracking. She'd recanted her previous assertion that she'd walked with the dog to Dillon's Park, admitting that she'd driven. Somehow she'd made it sound like she had just forgotten to mention it.

Now they had Mira in situ with means, motive and opportunity. However, proving whether she had pushed Lauren or if she had jumped looked like it would be down to the mathematicians at Headquarters to prove beyond reasonable doubt. Cathy knew there was a case in Australia where a conviction had been made based on the very same type of evidence. A husband had pushed his new wife off a cliff and between the angles and her weight and the landing point of the body, they'd been able to create a computer simulation showing exactly what had happened. O'Rourke had sounded confident that they could do the same here.

There was no shame in Lauren's jumping, but Cathy knew for her family that would be hard to deal with, whatever the circumstances. And Cathy didn't want to bring any more pain to her parents. If Mira had pushed her, they were going to nail her.

Mira had had a horrible childhood, had witnessed things that no young teenager should ever see. She'd lost everything and she was faced with losing everything again. But her first stop should have been to challenge Conor Quinn, to work it out with him, not to push a nineteen-year-old – whose life was only getting started – off a cliff. Cathy felt a physical ache when she thought about Lauren's death. She'd had some stuff happen to her, some pretty heavy stuff, she'd endured real pain, but through it all she'd known that there was a team of people who were all working their arses off to help her. If Lauren had still been conscious when she hit those rocks, she'd thought that the only person who knew she was there was Conor. What had Mira said to her? Had she told Lauren that Conor had sent her to end their relationship? How hopeless had Lauren felt as she had slipped from consciousness?

Cathy had shivered thinking about it. She'd almost lost her life three times and every single one of them would have been preferable to that scenario.

'You ready, Cat?' Starsky stuck his head around the detective office door just as she hit *Save* on her notes.

Clicking her seat belt on, Cathy listened to Starsky calling in their destination, nerves fluttering in her stomach again. She wasn't sure if she was nervous about seeing O'Rourke or about going to London. He was right that this would be good experience. They'd only be in New Scotland Yard for a few hours, but getting to see how the Met operated would be fascinating. O'Rourke's opposite number had organised a case conference with as many members of the original investigating teams as he could find so they could swap information.

It felt like it was suddenly all happening. Everything. All at once. She glanced at her phone. She'd half-expected O'Rourke to text at some stage this morning. But she knew something big must be happening to take him away from the station at this stage of the investigation.

She felt another flutter in her stomach. But it was definitely one of excitement this time. She should get a date for her interview with the ERU through soon. The tech and firepower she'd seen them use was just so impressive. She was dying to expand her firearms training, and getting paid to jump out of a helicopter? She'd be the first in the queue to do it for free. She was really trying hard not to get too excited – what if she didn't get in? Just because Eddie Flint, the ERU inspector, had been on to O'Rourke didn't mean it was a given. There could be hundreds of others applying, all with years more experience than her, she was quite sure.

But God, she hoped she got in. She couldn't stay in Dun Laoghaire much longer. And she needed to be busy, to stop her mind wandering to what O'Rourke might be doing. Like now. She wasn't sure if she was worried about his lack of communication, or if she was totally overreacting that he hadn't been in touch, and shouldn't be worried at all. He didn't owe her anything, really. He had a big job, was pulled in a million directions. Would he have been in touch normally by now if they hadn't had a mega snog?

Maybe, maybe not.

But, much as she hated to admit it, a part of her was trying not to be devastated that he hadn't contacted her. What was that about? She tried to shake off the feeling. He wasn't dead, he was just busy. He'd said he'd see her in the morning and something had come up. He'd called Frank, perhaps he was just too busy to text. *How busy was that exactly?*

Chapter 52

Thursday, 2 p.m.

Dublin Airport was always hectic. Cathy scanned her boarding pass and smiled at the security staff as the gate slid back. She recognised members the same way they recognised her. And there were loads of retired Gardaí on the airport security teams. If they had their thirty years' service done, or had reached the retirement age of fifty, they were still young enough to tackle a whole range of security jobs, and had the skills to know exactly what to look for.

Reaching the X-ray machines, she put her leather jacket, wallet and phone into the box on the conveyor belt, and walked through the gate, promptly setting off the alarms. She flipped open her ID, suddenly remembering the handcuffs clipped to her belt loop, concealed by her sweater. She showed them quickly to the security staff. Most members preferred plastic handcuffs these days but she'd always found the sound of steel to be very satisfying. She couldn't bring her gun into a foreign jurisdiction, though, and she felt a bit lost without the weight of it. Like her cuffs, it was part of her. But that wasn't a problem right now; she was going to a case conference, not into a war zone.

Weaving through the crowds heading for the departure gate, Cathy kept an eye out for O'Rourke, expecting to see him ahead of her in the crowds of travellers. As she passed WHSmith, the day's papers were displayed outside in angled boxes. A man standing in front of the display bent down to pick up his suitcase and she caught sight of the tabloid headlines. 'Karen Moves Out' was slapped across the front of the Irish *Daily Mail* with a full page photo of Karen Delaney, wearing dark glasses and a long black coat, throwing a holdall into the back of her white jeep. Cathy didn't need to buy the paper to guess at the press speculation, but her heart did a quiet cheer for Karen. She'd be so much better off without her husband.

As Cathy headed down to the departure gate her phone pipped with an incoming text. She felt her heart leap. *O'Rourke, had to be.* She stopped on one side of the broad walkway and pulled it out, her stomach fluttering with anticipation. But Sarah Jane's name flashed onto the screen: *Have fun!* with a series of emoji, boxing gloves and thumbs up symbols. Cathy was tempted to ring her back, to update her on everything that had been happening, but she could do that when she got back from London – when hopefully she'd have some real news. Sarah Jane was probably in the library at this time of day and wouldn't be able to answer anyway. She texted back: *TY, have news will call later xxx*

The area beside the departure gate was already filling as Cathy reached it, collecting a coffee on her way. But there was still no sign of O'Rourke. She had another half an hour to wait before boarding so there was lots of time. Sipping her coffee, she went to look out of the floor to ceiling plate glass window that overlooked the runway. Planes fascinated her. One day she'd love to learn to fly. She watched the aircraft taxiing in, passengers disembarking, thinking about each of their stories, wondering where they were going, why they were coming to Dublin. Completely absorbed in her thoughts, Cathy jumped as the flight was suddenly called and snapped back to the departure gate, looking around. *Where was O'Rourke?*

As Cathy reached into the pocket of her combats to pull out her passport, she heard a voice behind her.

'Cathy Connolly? What are you doing here?'

Cathy turned around to see Anna Lockharte, pulling a silver Samsonite cabin suitcase. She looked smart in what could only be a very expensive black trouser suit and high-heeled boots, a gauzy cream silk shirt setting off her pale skin. Her red curls tied back in a low ponytail, she looked like she'd stepped out of a photoshoot for executive women in *Vogue*.

Cathy looked at her for a second in total surprise.

'Anna? What are you doing here?'

Anna laughed. 'I'm speaking at a course in New Scotland Yard tomorrow, then we're going to see some shows. This is my niece, Hope.'

Anna looked around at a flame-haired teenager standing slightly away from her who was so absorbed in her phone that she hadn't noticed their exchange.

By way of explanation, Anna said, 'She's sixteen. We're going to see how much we can pack in before she has to be back in school on Monday.'

As she spoke, Cathy's phone pipped with a text. 'I'm sorry. Excuse me.'

O'Rourke at last.

Xavier Ayari drives a blue BMW. Looking for him. Running late have to get Heathrow flight. Meet u at NSY. They are sending a car to meet us, will collect you at London City.

Xavier Ayari again. A guy who has loads of cash and could travel freely on his French passport. A guy who is studying something to do with technology. Was he behind the websites and the hacking? If Tom had been about to blow his cover, he'd definitely have a reason to run him down. Perhaps Anna Lockharte's instincts had been correct. They'd know for sure as soon as they found his car – and took his fingerprints.

'Sorry. That was my inspector. We're heading to a meeting. Well, we were, he's catching a different flight now.'

Before Cathy could finish the flight was called again.

Anna smiled. 'Sounds like we'll be seeing you on the other side.'

It had been a smooth flight until the pilot had announced that they couldn't land in London City because of fog, so they were diverting to Luton. A collective groan swept down the plane like a Mexican wave. Cathy stretched. She was getting stiff, wasn't used to sitting still for so long. Further down the aircraft she could see Anna Lockharte's head beside her niece's, their shade of red distinctive.

The woman in the seat beside Cathy shook her head.

'Marvellous, I'm supposed to be going to the theatre.'

'How far is Luton from London?'

'Only about thirty minutes. The train runs straight from Luton into St Pancras – you can get the tube anywhere from there. I'll be lucky to make it to Covent Garden on time, though. Let's hope there's no fog in Luton.'

Great. Now they'd both be late.

And she didn't have details of O'Rourke's contact in London. Meeting at London City Airport seemed a bit of a mad idea now, but until she got hold of O'Rourke she'd have to stick with plan A – that's where the driver was meeting her. She'd text him as soon as she got reception, although presumably O'Rourke would still be in the air when she landed.

Cathy still couldn't believe that Anna Lockharte was on the same flight and heading to New Scotland Yard as well, but then, as O'Rourke had pointed out before, she was a world leader in her area. Which was one of the things that had made Cathy wonder what she was doing in Trinity College at all. It was one of Ireland's top universities but on a global scale there were others that ranked much higher. When O'Rourke had given her the full picture it made more sense. But Cathy was sure Anna Lockharte could have walked into a job anywhere in the world.

But what was going on with Xavier Ayari? She was desperate to know more. Did he have links to the cases in London too?

This trip should tell them more about the victims and the evidence the British police had gathered. Karen had said that Tom had planned to do something about the video of Lauren – had he known who was behind it, and perhaps behind Discovery Quay too? Or perhaps he was working with Xavier Ayari? Perhaps he followed in his mother's entrepreneurial footsteps? Could he be the link they were missing?

Cathy stretched in her seat. She had checked her phone one last time before she'd switched it to flight mode to see if O'Rourke had texted again. He hadn't. She sighed, closing her eyes. *What on earth was she going to say to him when they did finally meet?* He'd obviously been busy but why had he gone all quiet on her?

Maybe he was embarrassed. Maybe he didn't know what to say to *her*?

For feck's sake, he was old enough to be able to work it out. To be honest with her. And it wasn't like they'd only just met, but perhaps that was the problem.

As the wheels hit the tarmac, she felt an ache for him, for things to work out. She really didn't think she had the mental or emotional strength for this to fall apart. But if it did, at least they wouldn't be working together; they would be at opposite ends of the country. She reached for her phone as the plane taxied in and switched it on.

It pipped with a series of texts. Two missed calls from Orla Quinn. Still nothing from O'Rourke. She fired off a text to him explaining she'd been diverted to Luton. She'd ring Orla back as soon as she got a chance.

Chapter 53

The escalators heading up from the platform in St Pancras Station were packed. Cathy had forgotten how busy London was, just quite how many people there were constantly on the move. But the fog and extra train trip had meant they'd well and truly hit the rush hour – it was just past six. The meeting with the Met team had been scheduled for 6.30. They were going to be late one way or another.

Anna and Hope had been waiting for her just inside the terminal building in Luton when she'd eventually got off the plane, and she'd chatted easily to them all the way in on the train. Glancing out of the carriage window, they'd passed places Cathy recognised: Elstree, Mill Hill and Hendon, with its Air Force museum and the Peel Centre, the Police Training College where she'd been on a course a couple of years ago. Cathy had spent most of the journey trying not to look at her phone too often. The reception was patchy here, but she'd texted O'Rourke to say that she'd arrived safely – late and in the wrong place – but that she was on her way and would go directly to New Scotland Yard. Now she found herself waiting for him to text back. Again.

Arriving at the top of the escalators and following Anna and Hope out of the ticket barrier, Cathy was struck, as she always was, by how beautiful the station was. It was ages since she'd been here. The marble-tiled concourse with its mall of select boutiques and coffee shops was topped with an incredible arched glazed roof that was pure Victorian elegance. She'd read somewhere that when the station first opened it had been the largest building in the world, and it had a majesty to match.

'Where are we going?' Hope righted her wheelie suitcase and looked to Anna for direction.

'I've got to collect a dress in L.K.Bennett here in the station, so straight on. Then the tube to Tottenham Court Road. Our hotel's only a couple of minutes from there, the Bloomsbury on Great Russell Street. It's behind the Dominion Theatre – we can see what's on, on the way past. I think you can get to St James's Park on the circle line, Cathy. It's not far in a cab from here, but at this time of night the Euston Road is like a car park.'

Following Anna and Hope, Cathy could see a pair of armed police officers in the distance, walking across the concourse. They were glued to their radios. Then from somewhere above her a recorded voice came across the tannoy with a safety message: 'See it. Say it. Sorted'. They were obviously on high alert.

'Here, let me get a photo of you to show your dad and Uncle Rob that we've arrived.'

Smiling, Anna held up her phone, gesturing for Hope to take a step backwards. She turned it around to get in as much of the station as possible. Hope pulled a face and waved for the camera.

'There. Just let me send it.' Flicking open her email, Anna took a moment to attach the photo. She turned to Cathy, grinning. 'Rob made me promise to get lots of photos. He's Hope's uncle. It's her first trip here.'

Cathy kept her face straight but Anna Lockharte's close relationship with the CIA began to make even more sense.

'Come on, let's get this dress and head over to our hotel, I'm starving.'

Hope began pulling her case towards the shops. Anna caught up with her. Someone started playing a piano further along, filling the concourse with music. From the pocket in her combats, Cathy's phone suddenly pipped with a text. At the exact same moment as Anna's. Before Cathy could pull out her own phone, she could see Anna looking at her phone and her face creasing into a frown.

Anna looked around for Hope, who had gone on ahead to listen to the piano player. Then, as if she'd caught something out of the corner of her eye, Anna looked quickly over to the café on their left, its stainless steel tables crowded. Her expression changed abruptly from a puzzled frown to something much more serious. She glanced at Cathy.

Something was wrong.

Anna turned around so she was facing the middle of the concourse, her back to the café. Ahead of them, Hope had realised that her aunt had stopped and turned back, waiting for her expectantly. Cathy raised her eyebrows in question. Anna seemed to be gathering herself. *What could she have seen that shocked her like that?*

Cathy's phone began to ring. Realising she hadn't looked at her own text, she checked the screen. O'Rourke. *She had to give him full marks for timing.*

Cathy swiped to answer it but didn't have a chance to speak before he said, 'Where are you? There's some sort of attack going on in London.'

'I'm with Anna Lockharte and her niece in St Pancras. Where are you, what's happening?'

'My plane's been delayed, fog or something, then my battery died.' As if suddenly registering what she'd said, he continued, 'Anna Lockharte? Jesus Christ, what's she doing there? We've been trying to get hold of her all afternoon. The lads got a match on that print from the box of Modafinil in Lauren's room, the one that's linked to the Paris case. It's Xavier Ayari. Her instincts about him were right – she could be in danger.' *Whoa.* Cathy couldn't get a word in as he continued. 'That's what held me up. And his BMW was orbiting Ulverton Road the night Tom was killed. He was there all along, supposedly meeting Conor Quinn, but I'm starting to think that could be a fairy story. We've a warrant out for his arrest but we haven't found him or his car yet.'

Cathy turned to Anna, her mouth open to speak, but Anna pointed over her shoulder, keeping her voice low.

'I just got a text from Rob about Xavier Ayari.' Cathy nodded quickly to indicate that she was in the loop as Anna continued, 'His brother Olivier is sitting outside that cafe behind us. Long fringe. Laptop open. There are two of them.'

Cathy glanced behind her to see two dark-skinned student types sitting at one of the outside tables, both glued to their laptops. One of them flicked his fringe out of his face as she watched; the other had a thin pencil moustache.

Cathy whispered into the phone to O'Rourke, 'There's something weird happening, Olivier Ayari, Xavier's brother, is right here.'

Anna cut across her. 'He came to my office the other day, was asking about Tom, about the investigation, said he would get in touch with you. I gave him your number.'

Cathy raised her eyebrows. After her leaving countless messages, he'd got in touch eventually. 'One of our lads spoke to him – he said he was in the Trinity library the night Tom was killed. Their system showed him entering.'

Anna took a deep breath and pursed her lips, thinking for a moment. She shook her head.

'Maybe that's so, but this can't be a coincidence. I ordered a dress the other night and arranged to collect it here when we landed, it's easier than Oxford Street at this time of day. When Rob's guys cleaned my laptop they found spyware as well as the virus that accessed my webcam. But they never checked my desktop in the office.' She bit her lip for a moment, then continued calmly, 'I ordered the dress from the office. Olivier Ayari must have hacked my computer. What are the chances of him being here otherwise?'

Cathy put her hand on Anna's arm, her phone still to her ear as O'Rourke said, 'What's happening there, Cat?' Cathy could hear the impatience in his voice.

Glancing quickly behind her, Cathy looped her arm through Anna's and, glancing at Hope, indicated that she wanted her to follow them. Cathy guided Anna to the opposite side of the concourse. She kept her voice low as she repeated everything to O'Rourke.

His voice sounded strange as he replied, like he was trying to stay calm. That wasn't like him. He spoke slowly as he said, 'Listen to me, Cat. There's something big happening over there. Trains are colliding with each other all over the place.' He paused. 'It started in Scotland. There's been one in Birmingham and just now in Victoria. It's looking like terrorists.'

She cut him off. 'How many accidents?'

'Four so far, eight trains. All major stations.'

As he spoke there was an earth-shattering crash that felt like it came from the bowels of the earth.

'Holy feck.'

Anna was already reaching for Hope. Around them people continued to walk to wherever they were going, some of them glancing over their shoulders, looking up, their faces puzzled. This part of the station was packed; further up, what looked like a huge group of students and another of elderly Japanese tourists were crowded around their suitcases, standing outside the Eurostar departure gates. They looked around them, dazed.

Then came another huge bang, this time from the opposite end of the station, and people began to run towards the exits. The students turned and tried to drag their cases, falling over each other and anyone in their way as they headed for the outside entrance to the Eurostar terminal. Cathy froze for a moment. The second bang sounded like it had come from the Underground. She'd seen images of the 7/7 bombings on the Underground. It was a terrifying place to get caught in any sort of incident.

Hope had gone so pale she looked like she was going to faint, Anna pulled her close but Cathy could see that she was physically shaking. Around them, noise began to build – emergency announcements on the tannoy, running feet, shouting, the sound of sirens coming from outside the station, getting louder as the emergency services responded to whatever was happening. Fire, police, ambulance – Cathy was sure they were all on the way. But if this was part of what O'Rourke had been talking about, there was more than one incident and the emergency services would be stretched across the city.

Her phone still pressed to her ear, Cathy found herself shouting over the noise.

'Did you hear that?'

She could only just hear O'Rourke as he replied, 'It's all over the news. It looks like a series of simultaneous attacks. Euston as well.'

Cathy swung around, looking at Olivier Ayari and his friend sitting in the cafe, apparently oblivious to the increasing chaos. Too calm. Cathy's mind was flying, processing what little information they had. *Why weren't they reacting?* Everyone else was panicking, why not them?

Cathy spoke into the phone. 'There's a load of shit happening here, but there's no way those are all terrorist suicide missions. There's too many. How could you find that many people who wanted to die for Allah and could drive a fecking train? There's something else happening.'

Chapter 54

Londoners had been at the heart of terror attacks before. Now they moved fast.

Flipping her phone closed, Cathy grabbed Anna's hand and weaved through the people streaming around them, hauling her and Hope further up the station into a side alley beside the plate glass windows of a shoe shop. They pressed their backs up against the glass wall to keep from being knocked over by exiting commuters.

Cathy turned to Anna. 'You need to get Hope out. There's some sort of terrorist attack going on, they are hitting the train network, major stations.' Anna's eyes filled with anger as Cathy continued, pointing down the corridor behind them, to the mass of people heading out of the station. 'That must be a way out. Take Hope, I'll stay here and stick with Ayari. We can't lose him now.'

Cathy craned her head out of the alley to see if she could see what Olivier Ayari and his friend were doing. But they were too far down the station now, her view blocked by two banks of escalators. Cathy could feel all her senses kicking into high alert. She needed to get closer.

In just those few minutes the concourse had emptied. From where she was, Cathy could see dark-suited St Pancras staff manning the doors at the other end of the Eurostar section of the station, their pale blue vests bright against their uniforms, radios in their hands as they calmly ushered passengers outside to safety.

Cathy turned to Anna. 'Go, take Hope. I'll be fine. Keep your phone on.' Anna hesitated but Cathy didn't give her a chance to speak. 'Go!'

Anna grabbed Hope's hand and, dragging their cases, they ran down the broad corridor, disappearing around the corner. Cathy felt some of her tension lift. Anna and Hope had been mixed up in a horrific incident before, and Cathy knew she couldn't keep them safe and watch Ayari at the same time. She flicked her own phone to silent and slipped out of the end of the corridor.

While she couldn't see them, she could be pretty sure Ayari and his friend couldn't see her. Leaving the shelter of the corridor, she moved swiftly to the bottom of the first escalator and then on towards the lift. It was made completely of glass but on the near side, a black upright piano had been pushed up against it. Crouching low as she ran silently across the grey marble to the piano, she dropped down behind it, praying the refraction of light through the glass lift shaft and the lift itself would hide her movement.

Peeping out from behind the piano, Cathy looked down the concourse towards where Olivier Ayari and his friend had been sitting in the cafe. They were still there, looking around them as if they'd suddenly realised something was happening. But it wasn't distracting them from whatever they were doing. A moment later their eyes were back on their screens.

What was Ayari doing that was so important? Hacking some-one else's email or webcam? Why were they sitting so calmly when everyone around them was evacuating?

Cathy needed to get even closer. She was still a long way from them and she wanted to hear what they were saying. Crossing to the far side of the piano, keeping the lift shaft between herself and Ayari and his friend, she crept down the side wall of the lift furthest away from them. It was hard for her to see at this distance, but they seemed to be fully focused on whatever they were doing. Ahead of her, another escalator rose to the mez-zanine level. If she could just get to the base of that escalator without them seeing her, she reckoned she'd be close enough to hear their conversation but, protected by the glass and steel of the moving staircase, would still be hidden. Keeping low down, she peeped out again, glancing across at the cafe, working out how fast she could get to the escalator.

As she watched, Olivier Ayari pulled out his iPhone.

And she was suddenly sure what was happening.

'This way . . .' The end of the corridor Anna and Hope were running through opened out into the glazed side entrance to the station. Crowds of people were gathered on the pavements outside, a constantly moving row of black cabs collecting pas-sengers and peeling away into the already congested road.

Anna looked up and down the row of cabs, at the chaos of humanity trying to find their way out, and ducking left, headed past the top of the queue, her silver wheelie case bumping over the uneven paving stones. Hope followed her like a shadow. Pausing at the edge of the pavement, Anna waited a moment and threw her an encouraging smile.

'We'll head over there and regroup. I need to call your uncle Rob.'

Hope nodded, glancing anxiously behind her at the station, at the crowds milling around, further down the pavement.

Crossing the road, weaving through the slowly moving traffic, Anna pulled out her phone as she reached the other side. It was already starting to ring.

'Where are you exactly? The DI in Dublin just emailed me.'

'We're outside the station now, beside the British Library. Cathy's still inside, she's sticking with Olivier. It was him following me, not Xavier, I'm sure of it.'

'OK, honey, the guys in Dublin have found Xavier and they are bringing him in, but right now we need to get you somewhere safe. Stay right where you are. There's a team on the way to pick you up. Black SUV, diplomatic plates. They're going to take you to the embassy.'

How did he know where they were? Anna realised that he must be tracking her phone signal. She felt Hope tugging at her arm. A blacked out Mercedes had pulled up beside them. The driver got out, his head shaved, his crisp black suit and Ray-bans looking far too LA for downtown London. He opened the rear door for Hope and grabbing her case as the boot lid sprung open, threw it in the back.

'They're here. Thanks, Rob.'

'Stay on the line, honey, I don't want to lose you now.'

A moment later, her case in the back of the SUV, Anna was clipping on her safety belt and the driver was checking his mirrors and pulling out into the traffic. Insulated inside the bulletproof vehicle Anna began to relax; she turned to smile at Hope, the phone still to her ear. In the background she could hear the sounds of a busy office, Rob getting an update from one of his team.

'We're in the car. What's going on?'

'Some sort of attack. There are trains running into each other all over the goddamn place.'

Anna rubbed her hand across her forehead. She'd been involved in one terrorist incident – there wasn't room in her life for another.

'The embassy's in lockdown. You'll be safe there until we know what's happening.'

'I hope Cathy's OK, it was chaos in the station and Olivier was sitting there with another guy like nothing was happening.'

'What did he look like, the other guy?' Rob paused. 'Take a look at that photo of Hope you sent me. There are two dudes sitting down in a cafe in the background – is that them?'

'Hang on.' Anna turned to Hope. 'How do I look at that photo I took of you in the station and keep Rob on the line?'

Hope rolled her eyes, flicking the screens on Anna's phone, handing it back to her.

'Here.' Anna scanned the photograph. 'Now how do I . . .'

'Just talk, he's still there.' Hope tapped the phone impatiently.

'Hey, Rob, that's them, on the corner. Olivier Ayari is on the left.'

'Lucky strike, honey. Let's see if we can find out who this guy is and get the intel to the UK. Call me when you get to the embassy?'

'Of course.'

Anna sat back in the seat and put her arm around Hope.

'I'm sorry, this wasn't quite what I had in mind for your first day in London.'

Chapter 55

Thursday, 6.30 p.m.

Inside St Pancras station, Cathy crouched down beside the glass wall of the lift, pulled out her phone and hit O'Rourke's number.

He answered immediately but didn't get a chance to speak as she whispered, 'It's not the drivers crashing the trains. It's Olivier Ayari. I think he's hacked the system. They need to shut everything down, switch off the Wi-Fi in here and jam the phone signals so he can't set up a hotspot. Tell them to stop all the trains. I reckon he's got one of those worms into the signalling system.'

O'Rourke's voice was sharp. 'Got it. Are you OK?' In the background she could hear tannoy announcements. He must still be in Dublin Airport.

Her voice came out as a hiss. 'I'm fine. Anna and Hope have got out of the station. I'm watching Ayari.' Cathy fought to keep her voice low. 'I can't do anything on my own, I'm not armed, but we need to stop him.'

'Christ, Cat, why are you always in the middle of this stuff?' He sounded cross.

'I'm fine. Tell the Met they need to get a tech team on to the computers that run the trains.'

'On it. And, Cat? Don't do anything stupid.' He hung up.

As if she would.

Looking for the Met officers she'd seen earlier, or anyone from the British Transport Police, Cathy scanned the glazed mezzanine above her. The station was deserted. She was sure there were people somewhere but without a radio she had no way of finding out. Her phone vibrated in her hand with an incoming text message. She glanced quickly at the screen.

Karen Delaney: *Can you call me? V worried about Orla. Cannot reach her.*

Cathy mentally shook her head, puzzled. *What exactly could she do about that right now?*

Cathy stilled her irritation. Orla Quinn had been trying to contact her too. Cathy had called her back from the train but had got her voicemail. The messages Orla had left gave Cathy no clues as to why she needed to talk – she'd sounded under pressure, like she was rushing somewhere. She'd asked Cathy to call her back, but not said why. *Why did people do that?* It was one thing that really irked Cathy. She knew Orla was in a bad place but some idea of why she'd called would have been useful. Orla's words from their previous conversation still rang in Cathy's ears. *You need to find out who did this. I won't rest until whoever it is pays.* She bet Orla's call had something to do with her having a heart-to-heart with Karen Delaney yesterday about what had happened that night. When she'd heard Karen's story, had a few things gelled for her? Was that what she needed to talk to Cathy about? Had she tried to call O'Rourke too? Cathy hoped so.

Right now Cathy couldn't do anything else about Orla's calls and responding to Karen was definitely going to have to wait. Peeping out from the edge of the lift, Cathy scanned the concourse again.

Around her, the shops that lined both sides of the station mall were brightly lit but empty. The only people Cathy could see now were Olivier Ayari and his friend. Two innocuous students sitting at a table on their own, intent on their screens.

She needed to get even closer and she needed to do it now.

Crouching down, Cathy peeped out around the edge of the lift. Both Ayari and his friend had their backs to her. She needed to move. She hesitated for a split second, glancing over at them again, then, keeping as low as she could, she ran for it. *Thank God she was wearing runners.* Neither man looked up. Her heart pounding in her ears, Cathy reached the far side of the escalator and landed on the marble floor, curling up to make herself as small as possible. She caught her breath and, crawling around, peeped out again. She was close enough to hear them now.

Cathy felt her phone vibrate again. *What now?* Pulling it out of her pocket she saw O'Rourke's name beside a new text: *Another crash. Manchester, at least 10 dead. Met know ur inside. Have sent photos of Ayari. Wi-Fi jammed. Phones next. Be careful x*

He'd signed it with a kiss. But she didn't have time to think about that right now either.

What *were* Ayari and his friend doing? Whatever way they had set this up, sitting right in the middle of it was really taking the piss. They must be very sure that they weren't leaving a trail online, had so many layers of encryption and misdirection that the malicious programs they were using couldn't be traced back to them.

But Rob Power had a team dedicated to the viruses that had infected the girls' computers, and there was a whole operation working on Merchant's Quay and Discovery Quay. In Cathy's experience, when criminals got this cocky, they usually made a mistake somewhere. She sure hoped so.

As Cathy watched them, her thoughts flying, her phone vibrated yet again. *Boy, she was popular today.* She checked the screen, another text – Anna this time.

All safe. Heading 4 US Embassy. Guy with OA Karim Malik, known hacker, head of grp Unanimous. Rob onto UK cops.

Cathy did a double take. How the hell did Rob Power know who was sitting in St Pancras station right now? She knew the CIA were good, had read about the NSA monitoring communications, but really? Another text arrived.

Were in back of Hope photo. Facial recog conf.

Facial recog conf. Cathy wasn't sure what that meant. Then she got it. The Americans used facial recognition systems. Very sophisticated ones. Anna had spotted Ayari in the photo she'd taken of Hope and alerted Rob. The CIA computers did the rest.

She peeped out around the edge of the escalator again. They were frowning now, pointing to something on Ayari's laptop. Had they just realised the Wi-Fi was jammed?

Was she right about them hacking the train networks? Cathy was sure she was. If this Karim Malik character was a known hacker, the head of a group, he'd probably been working with Olivier Ayari, developing the worms he'd used to hack the girls' webcams, maybe working with him on Discovery Quay. She knew in her gut a well-planned sophisticated cyberattack could cause these catastrophic crashes. And all the evidence they'd seen from Lauren O'Reilly's and Anna's computers suggested that the people they were dealing with were very capable.

What Cathy couldn't work out was why they were here when they could attack the system remotely from anywhere?

Then Cathy felt a chill.

Anna was right, Olivier Ayari had been waiting for her; that's why he was here.

He was a hacker who got his kicks watching women on their webcams. Did he get his kicks from killing too? Had he taken it a step further, in Long Island, Paris and then London? Was Anna next on his list?

In the chaos of a terrorist attack, people went missing. It was the perfect cover.

Thank God Anna had spotted him before he spotted her.

Cathy's mind whirled. *How was Xavier involved?* His car had been circling Dalkey the night Tom was run down, and his fingerprints were on the boxes of drugs in Lauren's room. *Did they work as a team?*

It made sense – they were brothers – but it didn't feel right. Leaving your prints in a room that was bound to be searched; using your own car – it all felt a bit sloppy for a highly intelligent individual involved in this level of cybercrime. Wasn't secrecy and anonymity key to the whole thing? There had to be something else going on, but whatever the story was, Olivier Ayari and his friend needed to be stopped.

Suddenly they began to move, pulling their earphones out, putting their phones away, closing the lids on their laptops. Ayari's friend pulled out a backpack from under the table and slipped his laptop inside.

Where were they going next? She was sure these two knew their way around this station a lot better than she did, and that would make following them a challenge all of its own. But she wasn't about to lose them now.

Cathy's thoughts were cut off by the sound of a pair of heels crossing the marble, steps taken deliberately, echoing through the silent station like gunshots. Whoever it was knew exactly where they were going. Cathy peered down towards the Thames-link ticket barriers and the entrance they'd passed coming in.

What the . . .?

An elegant woman in a navy blue silk trouser suit was walking purposefully across the open concourse towards Olivier Ayari and his friend. Her blonde hair swept up in a chignon, a matching navy bag under her arm, she stood tall, in complete command of her space. And Cathy's heart almost stopped. Orla Quinn.

No wonder nobody could reach her. But what the feck was she doing here?

At the sound of footsteps, Ayari and his friend looked around, their faces frozen. Orla stopped about twenty feet from them. And as Cathy watched, she reached into the bag under her arm and drew out a gun.

Whoa.

Cathy almost said it out loud. She hadn't been expecting that. *Was this what Orla had wanted to talk to her about?* Must have been. Something had happened to bring her here, something big. And that something had to involve Tom.

Orla was determined they find and punish Tom's killer, like any mother would be, but she was a driven woman who got things done – she hadn't built her companies by sitting back and keeping her fingers crossed. The same focus that had got her onto the Irish Olympic Pentathlon team had earned her a fearsome reputation in business.

I won't rest until whoever it is pays.

Cathy suddenly felt like all the air had been sucked out of the building.

Taking her time, Orla checked the firearm was loaded, the safety off, and then pointed the gun at Ayari. Two-handed. Cathy could see she was relaxed and confident with the weapon. Orla had been a top sportswoman and pistol shooting was a vital part of the pentathlon. She knew exactly what she was doing.

But where had she got the gun from?

There was no way she could have brought it in through airport security. She must have bought it in London. Guns weren't hard to procure if you knew who to ask and had the cash. Something chimed in the back of Cathy's mind, something Fanning had said about Conor Quinn owning nightclubs – wasn't one of them in London? No doubt Orla took a hand in managing that business too. And nightclubs weren't always run according to the letter of the law. Orla must have known exactly who to ask to get her a gun. And fast. So much had happened in the last twenty-four hours that Cathy was losing track of time. Marie, their family liaison officer, had told her Karen Delaney had been at Orla's house when she'd called in with Tom's effects. Had they planned this together?

Cathy was close enough to recognise the gun was a 9 millimetre Glock – a self-loading pistol, with a 17-round magazine. Cathy wasn't as familiar with it as she was with her own SIG Sauer P226, but she'd used them on the range, knew its capability. It was proven, reliable and accurate. In the right hands it was absolutely deadly and Cathy was one hundred per cent sure Orla Quinn knew what she was doing. From the moment she'd drawn the weapon there had been no turning back.

Confirming her thoughts, Orla's voice rang out across the empty station.

'Did you think I wouldn't guess, Olivier? Did you?' Her voice was full of emotion, high-pitched, bouncing off the polished surfaces.

Ayari didn't respond, just looked at her, his mouth open, as if he was frozen in the middle of getting out of his chair. Beside him his friend slipped his phone into his backpack. Olivier Ayari was killing commuters with his hacking and his worms, but from the look on his face, Cathy reckoned this was the first time he'd been faced with his own imminent mortality.

'Did you think Tom hadn't worked out that it was your brother running those websites? You swore him to secrecy but you had to brag, didn't you, about knowing people, about how much "they" needed you to make the sites work. About how much money you were making? He knew straight away you didn't have the ability to set up an operation that big. He was my boy, he understands business. It didn't take him long to work out who the mastermind really was. And he knew how much you love your brother.' Her tone was dripping sarcasm. She paused, shaking her head. 'Tom told me about his suspicions, but we didn't have enough to go to the authorities. It could have all been hot air – a socially awkward nerd who was bragging because he needed to be liked – and he didn't know exactly which sites they even were. But then you showed him the video of Lauren, didn't you, and he worked it all out. He told you to stop, to leave her alone.' Orla's face twisted. 'My lovely, lovely boy. Always looking after everyone else.'

Xavier Ayari ran Merchant's Quay? And Olivier was the tech genius. It suddenly all made sense. Adrenaline coursed through Cathy's system as she assessed the scene, working out the distance between herself and Orla, between herself and Ayari. If ever she needed her own weapon it was now, but it was safely locked up in the gun locker in Dun Laoghaire station. Would Cathy be able to talk Orla down? She'd seen hostage negotiation in action, had studied the psychology of situations like these as part of her Master's. But this didn't look like a hostage situation. Cathy bet Orla Quinn had one thing in mind, and it wasn't holding Olivier Ayari for ransom.

Cathy could feel the nervous energy that always came before a fight building inside her. She couldn't let this escalate any more. She needed to come up with a way to distract and disarm Orla, ideally without getting herself shot in the process

She drew in a breath. The Met knew she was here, that Ayari was here, but they had a lot on their plate right now. Christ, this was a mess.

She hoped to God someone was watching them on CCTV. She couldn't call for backup – the phone signals were jammed by now. She was on her own. Assessing all the available options, Cathy kept her eyes fixed on Orla. Then at the edge of her vision Cathy caught Ayari's partner Karim Malik moving very slowly, easing out of his chair, trying to put one of the steel pillars that supported the roof between himself and Orla. Was he going to run? Part of her hoped so. He'd draw Orla's fire and Cathy might be able to get to her.

But Orla didn't seem to notice as she continued, 'You couldn't have Tom messing with your sleazy filming, though, could you? Couldn't risk him revealing what he knew? Karen told me. She came to see me to help me plan his funeral and she told me how much she loved him. And she told me about the video, about Lauren, about how he'd told her he was going to sort it out.'

As Orla paused, her voice suddenly husky, Cathy felt her stomach lurch – she'd been right. Orla's conversation with Karen had filled in the missing pieces. Orla continued, 'And then I knew. It took me a while, but you were his friend, the only person he might have told about Karen. You were the only person who could have known he was there that night.'

Cathy felt a bead of sweat run down her back. She had to stop this. Orla was here to kill Ayari, there was no question in her mind. And he knew it too. He was still paralysed behind the table, apparently unable to speak. Did Orla realise that there were likely to be armed officers in the building, that they could have their sights focused on her right now? Did she even care? She'd lost her only son and her husband was a lying bastard. Her whole world was crumbling.

Orla had her eyes fixed on Ayari. Would she see Cathy if she moved?

It was a risk. But life was a risk. Every time she went into the ring, Cathy took risks. Calculated risks. And right now, she reckoned she didn't have anything to lose. Completely focused, she planned her next move.

A few feet away, a backpack lay where it had been abandoned by someone desperate to get out of the station, a steel water bottle stashed in its side pocket. Cathy moved slowly towards it, her eyes never leaving Orla. Her gun trained on Ayari, Orla began speaking again.

'You think you're so clever, don't you, Olivier. But you forgot about your phone, didn't you? They gave me back Tom's phone yesterday. It's got that "find my friends" app on it. I could see exactly where you were. Friends?' She snorted. 'Tom was Lauren's friend. But she was so terrified of your video going public that she came to my husband for help. He told me that much before I threw him out. He pretended there was nothing going on between them but I'm not stupid.' Orla shook her head. 'How taken in, how conned, was Lauren O'Reilly that she thought Conor would help?' Orla laughed, a note of hysteria in her voice. 'The poor idiot girl.' She shook her head again in disbelief, as her voice took on a hard edge. 'Tom's phone was with his personal effects, Olivier. In a brown cardboard box. With his wallet and his student card. His belt. It's stained with his blood, Olivier.' She paused. 'I read his text to you: *You around? Need to talk to u. No more email.* Nobody knew what it meant, but after speaking to Karen, I did. Tom had told you to keep away from Lauren, hadn't he, told you not to send any more emails?'

With every word Cathy could see Orla was getting closer to the edge. Cathy watched as she licked her lips.

'You couldn't risk him telling anyone about your sick webcam hacking, about the websites. So you killed him?' Her voice went up a notch. '*You* ran him down in your brother's car, didn't you. I remember Xavier arriving at the opening of the Ayari Building in a blue BMW. I should have realised before. The Guards told me, Olivier, they told me it was a metallic blue BMW that hit Tom. But Xavier wouldn't have been stupid enough to use his own car. *You* killed my boy, didn't you?'

Cathy glanced up the concourse. There was no time to wait for backup. She needed to act. Kick-boxing was all about short sharp bursts of intense activity, it was what she was trained for. And she'd been up against a lone shooter before, one who was better trained and practised than Orla Quinn.

But she'd been armed then. This was going to be the test of all her skills.

Cathy reached out, slid the rucksack closer to her and pulled out the water bottle. She needed to create a distraction so that she could disarm Orla.

The water bottle was full, heavy in her hand, its smooth steel sides cold. Cathy got into a crouching position. Could she startle Orla enough to draw her fire away? She had to try.

Orla's voice rang out again across the concourse. 'Did you think you could get away with it, Olivier? *Did you?*'

In her peripheral vision Cathy could see Karim Malik beginning to back away from the table, his rucksack in his hand. He was staring at Orla, hadn't noticed Cathy's movement. It was all the cue she needed. If Orla saw him move she'd fire. Cathy launched the water bottle across the concourse, aiming for a point somewhere behind Orla. As it hit the ground with a clatter, Cathy exploded into a run.

The distance wasn't big and she'd never moved so fast in her life, but she was a moment too late. Cathy was only halfway to Orla when the first shot rang out. In her peripheral vision she saw Olivier Ayari crumple, blood plastering the glass wall behind him. The glass exploded, shattering as Karim Malik tried to run, stumbling over the tables and chairs in his path, his panic blind, the sound of falling furniture blending with the echo of the shot.

And a split second later, Orla turned the gun on herself.

Cathy was already springing into a kick, aiming to knock the gun out of Orla's hand.

This had worked the last time she'd done it, but she'd had the element of surprise then; it had been dark and she'd been attacking from above. Now she knew she needed speed and luck. And wings.

But a bullet had already left the chamber.

As Cathy's Nike reached her, the back of Orla's head exploded, but Cathy couldn't stop the momentum of her kick. Her body collided with Orla's as the older woman's knees collapsed, blood spraying across the smooth grey marble. Cathy landed heavily, her body tangled with Orla's.

And around her she could hear the sound of running feet, heavy boots on the hard floor. Cathy closed her eyes.

She was too late.

Chapter 56

'So just run that past me again.'

With the noise going on around her in the station concourse and the sirens outside in the street, Cathy could hardly hear O'Rourke. She pressed the phone closer to her ear, cradling it in her shoulder, wishing he was with her as she repeated what she'd just said.

'I was too late. I couldn't get to Orla fast enough. She shot Olivier Ayari and then she shot herself.' Cathy's voice caught. She took a deep breath, tears pricking her eyes. 'I tried to distract her, I thought I might be able to get to the gun. There was just no time.'

His tone softened. 'Are you OK?'

Cathy sighed. She was sitting on her own in the middle of a row of steel chairs in the centre of the station concourse, near the ticket barriers where Anna had taken her photo of Hope. Behind her, the cafe where Olivier Ayari and his friend had been sitting was taped off, the windows shattered. Ayari's blood was everywhere – copper-coloured skid marks on the pale grey tiles where his friend had slipped in it and fallen. Around her the station staff and police officers were milling about, a white plastic tent already erected over Orla's body, white-suited techs huddled in small groups. Karim Malik had given them a good run but they'd caught him in the Underground. Led him away in handcuffs. She shifted in her seat.

Was she OK?

Cathy looked down at the dried blood on her black sweater and combats, which would be going into an evidence bag as soon as she got a change of clothes. Her hair was a mess and she had a huge bruise on her hip where she'd hit the floor. But a few minutes before, as she'd pulled her phone out to call O'Rourke, a man with a dark beard who seemed to be the manager of a coffee shop further along the concourse had appeared with a takeaway cup of sweet, steaming milky coffee. She didn't think she'd ever been more grateful to see a cup of coffee. He'd handed it to her without speaking and patted her on the shoulder, and left her to it.

She sipped it now before she answered. She was starting to feel cold, the sides of the cardboard cup deliciously warm in her hand. It was the small acts that changed people's lives, unexpectedly locked a memory into a moment. Like when O'Rourke had pulled her to him as the helicopter had taken off from Keane's Field in Ballymun, airlifting Sarah Jane to hospital, like when he'd cradled her in his arms after the explosion.

'My hip's a bit sore, but everything else is grand.'

There was a pause, like he was about to say something but changed his mind. 'So what are you doing now?'

'Well, I'm guessing our meeting got cancelled so I'm having a coffee.' She took another sip. 'The Met Police have been lovely, I'm just waiting for the DI to finish up and he's going to take me to the station to clean up and give a statement.' She took a sip of her coffee. 'Can you ring Sarah Jane in case she sees it on the news? Just let her know I'm OK?'

Cathy had mentioned to Anna about knowing Sarah Jane's dad on the way into London, and they'd marvelled at how small the world was, agreed that they should all go out for a drink soon.

But right now Cathy was sure Anna had other things on her mind.

She'd been the target of a sexual predator who had murdered one of her students and been the cause of the murder of another. And her friend Orla had taken her own life. It was a massive fecking mess, particularly coming on top of Anna's previous experiences.

Olivier Ayari was some warped creep.

Cathy hadn't been one bit sorry when Orla had pulled the trigger, but she couldn't say that to anyone. Orla was an astute woman; she knew as well as Cathy did that even if they'd arrested Olivier and got a conviction for murder he could be out of prison after twelve years. Orla had wanted whoever had killed Tom to pay, she'd been very clear about that, and twelve years for her son's life was never going to be a deal she'd accept graciously. Cathy just wished she'd been armed. Not that she could have fired on an unarmed civilian, no matter now despicable his actions had been, but she could have disabled Orla, or at least have tried. And stopped her from killing herself.

O'Rourke's voice brought her back from the thoughts whirling around her head.

'Of course I'll ring her, no problem.'

She tried to smile. 'Thanks. I've got to do a full debrief, I'm not sure how long it will take.'

O'Rourke's voice hardened. 'So how's Olivier Ayari?'

At the other end Cathy heard someone say something in the background; it sounded like 007. Cathy smiled. She'd miss him and his antics when she left Dun Laoghaire. Not as much as she'd miss O'Rourke, but she didn't want to think about that now.

She answered quickly. 'He's in hospital on life support. The lads here have got his laptop, though, and they've already been in touch with Rob Power. They have a lot to work with. It's looking like his friend, this Karim Malik character, has been planning this thing with the trains for a while. He's head of a group of hackers who call themselves Unanimous. He's a big catch.' She took a sip of her coffee. 'Apparently the world of hacking is very competitive, they are always looking for something bigger and more damaging to make their group top dogs.' She paused. 'The Met lads reckon this Unanimous crowd wanted to do something bigger than that attack on the NHS. To be the best.'

The world of super-hackers made no sense to her; it was like they were all totally socially dysfunctional, couldn't see that their actions affected real people with real lives. People with hopes and dreams and families. She felt something shift inside her but she couldn't get emotional now; she needed to hold it together so she could give her statement. Which was likely to be a long one. She tried to move the conversation on.

'So what's the story now on the train crashes?'

'Sixty-eight dead, about two hundred injured. They were pretty catastrophic. Something called a Trojan worm infected the signalling, you were right on that. Basically it was sending trains into one another instead of separating them.'

'Jesus. We'd only got off the train from Luton Airport when all this kicked off.' Cathy felt herself chill. 'So tell me about Xavier. How did you come up with a match on his prints when the CIA and Interpol couldn't?' She knew he could hear the amusement in her voice.

O'Rourke half-laughed. 'Well, you may ask. We scored a hit on the biometric data from the marina. Fanning spotted the BMW first, orbiting the area prior to Tom's accident, then picked it up again on CCTV heading into town on the N11. As soon as we checked who it was registered to, we were almost there. But when Starsky fed the data from the marina into the system, hey presto, doesn't Xavier's name flash up in lights. Pearse Street have found the car now, in an underground car park in town and there's substantial damage to the offside. The car park CCTV tapes show Olivier driving it out of the car park the night Tom was hit.'

'Bloody hell. You'll get a gold star for that.'

'The lads picked Xavier up at his apartment in town late this afternoon. He's denying everything . . .'

'Obviously.'

'Almost. He's admitted the drugs in Lauren's room were his all right, but he says he never met her. He thought a prostitute his brother had engaged had stolen them from their apartment. He reckons his brother's set him up. They can't stand each other, apparently.'

'That sounds like an understatement.' She shifted in the hard steel chair, her hip beginning to ache. 'Can he explain how his print got onto that bracelet, the one the French victim was wearing?'

'Well, that's where things get interesting. Apparently Olivier had an exchange student staying with him at the time of the murder. A lad called Karim Malik from London. Malik bought the bracelet for his sister as a souvenir. Xavier said he looked at it, must have touched the disc . . .'

'And somehow it ended up with the girl's body in the park. And Olivier and Karim Malik form a lifetime allegiance.' Cathy shook her head.

'It turns out Olivier was in Long Island on another exchange programme when the girl there was killed. We have to check, but Xavier claims he was at home in Paris. Olivier was questioned along with everyone else as part of the investigation, didn't even have a concrete alibi, but the investigating team found images on the girl's computer and assumed she was meeting someone who had viewed them.'

'He's certainly been busy, and it sounds like he's been trying to frame Xavier for murder at every opportunity. Nice.'

'If we hadn't just seen Olivier in action, I'd say Xavier was being creative with the truth, but the evidence is mounting. Olivier used his car that night and if Tom had told him about Karen Delaney, like lads do, he'd have known exactly where Tom was going.'

'That's what Orla said – that he was the only person Tom might have told about his relationship with Karen. And Olivier would have known that the charity event was live streamed, which gave him a window of opportunity. Before she . . .' Cathy hesitated, clearing her throat. 'Orla said Karen came to tell her about Tom. Karen mentioned what Tom had said about Lauren and the video. Orla was a very clever lady, she put it together with what Tom had already told her about the websites. I think they were very close.' She sighed. 'But Olivier Ayari couldn't risk Tom exposing his involvement with the videos because they linked him to the killings. He knew he'd lose everything and be facing about a century in jail.'

'Which would be a fairly strong motive for murder. I'll be talking to Karen Delaney tomorrow – we'll see what she has to say.' He paused. 'Maybe Olivier recognised Conor Quinn in one of the videos of Lauren and was holding that over Tom too. We may never know. What we do know is that Olivier sending that video to Lauren kicked all this off.' O'Rourke paused. 'I think Olivier was planning to go after Lauren, but Mira Mandić got involved.'

Cathy cut in. 'I've been thinking about that. I reckon Olivier sent Lauren that sign-up email to Discovery Quay to frighten her – the one that arrived while we were in her room. He didn't know she was dead at that stage. He must have been wondering why he hadn't heard from her, got twitchy.'

'I bet he was twitchy. Rob Power is going over Xavier's laptop as well to see how he's linked to Merchant's Quay and Discovery Quay. Xavier claims his brother is the tech nerd, that he built the sites, that it was all him. Apparently he'd been hacking since he was a kid.'

Cathy watched as another white-suited tech arrived, but from the way everyone was standing back, she guessed it was the pathologist.

She paused for a moment, then said, 'Orla didn't seem to think Olivier was bright enough to set up such a big business. She thought Xavier was the mastermind behind the sites, that he got Olivier to build them. And at some stage Olivier must have realised that he could use Discovery Quay as a vehicle to attack women.'

'I think you're right. If Olivier had been successful and Xavier had been arrested for any one of these murders, he would have taken over running both sites and benefited to the tune of millions.'

'Which all fits.' Cathy took another sip of her coffee. 'Oh, you know Olivier's alibi about being in the library the night Tom was killed?' She sat forward in the seat. 'I've just realised that their system scans users' cards on the way in, but not on the way out. I'd say Olivier went in that night, changed his hoodie or something and came out again, hiding his face. Then he took his brother's car and waited for Tom.' Cathy paused. 'You would wonder why either of them needed to make that sort of money when they come from a family who are rolling in it.'

'I'm not so sure they are. Between them Rob and Pierre Beaussoleil have finally tracked down their parents. Xavier and Olivier's father is a technician with what was France Telecom, it's called Orange SA now. He's been working in some province in China. Their mother's French, but their parents have been divorced for years, she uses her maiden name, which was why they couldn't find her to start with. She's got MS, doesn't travel. She thought both boys were working through their degrees while they were here in Ireland. They went home regularly, and obviously spun her a tale about what they were doing here. She didn't know anything about the science block being built.' He paused, 'So it looks like the websites have been providing their income – Silk Road was worth $48 million when it was closed down by the FBI and it had only been trading for two years. We'll find out shortly what Merchant's Quay is worth now Rob and Operation Honey Bee are on it. It could be more. From what Pierre's team have found out so far, Olivier's definitely the black sheep, he didn't get on with his father at all.'

'You do surprise me.' Cathy paused, remembering Fanning explaining the value of Bitcoins on their way back from searching Lauren's room. The amount of money that could be made with these sites was mind-blowing. She sighed, exhaustion washing over her. 'I've been trying to work out why Xavier would draw attention to himself by funding that building in Trinity.'

O'Rourke snorted. Or at least it sounded like a snort. 'Arrogance? Maybe he wanted to leave some sort of tribute to his technical wizardry in one of the oldest universities in the world.' She could almost hear him shaking his head at the irony as he continued. 'I reckon it was a bit more practical than that, though – he had a stack of money he needed to get rid of. Sums as big as the ones he must have been bringing in start attracting attention. And there are only so many ways you can get rid of twenty or thirty million without it actually making you more money back. We should know more soon. Trinity's accountants checked out the company it came from. It appeared to be legit, or as legit as any company registered in the Cayman's is. It's an investment company, part of a group apparently. As far as they were concerned it was bona fide. Xavier doesn't pay tax in this state so the revenue wasn't interested.'

Cathy could see how that made sense. 'So what's the story with the marina? It wasn't Xavier breaking into the boats, was it?'

'Nope.' O'Rourke chuckled. 'Turns out it was your friend Nifty Quinn. He'd persuaded the marina staff that he was working on a boat and bypassed all their systems. Just kept on coming back. While the lads were down there getting Xavier Ayari's records, doesn't he walk right into the office with a bag of tools.'

Cathy smiled, shaking her head. Nifty Quinn was a house-breaker with some strange predilections who had been her and Thirsty's nemesis since the day she'd arrived in Dun Laoghaire. Suddenly feeling weary, she took another sip of her coffee. It was so good to hear O'Rourke's voice.

'So how's Anna Lockharte doing?' Cathy could hear the concern in O'Rourke's tone.

'She's supposed to be giving a lecture on political extremism and cybercrime at New Scotland Yard tomorrow morning.' The irony wasn't lost on either of them. 'But she texted to say she's safe at the US Embassy. Rob Power had her collected as soon as she got out of here. She doesn't know about Orla yet. I'll tell her as soon as I get away. She's arranged for them to put me up for the night.' Cathy took another sip of her coffee. 'She was sure Olivier chose St Pancras to work from because he's been following her and watching her online. He could have gone anywhere in the world to orchestrate this and watch his campaign in action. I think she was in very real danger, was most likely next on his list.'

O'Rourke sounded like he was thinking. 'Sounds like he thought he'd double job while he was in London.'

'That was his mistake. These cyber geeks think they are untouchable. It's always human emotion that fecks things up for gurriers like him.'

'I'm not sure about emotion. I think he's some sort of socio-path. Mike Wesley, the inspector in New Scotland Yard we were meeting, wants to see you before you go. I was just on the phone to him. In both the London cases, the girls were victims of cybercrime, received emails threatening that video from their webcams would be broadcast on Discovery Quay. But they have DNA that should give us a match now we have a suspect.'

'So we'll know for sure which of the brothers was involved in the killings.'

'Indeed. Now the cases have been linked, the evidence is building. It'll be complicated to construct a solid case that crosses jurisdictions like this, and the rail network hacking takes precedence, but we have the Ayari brothers in custody now and with time we'll get there.'

Time was the one thing they didn't have. It was as if they both realised it at the same moment.

'Are you coming over here now?' Her voice was tentative, but she already knew the answer.

'I can't, I have to interview Xavier Ayari and find out when we can interview Olivier. And I have to get down to Limerick. One of our lads has been abducted.'

Cathy winced. The criminal families in Limerick were worse than the Mafia – Jesus only knew what they were doing to him.

'Who?' Her voice was small; everyone knew everyone else in this job.

'I can't say. He was undercover. It's a big fucking mess.' O'Rourke paused. 'But can you come down as soon as you get back? You're supposed to be resting today, you'll be owed leave by the time you're done over there.'

She smiled. *As if he'd be able to get any time off to spend with her*. But the will was there. 'I will. I'll see you in Limerick.'

There were about five hundred million more romantic places in the world that they could have met, including St Pancras station, which, despite everything, she still adored, but she knew he wouldn't be able to get away until this new case was resolved.

O'Rourke's voice was soft when he replied. 'Good, I'd like that, I'd like that a lot.'

Cathy felt herself smiling. 'I would too.'

Acknowledgements

This book is, I hope, testimony to the fact that if you work hard enough and follow your dreams you can do anything you want in this world. As Oscar Wilde said, 'Shoot for the moon. Even if you miss, you'll land among the stars.'

All writers work alone to get a manuscript written, but it's a team that makes it into a book. Huge thanks have to go first to my (brave) readers, Jane Alger and Claire McKenna, but biggest thanks to my incredible and talented friend Niamh O'Connor who had the skill and wisdom to point out the mega problems in that first draft (ahem). Thank God you did.

Colm Dooley and Joe Griffin were invaluable in helping me get Garda procedure correct (or Cat would have been sacked about a thousand times over), huge thanks too, to Assistant Commissioner Fintan Fanning. Graham Penrose was an essential adviser on weaponry and terrorism. Thanks too, to Sophie Fox O'Loughlin and Alex Caan who put me right on the tech stuff. Kyle O'Connell gave huge advice on search and rescue procedures (it's just as well he's well trained – he also runs Irish Film and Television Services and whenever we work together, mad things happen). Any mistakes are entirely my own.

Thanks also to my extremely patient editor, Katherine Armstrong – this story 'developed' quite a lot between drafts, and her support was unwavering and enthusiastic at every turn. I owe an incredible debt to Steve O'Gorman who gave this book its final editorial polish and for whose sound advice I will be forever indebted.

This is the third in the Cat Connolly series, and I want to say a massive thank you to you, the reader, for sticking with Cat. She's just about to start on another exciting episode in her life and I've loved every minute of sharing her journey with you thus far. If you've only just met her, I hope you will check out Cat's earlier escapades in *Little Bones* and *In Deep Water*. Without my superstar agent Simon Trewin's faith in that first story, originally titled *The Dressmaker*, and in my writing, I may never have had the pleasure of sharing her story with anyone, so biggest thanks of all go to you, Simon, for making dreams come true.

This book is dedicated to all those who so tragically lost their lives in the Grenfell fire disaster on 14 June 2017, and to a wonderful lady named Nicole Dressen who was immensely generous in supporting the subsequent Authors for Grenfell auction.

I was immersed in writing in the middle of June, and will never forget the images on the TV, the utter tragedy of lives lost and the heroism of those who helped and supported. In the days that followed I read many reports but I was particularly struck by the incredible leadership of David Benson, the headmaster of Kensington Aldridge Academy, who stood watching the tower burn at 3.30 a.m. and who lost four pupils and one recently graduated pupil. His school was in the shadow of the tower, and the fact that fifty-six out of sixty of his students turned in for their exams that day stands testimony to his staff's dedication and commitment. David Benson ensured that his school reopened forty-eight hours later in a nearby temporary location, offering continuity and counselling to those involved. I doubt he slept in those forty-eight hours. I hope that this dedication, in a very small way, will help us remember those who were lost, and that their stories will live on.

If you enjoyed *No Turning Back*, read on for
an extract from Sam Blake's first novel,

LITTLE BONES

Available now

PART ONE

Coming Apart at the Seams
In clothing: where two pieces of material come apart and the garment can no longer be worn. Often caused by a weakness or break in the thread.

1

The door to the back bedroom hung open.

Pausing at the top of the narrow wooden stairs, Garda Cathy Connolly could just see inside, could see what looked like the entire contents of the wardrobe flung over the polished floorboards, underwear scattered across the room like litter. The sun, winter weak, played through a window opposite the door, its light falling on something cream, illuminating it bright against the dark denim and jewel colours of the tumbled clothes on the floor.

Cathy's stomach turned again and she closed her eyes, willing the sickness to pass. There was a riot of smells up here, beeswax, ghostly layers of stale perfume, something musty. She put her gloved hand to her mouth and the smell of the latex, like nails on a blackboard, set her teeth on edge.

Until thirty-six hours ago Cathy had been persuading herself that her incredibly heightened sense of smell and queasiness were the start of a bug. *Some bug.* But right now her problems were something she didn't have the headspace to deal with. She had a job to do. Later, when she was on her own in the gym, when it was just her and a punchbag, that was when she'd be able to think. *And boy did she have a lot to think about.*

Pulling her hand away from her mouth, Cathy impatiently pushed a dark corkscrew curl that had escaped from her ponytail back behind her ear. Too thick to dry quickly, her hair was still damp from her early-morning training session in the pool, but that was the least of her worries. She folded her arms tightly across her chest and breathed deeply, slowly fighting her nausea. Inside her head, images of the bedroom whirled, slightly out of focus, blurred at the edges.

When the neighbour had called the station this morning, this had presented as a straightforward forced entry. That was until the lads had entered the address into the system and PULSE had thrown up a report from the same property made only the previous night. The householder, Zoë Grant, had seen a man lurking in the garden. Watching her. Cathy would put money on him doing a bit more than just watching. One of the Dún Laoghaire patrol cars had been close by, had arrived in minutes, blue strobes illuminating the lane. But the man had vanished. More than likely up the footpath that ran through the woods from the dead end of the cul-de-sac to the top of Killiney Hill.

And now someone had broken in.

It was just as well Zoë Grant hadn't been at home.

Cathy thrust her hands into the pockets of her combats and fought to focus. *Christ, she was so sick of feeling sick.* The one thing that Niall McIntyre, her coach – 'The Boss' – drilled into her at every single training session was that winning was about staying in control. Staying in control of her training; her fitness; her diet.

Staying in control of her breakfast.

And she'd got to be the Women's National Full-Contact Kickboxing champion three times in a row by following his advice.

Below in the hallway, Cathy could hear Thirsty, the scenes-of-crime officer, bringing in his box of tricks, its steel shell reverberating off the black and white tiles as he called up to her.

'If this one *is* Quinn, O'Rourke will be delighted. Have a look at her shoes; he's got a thing about bloody shoes. Lines them up and does his thing . . .' The disgust was loud in his voice.

Trying to steady herself, Cathy took a deep breath. DI Dawson O'Rourke might be dying to nail 'Nifty' Quinn, but she knew he wouldn't be at all impressed if he could see her now. Dún Laoghaire was a new patch for him, but they went way back. And . . . *Christ, this wasn't the time to throw up.*

Shoes. Look for the shoes.

'The place is upside down, there's . . .' Her voice sounded hollow. But what could she say, there's a bad smell? No question that would bring guffaws of laughter from Thirsty. And she was quite sure no one else would be able to smell it; it was like the kitchen back at her shared house. If Decko, their landlord, or one of the other lads she rented with had left the fridge open or the lid off the bin, she couldn't even get in the door. *Thank God they hadn't noticed.* Yet. Decko fancied himself as an impersonator and there was no way she was ready to be the butt of his jokes.

Taking a deep breath, Cathy edged through the door, the heels on her boots echoing on the wooden floorboards. Downstairs she heard another voice. The neighbour this time, calling from outside the front door.

'How are you getting on?'

'Grand, thanks. A member of the detective unit is examining upstairs.' Cathy could tell from his response that Thirsty had his public smile in place. 'Any sign of Miss Grant?'

'Zoë? Not yet. I'll try her again in a minute. It's going to be an awful shock. He didn't take that big painting, did he? The old one of the harbour? I've always loved that.' The neighbour paused, then before Thirsty could comment continued: 'Is there anything I can do? Can I get you a cup of tea?'

Listening to Thirsty making small talk, Cathy focused back on the room. She needed to pull herself together and get on with this. They couldn't hold Nifty Quinn for ever. She could hear O'Rourke's voice in her head.

What had he been looking for? Cash? Jewellery? Or some sort of trophy? This didn't feel like a Nifty job to Cathy, and she'd seen enough that were. Whatever about him being picked up in the area this morning acting suspiciously, and his thing for single women, this felt different, more personal. But only Zoë Grant would know for sure if anything was missing. A lipstick? A pair of knickers?

Cathy had seen worse, but standing here in the ransacked bedroom, her six years on the force didn't help make her feel any less unclean. How would the woman who lived here feel when she got home? Someone had been in her *bedroom* . . .

Cathy scanned the tumble of fabrics on the floor. The cream silk was a misfit with the blacks, purples and embroidered blue denim. The colour of sour milk, it looked like a . . . wedding dress?

Bobbing down on her haunches, Cathy let the folds of milky fabric play through her fingers. The disturbance released more of the ancient perfume, the scent jangling like a set of keys. The silk had torn where it had caught on a nail in the wardrobe door, minute stitches unravelling along the hem, opening a deep cleft in the fabric. Tugging gently, Cathy tried to lift it from the pin. The seam widened and she caught a glimpse of something dark inside.

What the feck was that?

Whatever it was had fallen in deeper as she moved the silk. Leaning forward, Cathy teased the two edges apart with her fingertips, trying to get a better look.

She needed more light.

'Thirsty, have you got a torch down there?' Cathy's voice was too loud in the stillness of the room. Then she heard Thirsty's footsteps on the stairs and a moment later his greying head appeared in the doorway, a heavy rubber torch in his hand.

'Got something?'

'Not sure.' Frowning, she stood up to take the torch. 'There's –' A voice calling from downstairs interrupted her.

Thirsty rolled his eyes. 'Jesus, it's the bloody neighbour back. Call me if you need me.'

Cathy flashed him a grin and, crouching down again beside the pile of clothes, played the torch over them, double-checking before she went back to the dress. Looking for *what*? She wasn't sure. Fibres? Blood? She shook her head half to herself.

This was something different. She could feel it in the pit of her stomach, could feel the hairs rising on the back of her neck.

What was she expecting to find? Had the guy who had been here left some sort of gift? Like Nifty? Christ, she hoped not. Normally she could take all of that in her stride, but today she wasn't so sure.

Cathy suddenly realised she was feeling nervous – which was stupid. *What could possibly be in an old dress, in a room like this, that was making her heart pound?* She'd been in the force too long, had seen too much for this to spook her. But for some reason it was, and spooking her badly. Cathy could feel her palms sweating, absorbing the talc on the inside of her blue latex gloves. Were her hormones making her supersensitive? This was crazy.

Clearing her throat, she swung the beam of the torch onto the gap she had made in the creamy silk. There was definitely something there. Cathy eased back the seam, opening the fabric to the torchlight.

Pale grey shards. Hidden deep within the folds.

Shards of what? Something old. The rhyme took off like a kite inside her head. *Something old, something new . . .* Shaking it away, she lifted the weight of the silk and, holding the torch up, slipped her fingers into the seam, prising it apart. The stitches were minute, little more than a whisper along the hemmed edge.

Then she saw them. More shards. Tiny, twig-like, tumbling as the fabric moved. And in a moment of absolute clarity she realised what they were.

And the nausea came like a tidal wave.

Bones. Tiny bones. The unmistakable slant of a jaw, the curve of a rib.

'Thirsty, I need you up here now!'

This was going to make O'Rourke's day. First the FBI – and now this.